W9-BLA-169

"Dane's smooth style, believable characters, and intense pacing will remind readers of Lisa Jackson, Lisa Gardner, and Tami Hoag."
Publishers Weekly

"Her style is gritty, her writing sharp and concise."
Sharon Sala

"Jordan Dane will make you think twice before you ever walk alone in the dark again."
Robin Burcell

"High suspense and hot sex…"
Maggie Price

What had happened?

He pried through his memory, recalling nothing of how he ended up here. And where *was* here? He peered through the shadows of what looked like a cramped bathroom. And beyond where he was, the remnants of a cheap motel room, but none of it looked familiar.

Through it all, the flashing light persisted. Its grim color doused everything. He looked across two small beds and saw the light came from a window that had thin drapes partially drawn. Outside, a neon vacancy sign flared its message, but he couldn't see all of it. And after only a quick glimpse, the light sent shards of pain through his eye sockets and challenged his night vision. To recover, he shifted his gaze to the dark corners of the bathroom again, looking for anything that would trigger a memory.

Instead, he came face-to-face with a nightmare he would never forget.

By Jordan Dane

THE WRONG SIDE OF DEAD
EVIL WITHOUT A FACE
NO ONE LIVES FOREVER
NO ONE LEFT TO TELL
NO ONE HEARD HER SCREAM

ATTENTION: ORGANIZATIONS AND CORPORATIONS
Most Avon Books paperbacks are available at special quantity
discounts for bulk purchases for sales promotions, premiums,
or fund raising. For information, please call or write:

Special Markets Department, HarperCollins Publishers,
10 East 53rd Street, New York, New York 10022-5299.
Telephone: (212) 207-7528.   Fax: (212) 207-7222.

JORDAN DANE

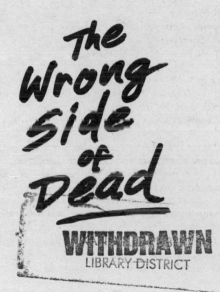

The Wrong Side of Dead

WITHDRAWN
LIBRARY DISTRICT

AVON

An Imprint of HarperCollinsPublishers

This is a work of fiction. Names, characters, places, and incidents are products of the author's imagination or are used fictitiously and are not to be construed as real. Any resemblance to actual events, locales, organizations, or persons, living or dead, is entirely coincidental.

AVON BOOKS
An Imprint of HarperCollins*Publishers*
10 East 53rd Street
New York, New York 10022-5299

Copyright © 2009 by Cosas Finas, LLC
Excerpt from Untitled copyright © 2010 by Cosas Finas, LLC
ISBN 978-0-06-147413-2
www.avonbooks.com

All rights reserved. No part of this book may be used or reproduced in any manner whatsoever without written permission, except in the case of brief quotations embodied in critical articles and reviews. For information address Avon Books, an Imprint of HarperCollins Publishers.

First Avon Books paperback printing: November 2009

Avon Trademark Reg. U.S. Pat. Off. and in Other Countries, Marca Registrada, Hecho en U.S.A.
HarperCollins® is a registered trademark of HarperCollins Publishers.

Printed in the U.S.A.

10 9 8 7 6 5 4 3 2 1

If you purchased this book without a cover, you should be aware that this book is stolen property. It was reported as "unsold and destroyed" to the publisher, and neither the author nor the publisher has received any payment for this "stripped book."

To my sisters Denise and Debbie—
in the cookies of life, you'd be the nuts.

ACKNOWLEDGMENTS

With each novel, an author learns more about the craft of writing. In the first book of my Sweet Justice series, *Evil Without a Face,* I worked on pacing and juggled multiple story lines with a diverse cast of characters. And a secondary character surprised me—Seth Harper, my quirky computer genius. I thought it would be fun to build on the mystery surrounding Harper's back story without providing answers until this second book. So I hope you enjoy getting to know how Seth Harper's life collides with the three strong women of this series: Jessie Beckett, Alexa Marlowe, and Sam Cooper. The Sweet Justice series wouldn't be the same without the enigmatic Harper.

Other real-life "characters" made significant contributions, too, not the least of who were my two gnome-ologists. As they say, gnome is where the heart is. And to answer all my many gnome-related questions, I brought in top experts in the field—award-winning author Jill Monroe and *New York Times* bestseller Gena Showalter.

Others helped, too. Special thanks to award-winning author Maggie Price (former police crime analyst and world traveler) for lending her expert feedback on police procedures. Mags, I swear you were hanging out in cyberspace waiting for me to ask a question. I appreciate your time and friendship. My dear friend and talented author Dana Taylor gave her insightful feedback. And thanks to my dementedly endearing friend Joe Collins, who gave his expertise in all things. I now consider him a God among men.

Retired Air Force Colonel Ed Torres traversed government bureaucracy with me when I had given thought to a different secondary plot in this book. In the end I had to scrap the excess pork, but I'm no less grateful for your time, Ed. You're still in my circle. And for his questionable prowess in the kitchen, I have to give a shout-out to my friend Tom for reasons only he will know. (I didn't share Tom's last name, because in this instance anonymity is a good thing when it comes to salsa recipes.) And to my former co-workers at OGE Energy Resources in Oklahoma City—who thought they had to wait until hell froze over to be mentioned in one of my books—thanks for tolerating my strange humor for years.

And to the usual suspects, I'd like to thank my husband and best friend, John, for his never-ending support, and my family for their generous tolerance. To my agent, Meredith Bernstein, you make me so thankful that we met. I love having you in my life. And to my editor, Lucia Macro, and everyone who contributed to this book from the amazing staff at Avon Books/HarperCollins—thanks for your creativity and unwavering professionalism. You made this collaboration a dream come true.

CHAPTER 1

Dirty Monty's Lounge
South Side of Chicago
Thursday, 9:20 P.M.
Late summer

At the end of the bar, Seth Harper slouched, nursing his lukewarm beer and keeping his dark eyes on the door, waiting. Not even a good beer buzz made him forget why he'd come— or why he still sat alone.

Given the grand scheme of the universe, he distracted himself by contemplating the big picture. Dirty Monty's and places like it existed for a reason. And several libations had given him the clarity of mind to reflect on it. Sleazy dumps gave the socially unacceptable a place to hang out, even on a Thursday night. And if these folks packed a thirst, Monty's served the cheap stuff and charged enough to trick its marginal clientele into believing it was worth it. When alcohol was involved, things *always* got real simple. And he appreciated the irony of his half-tanked epiphany, especially since he'd be counted among the socially unacceptable here tonight.

Yet he was a few beers shy of being easily duped by any redeeming nature of the shoddy bar. The pungent odor of cigarette smoke, liquor, and cheap perfume had marked him. And the carpet smelled of mold, a borderline improvement over the collective tang of the bar patrons. His dark tousled hair, well-worn jeans, and favorite black Jerry Springer tee already reeked of the bar's seedier elements. And well into the night, he'd be hearing a steady thrum of bass in his ears, courtesy of the nonstop jukebox music—a mix of country, classic heavy metal, and top 40 pop. He sighed and stared into his beer mug, bracing himself to accept what had happened and hail a cab home.

What the hell are you doing? The question had stuck in his head, reminding him he'd been played for a sucker. She wasn't coming *this* time.

And insult to injury, the piss factor had kicked in again. Every time the bartender shot tonic into a glass or hit the spigot for a draft beer, Seth's bladder reacted. He made a quick trip to drain the vein and slumped back on his stool. But after another fifteen minutes of nursing his beer and a fragile spirit—shifting his gaze between the front door and his watch—Seth decided to call it a night. He downed the rest of his drink and fumbled in his pocket for a tip.

As he stood, he caught sight of a blond woman near the door.

It *had* to be her, but from where he stood, her face had morphed into an unrecognizable blur. He narrowed his eyes and struggled for a better image, but nothing more would come. When he moved toward her, he staggered against the edge of the bar, feeling suddenly light-headed. The sensation took him by surprise. He hadn't drunk *that* much.

"What . . . the hell?" he slurred under his breath.

When the room undulated in shadows, he knew something was terribly wrong. He felt sluggish and weak. Out-of-sync voices and warped music amplified into an irritating blare. He looked around, but everything was the same. Faces of strangers and the distant memory of a blond woman jutted in and out of the dark, distorted and overlapping in a jumbled mess. Blinking hard, he couldn't change what he saw. Colors bled from the ceiling and walls, creating a macabre and shifting canvas.

Fear took a firmer grip.

"Help . . . m-me."

He imagined calling out, but wasn't sure the words were his. Could *anyone* hear him? His arms went slack. And when standing became a chore, he collapsed. Before he hit the floor, strong hands grabbed him. He turned to look for a face, but the room spiraled out of control. His world switched off.

And he was powerless to stop it.

Thursday—10:10 P.M.

Losing track of time, she worked the keyboard without effort, no longer the novice she'd been when she first started.

For the last two weeks, she had a MySpace account under the name of *NascarChic8*. Being cautious, she had created the anonymous handle as her main online identity. Most new friends to her page didn't bother to read her posts. If they did, they would have found the first name of Michelle buried in her blog entries. Anyone taking the time to address her by that name got extra attention when she rechecked their site.

Being picky, she hadn't gotten above a hundred friends, but she did her best to expand her cyber-reach. Although she'd worked hard to design her page, it hadn't been easy to attract the right people. With her profile marked as private from public viewing—except for her default photo—most didn't bother with sending a request to befriend her.

That left her with being the aggressor in searching for "friends" and she liked that.

Creating the most appropriate cyberpersona felt like assembling the pieces to an ever-changing puzzle with no right answer. She'd started with photos of driver Dale Earnhardt Jr., who graced the background of her blog page with his short reddish blond hair, chin stubble, and blue eyes covered in dark shades. Bit by bit she had added more images and designed the page, making sure anyone visiting the site would see her obsessive tribute to all things NASCAR. A cyberspace masterpiece in the making.

But compiling the photos had taken the most time.

The main photo on her blog—the one everyone saw online—had her standing next to a pudgy version of Dale Earnhardt Jr. with longer hair. A sunny day at the races with both of them wearing shades. But over the last week, she had posted a series of photos, each with personal commentary about the swollen pregnant belly she sported and had nicknamed *Junior*.

After her last photo upload, she got a new friend request that got her attention. And with it came a surprising message.

Hello Michelle—Saw your name at a friend's site. The young man in your photo is my son. How do you know him?

The message had been straightforward and to the point. She stared at the monitor and reread it.

Before sending a return message, she clicked over to the woman's blog and began reading. She wrote down the details that interested her. The woman's birthday checked out from what she knew. And she lived in the same city. So far, so good. But it took reading through a few blog posts and scanning the woman's online pics and slide shows to find what she'd been looking for. She took a deep breath and e-mailed her reply.

Everything hinged on how she worded her message.

She wrote, *Yes, ma'am. Looks like he's your son, all right. But I have to be honest. He's not exactly speaking to me since I told him about his baby. I don't even know where he is.*

The woman's reply came back fast.

Do you know what the baby is? A little girl or boy? Am I going to be a grandma?

She chewed her lower lip and typed a response.

I can't raise this baby by myself, without a daddy. I'm giving it up for adoption.

Once again, a return e-mail didn't take long.

Please. Don't do anything until we talk. I can make things right. You'll see.

But now it was her turn to plead.

If you tell your son that we talked, he'll think I contacted you first. He'll take off again and leave us BOTH.

You leave that boy to me, was all the woman wrote.

Her e-mail was short and to the point again, tough love from a momma who indeed knew her son. After another exchange of e-mails, she'd agreed to meet tomorrow morning. Risky business to make actual contact with an online stranger, but she'd run out of options with her search.

"Well, Junior," she said under her breath. "We may find your daddy yet."

Hours later

Seth stared into blackness, his thoughts the consistency of primordial ooze. Although his brain sent a questionable message to the rest of his body that he could move, he chose not to try. His senses were gathering intel, and he was content to let the process happen at its own pace.

He blinked his eyes—slow and easy—the only motion he could muster.

It took time for him to recognize that something else moved in the dark. A faint edge of red stabbed through the shadows, a light blinking at a steady and insistent rhythm. He had no idea where it came from and didn't care. The left cheek on his face hurt, and his head throbbed at the same measured beat as the light, inflicting a growing ache from behind his eyes and through the base of his skull. And with it, a chill sent a rush of pinpricks over his skin that cut deeper, especially with his back pressed against something cold and hard.

In front of him, images gradually took shape and emerged from the dark, pieces of a puzzle for his consideration. And like an artery, the red light pulsed, repeatedly teasing him with a glimpse and swiping it away. Crimson lunged across a blanched palette like a strobe effect, capturing a wild array of blotches that marred the surface. At first, the scene over his head looked like a harmless rendition of an artist gone berserk until a metallic sweet odor triggered something else.

Now a strong feeling of dread spoiled his creeping drift through oblivion. Muddled thoughts mercifully tempered the sensation, but he felt it all the same.

Do something!

Urging his body to move, he lifted an arm and dropped a hand to his belly, a sluggish, awkward struggle. His fingers felt dampness on his clothes. And a second bout with the cold swept over him, causing his teeth to chatter. He fumbled a hand to his cheek. It felt warm to the touch and throbbed a little, but he had no idea why. To get his blood moving, he rolled to his side and shoved an elbow under him, the cold tile pressed hard against his joint. When he lifted his head, dizziness brought on a surge of nausea. He nearly gagged but managed to control it.

What had happened? He pried through his memory, recalling nothing of how he ended up here. And where *was* here? He peered through the shadows of what looked like a cramped bathroom. And beyond where he was, the remnants of a cheap motel room, but none of it looked familiar.

Through it all, the flashing light persisted. Its grim red doused everything. He looked across two small beds and saw the light came from a window that had thin drapes partially drawn. Outside, a neon VACANCY sign flared its message, but he couldn't see all of it. And after only a quick glimpse, the light sent shards of pain through his eye sockets and challenged his night vision. To recover, he shifted his gaze to the dark corners of the bathroom again, looking for anything that would trigger a memory.

Instead, he came face-to-face with a nightmare he would never forget. Dead eyes stared back at him from the edge of a tub, opened wide and accusing. A slack head tilted at an odd and unnatural slant. A woman. Her mouth gagged with a soiled towel. Dark hair matted to her head, a bloodied mess.

"Holy shit!"

He gasped and shoved his back to the far wall,

scrambling for a place to hide. But he couldn't shift his gaze from the filmy white eyes and gagged mouth. A face frozen in terror and awash in flashing crimson that stippled eerie shadows over the corpse.

"No . . . no. What . . . ?" His mind couldn't grasp what he saw.

The body smelled of violent death, the metallic sweet odor tinged with something more than he wanted to imagine. And the artist's blotches he had seen when he first opened his eyes had morphed into the reality of blood splatter. He clutched at his damp shirt and pulled away his hand to see it colored by a dark substance. He knew in an instant that it was blood.

"Oh, God."

This time Seth couldn't hold back. He emptied his stomach, even knowing dead eyes stared down at him as he retched.

Sick and confused, Seth got to his feet and backed out of the bloody bathroom, but the eyes of the dead body followed him. He turned away from the gruesome scene and staggered off-balance. To catch himself, he leaned a shoulder into the doorjamb and gripped it with a hand. His legs barely supported him. And even in a stupor, he realized his brain was fried. Trusting his senses and his perceptions would be out of the question.

When he stumbled into the next room, he caught the motion of a shadow outside the window. He only had time to blink, but it was too late. A loud crack, and the door burst open. He lurched backward, his spine jammed against a wall, the only thing that kept him from falling.

"Move . . . MOVE!"

He heard a man yell and had no time to react. His heart hammered the inside of his chest. And when he sucked air into his lungs, he couldn't let it out.

Everything happened way too fast.

CHAPTER 2

Lights flooded the room, and beams spiraled through the dark, zeroing in on him. Seth raised an arm to shield his eyes. Angry voices filled his head. Words whipped by him and through him. Only a few stuck long enough to register a meaning.

"On your knees . . . NOW!"

He tried to react, but panic gripped him, making him sick again. He froze where he stood. His whole body shook. And he knew he had only heard a fraction of what these men had been yelling. Everything surged off-balance—too fast for him to keep up.

What the hell was happening? Who were these men?

"Hands behind your head. Do it!" One man's voice pummeled his ear, louder than the rest.

A bright glare blinded him. His eyes watered. He squinted between his fingers, filtering what little he saw through his muddled brain. It was all so surreal, like a bad movie, not happening to him. But when the silhouette of a man eclipsed the window, more shadows blocked the red blinking light. Now he felt the men close tighter around him. And in the flashes of light, he realized they had guns.

"Don't shoot . . . PLEASE don't shoot me," he begged, raising his hands.

This was real. It *was* happening. And when the yelling intensified, he shut down, too numb and afraid to reason it out. All he wanted to do was collapse and throw up again.

"Oh, God, I'm . . . gonna be sick," he mumbled, unsure they'd heard what he said.

When he bent over to empty his stomach, they rushed him. Strong hands grappled him to the floor. A knee dug into his back.

"Ah. . . . shit! Please," he pleaded. His face was pressed hard to the carpet, muffling his voice.

"Relax . . . RELAX," a man shouted. The way the man delivered his message would do little to calm anyone. "Don't fight," he added, yanking his arm back.

"He's down. We got him."

Seth felt the harsh slap of metal on his wrists, and for the first time, realized these men might be police. He forced his body to give up the fight, but that didn't translate to those who hauled his ass off the floor and frisked him. They manhandled him, but he knew the drill.

He'd grown up knowing way too much about how cops operated.

"Let's get light in here," one man said.

An overhead light came on, blinding him again. When he recovered, he watched two uniformed cops holster their weapons and sweep by him to look in the other room. They stopped before they crossed the threshold into the bathroom.

"Damn." One cop cursed under his breath and turned an angry glare on him. "You're some kind of freak, boy."

Another cop stepped closer and stared at his face, saying, "Yeah, and I suppose you got those scratches on your cheek from shaving." The cop shook his head in disgust.

Scratches? With eyes wide, he sucked a rush of air into his lungs, unable to let it go. And when all eyes turned on him, he avoided their stares, probably looking guilty as hell.

"I know you're not gonna believe me, but I didn't do this." He swallowed. His throat was parched. "I don't know how I got here. And I don't know that woman."

"Well, you're right about one thing, kid," one of them said. "I ain't gonna believe ya."

A cop behind him chuckled, but the ones closest to the bathroom weren't laughing.

While the cops worked at containing the scene and starting their investigation, Seth tried hard to think, connecting the dots through his doped-up brain. No doubt he'd been drugged, but he couldn't remember how or when it had happened. His memory had been wiped clean. And by the looks on these men's faces, another cold fact was undeniable.

In the next room, the body of a brutally slain woman lay sprawled in the tub. The shocking image was forged into his brain when he caught a better glimpse of the dark-haired woman steeped in gore, courtesy of the harsh light overhead. He looked away, but that only made things worse when he noticed his clothes covered in blood. Too much blood to be considered an accidental brush with the body. And the cuts on his cheek ached, another not so subtle reminder of how crazed he looked to the cops.

By the deranged splatter on the bathroom walls, he knew only a certifiable maniac with anger issues would have done such a thing. And Seth figured every cop in the room was convinced *he* was that maniac.

For them, the truth was as plain as the bloody scratches on his face.

Pullman Police Station
South Chicago
Friday, midmorning

"I'm Detective Cooper out of Harrison. I'm here to observe the questioning of a suspect, Seth Harper. Which interrogation room?" Detective Samantha Cooper showed her badge to the desk sergeant on duty, keeping the worry she felt for Seth under wraps.

"Yeah, I heard you was comin'." The sergeant gave her quick directions. "Someone's already up there. He's expectin' ya."

Sam headed for the observation room knowing Detective Ray Garza would be waiting, a homicide detective out of Harrison.

Chicago was split into five detective districts. Sam worked Vice out of Harrison Station, but because of where they'd picked up Seth Harper, he'd been taken for questioning to Pullman. Off the Calumet Expressway on 111th Street—not far from where she worked—Pullman Station covered sections of South Chicago. And Sam believed Garza would grease the skids to get her an inside track on Harper's case.

At least, she hoped the man would help her.

Detective Ray Garza had gotten wind of Harper's situation and given Sam a reluctant heads-up phone call an hour ago. He knew she'd want to know about the kid's troubles and had done the right thing. But he wasn't happy with her and Harper's close connection to Jessie Beckett, a local Fugitive Recovery Agent and her best friend since childhood.

Sam had heard the reluctance in Garza's voice when he called her earlier at work, but he made his point clearer when he said, "That bounty hunter is gonna ruin your career, but you know how I feel about her. 'Nuff said."

"Yeah, I do, Ray." She sighed, making sure he heard it over the phone. "But I sure wish you'd quit worrying about my career." She regretted saying it. Even though she'd spoken her mind, the last thing Sam wanted was to alienate the guy. "Thanks for letting me know. I'm going to Pullman. Will you meet me there?"

She had no right to ask, but she did anyway. Now it was Ray's turn to sigh on the phone, but without much hesitation, he had said, "Yeah, I'll meet you."

Sam headed for the observation room now, walking down a corridor near the elevators.

She took a deep breath, contemplating Harper's situation along with her looming face-to-face with Garza. Seth was up to his honey brown eyes in a brutal murder investigation. Ray had told her what he knew over the phone, but before she called Jessie, Sam had to size up the case for herself.

Whenever Jessie got involved, drama usually ensued. And her friend would do anything for Seth Harper, a kid she'd been looking for since she'd gotten back from her harrowing trip to Alaska three months ago. Harper was a young guy Jessie had called her summer intern and employed for a while before he disappeared from her life, taking his secrets with him. He'd played a major part in the rescue of a missing girl, but Jessie never got a chance to thank him. Harper had his own problems, Jess had told her. But she never said much more about him.

Now this. Seth Harper was definitely a puzzle.

Sam walked into the darkened observation room. And Ray Garza turned toward her, his handsome face and full head of dark hair silhouetted by the light coming from the interrogation room next door. Ray was dressed in khaki slacks and a navy sport coat with a white oxford shirt that looked good against his dark skin. His subtle cologne always triggered something feminine in her. It could have been his cologne, but she had a suspicion that his dark eyes had more to do with how she felt.

"They just started up again." He kept his voice low so she could hear the questioning from the overhead speakers. "But I gotta warn you. The kid looks guilty as hell."

Sam almost gasped when she saw Seth Harper under the stark fluorescent lights of the interrogation room. He was dressed in a faded red jumpsuit. And he had marks on one cheek that looked red and swollen. He'd been given a washcloth, but he'd missed more than a few spots, leaving streaks of red on his pale skin. And the dirty washrag, stained with blood, had been placed next to him on the table.

"What happened to his clothes?"

"Evidence. They were collected and bagged," he said. "And they printed him and got photos. You should've seen him. The kid was a real mess when they brought him in."

Seth's dark wavy hair looked disheveled. A departure from his normally endearing boyish appearance. And stubble had grown over his chin and jawline. With his normally alert eyes lacking their usual luster, he looked worn down and lost. She didn't know the kid like Jessie did, but she'd have bet money Harper would be the last guy to kill a woman.

"They ID the vic?" she asked, crossing her arms and watching Seth.

The detectives in the next room were repeating questions that Harper now refused to answer for the hundredth time, another ploy from a cop's playbook to break him.

"No, nothing yet." Ray glanced her way, enough for her to notice. "The crime scene was brutal, Sam. That woman was butchered with a knife. And she had small puncture wounds on her stomach and breasts like she was tortured. If you'd known her, I doubt you'd recognize her now. I'll spare you the details, but if that kid had anything to do with her murder . . ." Ray didn't finish, but she had a feeling he wasn't an advocate for death-penalty reform, an impression he reinforced when he added, "For some crimes, a needle in the arm is just not enough."

"You said they arrested him at a motel. How did the police hear about it?" she asked.

"They got an anonymous tip off a nearby pay phone. Techs are dusting for prints there, but you know how that goes. A real crapshoot."

"An anonymous caller, meaning no real witness to question?" After Ray shook his head, she continued, "How convenient. A brutal murder, and no one hears anything?"

"She was gagged, but a killing like that?" He winced. "It took some noise."

They'd both seen it before. A woman gets hacked to death, and no one had seen or heard a thing. A solid witness might have condemned Seth or helped him. Now, if no one came forward, circumstantial evidence would be all that remained. And Harper would make a convenient sacrificial lamb.

"Typical." She sighed. "Did they recover the murder weapon?"

"Yeah, at the scene." He grimaced. "And they think the bloody handprint they found on a doorjamb is his. They're still processing the scene. We'll know more soon."

Sam saw the circumstantial evidence piling up. A regular slam dunk for the DA. Without a witness or a solid base for reasonable doubt, Seth could go down without the DA's Office breaking a sweat.

"How long will they hold him?" she asked.

"They get him for forty-eight hours unless they come up with other charges to hold him over." Ray stared into the other room. "To question him, they Mirandized the kid, but no arrest yet. And he hasn't lawyered up either."

Ray was careful not to offer an opinion on Seth's situation, playing the part of the cagey homicide detective even with her. To make an arrest, they needed probable cause, but she suspected that wouldn't take long.

"He had alcohol on his breath when they brought him in. And he appeared intoxicated," he said. "They're getting a warrant to test him. Does he use drugs?"

Good question. She didn't know Seth well enough to give a solid answer. And Sam wondered if Jessie would know either. But once they got their warrant, any drugs Seth might have in his system would have dissipated by the time they had tested him. She wasn't sure if that would be good or bad. She glanced back at Garza, responding to the hint of compassion in his voice.

"I've only seen the kid a couple of times, but I'd wager he isn't a user."

"Gut instincts tell me that guy has more than alcohol in his system, that's all." Ray met her eyes. And in the tight and dark quarters of the observation room, being alone with him felt far too intimate. She forced herself to look away.

"Wish I could argue the point. Maybe Jessie knows more about him."

As a detective, Garza was as rock solid as they came, and she respected him as a man, too. Despite his strong feelings against Jessie, Ray would help if he could. Sam knew Harper's fate would be decided by the system, but if Ray could ease her burden, she knew he'd try.

He had never crossed a personal line with her, always remaining professional. Yet something in his eyes gave her the impression he wanted more. Woman's intuition or wishful thinking, Sam had no idea. Maybe Ray kept his distance, fearing he'd catch sparks off the blazing meltdown of her career, a reasonable certainty under Jessie's influence.

"Your call whether you bring your friend into this, but with someone like her on his side, that kid doesn't stand much of a chance."

Sam couldn't hold back any longer. Her eyes flared at Garza, and anger stirred hot in her craw.

"As I recall, you were just as sure Jessie was good for the murder of Lucas Baker a few months ago. Maybe you should cut her some slack. And giving Harper the benefit of the doubt wouldn't hurt either. Whatever happened to innocent before proven guilty?"

Ray rolled his eyes, a subtle show of insolence. Normally, she found the gesture appealing, but not when directed at her.

"I saw that." She glared, but he didn't give her the satisfaction of noticing.

Sam knew that Jessie had earned a name for herself

with the local cops. For the most part, her friend did her job well and without incident, but on more than one occasion, she'd demonstrated her more-obsessive nature when it came to pedophiles or other abusers. Lucas Baker, case in point. Jessie had her personal reasons. And even though Ray would back off if he understood Jessie's motivation, Sam would never betray her friend's trust by sharing her secrets.

Jessie's Achilles' heel had gained her a reputation that kept her from garnering better money in her line of work. The more successful bail bondsmen wouldn't work with her, so Jess hustled for money as a freelancer, catching odd jobs for lesser-paying recovery work. And the local cops resented her tenacity, especially if she targeted their paid snitches. Sam had learned to trust her friend's instincts, but Jessie had few advocates within CPD ranks.

She only hoped that when Jessie got involved in Seth's case, she wouldn't make matters worse. But there'd be no holding back the floodgates of Jessie's support after she found out what had happened to Harper.

Death, taxes, and Jessie's loyalty were things to count on.

"Do they have anything else on him that I should know about?" she asked.

"Since they're still working the scene, it's too early to tell. But the kid has been close-mouthed about where he's livin', and his background is real sketchy. Apparently he's been livin' off the grid, and that ain't helpin' his case any." Garza shook his head. "And he remembers goin' to meet someone at a bar, but so far, he's stickin' to some lame story that he . . . get this . . . he doesn't remember. Like forgettin' is a legit alibi."

"From what I know of the kid, he might be protecting someone," Sam speculated, then turned to face him. "And if he's telling the truth about not remembering, a smart detective might have to work hard to unravel what really happened."

She ventured a faint smile. "Are you gonna be that smart detective, or will I have to step in?"

He raised an eyebrow and crossed his arms. "This isn't my case. I was only doin' you a favor, Coop."

In the small, dark room, his low voice sent a gentle flurry of pinpricks over her skin.

"Does that mean you aren't up for a side wager, Raymundo?" She inched closer to him, rolling her tongue with the Spanish pronunciation of his name. "I mean, if CPD has such a strong case, what are you afraid of? That my instincts are better than yours?"

"This isn't about your instincts. It's about your loyalty to a friend . . ." He touched her cheek with a finger. " . . . somethin' I happen to respect." Then he grinned, cocksure of himself. "Besides, I'm not sure you can handle the truth about this case if it goes south."

"And I have serious doubts you can deal with a woman beating you to it, macho man." She matched his stance. "So what's it gonna be?"

Garza narrowed his eyes, and said, "What kind of bet do you have in mind?"

*   *   *

In a cramped room off her kitchen, Wilhelmina Smart sat at her worn Formica table, contriving ways to steal a baby.

She swapped a peek out her dingy miniblinds between swigs of lukewarm coffee and a suck of her cigarette. Dust from the blinds mixed with the smoke that stung her eyes as she stubbed out the cigarette in an ashtray that should have been dumped days ago. To ease the throbbing of her tailbone, Wilhelmina stood and lumbered to the kitchen for a refill on coffee, lighting up again as she did.

Michelle would be on her doorstep soon, pregnant with a grandbaby she might have a shot at keeping if she played her cards right. This girl, and plenty more like her, had spread their legs for her boy Eddie. She loved him, despite his ways, but he never had good taste when it came to women.

"That boy humps anythin' breathin'," she mumbled, pouring coffee and having second thoughts about the breathing part. "Never can keep it in his pants."

If she couldn't convince the girl to give her the baby outright, then she'd take it, legal or not. Knowing Eddie, that girl wouldn't make a fit mother.

"Would serve her right, the whore."

She unloaded her ample frame onto the chair again, sloshing coffee onto the stained tabletop. With a swipe of her hand, she made things right, tossing the spill to the floor. Her strapping boy Eddie carried sturdy seed, like his daddy, but a bitch like Michelle had no business raising his baby. Only family could do that.

Her boy didn't know what was good for him, but she'd make him see.

Eddie would be asleep for another hour, but he'd want to eat before heading to work. He serviced big-rig engines for a friend, with money passing under the table. Since he'd come to stay a month ago, avoiding the problems in his life, her small subleased rental house smelled of motor oil and the body odor only a man could make. And he constantly left lights burning, but since she didn't pay utilities separate, she didn't make a big deal about it.

But sharing one bathroom was a royal pain. Every day she dealt with the toilet seat being up and the boy's dribbles. Hell, sometimes he'd miss the bowl altogether. *Men!* She wouldn't mind if he paid her something for her troubles, but the boy had a nasty habit of being a taker, even with his own momma. How the hell did he get *that* way?

When she peeked out the window this time, she saw a girl walking to her front door.

"Well, I'll be." A smile spread across her face. "You're about ready to pop, ain't ya?"

The girl's round belly tented the oversized NASCAR sweatshirt she wore with swollen boobs bouncing underneath. She had on a faded ball cap, pulled down low. And a dark pair of sunglasses hid her plain-looking face. Getting knocked up was obviously an embarrassment.

Before her visitor rang the bell, she trudged for the door. When she opened it, the girl stood with one hand raised, ready to knock, with the other on her belly.

"You must be Michelle." She forced a smile and opened the screen door. "I recognized you from your pictures on MySpace. You're even prettier in person."

The girl was taller than she expected. And her pregnant belly looked to be filled with more than one kid. After she stepped inside the door, she took off her sunglasses, revealing a noticeable scar over her eye. Intense dark eyes stared back at her, and she wondered, for the first time, why such a woman would have anything to do with her son. A momma's gut reaction. Something didn't sit right, but before she said anything, Michelle beat her to it.

"You said Eddie would be here." Her eyes searched the room and peered down the hall toward the bedrooms. "So where is he?"

The way Michelle glared made her think twice about her chances at tricking the girl out of her baby. Something in her eyes wasn't right.

"If you were lying to me, I'm out." The girl turned to go, not waiting for her answer. She meant business.

"No . . . wait." She reached for Michelle's arm. "He's here. I just gotta get him up, that's all. You stay right there. Don't move."

She held both hands up as she headed for the hallway. A part of her didn't want to leave the girl alone, unsure whether she'd bolt or steal something.

"Eddie? We got us a visitor," she yelled. "Get your ass out here."

At the sound of her voice, the dog next door started to bark. But it took a while for Eddie to get moving. Eventually, he stumbled down the hall, his face scrunched, his eyes squinting from the light. And his reddish blond hair looked more like sunbleached tumbleweed.

All he had on was a pair of boxers, ones she'd given him last Christmas with the Superman logo on them. His trucker's tan made his skin look like a cotton tee—and with him scratching his bare belly with greasy nails—he looked a far cry from the man of steel, even through a momma's eyes.

"Where the hell are your manners, boy?" As he walked by, she smacked him upside the head and kept talking, "Get yourself dressed."

"Ow." He winced. "What did you do that for?"

But when he spotted the girl, his face blotched red. And his eyes flared in anger.

"Momma, what the hell did you do?"

"Hello, Eddie." The girl smiled, rubbing a hand over her swollen belly. "I'm fixin' to send Junior to college. What do you say? Care to make a contribution to our boy's college fund?"

What happened next took Wilhelmina by complete surprise. Michelle pulled a shiny silver gun from under her baby bump and leveled it at her son's face. That little girl was packing heat. And she'd brought this trouble to her own doorstep. All things considered, her day was swirling down the crapper. And she had no desire to find out what would come next.

"Now hold on, honey. What's going on?" She raised both hands, careful not to get between her son and the crazed girl holding him at gunpoint. After all, if that thing went off, she didn't want to get hit by mistake.

"She's a damned bounty hunter, Momma. Her name's Beckett."

"Jessica Beckett, ma'am." The girl pulled out something from around her neck that had been covered by her oversized sweatshirt—a badge as shiny as her gun. "And I prefer Fugitive Recovery Agent." To Eddie, she said, "You up for playin' nice, or are you gonna piss me off again?"

With a downright lethal glare, Eddie raised his hands, but faster than Wilhelmina knew he could move, her son bolted down the hall toward his bedroom. A half-naked Superman moved faster than a speeding bullet, his version of it.

"Oh, hell!" The bounty hunter lowered her weapon and chased after him, pregnant belly and all.

The girl ran by her, full tilt.

"What are you doin'?" she cried after her. "You're gonna hurt the baby."

CHAPTER 3

Chasing Eddie Smart, Jessica Beckett hit the déjà vu zone, remembering the last time this guy pulled a rabbit on her. She tucked her new .357 Magnum Colt Python away under her fake baby bump, knowing this would be another footrace. But this time, seeing his butt jiggling in Superman boxers would leave her scarred for life.

Another hazard not covered by workman's comp.

"Shut 'er down, NASCAR. You're only making me mad," she yelled, only seconds behind him.

But the guy slammed his bedroom door in her face. In stride and not stopping, she hit wood with her shoulder, hurling open the door. It hit a wall with a loud crack. And the dog next door went into a frenzy. Close on Eddie's heels, Jess had burst into the room and grappled him onto the mattress before he crashed through the nearest window.

"Oh, God." She winced as she pinned him to the bed.

His whole room smelled like feet.

"Get off me, damn it!" He drooled on the bedsheets. "Watch it!"

With his nose mashed to one side, it was a definite improvement. She straddled his body, fumbling to keep Junior out of the way. Her fake pregnancy gear had worn out its usefulness, leaving only one purpose now. It kept Eddie's hot sweaty skin at a distance.

"Eddie, come on, man." She bent his arm back and slapped on a cuff. "You skipped on bail. Did you honestly think Momma would be an asset?"

After she secured his other arm, she backed off him, heaving for air. She caught a peek from a dresser mirror. Eddie's momma stood in the doorway, her skin flushed.

"Honey, are you okay?" She shook her head. "You ought to not jostle the baby like that."

Jess stared for a long moment, taking in the absurdity of her situation. She glanced in the mirror again, seeing herself in NASCAR gear and baby bump. And a slow rumble of laughter started deep in her belly, her real one.

"I'm not kidding, honey. You maybe ought to go to a doctor or something."

And Momma Smart made it worse. She fought to keep her laughter to a minimum, but the harder she worked at it, the more maniacal she sounded. Jess knew Eddie's momma needed to see things for herself. As the woman's son lay sprawled on the bed, whining and complaining, Jess stripped off the fake pregnancy belly, a suffocating outer layer when worn with her Kevlar vest underneath. She tucked the phony belly under her arm and pulled her weapon again, not sure Eddie's momma would let her pass.

"Your son skipped on bail, and he's under arrest. You got anything more to say?" She stood over Eddie, waiting for his mother to register the truth on her face.

"So you ain't Michelle?"

"Not today." Jess rolled her eyes and pulled Eddie to his feet, heading him for the door.

The name Michelle had been a random pick. Jess had taken a chance with it, but she doubted Eddie would ever remember a woman's name, even if he'd slept with her.

"But your blog . . . the NASCAR. And your picture with my boy," the woman's voice trailed off as realization hit her between the eyes. Luckily, the woman kept her distance, allowing Jess to haul Eddie's ass safely to the curb.

"I heard Eddie used to be on MySpace. I figured it was worth a shot to set up a page with his picture on it . . . to see if someone recognized him."

Jess didn't explain the marvels of Photoshop, the only place where dismemberment wasn't against the law.

Seth Harper would have done a better job at splicing the two images together, but she hadn't found Harper yet. The guy she jokingly called her summer intern had vanished from her life without a word. Thinking about him made her sad. She sure missed her baby-faced computer genius, someone she had believed was her friend.

"But . . . what about my grandbaby?" the woman whined, her face knotted in a strange pout.

Jess had used Junior as bait for an old girlfriend or someone from Eddie's family. The gamble had paid off in spades. Even though she hated coming between a mother and her pride and joy, after meeting Momma Smart, she figured they deserved one another.

That nut hadn't fallen far enough from the tree.

Cursed by a name he could never live up to, Eddie Smart was dumber than a heaping pile of pea gravel. And taking him out of the gene pool, in any meaningful way, was too much to hope for. Men like Eddie always found a way to breed.

His original arrest had been in connection with an alleged assault of an old girlfriend. After taking his fists to that little snippet of a girl, Eddie didn't like his odds with the court system, so he'd skipped. Unfortunately, he wouldn't be incarcerated long enough to do the world any good. As a Fugitive Recovery Agent, she'd seen this drama played out far too often.

"Lady, just knowing Eddie could unleash his progeny on the world scares the hell out of me. But after meeting you? Well, it explains a lot."

The woman narrowed her eyes and pooched her thick lips, but she was done asking questions. She left the woman on the curb, still scratching her head over what had happened. Her boy walked slump shouldered down the sidewalk with his hands cuffed behind his back. She had her ride parked on the street, down the block.

Jess had figured right. It appeared Momma Smart harbored regrets about Eddie being the only legacy for her efforts as a reproducing human being. She craved a second chance to redeem herself with a brand-spanking-new grandbaby, fresh off the line.

Well, that wasn't going to happen—at least not any-time soon.

And Jess breathed a sigh of relief, empowered by the knowledge she'd saved a woman or two from the shock of waking up next to Eddie Smart, a man who single-handedly put the ugly back in coyote. She'd done her part for the sisterhood and earned some cash to boot.

After she'd secured Eddie Smart into the back of the blue monster—an old Econoline van Seth Harper had loaned her three months ago after her car had been blown up—she ditched the pregnancy contraption in the front seat and climbed behind the wheel. She called in her arrest to the bail bondsman on the job, but when she was done, her cell phone rang. Caller ID pegged the incoming call as coming from her best friend, Samantha Cooper, a cop with CPD Vice.

"Yo, girlie. What the hell ya doin'?" She grinned, grateful for the reminder that humanity wasn't wholly defined by the Smarts.

"Hey, Jessie. I know you've been looking for Seth." Her friend got down to business, minus her usual smart-ass banter. Not a good sign.

Getting a call from a cop regarding a missing friend sent chills over her skin, a wave of needle pricks that cut deep. Seth's sweet face flashed through her mind, a contradiction to the way her gut twisted under the grip of a dark premonition.

"Is he . . . is he still breathing, Sam?" It pained her

to ask, but waiting for *anything* wasn't in her nature, even bad news.

"Yeah, he's still with us, but he's in a lot of trouble." Sam gave her location, Pullman Station. "I'll explain when you get here. Where do you want to meet?"

"Booking works. I've got an arrest to drop off. I'm heading in." Before her friend hung up, she asked, "Sam, I gotta speak to Harper. Can you arrange it?"

"Already done. And Jess?" Sam's voice grew more somber. "You're gonna want to clear your plate. He'll need your undivided attention. They're booking Seth for murder."

Cook County Jail
Chicago

Jess couldn't claim to know Seth Harper well, but she'd be willing to bet big bucks that murder wasn't part of his playbook.

After she'd gotten the skinny on Harper from Sam, Jessie went to see him in lockup at the Cook County Jail, allowing her friend to report for her shift. She walked down a long hallway with dingy ceiling tiles and fluorescent lights overhead, escorted by a cop on jailer duty. Her steps echoed down the corridor, a lonely sound that she'd always associated with institutions. While she was being raised a ward of the state, she'd seen plenty.

Bland cinder-block walls were painted the color of oatmeal. And a few signs on rules of conduct were posted, screwed into the wall as if someone would steal

them even here. The holding-cell area carried a smell—
a mix of ammonia, glass cleaner, and an underlying
odor she didn't want identified.

When her escort got to the end of the hall, he unlocked a door with a keycard and gave her instructions
that went in one ear and out the other. Her eyes had
found Seth Harper sitting behind a wall of Plexiglas at
one of the five visitor stations. After the door slammed
shut, they had the room to themselves.

Under the stark lights, Seth looked tired, with dark
circles under his eyes. Jessie hadn't seen him in three
months. And until now, she hadn't realized how much
the boy had taken root in her world, like a damned te-
nacious weed. He had severed their tie, and it hurt to
know he had done it so easily.

Letting people into her life had never been easy.

From her earliest childhood memories, her best
friend Sam Cooper had always been part of her, like a
vital deep-seated bone marrow. And recently, Payton
Archer had gotten under her skin, too, even though
their paths had crossed in the blink of an eye. They still
talked on the phone, but distance had taken its toll. He
lived in Alaska, having chosen to stay and help his
family mend, a choice she respected. Months ago, the
abduction of his niece had given them common ground,
but for them to move forward in a real relationship,
they'd need more. She'd come to that conclusion far
sooner than Payton. He still called from time to time,
refusing to give up the ghost. And she missed him terribly.

Some people left marks, good and bad. But anyone

who'd gotten under her skin had come away with a piece of her. And Harper had been no exception.

"So . . . it took handcuffs to get you to look me up?" She turned the chair around and straddled it, resting her chin on the heel of a hand.

"I didn't exactly look you up, Jess." He shrugged and avoided her eyes. "Sam did."

"Thanks for reminding me you never lifted a finger. A woman doesn't like hearing she's been dropped from a guy's speed dial, Harper. You didn't give me much of a chance. I grow on people."

"So do tumors." He slouched deeper into his chair with arms crossed, fading behind smudged Plexiglas. His voice sounded tinny through the speaker, and it echoed in the room.

She'd seen Seth Harper in a diverse array of garments, from his signature jeans and Jerry Springer wear to slick upscale slacks and shirt suitable for a five-star hotel in downtown Chicago, the last residence she'd seen him. But in his red prison jumpsuit, he looked washed-out and sad. Warm puppy eyes had grown distant and lifeless. Jess didn't think she had a maternal bone in her body, but seeing Harper like this made her think twice about that prospect. She wanted to hug him and tell him it would be all right, but she wouldn't lie to a friend.

"You gonna tell me what happened?" When he didn't answer, she pressed, "Look, Harper, I'm not seeing a long line of acquaintances outside, clamoring to help. And unless you've got one of those Get Out of Jail game cards they sell on the streets of Hollywood, I suggest you think long and hard about answering me. Your options are limited."

When he resisted her considerable powers of persuasion, she made her point a different way.

"At the risk of stating the obvious, you're not like the guys you'll meet in prison, Harper." *Thank God,* she thought. "Not all of them are innocent, you know. And with your luck, you'll get bunked with a guy named Bruno who's just waiting for you to drop the soap."

"Thanks for the visual." He sat up and leaned forward. "You're not exactly helping."

"Then give me something. I thought we trusted each other."

"Trust isn't your strong suit, Jess. Who are you kidding? But I respect your privacy. Why can't you do the same for me?" he pleaded.

"Because being arrested for murder ranks a little higher than sneaking a peek in your diary, my friend."

Jess knew she'd be treading on thin ice if they continued to talk about trust and privacy. Harper had her pegged. A change in subject was in order.

"So where are you staying now? You noticed I used the word 'staying.' You like to keep your toiletries bag packed, ready so you can jump."

"I'm not giving you that."

"You've given me your addresses before, why not now?" When he stalled, she made a leap in logic. "Who are you protecting, genius?"

"I won't drag innocent people into this mess. So please drop it." He raised his voice for the first time. "I got myself into this. Me, alone. And I'm not protecting anyone 'cause no one else knows what happened. Hell, not even me."

He wasn't making much sense, and by the look on his face, he knew it, too. She needed another way under his defense mechanism.

"Look, let's start from the beginning. Tell me what you *do* remember," she said, then smirked. "And if it helps, picture me looking like a wart or some insidious skin rash. I'm not going away until you do something about it. Do us both a favor and throw me a bone, Harper."

Not even the skin-rash analogy worked. Her best material. He tightened the arms across his chest, his body language not telling her anything she didn't already know. But eventually he loosened up, ran a hand through his dark hair, and started to talk.

"I recall making a note of Dirty Monty's, a bar on the South Side. But I can't remember if I actually made it there."

She knew the joint. A sleazy bar that wasn't Seth's style. She had a feeling someone else would have made the suggestion. Jess tried picturing who could have gotten Harper to do it, and the extent of her wild machinations only reminded her how little she knew of the guy sitting across from her. Harper's life was clouded in mystery, and he liked it that way. As much as she wanted to believe she'd broken into his inner circle, she hadn't even scratched the surface in understanding what made him tick.

But having the name of the bar was more than the

cops had. And that gave her a place to start poking around.

"You gave me the blue monster for safekeeping, and I appreciate the loan. That old van has grown on me." She smiled. "But what are you driving these days?"

"A '65 Mustang. I'm restoring it, but I've got a long way to go." He stopped, probably considering the odds of him finishing his restoration project.

Murder had a way of mucking things up.

"What does my car have to do with this?" he added.

"Tracking it down might help establish where you went that night. Just another piece to the puzzle, that's all."

"Damn it! I hate this." He drew a hand through his hair. "I've racked my brain trying to remember anything, but it's all a blank. I can't tell the cops or you what I don't know, not even to help myself."

His frustration was showing, and he looked exhausted.

"What . . . you had some kind of blackout? From what?" She pushed him for more. When he didn't reply right away, she leaned forward and rested her elbows on the table. "If you don't have a plausible story, the cops won't buy this convenient flare-up of amnesia. Memory loss doesn't just come and go like a bad case of zits, Harper."

"I don't know, Jessie." He shook his head, looking dazed as he tried to recollect what had happened. "I remember leaving for the bar, but the only other thing I recall is opening my eyes and staring at . . ." His voice trailed off.

Jess had heard from Sam how they found Harper. No doubt the kid would have nightmares, and she knew all about those.

"There was all this blood . . . and that dead woman. Her eyes. The cops haven't told me who she is . . . was, I mean. I'd never seen her before, but I couldn't swear by it. She was so messed up, I didn't . . ." He shut his eyes for an instant, clenching his jaw. "I have no idea how I ended up there. Honest, Jessie. I have nothing to say in my defense because I don't *know* anything."

She'd hit a wall with this line of questioning, but now that she'd gotten him talking, she needed to find a way to keep him going. One thing she knew. To distract his mind from the horror of what he'd seen, it would take more than a clever segue.

She knew from personal experience that some images scarred the retinas with permanent damage, like the scars on her body from the horror of her childhood. Nightmares would surface on the rare occasion that her life got on track, a persistent reminder that she was anything but normal. Now, sitting here with Harper, she had a sense he'd always been a kindred spirit in that regard. And although he'd never shared that part of his life, maybe one day he would.

"Hard to picture you hangin' at Dirty Monty's." She softened her voice. "Had you been there before?"

It took him too long to answer. Jess cocked her head, letting him know that she noticed. After another roll of his eyes, he gave her the bare minimum.

"Yeah, once."

She stared at him in silence until he glanced up.

"What's her name?" she asked.

Harper flinched. It had been subtle, but it had been there all the same. And his cheeks blushed, spreading red streaks across his skin. She'd gotten a reaction that told her she'd hit pay dirt.

"Gotcha." She grinned and pointed a finger. "Now spill."

CHAPTER 4

New York City
Fifth Avenue at 56th Street

The city and its welcoming familiar sounds stirred with a newfound vitality as Alexa Marlowe stepped out of the exclusive jewelry salon of Harry Winston's on Fifth Avenue, unable to hide her smile. Amidst a throng of pedestrians, she glanced back over her shoulder at the magnificent stone archway with its black-gated entrance adorned in gold.

She had window-shopped but hadn't been inside until today.

"You've got style, Garrett," she muttered under her breath. "I'll give you that."

As she strode down Fifth Avenue with her mocha-colored Calvin Klein silk tank dress, vintage floral opera coat, and blond hair wafting in the breeze, her thoughts turned to the man who had impacted her life.

In cryptic fashion, her boss, Garrett Wheeler, had asked her to meet him at The House of Harry Winston, giving her a specific name to contact at the prestigious store. When she did, the saleswoman only smiled and gave her a magnificent velvet box containing the most beautiful diamond necklace she had ever seen. Her fingers shook as she held it to the light, each perfect gem holding tight to its precious trace of rainbow.

Garrett perplexed her. Her boss one minute, her amazing lover the next. He had opened her eyes to life in a way she had not expected—through her sensuality. And she'd been grateful but had come to recognize her addiction to his ways, making her hungry for her own experiences. Up until now, she had only played out her fantasies in her mind, imagining sexual encounters with strangers.

No names. No talking. Only satisfying her urgent need.

Somewhere along the way, she'd accepted Garrett as her teacher rather than a lover with the promise of a future together. It had been a painful discovery over the last several months—to accept their relationship for what it was—not for what she once hoped it would become. But once she let go of that hope—that conventional anchor—she gave in to Garrett's needs and discovered a few of her own. And perhaps she had known all along that he had a more-demanding mistress.

His job.

At first, after the way he'd phrased the message to meet him, she had thought it might have something to do with her job as an operative working for the Sentinels, a covert and well-funded international organization. She had never met the men behind this group, but Garrett had. He served as a go-between to protect their anonymity. These men waged a private war against criminals who'd found refuge in a global arena where multijurisdictional boundaries had created havens, making it impossible to prosecute. The Sentinels took matters into their own hands like vigilantes and remedied the problem, discreetly. And she was a cog in that wheel.

But Garrett loved surprises and had a knack for creative liaisons with her in the most unexpected places. As she walked, she only half expected to see him, unsure where he'd make his move. The man had been *that* unpredictable. Yet something reflected in a store window had caught her eye.

In a sea of yellow cabs, buses, and the occasional bike messenger, she spotted a sleek black limousine making its way toward the curb. Eventually, it trailed behind her, not making a secret of its presence. When she stopped, so did the limo. And as the rear door opened, Garrett grinned from his seat inside, that slick disarming smile that always took her breath. He was dressed in an elegant charcoal gray suit and hoisted a crystal champagne glass toward her.

"Care to join me?" His low voice teased her ear, making the city fade until there was only him. Even in an urban jungle, she would have recognized the familiar caress of his voice anywhere.

She climbed in next to him, ignoring the curiosity of people on the street.

"You really know how to make an entrance."

He kissed her and handed her a flute of champagne. The drink warmed her body as she sipped, but she wondered if Garrett had more to do with that.

"Nothing's too good for you, Alexa." He poured himself a glass as the limo pulled into traffic. "I had intended to catch you for dinner this evening, but something has come up. We need to talk."

Garrett had a way of mingling business with pleasure that made both very palatable, but his face looked more somber than usual. His steel gray eyes appeared darker in the subdued light, a color she imagined existed on the fragile edges of the sky before it turned to the pitch black of infinity.

"What's up?" she asked.

"I'd like you in Chicago by tonight. I've made all the arrangements. By the time you're packed, you'll have your itinerary and accommodations. But I'm leaving the trip up to you. Once you hear what I've got to say, you can decline if you'd like."

"Oh? What is this about?" She raised an eyebrow.

"It hasn't hit the papers yet, but it will. And I thought you'd want to know."

"Now you've really piqued my interest." She smiled. "And your network never ceases to amaze me."

Garrett had "associates" in key positions domestically and across the globe, those men and women sympathetic to the cause of the Sentinels. Such a network had taken years and perhaps decades to cultivate. Alexa had the impression it had existed before Garrett and would endure long after his influence. They appeared to be an ancient order of overseers who had adapted to the times.

"Jessica Beckett. You remember her?"

The bounty hunter. How could she forget? And hearing her name from Garrett's lips sent a ripple of jealousy through her that she had worked hard to suppress. Three months ago, the woman had helped her bring down Globe Harvest, a worldwide predator organization that bartered in human lives online. For them, everything had a price until the Sentinels dealt a crippling blow to their clandestine operation. Thanks in no small measure to Jessie Beckett.

Garrett had implied an interest when he'd first learned of Jessie and called her an "interesting woman," a term he had used to describe Alexa shortly before he hired her to work for him. Being intimate with Garrett had made her vulnerable to a pang of jealousy at the time, but she had gotten through the last assignment and put it behind her. Now the coincidence of his request for her to travel to Chicago made her question Garrett's real motives.

Was his request for legitimate reasons or did he have another more personal agenda in mind?

"Yes, I remember her." She forced a smile. "What's going on?"

"Her friend Seth Harper has been arrested for murder. He worked for her."

Alexa recognized Harper's name as someone connected to Jessie.

"Worked? As in past tense?" She narrowed her eyes. "Have you been keeping up with her?"

"Yes. She'd make an excellent asset," he replied without hesitation. "I thought you agreed."

"So we'll be capitalizing on Seth Harper's hardship to recruit Jessie. Is that what you had in mind?"

"Is that how you see it? Jessie could probably use the support, and if it nets us a new operative, I see no reason to pass up this opportunity." He cocked his head in question. "Do you have a problem with this? Like I said, you don't have to go, but I thought you'd want to."

He was leaving it up to her, but what choice did she really have? She respected Beckett and would want to help if she could. She had to deal with her unexpected jealousy to move on with her life. Perhaps a trip to Chicago wouldn't be a bad idea.

"No, I've got no problem with it. I just know how fast you seize an opportunity. And since you find Jessie Beckett an *interesting woman* . . ." She used his words from three months ago, words that had triggered her jealousy then. ". . . Seth Harper's situation may position us to take advantage of his troubles to gain leverage with her."

He considered her point as if it had never occurred to him, but she knew better.

"I suppose you're right. If we help Beckett's friend, she may be . . . grateful. Our organization could come off in a favorable light. And yes, she'd make a great addition to our team."

"Then I'd say the timing of this murder is perfect. Count me in," she said.

"You act as if I arranged it. Do you really think . . ." He laughed and took a sip of his champagne, not finishing his thought.

A part of her suspected Garrett was ruthless enough to do just that. When it fit his agenda, she knew him to be capable of far worse. All business, Garrett raised his chin and fixed his gaze on her.

"When you get to Chicago, contact Jessica. Let her know we're looking into her friend's case. And I'll have an associate send you a file with what we know."

In a slick maneuver, he had intervened and expanded the role Alexa had intended to play. She hadn't counted on making contact with Jessie until she had something to offer, but Garrett asked her to make a show of *his* support. She had become "we," and at some point, there might be a price to pay for Garrett's help.

Seth Harper had become a focus worthy of the Sentinels.

"Will do." She nodded. "Anything else?"

"No, that's it for now."

"If all goes well, I suppose you'll want to talk to Jessie."

"Yes, I will. Call me if the bounty hunter is receptive to the idea, and I'll make arrangements to meet you." His somber face warmed to a smile. "But whether she is or not, maybe we could take a few days off to ourselves in Chicago. It'd be nice to get away, just the two of us."

By the hungry look in his eyes, she knew he meant it. She felt the pull of their mutual addiction. Alexa sipped her champagne and leaned forward to loosen his tie.

"Now you're talking." Her throaty voice and sugges-

tive expression sent the message. The business part of
their meeting had concluded. "I'd love some downtime
with you . . . alone."

"We're alone now."

"Yes, we are."

Done with talking, she closed her eyes and kissed
him, breathing in the subtle smell of his cologne with
her fingers entwined in his dark hair. His lips and
tongue tasted like pricey champagne. She hadn't intended to do much more than kiss him, but when her
hand moved under his suit coat, she craved the feel of
his bare skin, especially as he nuzzled her neck. The
sensation sent a tingling shock wave over her body, and
things got out of control. Under the silk of her dress,
blood rushed down and through her, a surge of pleasure she couldn't restrain.

"I thought you'd be wearing it." Next to her ear, his
voice resonated against her, driving her crazy.

Alexa understood what he meant. She had slipped
the jewelers case into her vintage Dior envelope purse,
saving it for when Garrett could put it on her personally. But she didn't tell him that. She found another
way to say it.

"I wanted it to be the only thing I wore the next time
I saw you."

That made him smile. She heard it in her voice when
he said, "Now why didn't I think of that?"

He kissed the palm of her hand, then reached over
and punched a button on a control panel. She heard the
soft whir, and the window to the driver's compartment
closed. And even though every window in the vehicle

darkened with a screen for privacy, she still saw the people and traffic outside.

"Can they see in?" she whispered.

"I doubt it."

Without another word, he trailed his fingertips down her legs, unbuckling the straps to her platform Miu Miu shoes and tossing them aside. The carpet felt good against her bare feet.

"Garrett? We can't . . . not here."

"What if they *can* see us, Alexa?" He got to his knees between her legs and stripped out of his suit jacket and yanked off his tie, not taking his eyes off her. "Do you really care?"

Her cheeks flushed with heat. She wanted to glance toward the cab that had stopped next to them at a light. She saw the taxi driver turn his head from the corner of her eye. But she couldn't take her gaze off Garrett. The man's swarthy good looks mesmerized her, and behind those eyes was an enigmatic man far too complicated to understand in a lifetime.

On the outside, he wore pricey clothing like a mogul on Wall Street, but underneath it all, a wicked scar or two on his dark skin reminded her of the violence in his life. She'd seen him kill with the same passion she saw in his eyes now.

He'd become as adaptable as a chameleon with one foot in the civilized world and the other in places she was too scared to contemplate. Truth be told, that had been the part of him she wanted to understand but never would.

"What if they *are* watching us?" he asked again, his

voice lower. Her rapid breathing filled the quiet vacuum of the limo, mingling with his. As he unbuckled his belt, he kept talking to her. "Let's give them something to see."

He reached under her dress, his large hands gripping her hips and lingering.

"Tell me you want this, Alexa. Tell me how much you want it."

Garrett loved pushing her limits when it came to intimacy. Every new experience put his mark on her. And she knew it.

"I want this . . . I want you." She reached up to kiss him, but he only shook his head.

"Take it off. Everything."

Driven to the brink beyond caring, she didn't take long to make up her mind. Piece by piece, she took off her coat and silk dress as he watched. She didn't take her gaze off him, not wanting to break their connection. With every garment she removed, the hunger in his eyes intensified.

She turned her head toward the nearest window and found she wanted someone to see her. She even craved it, but before she told Garrett how she felt, he spoke first.

"Where is it? The necklace."

Alexa retrieved her purse and gave him the necklace. She held back her blond hair to let him slip it on her neck. The gold chain and diamonds dazzled on her warm skin as it flushed with arousal. It was all she wore.

"What do you think?" she asked as she posed for him, her inhibitions gone.

"Priceless." Drawing her closer, he lowered his lips to her body.

"Oh, Garrett. Yes."

He knew exactly how to touch her and took what he needed. Like an out-of-body experience, she pictured the scene in her mind's eye—in broad daylight, in the middle of traffic. She looked up into the urban landscape of New York City as the limousine stopped at another light and pedestrians crossed the street, peering into their tinted window.

And the sensation was . . . exhilarating.

She had changed and assumed Garrett had been the reason. Like an obsession, her need for sex had intensified. All she cared about was pleasing a man in every way he wanted, without holding back. For her, nothing else mattered. The effect Garrett had on her had been consuming.

But what if he'd only been the catalyst, a trigger that cultivated a darker side to her nature? Is that what he'd seen in her from the start? She closed her eyes tight—giving in to every subtle demand of Garrett's body—blocking that thought from her head.

Surviving the cutting edge of life and death had forced them to live every moment as if it would be their last—a mentality that had been a gift and a curse. Without regret or restraint, they had seized every opportunity to be together, living life to the fullest. Their gift.

Yet their curse had been living their lives without the naïve hope of a tomorrow. They couldn't count on anything. Perhaps that was why they were together in the first place—another facet of their relationship she refused to probe.

Examining her life too closely scared her more than a barrage of bullets.

Cook County Jail
Chicago

By the look on Harper's face, Jess knew she'd guessed right that a woman had been involved in his missing hours. But several questions later and her best tactics, she still hadn't gotten him to 'fess up. And time was running thin. The duty cop would be knocking on the door soon, and her time with him would be up.

"I don't want to bring her into this. She's got enough problems." He crossed his arms and slumped in his chair. "And she's not exactly a fan of law enforcement, if you know what I mean."

"I get that same sense from you, hotshot. What's up with you and the boys in blue?"

She'd hit another raw nerve, one she hadn't expected. He was definitely protecting a woman, but the cop thing got a reaction from him, one she'd file away for later.

"Talk to me, Seth. We're almost out of time."

"Look, you don't need to know everything, Jessie. If I don't remember making it to that bar, I probably didn't. And if that's so, then having her name won't help. She's not a part of this."

Jess sat back in her chair. Harper had a stubborn streak and had been a real pain in the ass. The whole experience had been like looking in a damned mirror.

"You know I won't narc for the cops. If this friend of yours wants to steer clear of the law, I'm okay with that. But we need all the pieces to the puzzle, and with your memory being Swiss cheese, we gotta start somewhere." She leaned forward and fixed her eyes on him until he returned her stare.

"You gotta trust me, Harper. Give me her name and where I can find her. We won't know what kind of help she'll be unless we ask. Maybe she can fill in the gaps of what happened that night, lead us somewhere worth going. Please . . . trust me. None of this is going to the cops. I'll keep her name out of it. I promise."

She'd finally struck a chord with him or had worn him down. She saw it in his eyes.

After a heavy sigh, he said, "Her name is Amanda Vincent, Mandy. But her street name is Desiree." He gave a general description of how to find the woman and what she looked like. A waiflike blonde who sold her soul every time she wanted to get high.

"And, Jess, be careful when you cross over into her world. It ain't safe there."

"Thanks, Harper, for trusting me." She reached into a pocket for her cell phone. "Now I need something from you. Try not to look like a booking photo."

She raised her cell phone to take his picture. She'd need it for her stop at Dirty Monty's. Someone might remember seeing him last night. After she got a reasonable likeness, she wanted to press him for more, but a loud knock interrupted their session. The on-duty cop opened the door, telling her what she already knew.

Her time with Harper was done. But as for his mystery blonde, Mandy "Desiree" Vincent—well, that was another story.

Given Harper's word of warning about the dangerous world Desiree lived in, she'd have to come up with a backup plan to make sure she walked away with all her body parts. Jess knew what to expect, but she'd need more than that to face it.

CHAPTER 5

South Side of Chicago
8:20 P.M.

Jess knew something about Desiree's world because she lived on its fringes, one of many reasons she didn't go alone. Her Colt Python made good company, plus she'd brought an unexpected surprise if she got cornered. Not being known for her subtlety, she firmly believed one thing.

Stun grenades made righteous icebreakers.

Englewood Police Station covered the 7th District, an area that ran north and south from 55th Street to 75th and west to east from the Penn Central Railroad to the Dan Ryan Expressway. The district had a vibe to it, even in daylight. But after dark, the place took on the razor's edge of a war zone. Street gangs protected their turf—boundaries defined in spray paint—each vying for control of their slice of the shit heap. Its seedy underbelly sprouted from every sidewalk crack, reflected off every shard of glass strewn down murky alleys, and snaked like caustic smoke from every discarded cigarette tossed on the street.

She equated the 'hood to a hostile living thing that stirred when provoked. And tonight had given her more faith in that analogy.

Jess had started with those she knew and trusted, then eventually hit the danger zone, resorting to a flash of cash to get someone talking. A calculated risk. In the 'hood, money had a way of multiplying influence like a modern-day miracle of biblical proportions. Sure, it would get her noticed, but not always by the right people. She had wanted information bad enough to pay, and that meant someone else could barter for the flip side of that morsel. After all, everyone had to eat. But not all negotiations were about money.

Favors could get someone in tight with the local powers that be. Long after she'd gone and taken her meager bankroll, others more influential endured. Information was king in most places. The 'hood was no different.

She had spent a few hours working her street connections. But no matter how cautious she'd been in her search, she suspected the word had leaked that she was looking for Desiree. Cooperation had dried up, and things had gotten real quiet—the eerie dead calm found in the eye of a storm.

Dirty Monty's would be her last stop of the night. By the time she'd get to the sleazy bar, it'd be in full swing. On her way there, she cruised the side streets around the bar looking for Harper's '65 Mustang, but came up empty. She made a mental note to try the crime-scene parking lot later—the last place she wanted to find his vehicle. Even though the cops probably weren't looking for Harper's Mustang, locating it at the scene of a grizzly murder would be another damning nail in his coffin.

So far tonight, she'd discovered nothing that would help Harper. And frustration closed in tight.

After she'd found a prime spot to park the blue van, a block down from Dirty Monty's, she hoped her luck had changed, but that didn't happen either. Not one waitress recalled seeing Harper, but a young bleached blonde shared her thoughts on what she'd like to do to the boy after seeing his photo on her phone.

"Thanks, honey," Jess raised an eyebrow. "I'll let him know. And just between you and me? Nothing says true love like a ball gag and paddle."

Oblivious to her sarcasm, the woman grinned, but before she walked off to serve drinks, Jess asked, "I need to talk to one of the bartenders. Which one?"

The waitress pointed to one of the guys behind the bar. "Try Jake Cordell. He's a prick, but he's in charge."

"They usually are." She tossed a tip on the woman's serving tray. "Thanks."

Jess claimed a barstool nearest Cordell and started a conversation with him. At first, the stout spiky-haired man with a nose ring had no recollection of the night Seth had been there. The guy hardly looked at Harper's digital photo when she held up her phone, but he kept up his end of the conversation as he served drinks.

"I see a lot of faces in a night. Sorry, lady. Don't remember him."

Money might jog his memory, but she opted for a cheaper tactic—lying.

"The kid got into a car accident leaving here," she said. "I do investigative work for his insurance company. They hired me to look into his DUI. I'm only trying to save you the hassle."

The bartender stopped and gave his full attention. "What hassle?"

"I've seen this before. A kid has too much to drink and everyone comes lookin' for the guy who let him get that way. Insurance is one thing, but civil lawsuits can get real ugly, man. When they arrested him, his blood-alcohol level was off the scale."

"No way, he only had a few beers." The man's memory suddenly became crystal clear. He tossed a wet rag onto the counter, ignoring a patron tinkling his raised glass for a refill. "And besides, he had a buddy take him home. I saw 'em leave."

"What did this buddy look like?" she asked.

"Oh hell, I don't know." He nudged his head to the other bartender, getting him to handle the insistent man with the hoisted glass, and kept talking. "The only reason I remembered your guy in the photo was because he made a scene. He nearly passed out, but someone came forward to help. He acted like a friend, but I never got a good look at him. Last I seen 'em, they were headin' out the door, and your guy was walking . . . sort of."

"So according to you, he only had a few beers. Yet he almost pulled a face plant and needed assistance to walk? That doesn't make sense. Which is it? Was he drunk or not?"

"Lady, I have no idea. I know what I served him. Maybe the kid had the flu."

The bartender stepped aside to serve a drink, but he soon came back with more.

"I only remember one thing about the guy who hauled him out last night." He raised his beefy arm, giving her a visual aid by pointing to his biceps. "He had a tattoo on his arm, right here. I never got a good look, but from a distance, it looked like something with a black curve to it. Maybe a letter or a snake."

She pressed him for more, but the guy came up dry. A tattoo of a black curve—a letter or snake—was the best he could do. It wasn't much, but more than she'd had.

"Do you know a woman named Desiree? Was she in last night when the kid was?"

Nose Ring Boy gave her the stink eye. Clearly she'd hit a nerve. At first, she wasn't sure he'd answer. Eventually, he did.

"Yeah I know who she is, but that girl is seriously messed up. She sells it for crank. If she was here last night, I didn't see her. Last time I saw her, I told her to beat it."

"When was that?"

"Maybe a month ago. I caught her working outside, in front of the bar. She'd hit up guys as they left. And she'd settle business in an alley down the block. Blow and go."

If what he'd told her was true, that meant Desiree might be freelancing, working without a pimp. No pimp would allow her to skim off enough to feed a habit. That would take low dollar and high volume, not a pretty picture and a real dangerous lifestyle. But the bartender avoided her eyes as he wiped down the bar. He was hiding something.

"Yeah, I can see how you'd be upset. Dirty Monty's has such an upstanding reputation. A hooker would only spoil the ambience." She cocked her head, letting him know she wasn't buying any of it. "You mean she never gave you a piece of the action for letting her conduct business out front?"

The guy took in a heavy breath, still having trouble looking her in the eye.

"Look, I don't begrudge anyone a livin'." He lowered his voice even though the place was loud enough, staying out of earshot of those at the bar. "And I'm all for free enterprise. She came to me first. All she asked me to do was keep my mouth shut about what she was doin'."

"For a piece of the action." Jess pushed him to admit it.

"I never saw it that way. For me, she was only feedin' the tip jar." He rattled the nearby glass decanter, filled with dollar bills and coins.

Jess had enough of his smug attitude. She leaned closer, putting her elbows on the bar. "You ever take it out in trade?"

She'd hit another soft spot. Score one for the home team. He shut his eyes tight and shook his head, no doubt regretting having started the conversation.

"Yeah, from time to time, she'd do me for free. What about it? It was consensual. She said she couldn't get enough of the old kielbasa." He shrugged with a smirk. "Me? I chalked it up to quality control. The girl doesn't look like much, but she has a lip-lock that makes your eyes water."

Thankfully, he shifted gears. "But I started gettin' complaints from the customers. Crank makes her crazy. Real paranoid. I was afraid someone might call the cops. And I knew if that bitch got hauled in, she'd spill her guts on anybody. And with our history, she'd drag me in out of spite."

"Yeah, I can see how you'd be concerned, you being completely innocent and all."

He shrugged again, ignoring her cynicism.

"Anyway, I kicked her ass out, and I hadn't seen her back. End of story." He pointed a finger at her. "I never did nothin' illegal. She did me for free, and it's her word against mine on anythin' else. Who'd believe a crank whore?"

The jerk walked away, saying, "I gotta get back to work."

Good move. Jess had heard all she could stand from the arrogant ass. She questioned a couple more waitresses but came up empty. Time to call it a night.

With her ears ringing and her clothes smelling of smoke, Jess needed a breath of fresh air. She had a lot on her mind as she walked out the front door of Dirty Monty's. How did Mandy Vincent turn into a pathetic street urchin named Desiree? And what connection did this woman have to Seth Harper? A part of her was scared to know the truth—the part with the nagging voice that questioned who Harper really was. He had too many secrets. And although she'd given him plenty of opportunity to speak up, he refused to share.

She reached for the car keys in her jean jacket, but as she headed for her van, a hulking man blocked her path, his ugly mug mercifully steeped in shadow. And another man, who looked Middle Eastern, leaned against a truck parked on the street, sucking on a cigarette. He tossed his smoke aside and joined the one who stood in her way.

Jess held her ground, assessing her options. She felt the weight of the Colt Python holstered under her jacket. But if she played her cards right, she wouldn't have to use it. Her backup plan had more potential to bail her out. She slipped a hand into her pocket, taking hold of the M84 stun grenade.

If the guys were the Welcome Wagon for the block, she wanted to make a good first impression.

With a smile, she said, "If you boys hurry, you can still make karaoke hour."

CHAPTER 6

"I hear you been looking for Desiree," the smoker said in accented English. "Who are you? And what's your interest in her?"

Dark skin with piercing eyes and a prominent nose, the guy kept his distance. Real cagey.

"Because I can see we're going to be such good friends, you can call me by my first name, Oprah. And my interest is personal." Inside her jacket pocket, she wrapped her fingers around the M84 stun grenade canister, feeling for the detonation pin and lever.

"Not good enough." The taller man joined the conversation. "And for the record, attitude don't work with us."

Jess sized up the two men. What Beef Boy lacked in gray matter, he made up for with brute strength and the ego of a bully who hadn't been bested. He was posturing to impress her with his bulk, but she had no doubt he worked for the smaller man with the nasty nicotine habit. And if things got dicey, the smoker would be the man to watch. He had the cold unreadable eyes of a predator who didn't have to prove himself.

"I got mixed feelings on that," she said. "Bad news

is, I gotta toss out all my best material 'cause attitude is all I got. But on the plus side, that means I've got nothin' to say."

She tried sidestepping the muscle, but he blocked her, saying, "We ain't done." His right eye twitched like a warning blinker.

"Then make your point. I might cooperate if we had a little give-and-take." She directed her question to the smoker. "What's your interest in Desiree? Does she work for you, or is she a good customer?"

From what the bartender told her, she didn't figure Desiree had a pimp, but she didn't want to make assumptions. If she had to guess, she'd put money that this guy was her dealer. Yet why would he take a personal interest in a small-time streetwalker turning tricks for product? More questions stirred in her mind than she had answers.

But one loomed larger than the rest.

Desiree had made herself scarce for a reason. Being a hooker with an addiction, she'd made a tough decision to lie low. What had scared her enough to stray from the demons she knew? Jess had a feeling the girl knew what had happened to Harper and didn't want to get dragged into it. Or maybe she'd set him up in the first place in exchange for money to feed her habit. Another real possibility. Jess knew that when she located the troubled girl, any answers she'd give would give her no more than a fifty-fifty shot at helping Seth.

Finding Desiree would either prove his innocence or lock him in a box for life.

"You're not understanding how things work here."

The smoker lowered his voice and stepped forward. His version of "less is more" had worked. "I ask the questions, and you answer. If you can't abide by this, then you've got a serious problem."

She kept her mouth shut for two reasons. One, if this asshole believed he had the upper hand, he might let his guard down enough to let her stun grenade do the talking. And two, keeping her trap shut gave her time to think up a lie worthy of her fierce skills.

"Now tell me why you're looking for Desiree," the smoker persisted.

The side of beef to his right crossed his arms, grimacing in thought. Apparently, thinking was a challenge.

"She's my sister." She shrugged. "Half sister, actually. Our mother wanted me to track her down. Any idea where I can find her?"

Jess always appreciated the irony in faking sincerity.

"What do I look like . . . 4–1–1?" The big guy smirked. His face made the effort look like it hurt. "I ain't interested in makin' this a family reunion."

"That's too bad. Havin' you in our family would've taken pressure off me bein' the black sheep."

Having a finger on a detonator gave her a whole new appreciation for the word "empowered."

"Just say the word, boss. Gimme a reason." He reached into his pocket and took out a switchblade. The whisper of its jutting blade caused the hair at the nape of her neck to stand on end. These guys wouldn't be satisfied with a hand slap.

"You don't look like the kind of guy who needs a

reason to hurt a woman." She locked eyes with his, not backing down. "I bet you ran with scissors when you were a kid. Didn't your momma teach you about the danger of sharp objects?"

"I ain't worried about that, but you should be." The eye twitched again.

"Taking a knife to an unarmed woman, that's the mark of a real coward."

"But it does get your attention, don't it?"

She stood her ground, her body taut and ready. Timing would be everything.

He clenched his jaw and made a move toward her. Jess clutched the grenade, primed to react, but a man and woman walked out of Dirty Monty's. They were talking and laughing too loud, a reaction to the noise inside. The man hesitated and stared at the two men next to Jess. And everything came to a grating stop.

"What are you lookin' at?" Muscle for Brains pocketed his blade and glared until the man backed off without a word.

The two latecomers to the party had assessed the situation and opted not to get involved. They headed around the corner with heads down and tails between their legs. In the 'hood, once the action went down, she'd be on her own. Good Samaritans these days were as rare as a straightforward politician.

"Whoever Desiree was before, she isn't now," the smoker reached in his pocket for another cigarette and lit up. "She is no longer your concern. If you're smart, you'll walk away. Forget about finding her."

Anytime the guy opened his mouth, she got a cold

chill. He had defused the tension, but she had the feeling he liked to strike when least expected. A primitive-yet-restrained cruelty hardened his words. Unleashed, the guy would do serious damage.

The question was—would he let her walk or would he feel the need to demonstrate?

"I appreciate the advice. And I'll certainly give your words of wisdom all the consideration they're due." Her friendly way of saying—hell, no, and mind your own damned business. "But I still need to find her."

Admittedly, she could have played it smarter. Provoking the guy wasn't the mark of a sane woman. The problem was that Jess wanted more from their exchange than these men were willing to give her voluntarily. Harper needed results—and answers. If she played the trump in her pocket, she had options—her way.

"Then you leave me no choice," he said, his voice low.

For the first time, the smoker curved his lips into a nicotine-stained grin. All in all, she wished he hadn't. She had enough trouble sleeping.

"That makes two of us." Jess fixed her eyes on him, sending the man a clear message that he'd misread her. She saw that he'd gotten the message, but his hired muscle wasn't a man of subtlety. Without waiting for an order, the big guy made his move.

And so did she.

The man lunged for her, his meaty hand reaching for her throat. With her left arm, she blocked his attack and grabbed his wrist. A quick yank and she wrenched his arm, thrusting it back. The move caught him off-balance. He compensated with a shift of his body, but as he leaned, she cocked her hip and swung a leg behind him. His momentum dumped him onto the sidewalk, slamming him hard to the concrete.

It happened fast, but time hadn't been her friend. The smoker had reached into his jacket. In the shadows, his moves were a blur. It didn't matter whether he'd pull a knife or a gun, either way she had no time to think—only react.

Her life would mean nothing to this man. She had seen it in his eyes.

Jess reached into her pocket and took out the stun grenade. She pulled the pin and lever, tossing it between them. She'd have only seconds. The disorienting effects of the blast would be over in a heartbeat. But unless she moved, she'd be swept up in the detonation.

A second later, a deafening blast thundered off walls. It echoed wave after wave down the block. And a blinding light stabbed the dark.

Her heart slugged the inside of her rib cage, her adrenaline on overload. She barely had enough time to lunge for cover. Jess felt intense heat at her back. It seared her exposed skin. For an instant, the grenade's brilliant flash stole her night vision. Pinpricks of light assaulted her eyesight. Her ears rang, but she wouldn't be as bad off as the men who had attacked her. They rolled on the ground with arms over their heads, moaning and dazed.

Although she wasn't in great shape, Jess had to move. In no time, these men would recover. A crowd had already started to form. And onlookers gazed cautiously down from windows along the street, silhouettes eclipsed in light. Hunched over, she kept her head down and crept toward the first man. Covering up what she was doing, Jess kept her back to the crowd and searched for his wallet, only having time to take his driver's license. She did the same with the smoker.

People had started to congregate, making a tightening circle around the men on the sidewalk. Now she'd have to improvise.

"What happened? Did anyone see anything?" she yelled. When no one pointed a finger at her, Jess took charge. She kept her head down and barked orders like she had a right. "Someone call 911. These men need help."

She kept up the chatter until it stirred others to act and take over. In the confusion, she slipped deeper into the shadows and melded with the crowd. She made sure no one noticed, waiting long enough before she climbed behind the wheel of Seth's blue monster and drove away.

She wasn't worried about the two men implicating her. They'd never talk to the police. As soon as they recovered—only a matter of minutes—they'd be gone, leaving the cops nothing to investigate. And if anyone remembered a mysterious blue van parked down the block, or if they had read the tag, they'd only find the vehicle registered to Seth. Being in jail gave him an airtight alibi. But Jess knew she'd made an enemy of the smoking man. He'd left her no choice. And he had looked like a man with a long memory.

Her heavy breathing mixed with road noise and muffled in her head, a lingering reaction from the detonation. Streetlamps cast ribbons of sparse light through the windshield and painted the dark interior of the van. The scrolling glow gave her enough light to read the names of the men she'd pissed off.

The hired muscle, Sal Pinzolo, and the smoker, Nadir Beladi. With Sam's help, she'd soon have more on these men. And maybe she'd be one step closer to finding Desiree, Harper's best shot at discovering who had framed him for murder.

But she had one more stop to make before heading home—and she sure as hell wasn't looking forward to it.

Outside Chicago

The Twilight Motel had seen better days, Jess thought as she sat in her van parked in the shadows.

The motel's cinder-block walls were colored in mottled aqua—the owner must have scored a deal on cheap paint—and it had a boxy construction any child could have designed in crayon. The place was totally forgettable except for one thing. Someone got off on ceramic gnomes. Several stuck out from under overgrown hedges and near the office door. Their faces were chipped, and their leprechaun clothes had faded with the sun, but no amount of damage had deemed them unworthy.

"God, I hate gnomes," she muttered. With an elbow propped on a door panel, she ran a finger along a scar over her eyebrow, an old habit.

Gnomes ranked top of the heap on the shudder scale, even above the imposed giddiness of a yellow smiley face. At one time, the elf-infested motel might have seen interstate traffic, but a new addition to the area changed that. A nuclear plant had taken residence down the street. She saw the lights of the large facility on the horizon. Some local businesses had moved out after the plant got up and running. Now the motel looked as if it barely supported itself.

A red flickering neon sign pulsed its message of vacancies available, one of the few indications the motel was even open. At this time of night, the neon cast a sickly red pallor onto the gnomes and reflected off the windshields of the three cars parked in the lot. No sign of activity or Harper's Mustang. Maybe the murder, and its crime-scene tape fluttering in the breeze, had deterred the usual patrons who rented rooms by the hour.

Jess checked her Colt Python, slipped out of her van, and locked up. She pulled her black White Sox ball cap down over her eyes and slipped through the shadows along the perimeter of the property, trailing an old cyclone fence toward the rear. If there was a back way in, she preferred to take it, but there wasn't. She was disappointed not to find a way into the crime scene from the more private rear of the property. She headed for the only way in.

Nothing like a little B&E before hitting the sack.

Jess walked around the front of the motel, acting as if she belonged. When she got close to the crime-scene tape across room number six, she retrieved her lock pick and got to work. Seconds later, she had the door wedged open, but an overzealous CSI tech had crisscrossed the entry with an overabundance of yellow barrier tape. Clipped to her jeans pocket, she carried a small knife. She used it to cut the tape, at least enough for her to squeeze through.

Once she got inside, Jess had to hold her breath. The unmistakable smell of death hung heavy in the room. An odor no one ever forgot.

Jess let the darkness close in, her vision adjusting to the pitch black. She crossed the room to close the drapes and flicked on her small flashlight. The dim light shed a frightening pallor over the scene. Blood had dried to dark burgundy and brown with castoff stains and crimson shoe prints marring the carpet, but as she headed for the bathroom, the blood splatter gripped her heart in its cruel fist.

In the dark, a flood of memories came back to haunt her. Her heart rate and breathing escalated out of control. Images of her dead tormentor's face raced out of the shadows, forcing her to flinch. And she felt his hands on her, still. Jess hadn't expected such a strong reaction. In her line of work, she never had to deal with dead bodies or this much blood.

She shut her eyes and clutched her hands together to stop them from shaking. In her head, the horror of the dead woman's last moments played out like a sick replay—her muffled screams, the terror in her eyes, the meaty sound of a knife striking her body again and again, and the frantic thrum of blood flung onto the walls and ceiling.

Unable to stand, Jess dropped to a knee and lowered her head, trying to stop the images from invading her mind. She forced herself to breathe, slow and easy, trying to quell a low and rumbling wave of nausea. She hated feeling this vulnerable . . . again.

Harper had nothing to do with the murder—but even as much as she wanted to clear him—Jess knew she had to take her investigation a step further. She had to hunt down the real killer. Whoever had done this had crossed her path, brutally taken a life, and framed a friend to get away with it.

And that was enough to really piss her off.

Jess left the motel office, knowing she'd hit another dead end. She drove the van from the motel parking lot and pulled onto a dark stretch of road, heading for home. It had been a long day, made worse by the deep exhaustion she felt in her bones and a troubled mind that wouldn't quit.

She grappled with the horror of the bloodied room, unable to leave it behind.

The smell of violent death had embedded in her nostrils and permeated her clothes. And from the shadows inside the van, images from her past continued to assault her memory. Distant and muffled screams in the middle of the night, a crying child she couldn't comfort, the heavy footsteps on wood that signaled more terror—all of these memories jutted from the gloom in strobe flashes. An unhealed wound exposed by her traumatized psyche.

With her thoughts scattered, she drove the murky two-lane highway of mostly farm country, barely noticing the yellow center lane whipping by. Switchgrass tossed in the breeze, and countless fence posts were caught in the funnel of pale light cast from her head-lights. In the solitude, she let the disturbing surge of emotion settle upon her, an affliction that had grown far too familiar over the years.

Jess tried to distance herself from the past without much luck. To crush the trembles, her hands gripped the steering wheel too tight, her lifeline to the present.

Long ago, she had been encouraged to embrace the tragedy of her childhood as an affirmation of her strength, turning a negative into a positive as if it were that simple. After all, being abducted by a sexual pred-ator and tortured hadn't killed her, exactly. Surely it must have made her stronger, at least that was what others had told her time and time again.

If she'd survived the ordeal, she could endure and overcome the traumatic memories now. But that mean-ingless drivel came mostly from the many therapists who had placated her over the years, making her a pet project while she was under foster care with the state of Illinois after her rescue. Eventually, they moved on to other kids and left her to figure it out for herself, leav-ing her with nothing more than a Band-Aid fix for the equivalent of a hemorrhage to her soul.

In reality, she hated her weakness, something she hadn't told anyone—not even Sam.

But after a quick glimpse in the rearview mirror, Jess caught something that forced her instincts to take over. A car in the distance. It appeared to be tailing her, staying far enough behind that she'd almost missed it. No headlights. Any normal person would have as-sumed the idiot had forgotten to flip on his lights, but

Jess had developed a paranoid sixth sense over the years.

She hit the accelerator to see if she had company, testing her suspicions. When the car behind her picked up speed to match hers, Jess knew it wasn't her imagination.

"Great, just great."

She floored the gas pedal and put the blue monster through its paces, knowing it would be a challenge to stay ahead. Harper's old van wasn't built for speed. Jess craned her neck, looking for the lights of the nearest interstate over her shoulder. Making a last-minute decision, she hit the next turn a little too fast.

The tires squealed in protest, and the van lurched.

"Shit!" she cursed under her breath. The sudden move jostled her off the seat, straining the seat belt. But the car behind her kept pace.

Her eyes darted between the dark road ahead and her rearview mirror. She couldn't see the tag or the make and model of the car, only an occasional glint off the dark windshield.

Safety in numbers, she needed to get to the interstate or a place she could lose her tail. Here in the open, she stood out. And she'd never outrun the guy. If the driver got close enough, he could shoot out a tire, run her off the road, or worse. And defending herself in this remote area would be tough.

"Damn it!" The heft of her Colt Python under her jacket gave her comfort, but not enough.

Not nearly enough.

CHAPTER 7

Once she hit the gas, the car behind her sped up and closed the gap between them—giving deadly chase. Her van hit its limits, but it wasn't enough. Bumper to bumper, her pursuer had no intention of playing it safe. If she got to the interstate, potential witnesses would complicate matters, and the driver had figured that out. He ramped up his game.

BANG! The asshole behind the wheel gave her a love tap on the bumper, grinding metal on metal. It knocked her teeth shut and jolted her neck.

"What the hell . . . ?" She shot a glance toward her mirrors, but the car swerved, not giving her a clear view.

Now the driver swung into the oncoming lane and hit the gas, passing on her left. In the dark, she saw nothing of the man inside, only heavily tinted windows on a dark sedan. She yanked the wheel to cut the bastard off. If he got beside her, he might fire a gun. She'd be a sitting duck.

She spotted the interstate ahead, not more than a few miles.

"Come on. Come on!" She urged the blue monster on, white-knuckling the wheel and keeping an eye on her mirrors.

All she had to do was stay ahead of the jerk. If she got to the freeway, she'd have a chance.

The sedan veered into the other lane again. This time, the driver gained the advantage, pulling alongside her. She clenched her teeth and kept driving, focusing on what lay ahead. A flashing red light marked the intersection of the farm road with the freeway. The entrance ramp was a hard right. She wasn't sure the blue whale could take it.

"Damn it."

And worse, she caught motion from the corner of her eye. The bastard was rolling down his window. And from the shadowy interior she saw the murky silhouette of a man raising a weapon. He was going to shoot. And with the turn up ahead, she'd have to slow down, making her an easier target.

"Oh, shit!"

Precious seconds. She had run out of time. Only one option remained.

Jess took a risk. She yanked the steering wheel left and collided with the sedan. *To hell with being a victim!* The crunch of metal sounded like the high-pitched grind of nails on a chalkboard. On impact, she sent the sedan hurtling for a ravine to the left. Traveling at high speed, the car went sailing over a ditch and bellied out on the other side.

"That's gonna leave a mark," she muttered as she hit the brake to slow down.

Jess made the turn onto the entrance ramp, watching over her shoulder as the sedan barreled for a wall, struggling for control. The vehicle scraped the embankment, sending up sparks like a Roman candle on steroids.

Once she got on an open road with streetlights, she took a ragged breath, her nerves catching up. Looking for Desiree had made her a target. But if she wanted to help Seth, she couldn't stop at the first sign of trouble.

"Damn it, Harper! What the hell did you get into?"

The next morning

"Yeah, I need to speak to Dispatch please." Jess gulped more lukewarm coffee and rubbed the back of her sore neck. "Yeah, I'll hold."

Last night's car chase had left Jess dealing with a stiff neck and aching muscles. And to add insult to injury, she hadn't slept at all, not with Harper in jail. For her to catch a few Z's felt like a complete waste of time and a betrayal of her solidarity with his predicament. And after seeing the remnants of the bloody crime scene, she was afraid the powerful images would stir her own demons.

Sleep had never been much of a friend.

"Dispatch. Arnie here."

"Hey, Arnie. I was wondering if you could help a girl out." She told him what she wanted and settled down for a wait after he put her on hold.

When he came back onto the line, he said, "Nope. I got nothing on that. Sorry, lady."

"Yeah, thanks." She hung up, striking out again.

Jess took a break from her morning phone calls and dumped her stale coffee in favor of fresh brewed. With coffee percolating, she thought about last night, an odd cluster of events, especially more surreal in the light of day.

Her trip to Dirty Monty's had started it all—setting her on a course with a major pack of scumbags—a collision course that earned Seth's blue whale a few more scrapes. But at the crack of dawn—after coming up empty on finding Harper's '65 Mustang at the motel parking lot last night—she throttled her mind into overdrive, running various scenarios through her plausibility meter. And her brain hadn't stopped since.

According to that sleazoid bartender, Harper had made it to Dirty Monty's, but Jess wondered how he had gotten there. Sometimes even the small details might be significant in the right context.

She hadn't found his Mustang parked near the bar or at the crime scene. If the real killer had taken it, that would have been a bonehead maneuver. The cops would be looking for it so crime scene techs could search for more damning evidence to lock Harper away for good. With a viable suspect in hand, CPD might not search too hard for the car. But if trace evidence of the murdered woman could be found in the vehicle, anyone caught with it could be hauled in for questioning as an accomplice.

With Harper remaining tight-lipped about where he lived, the police might not find his car anytime soon. Stalling the cops on the case didn't bother her. But with

Harper having major gaps in his memory about what had happened, he couldn't even help himself—or her. The whereabouts of his car was a loose thread she couldn't let go, but maybe she didn't have to. She had another option to explore.

What if Harper hadn't used his car at all?

Already on her second pot of coffee, she'd hit the yellow pages since dawn, calling cab companies operating in South Chicago, playing a hunch. If her boy genius had used a taxi, it would satisfy her curiosity on Harper's Mustang. But even better, she'd have a shot at finding out where the boy lived. Cab companies kept record of the location where fares originated.

"And me outsmarting you, my stubborn brainy friend, would be priceless," she muttered, pouring a fresh cup of coffee. But the ring of her cell phone intruded upon the solitude of her morning. She recognized the number.

"Hey, Sammie. How goes the war against crime?"

"We could use reinforcements. That's why you're on the front line." She heard the smile in her friend's voice. "I was calling to let you know that the medical examiner got an ID on the dead woman off her fingerprints, and we got lucky. She had an arrest record." Sam went into the woman's list of offenses, but when she was done, her friend added, "She doesn't sound like anyone Seth would hang with, but what do you think?"

After hearing about the victim, Jess had a bad feeling.

"You know, Sam, the kid's got baggage. And he's not real chatty about it, but from what I've seen, you're right. Someone like that doesn't fit. What's her name?"

Jess heard the rustle of paper in the background before Sam got back on the line. With every second it took, her gut twisted and tightened into a knot.

"Her name was Amanda Vincent, street name Desiree," Sam said.

Hearing that name jolted Jess wide-awake, confirming her fear. Harper had claimed not to know the dead woman. Had he lied to her? Why had he given Mandy's name and description—sending her on a wild-goose chase to find a dead woman?

Her hinky barometer crossed into the red zone—none of this made sense. Gut instinct forced her to keep her suspicions to herself. She didn't have enough to tell Sam, at least not yet. But with the evidence stacked against her boy, Jess didn't like the odds. Harper needed someone on his side. And tag, she was it.

She hoped Harper had kept his mouth shut when the cops questioned him again. By now, the detective in charge would have done that. With CPD having the woman's identity, they would have started a push for a confession. Any connection Harper had with the woman would be fair game and used against him. And if her boy genius had flinched when he heard the woman's name, the police would have seen it. His reaction would have been like blood in the water with great white sharks circling. *A feeding frenzy.*

"Can you arrange for me to see Harper again, Sam?"

This time Seth *had* to talk to her.

CHAPTER 8

Cook County Jail
Chicago

"I didn't lie to you, I swear," Seth insisted, sitting behind the Plexiglas of CPD's lockup. "I can't believe she's . . . dead." He looked washed-out, and the dark circles under his eyes looked stark.

"But you had me chasing a blonde. And Sam just told me Desiree was a brunette. What gives?" Jess asked, putting her elbows on the table.

"Last I'd seen Mandy, she *was* a blonde." He shut his eyes, looking tired. His lower lip trembled, but he covered that up by running both hands over his face. "And she was breathing."

He shook his head. "I didn't get a good look at the body. It was dark and . . . I just couldn't. Too much blood, and her face was . . . messed up."

Jess sat in silence, watching her friend. He didn't act or talk like a stone-cold killer. Mandy's death had taken a toll on him. Overnight, he looked older than his years, his innocence gone. But maybe Jess didn't know him as well as she thought.

"I had gotten through to her . . . finally. At least I thought I had." A tear trailed down his cheek, but he couldn't look her in the eye. Under the fluorescent light of the jail, the wetness was robbed of its sheen. "When she let her guard down, you could see . . ."

When she realized he wasn't going to finish—that he was mainly coming to terms with what had happened to Mandy in his own mind—she pushed him for an answer.

"See what, Harper?"

"She had the eyes of a little girl under all that makeup." A sad smile came and went. "She let me see her scrub faced one day. She was really pretty, you know? The kind of pretty that comes from inside." He swept a finger toward his face. "And she had freckles across her nose. She covered them with makeup, but she let me see them . . . once."

Mandy Vincent had only been twenty two years old when she died. The reality of a life cut short hit Jess hard. Considering her own twisted childhood, the same could have happened to her.

"You don't have to tell me this, but did you have feelings for the girl, Seth?"

Jess thought she knew the answer. Harper had secrets, sure. And he certainly was complicated. But when it came to his heart—and the people who mattered most in his life—he appeared to be an open book.

"I just felt . . . sorry for her. And besides, she had a

boyfriend. Jason somebody." He shrugged. "The first time he saw us together, he misread it and got all bent. That was why we arranged places to meet, away from him."

"Do you think he could've found out about you and Des . . ." She corrected herself. Out of respect for Seth's feelings, she wouldn't call the girl Desiree anymore, at least not in his presence. "—I mean, you and Mandy? Killing someone with a knife is an act of passion. Maybe he did it."

Jess wondered if Harper had said anything to the cops about the boyfriend. Anyone hearing his story would assume Harper had gotten involved in a love triangle gone bad. It wouldn't exonerate him, not hardly. Checking out the boyfriend could turn up something usable in his defense or give a motive to the DA. She'd talk to Sam about it, to see what the cops knew on the guy.

"I don't know, Jess. We never really talked about him. I was trying to get her clean. The crank was eating her alive, from the inside out. She already had hep C from sharing dirty needles. Her liver was a fuckin' time bomb."

"Oh man, Harper. I had no idea." Hearing him talk about Mandy raised questions in her mind. Not about the girl, but about the reason Harper had chosen her for his personal project. "How did you meet her? When did all this start?"

Harper slumped back in his chair with crossed arms. Defensive with a capital D.

"I can't talk about that." He shook his head. "But Jess, if you wanna be my friend, don't judge her. I couldn't take that coming from you. Just trust me when I say, Mandy had plenty of reasons for the way she turned out. Some people aren't strong enough to deal, that's all."

Jess heard the truth in what he said about judging people. She'd been on the receiving end of criticism plenty of times. But for her, Mandy had crossed a line. It was one thing to screw up your own life, but to take someone else with you was inexcusable.

To say Mandy had made bad decisions in her life was an understatement of mega proportions. Hooking up with a psychopathic jerk wad with a penchant for sharp objects could have been just one on a long list. She had ruined her life, but to play a hand in stealing the rest of Seth's wasn't right. Jess had sympathy for what her gullible boy genius had tried to do for this messed-up girl, but she found it hard to muster any sympathy until she knew more about her.

"Mandy got caught on the wrong side of dead, Harper. Her life was doing a 360 down the commode. You were only trying to throw her a lifeline. I get that, but the cops have tunnel vision. You being found with her gave them a slam-dunk case. They're not gonna believe that you were only trying to help her."

"Help? She's still dead, Jessie." He shook his head, chin low.

"Yeah, and you're still screwed."

"Thanks for the update."

"I just want you to start caring what happens, Seth. To you."

Harper looked too fragile for Jess to say what was

really on her mind—that his so-called friend had probably come close to destroying him. Even sporting a morgue Y-incision with her chest splayed like a lab rat, the girl still might take him down.

For some, misery loved company—even in death.

"So I guess that's it." He shrugged, defeat settling on his face. "The cops are gonna get me on this, aren't they?"

Jess didn't have much to lift Harper's spirits, but something Nadir Beladi said last night made her think. *Whoever Desiree was before, she isn't now. She is no longer your concern.* Had the smoker known about Mandy being dead before the story had appeared in the papers?

Plus, his beefy sidekick had been too quick with a knife. After he tried to bully her, imagining the bastard using his blade on a woman wasn't much of a stretch. Maybe Mandy had threatened Beladi's livelihood. After all, he'd been willing to cut her up for simply asking questions about Mandy. What did the girl know—being an insider to his dealings—that put a target on her back?

Jess had to get the cops to direct their investigative energy in another direction. *Any direction.* The cops would be building a case against Harper, compiling evidence for the DA to proceed. If she cast doubt on Seth's case—giving them a believable motive on anyone else—he might have a shot at bail. For them to drop the charges now was too much to ask, but that would eventually be the general idea.

"Don't give up on me, Harper." She grinned. "You gotta have faith."

"I do have faith in you, Jessie. And thanks."

"Well, I owe you one"—she shrugged—"or six."

After coercing a faint smile from him, she hit Seth with an unexpected question.

"Why did you take a cab to Dirty Monty's?" It was a bluff. Pretending to know more than she did, Jess stared him down and saw that her question had hit home, sort of. At least it got Harper thinking.

"A cab? I don't remember—" He struggled for glimpses of memory. "But I guess I could have. I grab a taxi when I know I'll be drinking."

She had to smile at the kid. He hadn't seen the irony in what he admitted.

"God, Harper. You're priceless." When he scrunched his face in confusion, she filled him in on the joke. "For cryin' out loud, you even drink responsibly. How could anyone think you hacked a woman to death?"

"Promise me you won't serve as my character witness."

She raised an eyebrow.

"Look, I'm makin' my way down a list of cab companies. If a driver remembers you, it could help build a timeline for that night. But I'm letting you know now that I plan to ask the cabby where he picked you up. You got a problem with that?"

She saw by his reaction, the kid knew what that meant.

"I need to make a phone call, Jess."

"Are you finally contacting a lawyer? If you need a name, I can check around, give you a good referral. You really shouldn't let them assign you a public defender."

"No, this is personal."

Harper was done answering questions. She saw it in his eyes. He'd made a decision, and he wouldn't share it with her. Seth had allowed her into his life in the past, but this time he chose to keep where he lived a secret—even from her.

Keeping his secret—and protecting someone else besides Mandy—was more important than he was.

Seth never thought he'd be on the wrong side of jail bars. And the reality of his situation made his stomach hurt.

Down the hall, a buzzer sounded, and a door slammed with a clang. Footsteps echoed and intensified as someone came closer. A dour-faced jailer stopped at his cell and escorted him down a hallway to a larger room with one phone on a far wall. Other prisoners stood in line. He kept his head down and didn't make eye contact, but they knew he was fresh meat and taunted him until they lost interest.

The rules for use of the phone were posted in more than one language. All prisoners had access to it during limited times of day. If he didn't make it through the line, he'd have to wait for the next time period. Since his call was not considered confidential or to a legal advisor, he had no right to privacy. His call would be monitored. Knowing this, he chose to call someone else, someone who would intervene.

And Harper prayed the man would.

When he got to the front of the line—with all eyes on him—Seth worked through the operator to place the collect call. On the other end of the line, a man with a low, gravelly voice picked up the phone. He acted as if he had expected the call and accepted the charges.

"Seth, is it really you?" the man asked after the operator got off the line.

He shut his eyes tight for an instant, wishing the call hadn't been necessary—not like this. Seth gripped the phone and realized he was holding his breath. Finally, he gulped air and got on with it.

"I need to reach him. It's urgent."

Silence. For a moment, he didn't know if the man would speak or hang up.

"Why haven't you called before now? He's been waiting."

Seth lowered his head and hugged the phone to his ear, saying, "I know."

CHAPTER 9

Harper was protecting someone else. At first, Jess thought it had been Mandy, but with the girl dead, he had no more reason to guard her identity. His reticence had something to do with where he was living now, but she had no idea why.

After leaving Harper, Jess drove to Harrison Station to see Sam. When she got there, her friend met her on the first floor and they walked to a nearby coffee shop to talk, away from prying eyes and ears.

"They took a blood sample on Seth and thanks to Ray Garza, the lab is gonna do a more extensive analysis, not just the standard screening. Ray thought Harper looked more drugged than drunk," Sam said. "But I doubt the final analysis will be back in time for Seth's bail hearing."

"That's too bad, but if Ray is right, the tox screen should help our boy, right?"

"Let's hope so. Harper couldn't remember anything other than heading for a bar, then waking up at that motel room. It would be nice if we had more of a timeline of what he did that night . . . and the name of that bar."

Good boy, Jess thought. Harper had held out with the cops, but the face of the bartender flashed in her mind. As much as she wanted to pin something on the bastard—to wipe the smirk off his arrogant face— anyone in the bar that night could have slipped a roofie into Harper's drink when he wasn't looking. And the tattooed Good Samaritan who had hauled Seth from the bar would be at the top of the suspect list.

"Well, maybe your guys didn't say 'pretty please,'" Jess said. ". . . 'cause Harper gave me the name of Dirty Monty's, a bar on the South Side. And I did a little recon last night."

Sam didn't act surprised to know Harper had withheld information.

"And?" her friend prompted.

"Harper didn't remember making it to the bar, so he didn't exactly lie to the police, but he told me he was supposed to meet Mandy there. She'd set it up." Jess pinched a corner off her Danish and popped it in her mouth. "The bartender remembered seein' him, but Mandy never showed. According to him, she knew better than to walk through the door. He'd kicked her out for conducting business outside with bar patrons."

"But why would Mandy arrange to meet Seth there if she knew she wouldn't be welcomed? That doesn't make sense."

"Yeah, I thought the same thing. The bartender's a big talker. He was coverin' his own ass about the money she gave him for lettin' her operate down the street. The guy's a real jerk wad."

Jess told her what she knew about Mandy hooking

near the bar to feed her crank habit. And she shared the news about the mystery man with a tattoo who helped Harper out of the bar.

"That's good stuff, Jess, but we need more." Sam lowered her voice so no one else would hear. "If Harper's blood test comes back positive for some drug and not just alcohol, the DA won't be happy; but that bit of news won't exactly kill her case. It would put a major dent in it depending on time of death, but Seth's not out of the woods. Right now, the DA's probably working a plausible timeline and gathering more evidence against our boy to solidify her charge. If she thinks she's got a strong enough case, she may go ahead with it."

Sam leaned forward after a peek over her shoulder, keeping her voice low.

"As it stands, Harper's got an uphill battle for bail. With his sketchy background and lack of cooperation on where he's living, the judge will probably hold him over, given the nature of the crime. But if we can show someone else had motive and that Harper was a convenient scapegoat, the charges might be dropped."

"Then you may want to find out why Nadir Beladi and his muscle-for-brains sidekick Sal Pinzolo pulled a knife on me outside Dirty Monty's. Apparently, me asking questions about Desiree got Beladi's tidy-whites in a bunch. And the guy seemed to know about the murder before it hit the paper." Jess pulled two driver's licenses from her pocket and tossed them on the table. "Pinzolo let his blade do the talkin' for Beladi. And he wasn't above using it on a defenseless woman."

"You, defenseless? You're friggin' Rambo with ovaries." Sam fought a smile as she got a closer look at the licenses. "And I'm not gonna ask how you got these. Tell me what happened."

Jess started talking, leaving out the minor detail of the stun grenade and finishing with her car chase in the boonies.

"You've been busy." Sam leaned forward, elbows on the table. "Any idea who was in the sedan?"

"No, it was too dark, but the guy flew solo, and he definitely had a gun. Plus he's now got a pretty big scrape on the driver's side of his vehicle. Kissing an embankment tends to do that."

"I'll look into these two boneheads and let you know what I find out." While the waitress refilled their coffee, Sam palmed the licenses in her hand until the woman left. Once they had their privacy, Jessie had something more on her mind.

"Okay, I gotta ask. What's this about Ray Garza getting involved? Isn't he the detective who tried to pin Baker's murder on me a few months back? He works out of Harrison Station like you, not Pullman. What's his interest?"

Sam smiled, a familiar expression Jess had come to recognize lately.

"Oh yeah, there it is." Jess pointed a finger and chuckled. "That goofy grin you get whenever you talk about Mr. Macho."

"Let's just say that I've got a bet going with Ray on who'll figure this out first. Harper can use the extra help, and if I play my cards right, I may get noticed by the brass. Homicide is where I'd like to be."

"I know you've been wanting out of Vice, but it probably doesn't hurt that a gorgeous Hispanic hunk works Homicide." Jess sipped her coffee. "But just remember, when your best friend makes a believable murder suspect, lesser men might hold it against you." She smirked. "So what about this bet? Spill it."

"Oh no, that's between him and me. Let's just say he's a good resource I can use."

"Yeah, I'll bet. Real good." Jess winked over the rim of her cup. "Does he know you're stacking the deck against him? Hell, you've got him and me both workin' the case with you having the inside track and poised to make the collar. Has he figured that out yet?"

"Nope."

"Oh Sammie, you make me proud, girl." Jess crooked a lip. "Hey, one more thing. Harper told me about Mandy having a boyfriend. Some guy named Jason. Did he mention that little detail to the cops?"

"Yeah, he did. We found out the guy's name is Jason Burke. And Burke's got a record of using his fists on a woman."

"That's great." Her quick grin shifted to a grimace. "I mean, not great like . . . great great."

"I know what you mean, but don't get your hopes up. Burke's got an alibi. He was out in Lombard at a bar. And his I-PASS confirms he wasn't anywhere near downtown when the medical examiner fixed time of death."

Sam gave her the rundown on Jason Burke. The guy was the same age as Mandy and worked hourly as a journeyman subcontractor doing on-site construction and repair wherever he was assigned. He'd been arrested once, two years ago, on charges of domestic abuse against his live-in girlfriend at the time. There had been more beatings, but the girlfriend never pressed charges.

"Are there any witnesses to corroborate his alibi? 'Cause I-PASS is only an electronic toll system. It proves his car was in the burbs, not that he was in it."

"I know, Jess. We're checking his story, but his toll pass trumps Harper's 'I forgot' defense."

She sighed, knowing Sam was right.

"You said Burke has an arrest record. Can you send it to me via e-mail?" Jess's e-mail was set to forward to her cell phone. Normally, that service allowed her to keep moving and not be tied to an office, but reading an arrest record would require a download to print. Once she got the word Sam had sent the document, she'd retrieve it from home.

"Yeah, I can. What are you thinking?"

"Jealousy. Harper said the guy got bent about him seeing his girl. Seth tried to clean her up, maybe that didn't sit well with Romeo. He could be the guy who drugged our boy and took him off the premises. If the bartender at Dirty Monty's can ID Burke from his booking photo and place him at the bar that night, we'll know he lied about Lombard, and his alibi is for shit."

"Yeah, that'd be worth a shot. I'm jammed with my caseload, but I'll send his booking record as soon as I get back to the station."

"And if that report had his work and home address

listed, that would be great. I might need to talk to him, too," she added, looking a little sheepish. ". . . to see if he's got tattoos."

Sam cocked her head and stared at her for a moment before opening her mouth.

"Talk to him? I know you, Jessie. You have no intention of just talking. And so you know? Checking him for tattoos doesn't require a full body-cavity search." Sam winced. "God, this better not come back to bite me in the ass. And if CPD gets wind of this, you wouldn't be doing Harper any favors either."

Jess tried to act insulted. "Hey, I can be discreet."

"Yeah, you and Paris Hilton." Sam shook her head. "Call me if you need anything. I'll keep you in the loop from my end. You do the same."

Her friend left her with a lot to think about—and the tab.

South Chicago
Off Cicero Avenue

True to her word, Sam sent the arrest record for Mandy's boyfriend, Jason Burke, in short order. By the time Jess made it back to her apartment and pulled into a parking spot, her cell phone signaled that she'd received the e-mail.

"Good girl." She muttered under her breath, shoving the phone back into her pocket. "Now let's see who you are, Burke."

Once inside her apartment, she booted up her computer to download and print the document. With the printer working, she made a few more calls to cab companies. On the third number, she got a hit.

"Well, I'll be damned." She grinned and grabbed a pen and paper near her phone. "Can you give me the location where you picked him up?"

Harper had been a responsible drinker and used a cab to cart his cute tush to Dirty Monty's that night. Part of his evening had an explanation, but more importantly, Jess felt a step closer to knowing where Harper was living these days—and whom he might be protecting.

"Yeah, I got it. Thanks." She hung up the phone and gazed at the address she'd jotted on a notepad.

She recognized it as being in downtown Chicago off Michigan Avenue. Posh real estate, but oddly enough, by now she'd come to expect that from Harper. She'd accepted his idiosyncrasies and the mysteries that surrounded the quirky kid, but that hadn't always been the case.

She'd first met him months ago after she hired him as a summer intern, her ploy to score cheap labor for computer research and skip tracing. Other than her immediate connection to him on a personal level, nothing about the guy raised a red flag. Her first impression had been that Harper was cute, smart, and in need of a job—not a bad combination. He'd been the only applicant for the position she advertised in a free ad and had been the original owner of the blue whale, the beat-up old van she now drove after he'd loaned it to her. The kid wore an unending assortment of Jerry Springer wear with worn jeans and sneaks. Yet in no time, the mysteries had begun to surface, compelling her to re-think her initial opinion of Seth Harper.

Off the top, he looked like a normal guy, but she soon found him living in upscale digs as if he'd been born to it—forcing her to question how he could afford such accommodations. ID theft came to mind when she caught him with a bootlegged crimeware program designed to install keystroke loggers on someone's computer to collect sensitive login and password data. Such information could later be utilized to perpetrate a financial crime.

At the time, he'd used the software at her request for a good cause in hacking the laptop of Lucas Baker, a suspected child pornographer. But Harper never explained how he'd gotten his hands on the program. And when she confronted him with her suspicions, he acted insulted and demanded she trust him, yet never once did he offer an explanation for why he had the illegal software. And she'd been too focused on stopping Baker to press Harper for answers.

Now she wished she had . . . for his sake.

Downtown Chicago

In perverse fashion, life had a nasty habit of carrying on for everyone else. But since Harper's life had been tilted off base, hers had followed like the tip of a domino reacting to gravity.

Jess pondered her domino theory as she waited for a traffic light to change, catching a glimpse of a sightseeing tour boat cruising along the Chicago River under the Michigan Avenue Bridge—the heart of Chicago's prime shopping. She made her turn and parked her van in an underground garage beneath the building she believed Harper called home, replaying the steps in the research that had brought her here.

She hoped that by doing so, she'd get a better handle on how to proceed once she got inside to talk to someone in security or the property manager. And given the prestige of the locale, she knew that it wouldn't be easy to pick a lock or trick her way inside, her normal mode of operation these days.

American Taxi had confirmed a call had been placed from the concierge desk on the premises the evening prior to Harper's arrest. A cab had been ordered to pick up a fare from the downtown address and dropped someone off at Dirty Monty's on Chicago's South Side with no return booked. Since Harper hadn't made the arrangements himself, that sent a clear message to her that his residence was upscale. She'd have to sweet-talk someone into giving her information on a resident who probably maintained a very low profile.

An elevator delivered her to a street-level lobby, the only option, for security reasons. And once the doors had opened, she knew she'd been right about Harper being accustomed to money. The lobby décor was stunning—only the best—furnishings gilded in gold and chic fabrics, huge displays of fresh flowers, real paintings in oil, with overhead speakers subtly playing classical music in the background. The minute she stepped into the atrium, all eyes were on her—a doorman, a maid in uniform wiping down windows to the revolving front door, and an older man in a fancy suit retrieving a newspaper.

Jess cleared her throat, feeling completely out of place. She hadn't given much thought to where she'd end up today after she'd dressed that morning. Her faded jeans and black Gold's Gym tee were second nature to her. And the lightweight jacket she wore covered her Colt Python. But one thing Jess had learned long ago. No one made her feel second-rate unless she let it happen. She dragged fingers through her dark hair in a nearby mirror, pretending to care what the Chicago wind had done to her locks, but in actuality she was scanning the lobby for the layout and the location of the elevators used by the residents.

After a respectable time, she held her chin high and walked toward the Concierge desk, forcing a smile. A short pudgy man with red cheeks, a tan-and-gold uniform, and thinning dark hair greeted her.

"May I help you, miss?" He grinned and cocked his head, an almost robotic move. Way too perky to suit her.

"Actually, you can." She tapped her fingernails on the counter between them, trying flirty on for size. "I'm pretty sure my younger brother lives here, but he doesn't know I've come to the city. I'd love to surprise him by knocking on his door. Could you please tell me his suite number?"

"I'm sorry, but I can't give out his room number. We protect the privacy of our guests. I'm sure you understand."

"Oh . . . sure. Then maybe someone could accompany me to his room? When he opens the door, you'll see it'll be okay with him, I promise."

Jess knew hotel personnel might resist giving her the suite number outright, but all she needed was the room number to come back after hours. Seeing the inside of Harper's suite might give her another lead about him and the person he might be protecting.

"And what's your brother's name?" the concierge asked, poised over a computer on his desk.

"Seth Harper. Like I said, he's not expecting me." She smiled and shrugged. "It's a surprise."

Yeah, a real surprise. Her plan had been to get confirmation that Harper lived here. And it looked as if the man behind the desk might just do that, but in an unexpected move, he narrowed his eyes, and said, "Excuse me. What did you say your name was?"

Harper's name had triggered a defense mechanism in the man, and Jess had no idea why. For a second, she contemplated lying about her name, but chose not to.

"Jessica Beckett. A married name." She mirrored the man's concern on her face. "Is there something wrong?"

"Do you mind if I see some identification?" he said, but when she looked surprised, he added, "Like I said, we like to protect the privacy of our guests."

"I've come to the right address, haven't I? I haven't been downtown since he moved in here." She handed him her driver's license. "Seth lives here, right?"

The man didn't answer. Something in his eyes told her he knew Harper, yet there was more at play. He did imply Harper was a guest, but she couldn't count on that as confirmation, not enough for breaking and entering.

"Excuse me." He took her license and stepped through a door to a suite of offices beyond the lobby.

Damn it! She wasn't sure why her visit had created such a stir. This could be a good thing or attention she didn't need. While she waited, she checked out the security cameras behind her. A girl could never be too careful when breaking into a guy's room.

After a long few minutes, the man returned.

"Would you please follow me? Mr. Humphries would like a word."

"Yeah, and what word would that be?" Her attitude was beginning to show. She wasn't going to get any cooperation, not today. " 'Cause if he doesn't have one in mind, I can make a suggestion or two."

"Please . . . this way."

She followed the uniformed man through the door by his desk and into the suite of offices she had spied earlier. Beyond a small break room, a reception area and a rather large office were at the end of the hallway, no doubt their final destination. A petite woman in a dark business suit with short auburn hair sat outside the office at a desk, presumably an administrative assistant to the head honcho. With a blank stare, the woman watched her walk by but didn't acknowledge her in any way.

Corporate America meets the Stepford wives in sensible pumps!

Jess figured Humphries to be the property manager or head of security; either way, she didn't like being summoned. And she hadn't gotten her driver's license back. At the threshold to the office, the concierge allowed her to enter and shut the door behind her, leaving her alone with a distinguished-looking man. His dark hair was streaked with gray, and he wore a sharp navy suit.

"My name is Jonathan Humphries. I manage this property and oversee security here. Please . . . have a seat." With a refined quality to his soft-spoken voice, the man offered a chair in front of his desk with a sweep of his hand.

"No thanks. I prefer to stand." She walked over to a nearby window and checked out the view of the bustling street beyond the reflective glass. "It's been years since I've been in high school, but your summons feels like a call to the principal's office."

"Ah, Ms. Beckett. Why does that not surprise me?" Humphries held her license in his hand, staring at it. When he looked up, he shook her by asking, "How is Seth?"

The initial sternness in the man's expression softened, and his voice reflected genuine concern. She narrowed her eyes.

"So you know what happened to him?"

"Yes, he contacted me a short while ago. And I know he considers you a friend. If that hadn't been the case, I can assure you that we wouldn't be having this conversation." He handed back her license. "Why are you here, Ms. Beckett?"

She thought she had known the answer to that question . . . until now.

CHAPTER 10

Jess pocketed her license and kept her eyes on Jonathan Humphries, sizing the man up. In the end she opted for a rare first step—honesty.

"I wanted to see who Seth was protecting at the expense of his freedom. He's cut himself off to fight this thing alone when he could use all the help he can get. Is he protecting you?"

"No, but I'm not at liberty to say any more on the subject."

The man sat behind his desk, looking worried and bone weary. Jess shoved her hands into her jeans pockets and remained standing, still feeling the edge of a faltering defiance.

"I'm arranging for legal counsel, and if bail money is required, I'll cover it," Humphries added.

"That's a start. Thanks." With his cooperation, she slumped into one of his chairs. "You know, I thought if I came here, I'd get to know more about Harper. The guy's a regular ghost. I definitely think of him as a friend, but I know nothing about him."

Humphries found humor in what she'd said. A sad

smile came and went. If she hadn't been watching him, she might have missed it.

"Do you form such loyalties for people you hardly know, Ms. Beckett?"

"Actually, no, but Harper is . . . special."

"Yes, he is." The man fixed his gaze on her. "Perhaps you've grown attached to him for other reasons."

"What?" She narrowed her eyes. "Look, whatever I feel for Seth Harper is none of your business. And he's just a kid, for cryin' out loud. Like I said before, I consider him a friend."

"He's not that much younger than you, Ms. Beckett." He stopped and heaved a sigh. "I'm sorry. As you say, it's none of my business."

Jess wasn't sure she was more concerned about the fact he'd done his homework on her age or that the man had speculated on a relationship between her and Harper. And she got the distinct feeling he wouldn't approve. The man was damned protective.

Glancing toward the window, Humphries looked lost in his memory.

"Seth may look young, but he had to grow up fast," he said. "And he's quite practiced at keeping secrets, but I often wonder what personal price he's paid for that privilege. Forgive me if I've overstepped."

"So you've known him for a long time?"

"Long enough," the man replied, reaching his tolerance for her prying. "I wanted to meet you . . . and to tell you I will assist if I can, now that he's asked for my help. But beyond that, I won't betray his confidence. I hope you understand."

Harper sure had a way of garnering unflinching loyalty from his friends, if Humphries could be counted as one. She had no idea how this man fit into Harper's life, yet he clearly held her boy genius in high regard. She saw it in his eyes.

"And I hope you understand, Mr. Humphries. Just because you have limits to what you'll share about Harper doesn't mean I won't find out what you're hiding. You've drawn a line in the sand where your cooperation ends, but as far as I'm concerned, areas marked as off-limits only make me more curious."

He pursed his lips and clenched his jaw, keeping his annoyance in check.

"Tell me, Mr. Humphries. Were you aware of Seth's connection with the murder victim, Amanda Vincent?" By the disapproving look on the man's face, she knew what his answer would be.

"Yes, I was. But like I said, I won't betray his confidence."

She smiled.

"I may not have known Harper as long as you, but for a guy who likes his secrets, I have a hard time believing he'd confide in you about her. You don't look very open-minded when it comes to drug-addicted hookers." When Humphries grimaced at her choice of words, she backed off the attitude. "The truth is, I would have been concerned for him, too."

He clearly did not approve of Seth's involvement with Mandy. And she couldn't blame him. But how far would he go to protect Seth from himself? And what about the man with the real clout, the one Humphries worked for? Did he feel the same?

"Yes, well, I think we understand each other. Here's my card." He handed her his business card with a sad expression on his face. "I know I have no right to ask this, but I'd appreciate a call if you learn something new."

"I can't make any promises. And I won't betray his confidence either."

"Have a good day, Ms. Beckett." In civil fashion, Jonathan Humphries gave her the boot.

Perhaps he only wanted to meet her, to size her up for himself. She wasn't complaining. His curiosity had given her the same opportunity. And having one more link to Harper got her closer to answers. She headed for the door to his office, but something made her turn around.

"There is one thing." Jess had no idea why she was in a sharing mood, but something in the way Humphries talked about Harper warmed her up to the notion. "The police took a blood sample from Seth that might help his case. Getting a quick turnaround on that tox screen sure wouldn't hurt."

She shrugged and left the man's office without waiting for a response, heading back the way she'd come. But when she walked by the door to the small-yet-spotless break room, she noticed an employee bulletin board and wandered in to check it out, playing a hunch.

Humphries struck her as someone who would take

his job seriously, going above and beyond his normal duties to see that his ship ran smoothly. A captain with enough resolve to go down with his sinking vessel rather than being the first rat off the ship. And it wouldn't be a stretch to think he'd be the gatekeeper to anyone above him, but how Harper fit into the puzzle was still a mystery.

She scanned the notices posted on the corkboard. Nothing stood out, except for one thing.

All employee notices were on the letterhead of Pinnacle Real Estate Corporation. Something about the name clicked with her, but not enough for the fog to clear from her memory.

"Can I help you?" A woman's voice came from behind her.

Jess turned and came face-to-face with the humorless administrative assistant to Jonathan Humphries.

"I was just looking to see if you had any openings." Jess grinned. "'Cause I can totally see me working here."

Surprisingly, the woman humored her with a smile, one of those enigmatic Mona Lisa numbers. "Come on, I'll show you out."

When she got to the door that led to the lobby, the woman let her pass, and added, "Tell Seth . . . let him know he's in our prayers."

More than a little speechless, Jess nodded and watched as the woman shut the door. Seth had a family here. People who didn't believe for one second that he could murder anyone. They knew a hell of a lot more about him and were willing to keep his secret. And

Jess had a feeling she hadn't even scratched the surface of what that secret might be.

As Jess climbed into the van in the parking garage, her cell phone rang. She recognized the number.

"Yeah, Sam. What's up?"

"Harper has got a bail hearing in an hour, give or take, depending on the docket. Thought you'd want to be there."

"An hour?" Even time was conspiring against Seth. Getting out on bail was a long shot at best, but without that tox result, the odds of him seeing daylight anytime soon just got shot to hell.

Sam gave her the particulars, and continued, "The DA wants Harper remanded without bail. They plan to argue he's a flight risk due to his sketchy background with no apparent ties to the community. And with the strong evidence they have against him and the brutal nature of the crime, they can make a convincing argument he's a danger to the community. Even his big, brown, puppy dog eyes won't help. It doesn't look good that he'll be out of jail anytime soon."

"Thanks, Sam. I'm on my way. And I'll call you later to let you know what happened." But Jess wasn't hopeful Harper would be with her when she made that call, even if she could scrounge up bail.

"Oh, and one more thing," Sam interrupted. "I looked into the police records for Beladi and Pinzolo. These are two nasty dudes. Beladi runs hookers and sells drugs, but he's real cagey, and some of his business dealings are legit. The DA has had a hard time making an arrest stick. And Pinzolo is his muscle, suspected in more than one murder. We may never know if Beladi was Desiree's pimp or dealer, but if Harper got between her and Beladi, he may have crossed paths with the wrong guy. And now, you have, too. Watch your backside, Jess."

"Oh, great. And here I thought Fugitive Recovery was a great way to meet people." She shook her head. "Call me when you know something more. And thanks, Sammie."

Jess ended the call and put the key in the ignition to start the van. Seth's blue monster. Driving his car—the one he had given her out of kindness—made her feel her connection to him all the more. The guy didn't have a malicious bone in his body. And forcing him to stay in jail while he waited for trial would drain what was left of his spirit. She had already seen the damage from his incarceration over a weekend.

"Damn it, Harper. You gotta let your friends help you." She headed for the exit and the courthouse at 26th and California Avenue. "Who the hell are you protecting?"

Cook County Criminal Courthouse

Being held in the Cook County Jail, Harper was a block down from one of the busiest felony courthouses in the country—*only a short hike to public humiliation.*

Jess had parked her car in a pay lot on a nearby street, not knowing how long she'd be waiting for Harper's bail hearing. After securing her Colt Python in the glove compartment of the van, she stood in line with the masses for the metal detector and finally made her way to the room where Harper would be taken. The wood-paneled courtroom was packed with the ebb and flow of concerned parties for every case heard before Judge Joseph Bellinger, the presiding judge of the criminal division.

Overworked public defenders with their bland expressions handled one case after another. Prisoners wore civilian clothes or DOC jumpsuits and were brought in from a side entrance. Family members and other interested parties crammed the small room. Controlled chaos.

Dressed in a red prison jumpsuit, Harper was escorted into the room. Jess craned her neck to get a better look at him and tried catching his eye. When that didn't work, she stood. Seth looked dazed, but eventually he found her standing toward the back of the room. He locked his gaze on her and with a subtle shake of his head, she knew he wished she hadn't come, but the kid was scared. *Really scared.*

When his lawyer sidled up next to him, Harper turned around and lowered his head, and the proceedings began as she sat back down.

Handing the judge a case file, a court clerk said loud enough for the courtroom to hear, "Docket number 34521 People v Seth Harper, voluntary manslaughter."

The judge flipped through the filing papers and cleared his throat.

"Voluntary manslaughter," Judge Bellinger repeated

the charge without looking up. "What's your plea, Mr. Harper?"

Seth kept his head down, barely looking up at the man in the black robe. Jess could only imagine the terrible blur his life had become. And today was another sickening spiral of degradation.

"Not guilty, Your Honor."

Jess barely heard his voice through all the commotion near her. After Harper choked out his plea, the judge asked for the People to present the evidence against him. Stacy Nichols, a slender blonde in a rust-colored suit spoke up, a young attorney with the DA's Office trying to make her mark. She knew of the woman and her ruthless reputation. Ruthless in a prosecutor was a good thing normally, as far as Jess was concerned, but not when directed at Harper.

"He was found with the body in a motel room, and he was covered in blood, Your Honor. A bloody handprint at the scene was identified as belonging to the defendant," the ADA said. "The People have strong and sufficient evidence against Mr. Harper, and we consider him a flight risk. He's got no ties here, and given the heinous nature of the crime, he's a danger to the community. We recommend he be remanded without bail, Your Honor."

Harper jerked his head up for a moment and stared at the woman but quickly dropped his chin to his chest. It broke Jess's heart to see him look so defeated.

The public defender appeared disorganized as he fumbled through paperwork. The older man in a rumpled suit looked burned-out and jaded, having seen far too many days as a public defender to be an effective advocate for Harper. Jess knew her first impression of the man wasn't fair, but she hated to see her friend not get a fair shake when he needed it most. Harper would have an uphill battle even if he had the best mouthpiece money could buy.

"I just got assigned this case, Judge, but my client has no priors. And he's . . ."

Before the man pleaded his hasty case for bail, a voice came from the back of the room and interrupted the proceedings.

"Please . . . may I interrupt, Your Honor?"

A tall, extraordinary-looking man with gray hair and riveting dark eyes came forward from the back of the room, dressed in a suit that screamed the word "money." He walked with fluid grace and the confidence of a wealthy man used to getting his way. And his deep baritone voice exuded poise, enough to make the judge look up.

"And who might you be?" he asked. "Please state your business before this court."

"My name is Anthony Salvatore. I'm a local business developer in town. My holdings are under the name of Pinnacle Real Estate Corporation."

When Jess heard the man's name, she knew exactly who he was, and by the look on the judge's face, he did, too.

CHAPTER 11

Now she knew why Anthony Salvatore's Pinnacle Real Estate Corporation had rung a bell when she first saw the reference at Harper's posh new hangout. The influential man owned half the prime real estate in Chicago, a major player on the local money scene. Chicago's version of Donald Trump—only with good hair.

"Well, I'll be damned," she said under her breath.

As Anthony Salvatore came forward, an officer of the court accompanied him. The uniformed man escorted him from the public seating area behind a wooden railing to the defense table.

"It's my understanding this young man has not been very forthcoming with his background, no doubt to his own detriment. But I believe he was mistakenly trying to hide his ties to me, to protect what he perceives to be a stellar reputation." With a charming smile, the man put his arm around Seth. Harper's head drooped as Salvatore continued, "And despite what the DA's Office has presented, Seth has very deep ties to this community. He was born and raised here and is the son of a very good friend of mine. A police detective by the name of Max Jenkins. After an unfortunate divorce, Seth's mother had the boy's name changed."

"I know Detective Jenkins." The judge nodded. "He testified in this court many times. He's a fine man and a good cop. Did he retire? Where is he these days?"

That name rushed from Jess's past like a sudden and icy wind that stifled the breath deep in her throat. She was suddenly bombarded by ugly memories. Jess wanted to stand again—to stare into the face of Seth Harper, who'd kept so many secrets from her—but she didn't think her legs would hold her. Salvatore kept talking, with Jess barely listening.

"Max is indeed a fine man, sir. And he would have been here today if he could." Salvatore cleared his throat and glanced at Harper. "He's not in the best of health. I believe the Danny Ray Millstone case took its toll on him. Seth is caring for his father at the Golden Palms Villa, a nursing home facility. So as you can see, this young man has deep connections and obligations to this community."

The courtroom quieted as the judge's face turned more somber. "I remember the Millstone case . . . all too clearly."

The name Danny Ray Millstone hit Jess like a punch to the gut. She'd blocked that name out of her memory even though it lingered in the dark fringes of her mind. *The man who had stolen her life!* She shut her eyes, and Millstone's old house on High Street leached into her brain like a chilling night terror, blocking out the courtroom and everyone in it.

With eyes still closed, she sat back and gripped her

hands together, struggling to regain her composure. But as her heart pounded out of control, and a trickle of sweat crawled down her spine, she tried to breathe and found the air stifling and hot. In a rush, the images pummeled her psyche.

She was back there again. In short bursts of memory—like the stark flicker of a strobe light—she was back at the house on High Street. When she recognized the symptoms of a panic attack, she took deep breaths and forced herself to calm down and listen.

Finally, the resonating voice of Salvatore served as a lifeline to bring her back. And she was grateful. *Very grateful.*

"Quite frankly, if this young man didn't already have an outstanding father, I'd proudly claim him as my son . . . if he'd lower his standards for parental material." Salvatore had deftly changed the subject. And his remark drew a soft chuckle through the courtroom. Even the judge smirked.

"Seth is one of the most trustworthy people I know," the man continued. "And he is no killer."

"A nice guy who happened to brutally stab a young woman to death. Let's not forget the victim here," the assistant district attorney objected.

"And what about the bloodwork you did on Seth?" Harper's wealthy advocate glared at Stacy Nichols and hit her with a roadblock she hadn't seen coming, given the look on her face.

Before the woman had a chance to regain her composure, he added, "I believe you're withholding the results of that tox screen to keep Seth in jail until you bolster your case." The man directed his attention to the judge. "This boy was drugged, Your Honor. And Ms. Nichols knows that the bloodwork will cast the shadow of reasonable doubt on her case."

"Is that true, Ms. Nichols?"

Surprises hit wave after wave. Salvatore had bluffed his way into making the ADA look bad on her own turf. And Jess had no doubt that Humphries had fed him the information he'd gotten from her. The bullet-proof Ms. Nichols suddenly looked off her game.

"We ran an extensive tox screen, Your Honor, not the standard analysis. That takes time, and I don't have the results. And I'm not required to share the findings until the preliminary hearing."

"Obviously you suspected more than alcohol was at play here, Ms. Nichols, or else you wouldn't have gotten a warrant to do the blood test in the first place. And the fact you didn't settle for a standard screening speaks volumes." The judge took a moment to consider his ruling before he said, "Bail is set for one million dollars."

The judge assigned a date for Harper's preliminary hearing and moved on to his next case. Harper was ushered from the courtroom, soon to be released if Salvatore had anything to do with raising bail.

But when Seth turned, he found Jess staring back, a look of shock still on her face. The secret he'd kept from her was now in the open—between the two of them. Harper's father was the cop who had saved her life. And in the process, Detective Max Jenkins had killed the man who took her from her mother. A good thing in her mind, but in killing the man, Seth's father had severed the only lifeline to her mother. She'd never found her. And in the wake of her rescue, nightmarish images remained to taint her childhood with dark memories of abuse and torture that no child should have had to endure.

Her skin prickled with Seth's betrayal. Trust had never come easy for her, but his deception hurt far more than it should. He'd been a friend, or so she thought. Why had he kept his father's identity from her? And why seek her out in the first place? She had far too many questions and needed time to think.

Jess wasn't sure she could handle anything Seth had to say—not the way she felt now.

Near the courthouse

A bar had a way of stopping time, luring patrons with the promise of oblivion and dark anonymity. Danny's Bar and Grill fit the bill and was conveniently located down the street from the courthouse. Utterly numb, Jess stared into a glass of single malt scotch, watching an ice cube melt and give way to gravity. She'd ordered the drink but only nursed it as she sat at the bar alone, losing track of time. Not even the jukebox music or the sounds of laughter from across the dark room had proved to be a distraction from her misery.

Her cell phone vibrated again, but she didn't have to look to see who was calling. Seth Harper had collided with her life. Or perhaps in hindsight, she realized her life had derailed his—the chicken and the egg argument.

"Something wrong with the drink?" the young bartender asked as he wiped down the counter in front of her. "I can freshen it up for you."

She smiled. If only life were that easy. *Hate your life, freshen it up.*

"No, I'm good. What do I owe you?" she asked. After he told her, she pulled cash from her pocket and tossed it onto the bar, leaving enough for a tip. "Thanks."

She walked out the door into the dying light of day, squinting until she put on her shades. The bar had been a convenient place to take a break from her world and stop for a while, but her mind didn't get the message. She pulled out her car keys and headed for the lot where she'd parked the van. She had good reason to wallow in pity like a pig in a mud bath, but she had better things to do.

Harper's behavior had been highly influenced by his sphincter—no doubt—but the guy still needed her help.

Cook County Jail

The bail hearing for Seth Harper had ended and apparently not gone as planned for one man. Private investigator Luís Dante had been retained to report the outcome to an anonymous man he'd never even seen. Everything had been arranged by phone. He'd been hired with cash delivered by a courier service—an impressive retainer—and he only had the number of a disposable phone to contact his new client. He'd checked into the number when he first got the business, not wanting to be played for a chump. But in Luís's world, money was money. And as long as he wasn't breaking the law much, he figured his dealings were business opportunities.

When his client heard about the kid getting bail set, he was pissed. But the bail amount of a million smackers calmed him down until he told the man about the involvement of Anthony Salvatore. Then the shit hit the fan again, as if his client had never seen it coming.

"I figured you'd want me to stick with the kid. I'm outside county lockup now. He's probably made bail already. But I gotta tell ya, it's real ugly here." He took a last drag off his cigarette and flicked the butt to the ground.

"What are you talking about?" the man asked.

"Media vultures are everywhere. They got crews with cameras staked out, waiting for Money Bags to show up for a photo op."

A simple maneuver of following the kid turned complicated with news crews at the jailhouse. The added foot traffic made it hard to keep track of one scrawny kid.

"Just find me that kid, where he's staying. I need an address, then you're done." He cleared his throat. "And like before, I'll courier a bonus to you if you make it quick, like we talked about."

"No problem. I'll call you when I've got something."

In the end, Salvatore never showed. And when the media lost interest, and the chaos died down, that left him with a slick black Lincoln Town Car to follow. He tailed the vehicle from the jail toward downtown. The car service hit a freeway entrance ramp, and he maintained his distance and followed the vehicle as planned.

It wasn't until the Town Car drove into O'Hare Airport that he wondered what was going on. With the kid out on bail, he had no business leaving town, but maybe he was picking someone up. Finally, the car pulled over to the curb designated for arrivals and parked. Luís did the same, pretending to be waiting to pick up a passenger. But when the driver looked as if he would go inside the terminal, he got out of his car prepared with a lie.

"I could use your service. Are you free to drive me downtown, man?"

"No, sir. I'm here to pick up a fare."

"Then can I have one of your cards. I'd like to hire your service the next time I'm in town." While the man fished out his business card from his pocket, Luís smiled and opened the rear door to the Town Car. "You have drinks back here. Hey, real nice."

The driver didn't make a fuss for good reason. The backseat was empty. He barely heard the man reply to his question on alcohol. Back at county jail, he'd been duped. Seth Harper must have gotten out another way.

When the driver gave him a card, he forced a nod, and said, "Thanks, man. Appreciate it. I'll let you get back to work."

Lighting up another cigarette, he wondered what he would say to his client about his screwup until he realized the man had promised a bonus if he got an address. He wouldn't have to admit that the kid gave him the slip. And he knew where to pick up his trail. With a little research, he'd have a way to cross Seth Harper's path again.

And this time, he wouldn't underestimate the kid.

Off Stevenson Expressway
I—55 at dusk

Jess had a healthy respect for the power of money even though her experience hadn't been firsthand.

She knew by the calls to her cell phone that Harper had made bail, helped by his wealthy friend and benefactor, Anthony Salvatore. Since his release, Seth had left several messages. She'd let them all roll into voice mail, afraid her emotions would flip the switch on her mouth and set it to autopilot. She wasn't mentally prepared to see him. Wiping the slate clean on their friendship wouldn't be enough. She knew they'd have to rebuild and redefine their connection or his betrayal would never be far from the surface.

Yet despite being royally pissed at him for lying to her and keeping her at arm's length, she grew antsy sitting around feeling sorry for herself. Moping wasn't in her nature. And she couldn't get into the distraction of a new bail-jumping case, not when things with Seth were dangling. She wasn't wired that way either.

And she had the home address and work location for

Mandy's so-called boyfriend, Jason Burke, burning a hole in her pocket. The guy worked an hourly job as a subcontractor doing construction and repair jobs. But, given the fact his assignments varied, he could be anywhere. And this time of day, she figured her best shot was finding him at home.

It might be quitting time for Burke, but for her the day was just kicking into high gear.

Jess drove west on I–55, the Adlai E. Stevenson Expressway, not far from her apartment by Chicago standards. Burke lived off 79th Street and Roberts Road under the shadow of I–294, the Tri-State Tollway. His noisy piece of the urban jungle was a redbrick building faded by the sun and surrounded by a cracked, uneven sidewalk with a weed-choked patch of grass in front.

There was only one good thing about his place. It made her dump look upscale.

She parked the blue van around the corner on a side street and walked on the buckling sidewalk to the front entrance of the building. But when she got to a breezeway lined with mailboxes that led into an interior courtyard, she stopped cold. In the shadows, a woman wearing jeans and a stylish gray jacket leaned a shoulder against a brick wall with arms crossed, shaking her head with a half smirk.

"Do you consider meeting like this a good thing . . . or bad?" the blonde asked.

Jess stared into the face of Alexa Marlowe, a mysterious woman she never thought she'd see again. Not in this lifetime. To cross paths with a woman like her, once had been quite enough. Although Alexa had saved her life months earlier, she guarded her secrets and generally traveled with bad news on her heels—reminding Jess of a vulture. Sooner or later, picking bones clean would be the order of the day. And the woman had a habit of turning up with disaster not far behind.

"What the hell are you doing here?"

Alexa raised an eyebrow. "Bad, it is."

Jess shrugged. "Chatting over old times won't get us very far. And a trip down memory lane would only give me nightmares. Why are you here?"

She prided herself on being able to roll with the hefty punches that life doled out, but Alexa's appearance had really taken her by surprise.

"I heard about your friend Seth Harper and I . . ." the woman hesitated. "I came to help."

Jess narrowed her eyes, content to let the silence build between them. If she'd been the one in trouble, she might have refused the woman's help, preferring to go it alone. But this was about Harper.

"You flew here—from wherever—to help Harper? Gee, I didn't know you two were so close." She matched Alexa's stance with arms crossed. "You don't strike me as the charitable type. At least, not without something in it for you. What's your agenda?"

"I saved your life. Don't I get the benefit of a doubt?" Alexa walked toward her.

Jess couldn't see any ulterior motive for Alexa wanting to help Seth, but she also found it hard to trust the woman blindly. And just because she couldn't connect the dots, that didn't mean the connection wasn't there.

"Saving my life earns you a Hallmark card. Send me your address." She cocked her head, deciding to shift gears. "Are you tailing me, or did you find this address on your own?"

With old habits hard to break, Jess was careful not to mention Burke's name, in case Alexa was fishing for information she didn't already have. Jess knew she was being paranoid, but by not answering her questions, Alexa was playing it cagey, too.

"Look, I can see why you'd be leery of my interest, but this isn't about you and me. It's about your friend." Alexa laid it on thick, filling her voice with compassion.

She knew Jessie would be a tough sell, but she needed to break down the bounty hunter's barriers if she was going to recruit her for Garrett. Sure, she had an agenda, but what Jessie didn't know, wouldn't hurt her . . . for now.

"And in the interest of full disclosure, the guy who lives here is named Jason Burke. He's the boyfriend to the murder victim. My employer would like to help your friend Harper, so I'm on loan."

"And what business would that be? I remember you saying something before about working for an alliance. I figured a group of rich vigilantes," Jessie speculated. "Who's your employer?"

"I can't exactly say . . . just yet."

"So much for full disclosure."

The bounty hunter tried to walk by her, but she reached out a hand. Knowing what she did of the woman, she suspected the straight-up truth would be the only way to go, but she'd have to tread a thin line to give what she could.

"My boss is Garrett Wheeler. He'd like to meet you, but in the meantime, he's authorized me to look into Seth's case."

"For what reason? He doesn't know Seth. And why does he want to meet me?"

Alexa knew Jessie wouldn't give an inch without more of the truth, the sanitized version of it.

"Truth is, he figures that if he can help Seth, you might be grateful enough to at least listen to what he has to say. He's interested in hiring you, to work with . . . me. With us."

Jessie chuckled under her breath and turned to face her. The evening shadows closed in, fringed by the dim glow of streetlights in front of Burke's apartment building.

"I'm not sure I even like you. What makes you think we can work together?" The bounty hunter didn't pull her punches. Yet despite their differences, Alexa admired Jessie and her head-on approach to trouble. Garrett had seen potential in recruiting the bounty hunter, and so did she.

"Because we want the same thing." She locked her gaze on Jessie. "You've been going it alone, picking your battles as a one-woman wrecking crew. But what if we could offer you the resources and the leads to make a real difference? Would that interest you?"

Alexa had to smile. She'd never seen the bounty hunter speechless. The woman had truly heard what she had to say and thought about it before opening her mouth. It was a good start.

"Look, all you have to do is listen to what Garrett has to say, then make up your mind. I can arrange a meeting when you're ready. And whatever you decide goes. But for now, let's talk to the boyfriend together. You don't know much about Burke, and having backup can't hurt. I'd like to help. And with the resources Garrett has, you won't regret letting us in on Harper's case. What do you say?"

After a long, strained moment, the bounty hunter said, "I'm not committing to anything, no matter how much you help Harper. This is my case. I call the shots. But for Harper's sake, let's get moving. We're burning moonlight."

Jessie hadn't turned her down cold. Alexa took this as a good sign. Shoulder to shoulder, they headed for Burke's place, neither of them in the mood to tolerate a man who used his fists on a woman to settle an argument.

CHAPTER 12

"Who says opportunity don't come knockin'?"

Jason Burke sucked in his gut and threw his chest out when he saw two women at his door—like that was all he needed to improve his looks. Dressed in an old pair of gray sweats and green flip-flops, the guy had a slick, bald head buffed to a high sheen and his grin showed stained teeth . He had tattoos on his arms and chest. A regular piece of work.

With enough piercings to set off a metal detector, he looked like a beefy bag of testosterone with pull tabs. Rings and studs adorned his nose, an eyebrow, and both ears. And through his wife-beater tee, Jess caught the faint impression of nipple rings. *No way he did those sober.* She shuddered.

"Yeah, and I have to admit. I feel like I've been slapped upside the head with the lucky stick myself. We saw your name and apartment number on your mailbox. You're Jason Burke, right?" When he nodded, it took everything Jess had to force a smile. She'd never been good at flirting, but her companion had no trouble slipping into character.

"Hi, my name is Hilary and this is Chelsea," Alexa jumped in, shaking hands with Burke.

Jess shot her a glance and carried on.

"We were interested in renting in the building and wanted to talk to someone who lived here. Can we come in?"

"Uh, sure." With a goofy grin, Burke stepped back to let them in, acting as if he'd scored a major prize. "Come in. Sit. Can I get you two a beer?"

"Not right now. Maybe later," she said.

Burke liked the sound of "later." And by the look on his face, he was ready to party. He rushed to his ratty brown sofa, picked up a stash of old newspapers, and shoved aside an overloaded ashtray on a smudged glass coffee table littered with dirty dishes and empty beer bottles. Jess was thankful the man smoked. The smell of old cigarettes covered up something worse.

"What did you say your names were?" he asked, hauling dishes and bottles to the kitchen as they sat.

"I'm Ashley." Jess pointed to Alexa. "And she's Mary Kate."

"Hey there." Alexa grinned and waved a hand, looking . . . *blond.* "Love what you've done to the place. Very . . . lived in." Before he replied, she asked, "You got any music? Let's crank some tunes. Do you think your neighbors would mind?"

"Hell, I don't care. I always play my music loud." He dumped what he had in his hands. Dishes clattered into the sink as he raced to his stereo system. "You want music, sweet cheeks? It's comin' right up."

As Burke moved, Jess noticed his body art. He had

the tattoo of a coiled snake on one bicep and a tribal band of thorns on the other. The bartender at Dirty Monty's had told her that the mystery guy who dragged Harper from the bar had a tattoo on his arm. Although he hadn't gotten a good look at it, he described it as black and curved, maybe a letter or snake.

From a distance both Burke's tattoos, the tribal band and the snake, could pass for black and curved—at least enough to get her interest. But if Harper's case went to trial, she'd need more than just the bartender's vague recollection of a tattoo to keep Seth out of the gray-bar hotel for the rest of his life. Busting Burke's I-PASS alibi would make a solid case for reasonable doubt, especially if that choice tidbit was coupled with Harper's bloodwork testing positive for the date-rape drug. CPD and the DA's Office would have to investigate Burke as a suspect.

For the first time since she'd learned about Seth's trouble, Jess was hopeful.

"So how long have you lived here?"

Over a beer, they talked loud enough to be heard above the blaring music, a strange mix of metal and rap. And Burke interrupted the conversation to jerk his head and bite his lower lip in time with the beat.

His idea of sexy. Her idea of a self-inflicted wound.

There were times she fought to keep from laughing, but she didn't dare look at Alexa. And if the jerk launched into his version of air guitar, she'd cut to the chase and pull her Colt Python—a clear-cut case of self-defense.

"We noticed these apartments are close to the bus

line. It's one of the reasons we were lookin' here." She wove her lie. "Sharing a car hasn't been too bad since we moved to town. Neither of us has a job yet, but when that changes, it's gonna be tough."

"I might be able to help you with that . . . if you moved here, that is." He winked. "What kind of work do you two do?"

Burke was circling the bait. She needed a hook, but didn't want to appear too eager.

"Thelma here is a real good dancer." Jess smiled at Alexa. "She does this routine with spinning rhinestone pasties that always gets good tips."

Alexa grinned back.

"And Louise is just being modest . . . again. No one works a pole like she does."

"You *both* are exotic dancers? Damn, that's hot!" The look on Burke's face told it all.

He thought he'd won the sex-fantasy lotto. The guy undressed them with his eyes, probably imagining girl-on-girl action. Hell, the jerk was so balled up in testosterone and his own agenda, he hadn't noticed they'd changed their names three times since they arrived.

"Yeah, we like it. The money's decent." Alexa took a pull of her beer, giving him a visual aid, then asked with perfect timing, "What were you saying about helping us out if we moved here?"

It took Burke a long moment to recall what he'd said.

"Oh, yeah . . . right." A bead of sweat trickled down from his temple. The air was stale and muggy, but Burke had his internal furnace working overtime. He took a swig of beer to cool off. "For gas money plus change, I loan out my car, mainly to friends and people in the building. But with you two, maybe we could work out a . . . trade."

"Wow, that's very generous of you, Jason." She turned to Alexa, and said, "He's sure making it easy for us."

"Yeah, I was thinking the same thing." The blonde returned her smile. "So what now?"

Good question. And from the look in Alexa's eyes, Jess knew she was on the same page.

With a little legwork, the cops could run down Burke's friends and others in the apartment building to see who might have used his car on the night Mandy was killed. At least she had enough to tip off Sam. In her mind, there was no need to continue questioning him on the car. If he were guilty, it would only give him a heads-up that CPD hadn't bought his story on the I-PASS.

"I'm thinking I'd like to have a little one-on-one time with our new friend," she told Alexa.

She knew the woman understood her meaning, but Burke remained entrenched in his delusional male fantasies. All that remained were questions about Mandy, and Jess was relieved. That meant she could drop playing nice. He'd need incentive to talk about his murdered ex-girlfriend, especially if they wanted to get at the truth. And taking the gloves off with a guy like Burke fit into her comfort zone of dealing with sleazeballs. No pretense required.

"If you don't have a stomach for this, hang outside in

the hall." Jess stood, her gaze fixed on Alexa. "Be my eyes and ears?"

The tall blonde got to her feet.

"You don't know me very well." Alexa shifted her glare to Burke. "I want in on this."

"What? What's happening?" he asked.

His goofy grin had returned. And the man's eyes were bugging from his shiny bald head, shifting between Jess and Alexa.

"Ladies, there's plenty of Burke to go around. You don't have to fight. Why not all three of us?" He shrugged, acting like threesomes happened to him all the time.

Yeah, right! In your dreams, dude! Like all they needed to get the party going was picking a safe word.

"I could go for that." Alexa nodded. "Why not?"

"Oh, wow. Cool." Burke looked like he was about to wet himself.

But she busted his mood by drawing her Colt Python— the muzzle aimed between his eyes—and said, "Let's skip the foreplay."

"Hey, what the hell is this?" he blustered.

"I've got Flexicuffs on my belt in a dispenser. Use 'em." Jess ignored Burke and took charge, directing her comment to Alexa. "That radiator should work."

Before Burke made a fuss, Jess said, "There's a reason we wanted the music up loud, Jason. Think about it. And don't make me shoot you."

Alexa got to work and cuffed him to the radiator. She used the plastic restraints Jess carried with her for multiple arrests. With his hands tied to opposite ends, he sat with hunched shoulders and his butt on metal. For good measure, Alexa bound his ankles, too.

They'd have his undivided attention now.

"What's this all about? It ain't right, you comin' in here like this."

"We wanna hear what you've got to say about Mandy," Jess told him.

"Mandy? How do you know her?" Staring into the Colt Python, Burke didn't wait for an answer. "Hey, I got an alibi. I wasn't anywhere near that motel. The cops know all about it."

"Yeah, that's what we hear, but humor us. She ever live here with you?"

Jess holstered her weapon, and Alexa backed off, giving her room to "work."

"Yeah, but she moved out a month ago. We had a fight."

"I find that hard to believe. An easygoing guy like you? What was the fight about?"

"Money. It was always about money."

"When was the last time you saw her?"

"I saw her a few days before she was killed. She tried to make me feel sorry for her, but I'd had enough of her act. That scrawny bitch used men to get what she wanted." He sneered. "All she cared about was cash to feed her habit. And she didn't give a rat's ass what she had to do to get it neither. She was playin' that asshole, the guy who killed her. I seen him with her. Who knows what she did to piss *him* off?"

"Try again, asshole. 'Cause that damned tune ain't gonna play with us." Jess stepped closer. And when he flashed another arrogant smirk, she reached for a shiny gold ring that pierced his eyebrow and gave it a sharp twist.

"Damn it, bitch!" he spat.

Burke had squirmed and pulled his head back. Now the ring dangled loose, nearly ripping through his skin. Blood trickled down his cheek, mixing with sweat.

"Oops. You shouldn't have moved, slick."

"You better hope I don't get loose," he threatened.

"Actually, I hope you do." She fixed her eyes on him. "In fact, I'm counting on it."

To make her point, Jess retrieved a knife from her boot. Dim light from a nearby lamp reflected off the blade. And his eyes grew wide.

"Hey, you don't need that. What do you want to know?"

"The truth, Jason. We just want the truth." After he settled down, she asked, "Besides hooking, did Mandy have other ways to earn coin? And don't bother to lie 'cause I'll know it."

When Burke didn't speak fast enough, Jess reached for another pull tab.

"Okay, okay. Just lay off the metal." He jerked his head, trying to stay clear of her hand. "Right before our fight, Mandy came into some dough."

"I thought you said the fight was over money, not having enough."

"It was more like, she lived under my roof, and I wanted my share." He shook his head. "I never actually saw her stash, but I always knew when she was holding out on me. I figured she scored big bucks off a guy.

When I asked her about it, she didn't have much to say. We fought. She left. End of story. She packed her stuff and took off when I was at work."

"So you were wanting a piece of *her* action. Real nice, slick. You have any ideas on how she got the money?"

"Blackmail, lady. That little bitch was blackmailing someone. At least, that's what I figured out after I asked around, but no one could tell me nuthin' for sure."

"Any ideas who she was bleeding?"

"The guy who killed her, that's who. He looked like he had deep pockets. Real used to money, you know what I mean?"

"But you don't know this for a fact."

He shook his head. "No, but I had a bad feeling about that kid from the first time I saw him. He didn't look right. I always thought he was obsessed with Mandy for some reason, the way he kept coming around. I thought she put an end to that, but I guess not. Not if they were at a motel when he whacked her."

Even a jerk like Jason Burke could damage Harper's chances in court. He'd seen Seth with Mandy and could testify that Seth had been obsessed with her. Jess clenched her jaw. And Burke's story had a ring of despicable truth since the bastard hadn't tried to hide the fact he wanted to cut in on her action, whatever it was.

And if Mandy had put the squeeze on someone for money, Burke asking around might have called attention to what she'd done and put a target on her back. Plus the girl's drug habit had been eating her alive. Jess had seen it more than once in her line of work. And common sense would be the first to go when it came to the choices that the strung-out girl had made to feed her nasty habit.

Mandy had put herself in the line of fire—and she'd dragged Harper with her. Knowing Seth, he would have done it again and again if it meant he had a shot at saving her. And being the son of Detective Max Jenkins, her boy genius had a strong measure of the hero gene in his DNA. She'd seen it in Harper before.

"All I know is, it kept her in crank for a while," Burke kept talking. "Then one day, she came to me, acting real scared."

"When was this?"

"I don't remember. I was a little wasted at the time."

"What was she scared of?"

"I don't know. But coming to me, she had to be desperate," he admitted. "She wanted to move back and crash here, but I had enough of that bitch, and I told her so."

"Real compassionate of you, big man." Jess pressed the blade to his cheek. Having learned his lesson about moving, Burke stiffened and held his breath. A white crease on his skin filled with blood, tiny beads of red. "Go on."

"Damn it! I swear, that's all I know. You gotta believe me."

"Yeah, like you believed Mandy when she came to you for help?"

She looked at Alexa.

"Cut him loose . . . and step aside."

Until now, Alexa's expression had been unreadable.

But by the look on her face, her companion clearly had an issue at letting Burke go without giving them a head start. Yet to her credit, the woman never said a word. Jess handed her the knife and Alexa freed the man.

Burke stood and rubbed his wrists, glaring at her. With her body tensed for action, she handed Alexa her gun, not taking her eyes off Burke.

"You wanted loose, asshole. Now what?"

Burke came at her, bristling with anger—and the man was done talking.

CHAPTER 13

All Jess thought about was taking a long, hot shower to get the smell of Jason Burke off her. She reeked of sleaze.

She shook her right hand and checked her bruised knuckles as she accompanied Alexa outside. They walked through the center courtyard toward the front of the complex. Inky darkness had spread its shadows and transformed the neighborhood into a real creep-fest. And the familiar drone of traffic off the interstate had never let up.

"You got anything to say?"

"Nope, nada." Alexa shrugged, not stopping and looking straight ahead.

"The guy had it comin'. He came at me. And I figured if he got a few bruises from a woman, he'd be less inclined to say anything."

The blonde pursed her lips and nodded, "Yeah . . . good call. Sounds logical to me."

Jess expected more of a reaction.

"Hell, you'd think a guy with two nipple rings could take a little pain." She ran a hand through her dark hair and made sure her Colt Python was secure.

"An astute observation."

A moment of silence drifted by, but Jess couldn't stand it any longer. She stopped in front of Alexa and had to say it.

"You think I lost it in there. And you're planning to report that I'm a loose cannon and not fit for your team, aren't you?" She pointed a finger. "You know, I may not work and play well with others, but I've got skills . . . on occasion." She jutted her chin out. "And nothing sticks in my craw worse than getting counted out before I've had a chance to prove myself."

"Are you done?" After she nodded, the woman crossed her arms and cocked her head. "Now . . . are you ready to listen?"

"Can I get back to you on that?"

Alexa rolled her eyes as an eighteen-wheeler blasted its horn from the freeway. When things quieted to a dull thunder, she gave her opinion.

"You *are* a loose cannon, Jessie. And I think you know that, but your instincts are solid. We'd make a good team, and I could use the help." A faint smile curved her lips. "Most days, I like working alone. I think you're the same, but I gotta say it. You and me were in sync with Burke, and it felt good. And I've seen you in action. I don't know how Garrett does it, but he can really pick 'em."

Alexa walked by her, leaving her stunned.

"Besides, I think I'd be a good influence on you . . . if you're willing to learn," the blonde said over her shoulder.

"And a few pointers from me would up your game to an acceptable level . . . at least enough for me to consider taking you on," Jess countered.

Ego aside, Jess had thought they'd made a good team, too, but it surprised her to know the more sophisticated blonde agreed. They were complete opposites, yet when it came to working Burke, everything had gone real smooth. The woman anticipated her moves—for the most part—and went with the flow. Jess liked that, especially when Alexa cut Burke loose without even a question. And getting him to crank up the music had been a stroke of genius.

Jess had always worked alone and wasn't sure she could be a team player like Alexa had said, but questioning Burke with her had definitely come easy. Of course, it would take much more to convince her to join Garrett Wheeler, but she was curious about his proposal, at least enough to hear the man out. And the idea of having resources to back up her agenda had appeal.

She could wield justice on a grander scale. And do it her way—giving Lady Justice a whole new reason to wear blinders. Yeah, she liked that idea, real fine.

"Slick set of wheels, bounty hunter." Alexa had stopped by her blue van, given it the once-over, and asked, "Can you drop me off?" The blonde disappeared behind the rear of the blue whale, giving the van a thorough inspection.

"Yeah, but don't be slammin' my ride. Not when you're beggin' for a hitch," she said as she hit the speed dial on her phone. "I gotta make a call first."

She held the phone to her ear and plugged a finger to her other ear, listening. On the second ring, her friend answered.

"Hey, Sam. It's Jess. Where are you?"

"I'm at work but heading out. What's up?"

"Can you meet me at my place? I've got new developments on Harper's case. I can be there in thirty."

"Yeah, perfect."

Alexa caught her eye and gestured that she wanted to be included. Jess shot her a questioning look but decided it couldn't hurt to have the extra help for Harper's sake.

"Oh and Sammie, I'll have someone with me. Alexa Marlowe is in town. You have a problem with that?"

Her friend didn't reply at first, then said, "No, not really. If you think it's okay to talk about Harper's case in front of her, then I'm good."

"Yeah, thanks. See you soon." She ended the call, and said to Alexa, "You remember my friend Sam Cooper, a local vice cop?"

"Yeah, sure." The blonde climbed into the van. "I hope you have munchies. I'm starving."

"I got you covered. No problem." *She lied.*

As she drove, Jess felt good about how things had gone at Jason Burke's place. She had a possible tattoo match from what the bartender at Dirty Monty's had told her. And CPD could run down Burke loaning his car out, but Mandy's blackmail scheme had caught her by surprise.

Whoever the girl had demanded money from—for whatever reason—the mark would have had motive to kill her, especially if she'd gotten greedy. Blackmail always brought out the worst in folks. If Burke's story held up, she'd have a slim lead on Mandy's killer, someone who had framed Harper in an elaborate ruse.

But from here on, she'd be treading on thin ice—hunting a crafty killer who knew how to get away with murder.

"All you have is beer and condiments," Alexa said, staring into a nearly empty fridge with her face awash in its light. "I thought you said you had food."

"Who do I look like, Rachael Ray?" Jess replied over her shoulder to the blonde in her kitchen.

"Actually you do kind of . . ." Sam grinned, but stopped short when she saw the perturbed expression on her face. "Never mind."

With Alexa in the other room, Sam ventured a more personal topic.

"Have you heard from your boy genius?" her friend asked, hugging a sofa pillow to her chest as she sat next to her on the sofa. "You haven't talked much about Seth since his bail hearing."

Sam had read her well. Good friends had a nasty habit of doing that. She hadn't told Sam about Harper's connection to the man who had rescued her all those years ago. There was something much too personal about it. The only person she wanted to talk to was Harper. She needed to confront him, but she wasn't sure she was ready to do it.

And talking about it with anyone else, even Sam, would only gain her a liberal dose of pity. Only Seth had the answers she needed, and she wasn't sure she could look him in the eye without losing her temper. His betrayal still carried its sting.

"He's left me messages, but we keep missing each other."

To change the subject of her avoiding Seth, Jess gave Sam the CliffsNotes version of her encounter with Jason Burke. And she left Alexa's name out of it, a fact that hadn't been missed by the blonde in the kitchen. In the midst of foraging for food, Alexa looked over her shoulder and winked. Her only reaction.

She told Sam about Burke's possible tattoo match based on the recollection of the bartender at Dirty Monty's and about Burke loaning out his car to anyone with cash. But she saved Mandy's blackmail for last.

"You think there's anything to the blackmail thing? I mean, not about her hitting up Harper, but someone else?" her friend asked.

"It could explain everything, but the DA would love to get ahold of Burke," Jess said. "The guy may not be much, but his testimony could hurt Harper's chances with a jury. I'm gonna check my sources, but maybe your boys in blue can chase down these other leads, huh?"

"Yeah. And I'll tell Ray, too, Jess."

Sam took out a pad and pen from a pocket and made notes as Alexa's voice came from the kitchen.

"Hey, do ramen noodles expire . . . ever?"

Jess fought back a smile, and Sam shook her head. With her crazy work hours, she wasn't much for stocking her pantry except with food that had the never-ending shelf life of Spam.

"We're gonna find out what happened that night, Jess. You'll see. Seth isn't going down for something he didn't do."

Her friend's reassurance was as good as a hug, but Jess felt antsy, as if she were spinning in circles with a clock ticking on Harper's life. And although Sam had an unshakable idealistic belief in the justice system, it was an opinion she didn't share. She'd seen it fail too many times, and being cynical came far too easily.

"What's with the drawerful of unopened fortune cookies?" Alexa called out from the kitchen again. "Isn't that bad luck?"

Sam pursed her lips and nodded. "She has a point."

"Don't encourage her." Jess rolled her eyes, and Alexa interrupted again, still conducting an inventory of her kitchen.

"Malt-O-Meal?" The woman chuckled. "What are you . . . ten years old? Did you get a supersecret decoder ring with this?"

Jess finally had enough and got up to deal with her hungry guest.

"Quit rummaging through my kitchen." She grabbed the half-empty bag of chips Alexa carried in her hand. "Go sit. And I'll make something to stop your whining."

Alexa joined Sam in the small living room and slumped into a chair. The cop shrugged and raised both eyebrows in commiseration, but didn't say a word. Jess flipped the overhead light on in her kitchen and rummaged through her pots and pans for what she needed. Idle chatter filled the next ten minutes until she came out with a serving platter of chips and dip.

"Will this work?" she asked, setting the hot snack and napkins on her coffee table.

"Uh, sure. Looks great." Alexa grabbed a chip and tried the dip. "Hey, not bad."

She waited until the blonde had her mouth full before she asked, "Now that we can get down to business, if I give you some names, can you run financials and a thorough background check on them? Sammie needs a warrant, but it sure would be nice to avoid the red tape. Can you deliver that?"

Not one to waste time, Jess thought it would be a good idea to test the resources Garrett and Alexa claimed to have at their fingertips. And working on Harper's case with her new wannabe ally would also give her an opportunity to try Garrett's resources on for size, to see how they'd fit.

Alexa wiped her mouth and nodded. "Yeah, I could do that. But my people's turnaround is going to depend on how many names you give me."

Jess wondered what it would feel like to have "people," but if Alexa came through with help for Harper, she might take it as a good sign for the prospect of their working together in the future. Trust started with a single step. And that first step never came easy for her.

"That won't be a problem. I've only got a few names for you now. The smoker, Nipple Rings, and Mandy."

"Sounds like a porn flick," Sam said as she handed her a sheet of paper from her notebook and a pen.

Jess wrote the names Nadir Beladi, Jason Burke, and Amanda Vincent. Following the trail of blackmail, it would involve tracking any money that had changed hands. And the murder victim might be the cog to the wheel. The list was a start.

She gave Alexa the names.

"I'll let you know what I find out," the blonde said. "But hey, how come neither of you are eating?" She narrowed her eyes in suspicion.

"Oh, I never eat what she serves me," Sam said without hesitating. "Not unless I brought it."

Alexa shot an accusing stare to Jess. "Come to think of it, I never saw any salsa in your fridge. How'd you make this?"

"Malt-O-Meal and ketchup with a dash of Tabasco, the single girl's best friend. You want me to write down the recipe?"

Alexa looked stunned. She stood with urgency in her eyes. "I think I'm gonna hurl."

"Down the hall, first door on the right," she said, as the blonde rushed by her.

Sam shook her head. "She can outrun explosives, but condiments take her down."

"Yeah, a real lightweight." She winked at Sam, but a knock at the door surprised her.

"Who could that be?" she wondered as she stood, glancing at Sam.

Focused on her life and keeping odd hours made it impossible for her to have a huge circle of acquaintances. Friends were a garden she didn't have the green thumb to cultivate, despite her preaching to Harper how much *he* needed them. And after Lucas Baker had paid a call and trashed her place not too long ago, Jess felt the urge for caution and grabbed her gun.

In her world, old habits died hard, especially those stemming from self-preservation. She doused a nearby lamp and glanced out a side window, barely moving the curtain. She didn't want to leave herself vulnerable by peering through the peephole, making her head an easy target for a shooter with a sick imagination.

She saw the silhouette of a man outside her door. It didn't take long to recognize him. Not saying a word to Sam, she holstered her Colt Python and opened the door.

"We gotta talk, Jessie." Seth Harper stood in her doorway.

Apparently he'd called a moratorium on voice mail and text messages. And she had to admit—looking into Harper's sad, dark eyes—she felt the pull of their bruised friendship.

It was time to talk face-to-face, whether she was ready or not.

—

CHAPTER 14

Her day of reckoning had come, wearing worn jeans, a House of Blues tee, and sneaks.

Seth paced her living room as Jess ushered her guests out the door without much of an introduction. Sam would take Alexa back to her hotel. But before they left, she exchanged cell phone numbers with Alexa. If something came up, Jess wanted a way to contact her.

That left her alone to confront Harper. Despite his personal problems—the glitch of a manslaughter charge hanging over his head—she knew by the look in his eyes that he would finally tell her about his father.

And the reason he'd crossed her path in the first place.

Harper looked tired, in need of a good sleep. And his antsy behavior would have been contagious if she didn't feel wrung out tired herself. She fought the urge to make this about him. After all, he was the one who had knowingly chosen to keep his secrets and betray their friendship. For her to forgive him now would depend entirely on what he had to say.

"You took a chance comin' here. I could've slammed the door in your face."

"Wouldn't be the first time a woman had that notion."

"Oh, Harper . . . I doubt that." She stuffed her hands in her jeans. "Can I get you a beer?"

Harper had a dismal expression. And he hadn't settled down since he walked through the door. He had something in his craw that needed to come out. And with an unrelenting glare, she wasn't making it any easier on him.

That would have to change if she expected him to open up.

"No." He shook his head, avoiding her eyes. "I just . . ."

She plopped down on her sofa and patted the seat next to her, taking a deep breath and reining back the attitude.

"Hey, you're wearing me out," she admitted. "You're like a moving target in an arcade game. Sit down before I shoot you."

"That might not be a bad idea. Put me out of my misery."

"Nah, like I said before, Harper. You gotta have faith." She could have told him the latest developments, but judging by his guilt-ridden face, Seth had something to say.

"Spit it out," she said. "Just say it."

An awkward silence filled the room as he slouched beside her, sprawled in the farthest corner of her sofa. He crossed his arms, still not looking her in the eye. It suddenly dawned on her that his outward appearance and easygoing attitude had been a wall he'd crafted to hide who he really was.

She'd thought she knew him, and that simply wasn't true.

In the past, Seth sometimes refused to answer the occasional question she'd thrown him, but it had never seemed important for her to press him for answers. She'd always believed his basic nature was trustworthy. He was an open book, a simple guy who was easy to read. If he had something to hide, she thought she could always spot it lurking in his dark eyes. And all it would take to get him to open up would be persistence on her part.

But after learning about Harper's connection to the man who had saved her life as a kid—and how well he had kept his secret from her—she realized Seth was far more complicated than she had ever given him credit for. She had to take off the blinders and see him in a different light.

She wasn't sure she could do that.

"I had no intention of you finding out about my father that way. At my damned bail hearing. I'm sorry, Jessie." He struggled for words. "I wanted to tell you. But when you were leaving for Alaska, Mandy hit a new low. She needed . . . someone."

Before her unforeseen trek to Alaska, she remembered how lost and utterly alone Harper looked the day she came to him for help in tracking down Payton Archer's missing niece. She knew something was up and even asked him about it, but he deflected her pointed questions about his personal life and changed the subject. And she'd been too distracted to push him. The hunt for Globe Harvest—the insidious organization behind the girl's abduction—had heated up and taken all her concentration.

Backtracking to that moment, his behavior now made sense. It had seemed harmless at the time, and she hadn't pressed him out of respect for his privacy. Her mind raced with all the other times he had been evasive about his life, but she tried to stay focused.

"But why did you disappear like that? Sam had to tell me you were gone over the phone, even before I came back. What happened?" She touched his thigh. The intimacy of her gesture got his attention. His eyes met hers and stayed. "Did you think I wouldn't notice you were AWOL? Did you think I'd be okay with that?"

Jess was surprised at the hurt in her voice—and in her heart. She had made room in her life for Harper, and his disappearing act felt too much like rejection.

"You didn't need me anymore. Not really. Maybe you never did, but Mandy had no one. And the men in her life always took from her."

Harper was the kind of guy who took in strays of the two-legged variety. She wondered if that was all she had meant to him in the beginning, but questions about Mandy surfaced.

"Was she in more trouble, Seth? I mean beyond her self-inflicted bullet to the brain of using drugs. Did she ever mention being scared of someone?"

"She was so messed up, Jessie . . . because of her addiction and other stuff."

"What other stuff?"

"Life, her boyfriend, everyone was out to get her. You know the drill with addicts. They're paranoid and delusional."

"Did she ever say anything about blackmailing someone?"

"No, but I doubt she would have told me if she was. I wanted her clean. And breaking the law wouldn't be a part of that. Besides, I hadn't talked to her in weeks, not until the night I was supposed to meet her. And I have no idea why she called me out of the blue like that. She never said."

Harper was a regular Boy Scout. His good nature reinforced her judgment that he was a solid, well-meaning guy when it came to others, but something else lurked deeper. Something personal that he was keeping from her. She could have accepted his explanation on its merits and gotten balled up in his angst over Mandy, but a major piece of the puzzle was missing.

"So why did you pick me . . . and Mandy? Does this have anything to do with your father, Seth?"

Jess held her breath, waiting for his answer. And by the look on his face, she knew what he had to say wouldn't be easy to hear.

A flood of images from the day she was rescued filled her mind—an overload of horror that threatened to suffocate her. She struggled to picture the face of Detective Max Jenkins, Harper's father. But all that came to mind were his strong hands and reassuring voice when he hauled her out of that house in his arms, freeing her from a living hell. She'd blocked too much from her memory. Even the good got jumbled into the bad. *The torture. The muffled screams. Her abuser's face. That house on High Street.* It made her sad that she couldn't recall Seth's father—the man who had saved her life.

"You've got to understand, Jessie. My father was a hero to everyone . . ." He lowered his chin and muttered, ". . . to everyone except me."

Harper shut his eyes tight until he could start over. It took courage to talk about an ugly truth, one he probably had never intended to share. The least she could do was listen without passing judgment.

"I never understood why he chose other people . . . over me. My mother tried to explain it, but after a while, she just stopped. I think she felt it, too." His voice took on the sharp edge of resentment. The years hadn't tempered his pain, something she understood. "He gave everything he had to the job. And there was nothing left. Not for me . . . or her."

When his eyes watered, he took a breath and sank deeper into her sofa. Misery personified.

"I cut him out of my life, Jessie. A preemptive strike. A kid's way of saving face, I guess." He shook his head, unable to look her in the eye. "As a kid, I was so angry all the time. Somehow, I lost my place. I let my anger take over until I didn't know who I was or where I fit anymore. It became easier to be alone."

She understood what he meant, completely.

"And I wanted to distance myself from my old man, and changing my name seemed like a good idea at the time my parents got their divorce. After that, it got simpler to reinvent a whole new me."

A tear lost its hold and trailed down his cheek. He never bothered wiping it away. "But my dad's investigation . . . when he rescued you and those kids? That really ate him up. There wasn't much left, especially after . . ."

"What happened, Seth? Tell me." She reached for his hand and held it.

Guilt grabbed her. Until Seth's bail hearing, she hadn't thought about the man who'd saved her life—a self-preservation tactic. Those days of terror were buried deep in the damaged psyche of a child—only resurrected by the nightmares that still plagued her.

"My dad began to drink . . . a lot. Eventually, we noticed he'd changed. Doctors told us the alcohol masked the symptoms of dementia caused by a series of strokes. But by then it was too late. We had to hospitalize him. He needed long-term care." He clenched his jaw. "I got used to him being absent from my life, but inside it still hurts, you know? And I never got a chance to really talk with him. Hell, I've got more baggage than Samsonite."

She knew his attempt at humor was a defense mechanism, a familiar tactic she favored, too. But of all people, she saw behind it, recognizing the crack in the foundation of his life that would remain broken.

"I've never heard you mention family. I always got the sense you were alone, Seth. How's your mom holding up?"

"She isn't, not anymore." He shook his head and squeezed her hand. "Mom died a year ago. And now my father's care is my responsibility. Ironic, huh? He's got no one else. Not really. So I'm taking time to sort things out."

Seth had revealed a great deal, but she saw there was more.

"You're not telling me something. What is it?"

For the first time, he fixed his gaze on her.

"Look, Jessie. This thing with my dad had been between him and me. But as his mind deteriorated, I had to find answers somewhere. I had to come to terms with it, but I want you to know the real reason I made contact with you . . . after all these years."

"What do you mean . . . made contact?"

"I used my dad's old case files to find you. I had your name and other information to track you down," he finally admitted, and let go of her hand. "It was my only way to understand him. Don't you see?"

"How did you get the Millstone files? That's police property." She asked the question, more out of shock than any real concern for police protocol.

"He kept copies of everything. He'd been obsessed with that case. As far as I know, it still haunts him, even in his condition." He leaned forward and grabbed her arm after a tear slid down her cheek.

"Jessie, I needed to understand his fixation." He brushed her tear away with a finger. "And the way I saw it, there was only one way to do that. I had to track down his kids, the ones he'd saved—to know my family's sacrifice had been worth it."

He let the revelation sink in, but when she only stared at him in disbelief, he added, "I'm not proud of why I did it, but, Jessie, I'm beginning to understand how he felt. It's something I have to finish, so I can . . . let it go."

"And Mandy? Was she . . . ?" She fought the emotion welling in her throat, dreading his answer.

"Yes. She was part of your nightmare, Jessie. She was there . . . in that house. Mandy was one of my father's kids."

Jess shut her eyes and took a deep breath, desperately trying to stifle the sickening feeling that gripped her now. She tried digesting what he'd told her, to put it into perspective, but a stark image assaulted her mind like a virulent disease. The blurred face of a crank-addicted hooker—stabbed to death in a cheap motel room—suddenly shifted into focus.

And it was like looking in a mirror.

"We were both there . . . in that house?" She opened her eyes and stared past him, not really seeing Seth, only feeling his hands pulling her close. "Her life could have been mine."

"No, Jessie. You survived. You were stronger than Mandy," he insisted. "Hell, you're the strongest person I know. I've never met anyone like you."

Seth nudged her chin with his finger and fixed his dark eyes on her, forcing her to look at him. He brushed a strand of hair from her face and let his finger trail down her cheek. His tenderness had shocked her, but when he lowered his lips to hers—for an instant—she simply let go. His lips pressed to hers, a warm, comforting touch. She craved the intimacy. It felt right, and she gave in to the sensation, needing to be held. He pulled her to his chest and caressed her.

But eventually, the shock had worn off, and she realized what was happening. That was when she reacted.

"Seth, what are you . . ." Blood rushed to her cheeks, and she pulled away from him.

"I'm sorry. I didn't mean to . . ." Seth scrambled to his feet and stood. He backed away from the sofa and headed across the room. His face flushed pink.

Jess had never seen it coming. Had she misread what he'd done, made more out of it than was there? She replayed the moment in her head and found it hard to misinterpret what had happened.

Seth had kissed her. And damned if she hadn't returned the favor.

CHAPTER 15

Chicago suburbs
Two hours later

Being the bearer of bad news about Seth Harper didn't
sit well with Ray Garza, but it was a hair better than
sharing it over the phone. He hoped Sam Cooper would
appreciate the difference.

With a hand on his steering wheel, he leaned forward and held up a note with an address scribbled on
it. The light coming off a nearby streetlamp was
enough to see the house number as he drove through
the older residential neighborhood, a street lined
with small, well-kept bungalows. He'd never been to
Sam Cooper's house, but the homey street suited
her.

One more block.

Nudging the gas pedal, he felt anxious about seeing
her, a strange mix of feelings that were hard to unravel.
Emotions were a black hole he had no patience for. Part
of him couldn't wait to see her—like a damned kid
with a crush—but another side wished he were in better

control. Hell, he was a seasoned cop. He should know better.

From the first day he'd seen her in the squad room, he had to stifle how he felt. And her being smart and a good cop made his infatuation worse. He wondered if she felt the same, but he didn't trust his instincts where women were concerned. Taking things slow worked best. At least, that was what he told himself.

Ray knew he'd taken a risk coming to her home, when he could have called. But in his mind, a phone call wouldn't cut it. Not with the news he had. It was late, but not completely out of line. He only wished he had a better reason for showing up on her doorstep.

He found her home and parked behind her vehicle in the drive. The small brick bungalow had interior lights coming from what he guessed was a living-room window with curtains drawn. The front stoop and the flower beds beneath the porch were lit. It reminded him of his parents' place, when they were alive.

He hit the front buzzer, and she answered the door wearing jeans and a black CPD T-shirt, her hair in a ponytail. The word—CUTE—could have been stamped on her forehead without lying.

"Ray, what are you doing here?"

When she first saw him through the curtain, her heart leapt. She ran fingers across her hair and fiddled with her clothes—fighting the urge to stall until she could change. But that wasn't going to happen. Sam prided herself on being a low-maintenance woman.

But that was before Ray Garza showed up on her doorstep.

"Hey, Sam. I was . . . ah . . ." He gestured over his shoulder, pointing toward his car, as if the vehicle had brought him against his will.

"You were in the neighborhood?"

She tried to bail him out, but a smile gave her away. She was enjoying herself. Normally, Ray was the picture of confidence, but not tonight. Seeing him like this made her cheeks heat up.

"Come in. Can I get you a beer?" She stood back and let him in.

"No, but thanks. I'm on duty."

The man looked good in her house, but by the expression on his face, he'd come for a reason. This wasn't a social call. She stepped toward her small living room, but he stayed in the foyer.

"What's up, Ray?"

"We gotta talk, Coop. There's something you need to know about Seth Harper." Ray Garza took a deep breath and told her, "I've got news, and I figured you'd want to hear . . . in person."

"Yeah, sure. What's going on?" A worry knot clenched Sam's stomach.

"Another hooker filed charges against him a few hours ago. Camille Regan, street name Jade. She claimed he beat her up earlier today . . . and she says it had something to do with that dead hooker. Detective Loren Clampitt out of Central is checking her story." He gave her the time of the alleged assault. "The woman was stitched up at an ER, but she's out now. We've got an APB on Harper, but so far no luck. I think the kid skipped."

"Oh, my God. I can't believe this." She slumped to the armrest of her sofa. "Ray, that doesn't make sense. You don't know this kid, but I swear . . ."

"For what it's worth, it doesn't make sense to me either. That guy would have to be an idiot to take his fists to a hooker right after makin' bail. But until we talk to him, we've got only her side of the story. You got any idea where he is?"

"No, but I'll call Jess. Maybe she'll know."

She had left Seth at Jessie's place not long ago. The guy had looked antsy and wired, but she had a hard time picturing him doing anything violent. Keeping what she knew from Ray went against the grain, but she owed Jessie a heads-up. And it would look better for Harper if he turned himself in. She had to give him that chance.

"You think she'd tell you?" He cocked his head, his cynicism showing. "You care to make a wager on that?"

"Nope." Sam heaved a sigh. "No bet, Ray. Not this time."

When he had delivered his news, Ray headed for the door, but turned around, waggling a finger. "Hey, did you know that kid is the son of a cop?"

"What?" She wondered if Jessie knew. "No, I didn't know that."

"Yeah, Max Jenkins. He used to serve at Central, detective division. He cracked a big case in his day before he retired. The Danny Ray Millstone case, the serial pedophile who killed and abused all those kids? You and me, we were pretty young back then, but people still talk about it."

Sam felt like someone had smacked her in the head. That name, Danny Ray Millstone, had triggered a gut-wrenching sensation. Jessie had been one of Millstone's young victims. And Sam carried her own memories of how her path had crossed Jessie's all those years ago—a secret she had kept between them.

As a kid, she had seen Jessie poke her finger out of a dark basement one day, but she didn't mention it to her parents or anyone else. Later, she admitted it struck her as odd, but as a kid she had no idea the old man in that house could have done such vile things. Detective Max Jenkins eventually rescued Jessie and the others, but not before weeks of abuse continued, and another little girl had been taken. Even after all these years, Sam held on to the guilt of not telling—and became another victim herself.

"When did you find this out, Ray?" She barely recognized her own voice.

"I heard it came out at the kid's bail hearing. Some big developer named Anthony Salvatore made his bail. The guy was a friend of old Max. Guess the kid has ties to the community after all. Big ones." He narrowed his eyes when she didn't respond.

"You okay?" he asked.

"Yeah. I just got a lot on my mind, that's all." She waved him off and forced a smile that had all the staying power of a snowflake on a hot sidewalk.

"Well, I gotta go." He wanted nothing more than to stay, but something in her eyes told him he wouldn't be welcomed. Nothing personal. "Good night, Coop."

"Yeah . . . good night, Ray. And thanks."

She closed the door behind him and locked it, then leaned against the doorframe, stunned. Jessie had heard about Seth's father at the bail hearing. And she'd deliberately not told her about it. Her friend's life had its dark corners, ones she'd never get to see. And of all people, she understood Jessie's reasons.

But that didn't stop the guilt she felt for playing a part in Jessie's childhood torment. The dark memory rose hot, like bile in her stomach—and always would.

Jess hated to let Harper go, but she had no choice. With his cheeks flushed red, he had refused to stay. His bruised male ego had taken over, and she completely understood. He'd left her place looking more depressed than when he'd arrived—and that was saying something. She understood his need to be alone, especially after she'd overreacted to his sudden show of affection. She'd been guilty, too. She had not only let it happen, she'd kissed him back. The awkwardness of the moment hadn't helped their strained relationship, but why hadn't she seen it coming?

"Damn it," she cursed under her breath. She could have handled it better. Her shock had hurt him. She'd seen it in his eyes. In hindsight, they had both been vulnerable and had probably only reacted out of need for comfort. Maybe he hadn't meant anything more than that, and she had overreacted and embarrassed him.

And after getting Sam's call about the downhill slide of Seth's life, she wouldn't wait until morning to go looking for him. It gave her more of a legitimate reason to search for him, beyond the personal one that had left her baffled. She only wished that she'd insisted they talk about what had happened between them rather than letting him walk out the door.

After all, she had a roll of duct tape and a gun. She could have convinced him to stay.

And on top of it all, Sam had sounded distant on the phone: but when Jess asked her about it, her friend denied it and told her to focus on finding Harper.

Not an easy task.

The first place she looked was his downtown residence, the one she'd found with her taxi-company search. According to the late-night concierge, Harper had cleared out in a hurry without explanation. As usual, he had packed light, carrying only a knapsack on his back, but she had no idea if she could trust what the concierge had said.

If Harper was on the run again, his living nightmare would be ramped up with no end in sight. Even if his bloodwork came back positive for the date-rape drug that had taken his memory—casting doubt on the state's case against him—the cops could arrest him for the assault if he didn't have an alibi. And if this new charge could be linked to Mandy's murder, even if the accusation was false, it would be damaging to his defense. With the evidence piling up against him, the ADA would have plenty of time to make her case without a hitch.

She had one other location to check, a posh condominium project off Lakeshore Drive near the Chicago Harbor, but it would be a long shot. Harper had vacated the premises months ago, and she had the feeling he never covered the same ground twice. But searching the address would make her feel like she was doing something.

Jess found a spot to park along the curb outside the six-story building, but before she got out, her cell rang. Her phone display gave no caller ID, but that didn't stop her from hoping she knew who was on the line.

"Yeah, Beckett here."

"Hey, it's me." Harper's voice sounded distant. "I don't suppose you'd agree to the Vulcan mind meld to forget what happened."

"I'm not sure I want Leonard Nimoy messing with my head, Harper. I'm screwed up enough." Like Seth, she resorted to humor to broach the subject, but before she could tell him how she really felt, he interrupted her.

"If you can forget it ever happened, I'm okay with that," he said. "Irrational behavior is part of an insanity plea I'm building."

When Humphries had reminded her that Seth wasn't as young as she thought, the notion had surprised her. She'd always thought of him as a kid, probably because the harsh life she led had hardened her beyond her years. And Harper struck her as a naïve kid trying to find his way.

He had an open innocence to everything he did. Seeing him in this new light—as a man—had taken her off guard.

"I'm not sure I want to forget it happened, but we do have other things to worry about."

"Yeah, I know the cops are looking for me again. What they're saying . . . it isn't true, Jessie."

His frustration came through over the phone, despite the loud traffic noise in the background on his end.

"You didn't have to tell me that, Harper." She plugged an ear to hear him better. "Where are you?"

"I haven't landed yet." His polite way of saying he had no intention of putting her in the middle with the cops. "And I'm on my own this time. I won't drag Tony Salvatore into the shambles of my life. Man, how did things get so screwed up?"

"I don't know, Harper, but I'm gonna find out. You have an alibi for when the hooker got beat up?" She gave him the time she'd gotten from Sam.

"With the way my luck has been going, what do you think? And I'm too stupid to lie."

Too honest, she thought.

But Jess had to give Harper strokes for more than just honesty. This time he hadn't pulled his usual vanishing act in stealth mode. He'd reached out to call her. But she had a sickening feeling this would be the last time she'd hear his voice. If he'd severed his tight link to Salvatore, it wouldn't take much for him to shut her out.

Jess closed her eyes to imagine him standing in front of her now, to help her focus on his words—but picturing him wasn't enough. Knowing Harper, he had a throwaway phone, and he had probably made arrangements to bury himself deep. If she had any lifeline to him, the rope was fraying.

She had failed him. That was all she knew. And fail-

ing the son of Max Jenkins—the man who had sacri-
ficed so much to rescue her—was unacceptable.

"No one ever tells you how important it is to eat
black-eyed peas at New Year's," he said. "Now my luck
is for shit."

"Yeah, and being framed for murder really blows,
but this isn't over."

"Come on, Jess. I think it's time to cut your losses.
The odds of me getting out of this are slim to none." He
sighed. "I'm not running away, but I just can't sit in
jail."

"I completely understand, Harper. And I commend
you for thinking outside the box, but the cops aren't
likely to embrace your exile strategy—especially if
you have room service and cable. Your taste in upscale
digs would piss them off."

"You think they'd go for it if I stayed at Motel 6?"
The old Harper she knew and loved rose to the occasion—
black humor and all—but he didn't stay long.

"I can't do this, Jess." Fear edged his voice. "And if
they lock me away and someone finds out I'm a cop's
son, what do you think will happen? Hell, maybe I've
seen too many prison movies."

He tried to laugh but failed miserably. It only made
her sad.

"Oh man, I have enough trouble sleeping," she admitted, fighting back tears and a fierce lump in her
throat. "But Seth, you're only making things worse. If
the cops find you . . ."

"That's my new job, Jess"—his voice sounded far

off, like he'd turned his head away from the receiver—
"making sure they don't."

"That isn't a solution."

"I know, but it's all I've got," he said.

Silence. She knew he'd said everything he had intended. Dial tone would be next.

"What about your father, Seth? If you leave, what
will happen to him?" Desperation left her grasping at
straws, even if it meant hurting him to do it. She hated
trumping him with the father card, but she had nothing
else.

"Low blow, Jess." He sighed. "With me in jail, all
he's got is Tony Salvatore anyway, but good try." An
awkward silence reminded her how fragile their connection had always been. "Have a nice life, Jessie. I
think my dad would have been proud how you turned
out. I know I am."

Harper didn't wait for her reply. With a catch in his
voice, he ended the call, leaving her wallowing in dial
tone.

"Damn it."

Someone was determined to frame Harper. And to
cover their tracks, they'd taken a second shot at it,
adding an assault charge for good measure. Yet Jess
knew from experience that if the boy didn't want to be
found, he could shape-shift into a damned ghost—for
real. But that wouldn't fix the hole left in her life where
he'd been.

Jess had to turn things around with a new game
plan. Up until now, the real killer had dictated the

action. *The coward!* She'd been reacting—shoring up Harper's defenses—but that hadn't worked. Jess needed results, and there was only one way to meet that challenge.

Head-on!

She had to stir things up, even if it meant becoming a target for a killer. And, unfortunately for her, she knew exactly where to start.

CHAPTER 16

South Side of Chicago
1:10 A.M.

Hookers don't get workman's comp. And forget about sick days, not even in Nevada, where prostitution is legal. Being an independent contractor herself—*of a different sort*—Jess knew all about operating without benefits.

So she had a pretty good notion where to find Jade.

And if the woman had known Mandy, she figured chances were that they traveled in the same circles. She didn't have to start from scratch to track her down. It was a theory—one that had paid off. And she didn't have to shell out much coin to score Jade's favorite spots. Even if someone hadn't given her a usable description, she recognized Jade by her fresh stitches and distinctive limp in stilettos as Jess drove by her on the street.

Finding a spot under the pale glow of blue and red neon, the woman lit up a cigarette with her back to the wall of Phat Jack's. Next to the lounge was a dark alley, probably the closest thing a streetwalker had to an office. Jade wasn't working it hard, judging by her slouch and lack of interest in the few men who came out of the bar.

Jess parked the blue van down the street and approached Jade on foot, keeping her hand near the butt of the Colt Python, which she wore under a jeans jacket. When she got close, she heaped on the familiar and added a dash of honey to her voice.

"Well . . . what happened to you?" She smiled as if she were an old friend, but Jade gave her the stink eye, clearly not in the mood.

"None of yo' business. Now get outta my face." The woman flipped a hand—flashing an insane set of long red nails—and turned her shoulder like that would discourage her. *Who was she kidding?*

"Okay, I get it. You're a businesswoman." She moved, staying in front of the woman. "What's your price?"

"No way. I don't go for none o' that. Beat it." Jade hobbled away, sucking on her smoke. Two other hookers down the block took notice. And a group of men rounded a corner down the street.

"Hey, I just wanna talk. Nothin' wrong with that, is there . . . just talkin'?" Grinning, Jess caught up to her and lowered her voice, turning her back on the unwanted attention from the outsiders. "Come on. I'll buy you a drink inside, and you can take a load off. And I'll even pay for your time. What's not to love? Those shoes would be killin' my feet 'bout now. What do ya say?"

Jade stopped and listened, her tough street act fading as she stubbed out her cigarette. Jess could have been angered by her false accusation against Seth, but she knew the woman had probably had no say in it.

"You buyin'?" she asked, raising her chin in challenge.

"Yep. Whatever you're having, I'm good for it."

"I normally get fifty for my time. And I leave, when I say I do." Jade narrowed her eyes, defying an objection.

Jess grimaced but forced a smile. "I have no doubt you're worth every penny. Now prove it."

"Okay, then." Jade made a beeline for the front door of Phat Jack's, not waiting for her. But a voice came from behind Jess.

"Don't move."

A dark shadow reflected off a nearby window and forced her to stop. On instinct, she inched a hand toward her gun.

"Put your hands up." A gruff hostile voice. "Don't turn around."

The crunch of a shoe on cement gave her an indication where the man stood, too far away for a sucker punch. And the reflected glint of metal under neon warned her the man had a weapon—and two other men at his side, standing in murky shadows. *Not good!*

Jade turned, and her eyes grew wide when she saw the men. She looked scared shitless. Her gaze darted from Jess to whoever stood behind her. In sympathy, the woman slowly shook her head. Jess took it to mean the men would be trouble, but the hooker wanted no part in the beef.

"Beat it, Jade." One of the men gave her a reprieve. And by using her name, he reminded her that he knew who she was.

No one had to tell Jade a second time. She limped out of sight, leaving only the unsteady clack of her stilettos on the sidewalk for Jess to know which way she went.

"Now turn around . . . bounty hunter." The man's voice made her skin crawl, like an unwanted touch. "And keep your hands where I can see 'em."

Jess took a deep breath. She had a real bad feeling. And when she turned, she faced three men who had done their homework and knew who she was. And one of them pointed a gun at her chest.

"Gentlemen . . . good to see you again. Last time we met, we got off on the wrong foot. What can I do to make amends?" She kept her hands waist high.

Flickering neon washed over Sal Pinzolo, casting his brand of ugly in an eerie glow. The man clenched his weapon, taking perverse pleasure in his threat. And by the looks of him, a well-timed stun grenade exploding at his feet hadn't improved his looks or his disposition any. Another man she hadn't seen before looked like Pinzolo's twin, nothing more than muscle for hire with a vacant stare and no neck. And stepping between them was Nadir Beladi, cigarette smoke wafting in his wake. His cruel eyes were the color of obsidian.

This time she had no surprises up her sleeve.

"It's not that simple, Ms. Beckett," Beladi said. "You've put me in the awkward position of having to make you an example. You wouldn't answer my questions about your interest in that crank whore. And you came to my turf, my place of business, giving me attitude and setting off grenades at my feet?"

She had no idea a man could be so sensitive about a small incendiary device.

"Forgive me, Nadir. I didn't mean any disrespect. But I took exception to Sal using me as a pincushion for his blade. But if you say it was all a big misunderstanding, I'm good with that. We can call it a night."

"It is too late for that, I'm afraid. For a man of my stature in the community, I must save face."

"I won't tell if you won't."

"You have a very smart mouth, Jessica. I would say that it will get you in trouble one day, but you see? It already has." The smoker was done talking. He nudged his head toward Pinzolo and No Neck. "Do it."

Beladi took off, leaving her alone with his men. They stepped toward her, forcing her back. She had nowhere to go except deeper into the alley behind her. And insult to injury, No Neck took her Colt Python and shoved it under his belt as Pinzolo jacked his smug face into a grin. They drove her deeper into the shadows. Her eyes searched the gloom, looking for a way out, but she found nothing to help her. When she got toward the end, the alley looked as if it veered right, but she couldn't be sure. Old crates and a rusted Dumpster blocked her view.

Jess squared her feet and braced for a fight. She hoped the bastard wouldn't just shoot her where she stood. Pinzolo guessed what she was thinking and laughed, a sound that echoed off the brick walls.

"I'm not gonna waste a bullet on you, but when we're done, you're gonna wish we had." The smirk on his face told her he wasn't done taunting her. "You know, there's a reason they say paybacks are a bitch."

The coward stuffed his gun in a holster and both men lunged at her. She got in a few good licks but not before No Neck grappled her from behind. He held her arms, wrenching them back until she thought he'd break bone. Jess shoved as hard as she could, putting all her weight behind it, as Pinzolo leered and balled his meaty fists, waiting his turn.

No Neck toppled to one side, but held strong until Pinzolo blocked the light coming from the street. He towered above her, looking like a ghost from one of her nightmares. She clenched her stomach, but nothing prepared her for his vicious first punch. It took the wind out of her and hurt like a mother.

"I have to say it," she gasped, barely able to speak. "I'm not liking . . . where this is going."

She kicked and jerked her body as Pinzolo pummeled her. Two more to the gut, and her legs gave out. Her head lolled to her chest, and he hit her with an uppercut. She saw stars, and her mind faded in and out of shadows.

The punishment continued. She fought to stay conscious although she wasn't sure why. Oblivion would have been a mercy. But in one swift motion, No Neck let go of her arms and she dropped like a rock. Her kneecaps hit asphalt, jarring her whole body. She fell against something hard. And her head snapped back, sending streetlights spiraling out of control in a blur.

For a brief instance, she lay flat with her swollen cheek on a cold surface. All she wanted was to lie there, not be touched. But the scuff of a shoe near her head made her flinch. She cocked her face to one side and saw a man reaching for her. Jess braced her body, still fighting back, but a movement in the distance caught her fragile attention. A car had blocked the alley. Its headlights cut through the darkness.

And now a lone shadow eclipsed the light, nothing more than an eerie silhouette.

The men saw what had happened. They gaped over their shoulders at the intruder. As they moved aside, the lights from the street blinded her. Jess raised a hand to block the glare, fighting hard not to pass out. She winced and gasped for air, feeling a thousand pinpricks stabbing her eyes. The distant shadow wavered, a blurred spiraling illusion.

Eventually it came into focus.

A tall blonde wearing a long, dark trench coat walked toward them.

"Stop where you are." Pinzolo's voice came from the darkness. "Who the hell are you?"

"Is that any way to treat a lady?"

Quiet, but no less threatening, Alexa's voice was nothing but a chilling whisper. In one fluid motion, she reached under her long coat and pulled out a twelve-gauge Mossberg pump-action shotgun slung under her arm—a fierce-looking weapon with a pistol grip and flash suppressor.

Without hesitation, Alexa racked the slide and took aim. Pinzolo and No Neck fumbled for their guns, shocked that a woman had gotten the drop on them.

"What the hell?" One of them cried out.

"Oh shit." Jess scrambled for the Dumpster.

Boom! Thud! A shot roared and a muted muzzle flash lit the dark alley. Brick shards sprayed and pinged off metal. *Boom! Thwack!* A second blast, and the meaty thump of lead hitting flesh resonated down the alley. And Jess heard a pitiable groan behind her.

The shotgun had done its damage—and so had Alexa.

CHAPTER 17

Alexa hadn't come to kill, but if these men were intent on using deadly force, she knew how to respond. Her prime objective was to stay alive and get Jessie to safety. With her first round, she'd aimed over their heads, raining brick down to get their attention. And with the second, she drew blood. This time when she pumped the shotgun, the men would have a choice.

She stepped closer and aimed the barrel between the eyes of the bully with the fists. He had fallen to the asphalt when he got hit.

"That last one was birdshot. You won't sit for a while, but you'll live. The rest are double-ought buckshot and deer slugs. And as far as I'm concerned, it's open season. You wanna see if I'm bluffing?"

The man glared, but she saw his fear.

"No, I'll take your word for it, but this ain't over." He tried a weak attempt at bravado for his friend's benefit, but a load of lead in his ass had taken the fight from his eyes.

"You have no idea who you're dealing with. You mess with us, and the CIA will take it real personal.

You got that?" To make her point, Alexa flashed a badge. "If you don't want feds crawling up your riddled butt, you better let this one go."

The man's eyes grew wide as he stared at her badge and picture ID. He cursed and stumbled to his feet with the help of his buddy, then turned to limp away. Knowing the area, they took a different way out of the alley, through the shadows behind them.

And with relief, Jessie watched them go.

"Hold on," the blonde called out before they got too far. Alexa grabbed her Colt Python from No Neck's belt. "And you might consider taking your friend to a veterinarian. They've got plenty of experience picking birdshot out of mutts."

"I don't care who you are. This ain't over," Pinzolo spat, venom in his eyes. Jess knew that look, had seen it up close. And his eye twitch was back.

"Then you're dumber than you look." Alexa stared him down. "Now move it."

She watched them go, and the blonde made sure the fight was over before she got down to business.

"You sure know how to pick 'em, Beckett. But looking at you, I think we can make a good case for self-defense if the local law comes calling." Alexa picked up her spent shell casings as she spoke. She wouldn't leave evidence behind. "Come on. Let's go before we draw a crowd. I'll drop you off at your van, but I'm following you home. We need to patch you up."

"I thought you didn't have wheels." She wiped blood from her brow, feeling every new ache.

"It's a rental. Figured I could use it." Alexa pocketed her shells. "Any bones broken? Can you walk?"

"My pride is a little bent. Help me up, will ya?" With a hand from her new friend, she winced and struggled to her feet, stretching her bruised muscles and stiff joints. "Ow, damn it. How'd you find me anyway?"

Jess steadied herself, making sure she could stand before she took a step. Once she got her wind, she hobbled alongside her tall companion, heading for the lights coming from the street. After a quick glance, Alexa returned her Colt Python and stared straight ahead, her blond hair wafting in the faint breeze. She noticed the woman shortened her long strides to let her keep up.

"Old habits die hard. When I hitched a ride in that monstrosity you call a vehicle, I put a tracking beacon on it. You have a habit of going off the reservation. I figured it wouldn't hurt to have a little insurance."

Alexa had done that once before, a few months back. The woman was neck deep in high-tech spy gear. And she knew when and how to use it.

"But tracking me in the middle of the night? What's up with that?"

"I couldn't sleep anyway. And Conan O'Brien was a rerun." She glanced over her shoulder as she hobbled a step behind. "Besides, I didn't like your odds this time."

"I could've taken 'em." She moved her jaw, making sure it still worked. "I was wearin' 'em down."

"Yeah, their knuckles will be real bruised tomorrow. I know how hard your head is." Alexa smiled and raised an eyebrow. "I hope you realize I didn't have to tell you the truth about that tracking beacon. And I probably messed up a perfectly fine manicure for you. Consider this my way of bonding."

"Yeah? Well, next time . . . let's go bowling instead." Even aching, she forced a smile, pondering what had just happened. "And what's with the CIA badge? On St. Lawrence Island, you were wearing FBI gear."

The blonde shrugged. "A girl has to know how to accessorize."

Jess knew she wasn't going to get any more out of her. But as she turned to get a better look at the woman, she took stock of the black trench coat with matching Kevlar. It felt good to have someone backing her up, even if the woman had a flair for drama.

"So what's with the Matrix knockoff, Trinity?"

"A little over the top?"

"Maybe." Jess shrugged. "But it worked for Keanu Reeves."

Alexa grinned. "Damned straight."

Buena Vista Motel
Off Madison Street
4:20 A.M.

Even at this hour, the Eisenhower Expressway droned, nothing more than white noise to urban sprawl as Ray Garza drove by Garfield Park on his way to another murder. He pulled into a motel parking lot after spying the rotating red-and-blue beacons of police cruisers and the Mobile Crime Lab on the scene. ET-South drew the short straw, and evidence techs were hard at work as he walked through the police barrier, past the curious onlookers who had already gathered outside the yellow tape. And the usual media crews were on duty, making the most of the show.

"Detective Garza, can we have a word?" a woman reporter called to him, holding out a microphone with camera rolling and bright lights.

"Yeah, have two. No comment." Avoiding the bright lights, he never bothered to look to see who'd asked the question.

With his badge clipped to his belt, he didn't need an introduction to the beat cops who'd secured the scene. Too many déjà vu scenes like this had played out before, giving them the inside track on depravity no one should have to witness firsthand.

He nodded a greeting and headed for the motel room, the one with all the traffic. As he got closer, a young cop in uniform heaved the contents of his stomach onto the asphalt sidewalk two doors down. Worse timing on his part, and he might have caught the splatter.

"Hey, watch the shoes," he said as he walked by.

Rousted in the middle of the night, Ray wore a navy polo shirt and jeans with running shoes and a CPD windbreaker. When he walked over the threshold, a wave of stench hit him as he hit the door. Moldy stale air mixed with the metallic tang of blood, excrement, and other bodily fluids, the rank smell of violent death.

He kept his expression blank as he looked onto the scene, but he never got used to it. *Never.*

The day he did, that would be the day he'd quit.

A woman's nude body lay sprawled on the blood-stained and soiled mattress. Her skimpy clothes were tossed onto the floor, nothing more than a heap of spandex and torn lace. From where he stood, her face was partially covered by a pillow. Deep gouges cut into her flesh, too many to count with all the blood, especially around her neck. And blood splatter streaked the walls and ceiling, a grisly tableau.

Dim lighting in the room had been a blessing until an evidence tech took photos. Every time the camera flashed, the harsh light assaulted the body and added another stark image to his memory.

"What do we have, Nigel?" He breathed through his mouth and pulled out his notepad and pen. "Talk to me."

"Dead hooker. Killer used a knife, but we haven't found the murder weapon." His partner, Detective Nigel Walker, gave him the lowdown. "Castoff suggests there was a lot of rage involved once the killer got into it. TOD is estimated at no more than two hours ago. Around two, I'd guess."

Tall and lanky with thinning hair, Walker had the drawn face of a human basset hound. And his slow Southern drawl came from Texas, but his eyes took in every aspect of a crime scene. The man was thorough and knew his stuff.

"Who found the body?"

"The night manager," Walker replied. "He got a

complaint about a TV playing too loud. When he didn't get a response from his knock, he used his key. He phoned 911 after he backed out of the room . . . said he didn't touch anything."

"He didn't come in and turn off the TV?"

"No. It was still on when I got here. I turned it off myself. *Twilight Zone* reruns give me nightmares."

The man's deadpan expression didn't flinch. Ray might have chuckled at his dry sense of humor, but he shifted his focus back to the body. No amount of training ever prepared him for a scene like this. And no one deserved to die in such a brutal way—naked and degraded. Whoever had done this wasn't stable—at least that's what he preferred to believe.

"We get any bloody prints?" he asked.

Fingerprints in a motel room could be easily explained away unless they were marred in blood or confirmed as part of the murder scene.

"Mostly smudges, but we're still workin' it," Walker replied, and added, "Hard to tell with all the blood, but it looks like she'd been beaten recently. New stitches and all. M.E. will tell us more. And here's something you should see."

His partner pointed to a series of shallow wounds to the victim's stomach.

"These don't appear to be very deep," Walker said. "M.E. will have to make the final determination, but it looks like the killer jabbed and poked her."

Ray had seen this type of wound before—and recently. Apprehension twisted his gut.

"She didn't die fast," his partner continued. "She

was mutilated and tortured. And these shallow punctures don't look postmortem either. You ready to have a look?"

Without answering, Ray stepped closer to the bed and leaned in as Walker lifted the pillow off the dead woman's face. He stared into glazed dead eyes, sightless and wide with terror. Her mouth gaped open.

Despite the horror on her face that distorted her features, he recognized her. He'd seen her booking photo.

"DL says her name is . . ." His partner read from a driver's license taken from a purse on the nightstand.

"I know who she is." Ray straightened up and shook his head. "Camille Regan, aka Jade. And, Nigel, things just got more complicated."

CHAPTER 18

Late morning

After Ray Garza's visit to her home last night, Sam hadn't slept much since hearing his news on Harper and the kid's connection to Jessie's past. She had no doubt her friend was battling old demons again—shutting her out one more time—but some battles were best waged alone. And she understood that. Her guilt over Jessie had been her lifetime obsession and had driven her to "fix" things for her childhood friend—making up for when she hadn't helped at all.

Of course, understanding her problem and overcoming it were two different animals. It was a compulsion she had accepted as her penance long ago. And Jessie had every right to deal with her past in her own way. But Sam could help Harper, something she knew Jessie would want, too.

So her day had included a step in that direction.

From a distance, she stared at Ray Garza at his desk in the detective's bullpen. She sipped coffee as she did, enjoying the anonymity of her spot across the busy room. She liked watching him in unguarded moments, a cop hard at work. He was on the phone and taking notes, looking especially sharp in a navy suit and tie. The man cleaned up real nice, although he looked a little tired. She'd left a message for him early, and he'd returned it, but both calls had rolled into voice mail so she'd decided to leave the next one in person.

Seeing Ray in the flesh was always a good move.

As she made her way down the aisle toward his desk, he looked up and did a noticeable double take with the phone to his ear, a gesture that had taken her by surprise, too. His all-business expression softened, and she couldn't help but smile. And although he held up his end of the conversation, he kept his eyes on her.

It was a seductive gaze she could get used to.

Since she'd first met Ray, the connection between them had grown. And she loved every moment of their innocent cat-and-mouse game of flirtation. She knew they would eventually cross the line into something more, and she wanted that, too—one of the reasons she had instigated their bet in the first place.

But things had changed since they'd made the bet.

She pulled up a chair next to his desk and sat waiting, content with the view. When he got off the phone, he tossed his pen on the desktop and slouched back in his chair.

"Hey, Coop. We've been playing phone tag, but you look like a woman with something on her mind. You go first."

"You have no idea, Raymundo." She smiled and placed her coffee cup on a corner of his desk. "Look, I know we have a bet, but I think it's time we compare notes on Harper's case. If we pool our resources, we might make more headway. What do you say?"

"It sounds like you're conceding." Ray teased her. "I didn't figure you for a quitter."

Despite a grin on his face, she saw the concern in his dark eyes, a charming contradiction.

"I'm not a quitter, but I'm leaving it up to you. If I have to wave a white flag, I'll do it." She sighed. "This thing with Harper has gotten worse, and with him being in the wind, I think we should work together, that's all. Our bet makes this seem like a game when it's anything but that. He's a cop's son, Ray. We owe it to his old man."

He thought about what she'd said for a moment, then began, "You don't have to throw in the towel, Coop. I think we can keep a scorecard and give credit where it's due."

"Glad to hear you say that," she said with a smile. "I've got something to share on Jason Burke, Mandy's ex. That guy's a piece of work."

Sam kept Jessie's activities to herself. Not because of their bet, but secondhand hearsay obtained by an outsider to the investigation would have little bearing on the case. Anything Jessie had acquired would not be admissible in court unless CPD's investigation had uncovered the same findings legally.

"Yeah? What do you have?" Ray asked.

"I didn't buy Burke's I-PASS alibi, so I did some checking on my own. Jessie doesn't even know about this. I didn't want to get her hopes up if it turned out to be a dead end." She had spent most of her morning chasing down her hunch.

"Checking on what?" he asked.

"I pulled his cell-phone records." She raised an eyebrow. "And it would appear our man Burke is something of a superhero."

"Yeah? How so?"

"Tracing his movements by cell-phone tower on the night Mandy was murdered, the guy used his phone in South Chicago at the same time he was supposed to be on the West Side in Lombard. Now if we search his apartment and find he's got spandex and a cape in his closet, then I might change my mind, but I think he lied to us about being in the burbs, and I'd like to know why."

"Yeah, so would I. I'd say Jason Burke has a solid spot on our suspect list. Culver's lead on this. I'll tell him and make sure he knows the tip came from you. He'll bring Burke in for questioning." He shrugged. "But you had that morsel in your hip pocket all along. Did you set me up about calling off our bet?"

"I wouldn't exactly call it a setup. I had faith that you'd do the right thing." She smiled.

"Thanks . . . I think."

"You're a good man, Raymundo."

"I'd appreciate it if you'd keep that to yourself. I've got a reputation to think about."

She took a sip of her coffee, and asked, "So what's your news?"

His face turned grim. "I'm glad you're sitting down."

South Chicago
Off Cicero Avenue

Why did morning have to come so damned early?

Feeling every ache in her body, Jess glanced at the clock to see morning had actually come and gone. It was past noon when she rolled to her side and pulled a pillow over her head to block the daylight that filtered its fingers through her bedroom blinds like a rude poke in the eye.

Sleep had not been her friend. And despite the repair job on her face with butterfly stitches over her eye, she'd messed up her bed linens with smears of blood. When she caught a glimpse of smudged red on the pillow, she had enough and tossed it aside.

Nice, real nice. She stumbled out of bed and trudged down the hall, grabbing a change of clothes as she went. After getting a look at her face in the mirror—the bruise on her cheek, the busted lip, and the new cut on her brow next to her old scar—she winced and shook her head.

"Harper . . . only for you, pal."

As she got dressed, she replayed the events of last night, the ones she remembered. After her run-in with Nadir Beladi, Jess had way more to think about than her latest bruises that made her body look like a shrink's Rorschach test.

Something Beladi had said bothered her.

. . . you came to my turf . . . my place of business . . . setting off grenades at my feet . . .

Sure, a grenade could be construed in a negative

light, but the man had taken the whole thing personally. At first she thought he'd taken exception to her
treading on his turf, but having the crap beat out of her
had triggered an epiphany—and there was nothing like
head trauma to render clarity.

"'My place of business'?" she muttered.

Jess headed for her kitchen to make coffee, the
caffeine-laden ambrosia of the gods, pretending it was
still morning . . . somewhere. But a look into her living
room stopped her. Looking cramped and bent, Alexa
lay asleep on her short sofa. Fully clothed, the woman
still wore her black Matrix gear and had a small com-
forter over her.

"Hey, Goldilocks. Rise and shine." She waited until
the woman opened her eyes. "I thought you left after
you patched me up last night."

"Last night? Try this morning." Alexa yawned and
was slow to sit up. She ran fingers through her hair
when she was upright. "And yeah, I was going to, but
you might have had a concussion. You don't remember
me waking you? I thought you'd slug me the last
time."

"Sorry I missed the opportunity. Normally, I don't
pass up a free poke." Jess rounded the corner into her
kitchen and checked her fridge.

"You hungry?" Jess turned toward her houseguest
and grinned. "I've got Malt-O-Meal."

"Oh no, not on your life," the blonde objected.
"We're going out to eat, and you're buying."

Alexa stood and stretched, but a knock on the door

saved Jess's pocketbook. She peeked out the window and grimaced when she saw who it was.

"This can't be good," she muttered.

She opened the door to find Ray Garza and Sam on her doorstep. But before she said a word, Ray got in a quick jab.

"I always thought you were tougher than a three-dollar T-bone." He shook his head and gazed at her cuts and bruises. "But maybe I should check out the other guy."

"Yeah, you do that. He'll be the one with the new corn shoot."

Ray tried not to laugh, but he lost his fight with a smile.

"What happened, Jessie?" Sam rushed through the door, but when she saw Alexa smile and wave, she narrowed her eyes. "Actually, maybe I don't want to know."

"Good idea." Jess shut the door behind them and quickly introduced Ray to Alexa. "I'd get you guys some coffee, but I get the feeling this isn't a social call. What's up?"

She looked at Sam, but when her friend kept quiet and shifted her gaze to Ray, Jess knew something was terribly wrong.

"Someone start talking . . . please," she pleaded.

"Sam told me she called you about Jade filing charges against your friend Harper," he said.

"Yeah, what about her?" Jess didn't dare look at Alexa.

Her confrontation with Jade and her head-on collision with Beladi last night weren't up for discussion
until she knew more. Sam was her friend, but Ray was
the cop who'd nearly gotten her arrested for the murder
of Lucas Baker a few months ago. Just because Sam
had the hots for the guy didn't mean he deserved her
complete trust.

He'd have to earn that.

"She was killed early this morning," he said. "Butchered with a knife, same as Desiree—right down to a
series of distinctive puncture wounds. If the DA wants
to proceed with charging Harper for Desiree's murder,
those shallow wounds will tie him to Jade's killing
even if the link is only circumstantial. And Jade's assault charges against him don't help his case. We've got
an APB on Harper."

"And I suppose you want me to magically produce
him, like I know where he is." She turned on him,
walking into her living room to slump onto her couch.
Things had gone from bad to worse in seconds flat.
And she had a headache brewing at the base of her
skull.

"Actually, we're here to update you on other developments. Then we can talk about what's best for Seth."
Sam sat next to her on the sofa, with Ray taking a spot
on the armrest near her friend. Alexa remained standing, her face stern.

"This morning I put a hole through Jason Burke's
I-PASS alibi," Sam began.

"She's being modest," Ray said. "She annihilated
it."

Sam touched a hand to his thigh and smiled. Jess hadn't missed the gesture. And neither had Alexa.

"Talk to me, Sammie. What's going on?" Jess didn't want to get her hopes up, but this was the first bright spot she'd heard in Harper's case.

"I had a hunch about Burke. Remember, the guy claimed to be in Lombard at a club and he used his I-PASS for an alibi?" After she nodded, Sam went on, "Well I ran his cell-phone bill and checked it against the night of the killing. He lied to us about being in the burbs."

Sam explained about triangulating cell-phone towers and how she had determined Burke's location and exposed his lie.

"That's good news, right?"

"Yeah, I'd say so. Detective Culver is bringing Burke in for questioning. We'll have him for forty-eight hours if he doesn't lawyer up. It'll give us time to check him out."

"And we should have Harper's drug test soon," Ray said.

"That should help with reasonable doubt," Sam nodded.

"Yeah, but we still have to find out who killed these women," he said. "With Burke being Desiree's ex and having a history of violence toward women, he's a likely candidate. But Jade is another story. Her killing may have similarities, but my gut tells me this doesn't add up. Something else is at work."

Jess clenched her teeth. Ray's hunch was spot on. Beladi and Pinzolo had seen her with Jade in front of

Phat Jack's. If the woman were perceived to be a loose end, Pinzolo would have no problem with cutting her out of the picture, literally.

Had she gotten Jade killed? Her stomach turned at the thought. It was one thing to put *her* life on the line, but taking Jade with her made her sick.

"So Harper might—and I stress the word 'might'— have reasonable doubt in his favor for Desiree, but for Jade he's got nothing. If anything, that killing might strengthen the DA's case." Alexa jumped in with the harsh reality of Seth's situation and locked her gaze on Jess. "They turn up any of his prints at the scene?"

"No, but they're still working evidence," Ray admitted.

Jess knew Alexa was making a point to be careful and not expect too much—at least not until they had a chance to talk one-on-one. Beladi was a viable suspect, but she had nothing to go on except gut instinct. Although Alexa had promised a thorough background check on the man, all Jess had were theories and the bruises to go along with them.

But Ray was not happy with Alexa's take on Harper's predicament. She could see it on his face.

"It's time for a little tough love, Jessie," he said. "That's why we both came, to plead our case."

Sam reached for her hand and held it. She was straddling the line between being a friend and a cop, a familiar place.

"You gotta bring in your friend for his own good." Ray's usually somber expression softened, and he lowered his voice. "If you care for him, you gotta bring him in whether he wants to come or not. With him on the loose, whoever is framing him is racking up the charges and making it look easy. And the killing may not stop with Jade. Other lives could be at stake."

Jess knew this was difficult for Ray, too. The guy was pretty cut-and-dried where the law was concerned. But for Sam, he was making an effort.

"I know this will be hard." He fixed his gaze on her. "But the way I see it, it's up to you now. Do what's right, even if your friend can't see it."

Jessie gritted her teeth, fighting back nausea. Her loyalty to Seth Harper clashed with the sickening guilt over playing a part in Jade's death. Her path and Seth's had crossed when they were both kids, and it was happening again. And all the darkness lurking under her skin and wedged deep in her memory had been stirred awake. She'd have to deal whether she wanted to or not.

But in the end it might come down to one thing.

Could she track down a friend to stop a killer? She hoped Seth would understand.

After Ray and Sam left, Jess sat with Alexa in silence on her living-room sofa. Her appetite had bitten the dust. And to her credit, her new companion gave her plenty of time to think—an intuitive gesture she appreciated.

Finally, she spoke. "Did I get Jade killed?"

Jess stared across the room, unable to look the woman in the eye. She had only thought about finding Mandy's killer so Harper would walk on the charges.

Her sole focus had been on her friend. Had she known someone else would have been murdered, would she have acted differently? The fact that she had to think about the answer scared her.

"Jessie, look at me." The blonde waited until she did. "You had nothing to do with that woman's death. My theory is that she got picked because she knew her killer. Whoever did this knew she'd file charges against Harper and probably beat her up to make it look good. You can't take credit for all the bad choices Jade made in her life. She became a loose end, and someone felt the need to eliminate the threat. You had nothing to do with that."

"I wouldn't exactly say I had nothing to do with it." She shook her head and pulled a pillow to her chest. "My gut tells me Harper would be safer in police custody, like Ray said. But I'm not sure I can be the one who takes him in."

Duping Harper and betraying his trust felt so wrong. Even though Ray and Sam made a good point that it was time for tough love, she found herself flogging her brain for another option.

"I can do it, if you want," Alexa offered.

"No, that would only be a cheap shot. He'd know I had something to do with it anyway. No, I gotta do this or find another option." She took a deep breath. "But I could still use your help. Get me those financials. Maybe we can find something to chase while I'm looking for Harper. Can you put a rush on that?"

"Yeah, I'm on it." Alexa stood and headed for the door, but turned to add, "You're not alone in this, Jessie.

And neither is Harper. We're gonna find the bastard who's really to blame."

"Thanks, Alexa." She forced a smile until the woman shut the door, then her smile faded.

Before she devised a scheme to track down Harper, she had a stop to make that was long overdue. Thinking about it brought on a rush of nausea. And her heart ramped up to the rhythm of her shallow breaths, the start of a panic attack she'd experienced far too many times whenever her past threatened to erode the makeshift foundation of her present.

But she had a feeling that facing Detective Max Jenkins alone would be important, an ordeal that fate had set in her path to try out her courage, taking it for a test drive. Confronting the demons of her childhood had always been her destiny—her way of dealing with it. In the back of her mind, she had always known that. Surviving her ordeal and being rescued had only been the beginning.

The real test was yet to come.

CHAPTER 19

Golden Palms Villa
Late afternoon

In the back of her mind, Jess always suspected this day would come—and with it, a flood of mixed emotions gripped her. Driving up to the nursing home gave her a sense that her life was about to come full circle. And even though the prospect of that scared the hell out of her, she felt on the verge of change.

"Max Jenkins."

She said his name aloud, a mantra that grounded her in the reality she'd soon be looking into the man's eyes—the detective who had saved her life, taking her from darkness into the light. Seth's father. She knew that seeing Max again would dredge up the ugliness of her childhood, but in order to confront her fears, she had to see him—to make him real and fix his face in her memory.

She owed him that much and more.

And for the first time, she felt strong enough to do it. This wasn't about locating Seth. It was more about confronting her demons. Jess didn't want to believe in fate. The concept was not only depressing, but she couldn't fathom living in a world that had condemned her to the fate she had experienced as a once-innocent child. Yet how Seth's life had crossed hers then and now had haunted her thoughts ever since she'd first learned of his connection to her past.

"Another puzzler from Harperworld." She tried to smile but couldn't summon one.

She parked her vehicle on the street facing the property, choosing to walk the rest of the way and work out the kinks in her sore muscles. The sunny afternoon carried a nice breeze, downright cheery. But she had serious doubts the good cheer would rub off.

"It's now or never, Beckett." She headed for the front door.

Located at the end of a street, the nursing home was set off the road, with a well-manicured front lawn and a wide, curved drive that led to the main entrance. A four-story building of red brick with a white column portico. Toward the back, a wall gave the residents privacy when they ventured outdoors onto the grounds. And a mix of commercial properties and older residences lined the street. The setting was modest but real homey. She'd seen fancier places. And if Anthony Salvatore had had more say in where Max lived, his accommodations might have been different. But she got the distinct impression that Seth had picked this place for his father.

Double glass doors listed the hours the facility would be open for guests. She had called ahead to make sure when she arrived that visiting hours would be under way. Stepping inside, she was greeted by a friendly face behind a reception desk. The young woman chose to ignore the bruises and cuts on her face, treating them as if they were invisible, a gesture Jess appreciated.

"Can I help you?"

"Yeah, I'm looking for Max Jenkins. Can you tell me which room he's in?"

"I'll need you to sign in please." While the woman hit a few keystrokes to pull up the information on her computer, Jess signed in under a fake name, not wanting to leave a trace she'd been to the place. But she took her time discreetly looking for Seth on the roster of guests. It didn't take long to find his name, and she recognized his handwriting. He'd last visited late on a Friday—the week before his life went into the crapper— nearly two weeks ago.

"Mr. Jenkins is on the second floor. Number 204." The woman smiled and pointed down the hall. "The elevators are to your right. And you'll find signs upstairs to help you locate his room. Is there anything else I can do for you?"

"Actually, I'd like to speak to someone about Uncle Max. One of his nurses maybe. I live out of town, and this is my first visit. I'd like to get an update."

"Then you'll want to speak to Bernice Withers. She's the second-floor nurse on duty. Her station is by the elevators. You can't miss it."

"Thanks."

When Jess got to the second floor, she found the

nurses' station, but no one was there. That left her only one option. She took a deep breath and went looking for room 204, Max's room. When she got there, his room was empty, but that didn't stop her from looking around.

She wandered in and checked the view from his window, noticing his room faced the front entrance, a convenient situation for the stakeout she had planned. Even though seeing Max had been a huge part of why she'd come, the other reason for her visit left her feeling guilty. Jess had come to track down his son. And no amount of justifications or sugarcoating would change that fact.

"Excuse me. Can I help you?" A woman's voice. Jess turned to see a nurse at the door.

The nurse wore a name tag, and Jess smiled when she saw it. Bernice had found her—a sturdy woman in white uniform and sensible shoes. She looked to be in her forties, with short brown hair streaked with gray. And she had a no nonsense expression with the twinkle of good humor in her blue eyes—a face easy to trust.

"Yes, I've come to see Uncle Max. Is he here? I just got to town and wanted to see him before I headed out again."

"I'm Bernice, honey. What's your name?"

"I'm Michelle. Hi."

"Michelle, come with me, dear. I took him to the dayroom. I'll show you where it is."

Jess accompanied the woman down a corridor toward a large sunny room at the end of the hallway.

She took advantage of their time together by asking Bernice about Harper.

"I was hoping to see his son Seth while I was here. Has he been in lately?" She took the risk that this woman hadn't seen Harper's booking photo in the paper, but she'd know soon enough.

"You know, he missed last week, and that's not like him. He comes every Friday, the last visiting hours of the day." She smiled. "I told him once that his father isn't aware of his punctuality, but he always said he wanted Max to count on him. Something about a promise to his father that he wanted to keep. I never had kids, but if I knew mine would turn out like that boy, I might've reconsidered."

"Yeah, I know what you mean."

Jess wondered how badly Seth wanted to keep the promise he'd made to his father. Getting arrested for murder had mucked up his last visit. And the cops seeking Harper as a person of interest in a second killing had "train wreck" written all over this week's visit. And black humor aside, Harper would probably avoid daytime hours as too big a risk. To play it safe, she'd made up her mind to stake out the nursing home at night for as long as it took.

One thing she knew to count on was Harper's loyalty. He'd told her once never to question it, that some things about him never changed. Of course at the time he was talking about his peculiar devotion to all things Jerry Springer, but she knew he'd intended to make a point, and she totally got it.

People who mattered to Harper got his full attention—the legacy of a father's unintentional neglect.

Bernice led her across an airy room of sofa and chair groupings, card tables, and two televisions set to low. Windows along the far wall looked onto the grounds behind the nursing home, a pristine setting. Other residents took advantage of the inviting room and the view.

But one man in a wheelchair captured her attention. It had to be Max.

He sat alone, staring out a window. His body twitched and moved, and he muttered words she couldn't hear. When she got close enough, his frailty shocked her. She remembered, as a child, being carried in his strong arms and hearing the comforting reassurance of his voice. It was all her young traumatized mind had grasped.

Time had changed everything—for both of them.

"Max, you've got a visitor." Bernice raised her voice to make sure he heard. And to Jess, she gave advice. "It helps not to expect too much, honey. He's got good days and bad. But you have a nice visit."

She waited until Bernice walked away.

"Hello, Max." She knelt in front of him and touched his hand. Nothing about this man triggered her recollection of his face until she looked into his eyes. Then it all came back in a rush, a flicker of images that connected.

"You may not remember me, but I sure as hell can't forget you. You're the man who saved my life. My name's Jessica Beckett. You used to call me little Jessie, remember?"

For a brief instant, she saw recognition in his eyes. And he stopped his fidgeting and looked straight at her. But as quickly as their connection came, it faded away when his eyes glazed over again. Maybe it was only wishful thinking on her part that it had been there at all.

Undaunted, she pulled up a chair and began to talk—without a plan and without any expectation he'd understand. She would search for the words to explain what it meant to see him again and how things had been for her, then and now. And Jess wanted to tell him about his incredible son.

She hoped he would hear her.

10:15 P.M.

The stakeout looked to be a bust. Harper was a no-show, and the nursing home would soon shut its doors for the night. Jess finished the last of her cold coffee and stretched her aching back one more time. She'd moved the van down a side street and now sat steeped in the murky shadows of her vehicle. A bruise on her cheek throbbed with an aching heat, the aftermath of Pinzolo's message from Nadir Beladi.

But Jess killed time by replaying the afternoon she'd spent with Harper's father.

It had been a long day. Emotionally draining yet cathartic. Jess had told Max things she hadn't even admitted to herself, knowing the one-way conversation had all the privacy of confessing to a priest. At the end of her visit, she had no delusions the truth would set her free, but it felt like a step in the right direction.

When she was a kid, the counseling sessions provided by the state had seemed like nothing more than a requirement, a box for an adult to check on a form. She preferred silence and isolation to the lip service of a state-provided psychiatrist. But after all these years, she felt ready to reopen the wounds that had never healed because talking to Max had been her choice.

The rush of emotions, old and new, had been instigated by Seth's impact on her life. She was still grappling with those feelings when she noticed movement at the entrance to the nursing home. With binoculars, she confirmed the night nurse had shut the front doors for the evening. Visiting hours were officially over, and Harper hadn't made an appearance. She took a deep breath and reached for the key dangling in the ignition to give it a turn when her cell phone rang.

"Yeah."

Without any semblance of a greeting, Alexa got down to it. "You do realize I still have that tracking beacon on your van, right?"

Jess started to smile, but the effort hurt too much. "Yeah, I kind of like you knowing. You're my anchor to a saner world."

"That's a scary thought," she said. "What's so fascinating? You've been in one spot for hours."

"And you apparently have no life. Who's worse off?" She sighed, and added, "I'm parked outside a nursing home."

"You catch many bail jumpers in the blue-hair set?"

She would have made an effort to laugh, but she didn't want to encourage her. "No, my money is on Harper keeping a promise. And I want to be here when he does. What's up?"

"I received an encrypted file for the background checks and financials you requested. I've been digging into them today. You want the short version?"

She hoped having more information on Beladi, Burke, and Mandy would leave bread crumbs to follow. Harper could use a break.

"Yeah. Short works."

"As you might have guessed, the smoker is cagey. We had to modify our searches to only his last name, and we found links to a series of corporations. Sleaze goes Wall Street. If I had to speculate, I'd say the man has family. And he's been generous doling out his assets for the legitimate side of his enterprises, a way to launder his more lucrative business dollars."

"You've got a list of assets I can see?"

"Yeah, I'll send you what I've got. Give me an e-mail address."

Jess gave her what she needed. And as curious as she was to see the material, she wouldn't sneak a peek via her high-tech cell phone. These documents would require downloading and quality time for her to focus on each page.

"Hard to imagine Mandy hitting this guy up for cash."

"Yeah. Now *that's* a scary thought."

Nadir Beladi certainly had the maliciousness and

the deadly connections to be the bastard behind Harper's frame job. But why? Had Mandy been stupid enough to blackmail him and drag Harper into her mess, guilt by association? Sure the smoker had deep pockets, but someone like Beladi would squash her like a roach underfoot. And he'd get Pinzolo to do the dirty work. She'd seen that firsthand.

Jess had a hard time imagining the self-destructive nerve it would have taken for Mandy to demand money from the smoker. But good sense was the first casualty when it came to drug addiction. More than likely, the crank did the thinking and talking for her.

"I'm thinking aloud here, but what would Mandy have on Mister Nicotine?" Alexa asked. "It wouldn't take much for a guy like him to kill her. He doesn't need a reason. Did she witness something that made her a target?"

"Could be. And Pinzolo looks like a guy who'd have a tattoo. Body art would be an improvement to butt ugly." Thinking of him made her ache all over. "Anything on Mandy?"

"No, not much. She wasn't exactly living on the grid like you and me. Well, like me," she corrected. "I figured she did everything on a cash basis. Not much of a trail, and nothing current, but Burke is another story, one of the reasons this couldn't wait for morning."

More lights blinked off at the nursing home. And security lights kicked on.

"What's up with Nipple Rings?"

"He's not a financial wizard. No surprise there. But if he's got cash stashed, it's not showing on his bank statements or being reported to the IRS, which could be a nice club for the feds to wield if we find out otherwise. A couple of steady payments do stand out. Automatic debits. Nipples has a safe-deposit box and a storage unit he's maintaining."

"Nice. We won't get close to the safe-deposit box, but that storage unit is another story."

"That's what I was thinking. And with him under wraps for forty-eight hours with the cops, I thought we could check it out. I dug up the address for the facility."

"The address is one thing, but unless you've got a unit number . . ."

"You're gonna have to trust me on this one, but I've got his number. I just can't tell you how I got it. So if you can spare a few hours off geezer patrol to break and enter, you can meet me." Alexa gave her the address. "And gloves are the new black. Bring 'em if you've got 'em."

"No problem. I'm on my way," she said, indulging in a smile as she ended the call and hit the ignition. "Harper . . . until tomorrow, my fine friend."

Luís Dante remembered one important thing about Seth Harper from the bail hearing—he had an old man who meant something to him—Detective Max Jenkins—someone he might risk coming to see at the Golden Palms Villa Nursing Home. Checking out the nursing home would be worth a shot since he'd come up empty on Harper's background. And being a private investigator, he knew how to research the kid's visiting routine, if he had one. Earlier, Luís had called the nursing home to ask about Harper's father over the phone, getting his room number on the pretense of sending flowers, which he did. The cheapest batch of carnations he could find. The administrative staff had been very accommodating, especially when it came to the kid's visiting pattern.

Not taking anything for granted, Luís also had done his homework on the Millstone case by searching newspaper archives and making copies to read later. His client might appreciate his initiative if he found something worthwhile in the old news articles.

Now all that remained to track Seth Harper was setting up a vigil both day and night outside the nursing home. Since the kid was more savvy than he'd first thought, he'd have to play it smart if and when he got a second shot at him.

But near dusk, Luís spotted an ugly blue van when he first staked out the facility after cruising side streets looking for a good surveillance spot. From a distance, he'd taken a few discreet photos as he sat in his car. A woman sitting alone had caught his eye, but when she stayed parked, it made him wonder enough to ask for help from an old buddy.

"Yo, Frankie. How's it going?" He chatted up his cop friend, a guy he'd known since high school, and caught up on family and sports until he got down to business. "Can I get you to run me a tag, *pendejo*?"

"Sure, dickweed. Shoot."

He gave his friend the tag number for the blue van. After a few minutes, his old pal Frankie came back with the make and model of the vehicle.

"It's registered to Seth Harper at Pinnacle Real Estate Corporation. You need the address?"

"Yeah, give it to me." After he took down the information, he asked, "You sure the van isn't registered to some chick? Maybe it's a company vehicle, but if that's so, business must not be good. It's a piece of crap, bro."

"Hey, you asked for the registration, I gave it. You need anything else?"

"*Nada.* That'll do it." And with a grin, he added, "Give a kiss to that beautiful wife of yours for me. Use some tongue. She likes that."

"And if you had a woman, I'd have more to say than fuck off, Dante. Later, bro."

After the call ended, he puzzled over why a woman would be camped out at the nursing home and driving Seth Harper's van. Luís kept watch at the location through the evening, looking for the kid and maintaining surveillance on the blue van. The longer the woman stayed, the more she fueled his curiosity.

"What are you up to, *chica*?" he muttered, snapping a few night shots to give a time reference.

Now he had more to say to his client than merely reporting the van color. And he had a feeling he'd be coming into bonus money if he worked it right. The man answered on the second ring and wasn't pleased to hear about the added wrinkle.

"A blue van?" the man asked.

"Yeah, she's still here," Luís said. "But vehicle registration is under Seth Harper. And there's more."

He told his client about Harper's connection to the old Danny Ray Millstone case, even reading some of the news articles over the phone. The man sounded pleased by what he'd found.

"So what do you want me to do?" he asked.

"She may lead you to Harper. Use your judgment, but your priority is the same. Find him. And call me when you know where he is."

The man ended the call, leaving it up to him to decide what to do where the woman was concerned. So when she started her vehicle, Luís followed and gave her plenty of room. He didn't want to lose her or give himself away. But the mystery surrounding Seth Harper deepened.

And his new case just got more interesting.

South Chicago
11:20 P.M.

Burke had a commercial storage unit near the Dan Ryan Expressway off 87th Street. Located amid a cluster of warehouses and local businesses, it was a middle-of-the-road unit. Not too high-end to make his brand of sleaze stand out as a patron, but upscale enough to have decent security measures. The units had video cameras and were gated with keycard access at the entrance and at each unit.

From experience, she knew such facilities gave after-hours and weekend access upon request. But with her twenty-four/seven five-finger skills, she didn't have to worry about that. All she had to do was figure a way in and not get caught in the flesh or on digital.

Alexa pulled behind her van, no doubt aided by her active tracking beacon, and joined her in the front seat. She dumped a knapsack on the floorboard and slipped on a pair of black gloves and a stocking cap to cover her blond hair. But after getting a good look at Jessie's bruised face, the woman had plenty to say.

"You look pretty rough. And I know you're not getting enough sleep." She turned to face her. "Tracking your friend may take time. You gotta pace yourself."

"I'll sleep when I'm dead." She looked across the street, avoiding the woman's stare.

"Suit yourself." The blonde got down to business. "Burke doesn't strike me as the kind of guy who'd lease a unit like this. He must have something worth stealing to pay the extra bucks, which I'm expecting to find a little ironic by the time we're done."

"Yeah, I was thinking the same." She retrieved the night-vision binoculars from her glove compartment and checked out Burke's storage facility. "Looks like we'll have the place to ourselves. I don't see anyone else on the property, but video poses a problem. It might limit our time."

"Not so, grasshoppa." Alexa rummaged through the rucksack at her feet and pulled out her gear. "I've got countersurveillance to take out the video. We won't have all night, but whoever is monitoring will think it's a power outage, at least for a while."

"Slick." Jess tied back her hair and tugged on her gloves. "I saw one of those on eBay."

"And I've got a device to plug into every keycard lock. It'll pop it in seconds. No climbing over the gate or crowbars." Now the blonde was just showing off.

"Is this another convincing argument for me to join the team?" She grinned and grabbed the lock device for closer inspection. "'Cause I'm a girl who likes toys."

"Whatever works, Beckett." Alexa raised an eyebrow. "Let's go."

CHAPTER 20

Luís Dante had followed the blue van from the nursing home, nearly losing the woman as he maintained a safe distance. Now, as she slowed to park on a deserted street, he doused his headlights and pulled into the shadows a few blocks down and kept watch with binoculars.

Another vehicle pulled behind the van, coming off a side street. A blond woman joined her, dressed in dark clothing and carrying a bag. Luís had no idea what the women were doing, especially at this time of night. Businesses were closed, and there were no bars on the street that he could see. And when they didn't get out of the van right away, his suspicious nature kicked into high gear.

"¿Qué estas pensando, chica? ¿Y quién es tu amiga?" he muttered, wondering what was on her mind and who the other woman was. He made a note of the license tag for the second car and hit the speed dial on his phone.

When his cop friend answered, he said, "Hey, Frankie, I got another tag. You got time to run it?"

"Yeah, give it to me."

He read the tag and waited on hold while his friend pulled up the record, but when Frankie didn't come back with a quick answer, he knew something was up. He lit a fresh cigarette, expecting to wait, but the women got out of the van and headed across the street on foot. As they disappeared around a corner, he lost sight of them at an intersection. From where he was parked, he couldn't see where they went.

"Damn it," he cursed under his breath, blowing smoke through his nose.

He had a decision to make. Would he stay put and wait for them to return or would he follow to find out what they were up to? Curiosity won out. With the phone to his ear, he got out of his car and flicked his cigarette to the curb. He locked his vehicle and followed the women. Using binoculars that he carried on a strap around his neck, he could watch them from a distance.

Luís crept to the intersection and peered around the corner, spying them at the secured gate to a storage complex. If they were accessing a unit, why would they park far away? And what was so important this time of night?

Something didn't add up. Under his shirt, he felt for the Glock 19 that he kept in a holster on his belt. But when his friend came back on the line, he stopped short of pulling his weapon.

"Looks like your car is a rental," Frankie said. "But the ID of the driver came up a dead end. The only time I've ever seen this is with the feds. CIA, NSA, whatever. What are you into, Luís?"

"I have no idea, but when I do, I'll call you," he replied, lowering his voice.

"Watch your ass, *mi amigo.*"

"Later, bro."

Luís ended the call and tucked the cell phone in his pocket. He held up the binoculars and followed the movements of the women, knowing he'd have to get closer. He headed down the block to cross the street without being noticed and after he got to the other side, he pulled his weapon.

Curiosity definitely had him by the throat. And he couldn't fault his client for that.

On foot, Jess crossed the street and followed Alexa, sticking close to the shadows. They didn't want to drive onto the property using her van or the rental car and take the chance a bystander might remember the vehicle. As they got closer to the storage complex, her companion pulled gear from her knapsack and got to work, employing the devices she'd brought with her.

"I've taken out the video cams." Alexa stashed her countersurveillance gear and retrieved the keycard equipment, a simple-looking black-box device with electronic leads. "Once we get inside, we'll need to move. We won't have much time."

Alexa attached the gear to the numbered keycard pad located on a brick pillar at the main drive-through entrance. When the black box flashed a green light, she opened the secured gate in one slick move, operating with practiced efficiency. The metal electronic gate slid to one side, rattling a pulley chain as it moved. It would stay open for a while, but sensors would allow it to close behind them.

"Look for unit number 168," the blonde said.

The rows were well numbered, and it didn't take long to find Jason Burke's unit. It was large enough to have a door as well as a small loading bay. The larger door looked like a residential garage with either remote-control access or a manual locking lever. They'd have no way of knowing until they got inside. To maintain their privacy, Alexa went to work on the smaller door's keycard lock.

In seconds, they were inside. Nothing but pitch black.

With the door to Jason Burke's storage unit closed behind them, it might have been tempting to flip on the overhead light for better visibility. But Jess reached into her pocket and retrieved her flashlight, pleased to see Alexa had instinctively done the same. By using flashlights, they wouldn't risk having the brighter overhead lighting shine under the bottom of the storage doors, a dead giveaway they were inside.

Jess raised her hand and cast her beam into the darkness. She heard Alexa move and saw her flashlight cut through inky black. With her body silhouetted in pale light, Jess could track her movements in the dark. Their flashlight beams landed on boxes and reflected off glass and chrome. It didn't take long to assess what they'd found. Large cardboard boxes were stacked amidst furniture pieces and electronic equipment.

"This could be his personal property," Jess began, speaking in a hushed tone. "But since when does he need this many big-screen TVs?"

She didn't expect an answer. According to what Alexa had learned about Jason Burke, he was a construction worker by trade, at least on paper. If he operated another legitimate business on the side, as sole owner or a partner, he wasn't reporting it to the IRS.

"I'd bet money Burke's got a stash of stolen goods here, but we're going to need proof." Alexa wedged herself behind a TV monitor and directed her light to the back of the console for a better look. She took out a pen and paper and jotted something down. "I'm taking serial numbers. I'll cross-reference them to police reports . . . see what turns up."

"If Burke is a middleman for stolen property, you think he'd kill to protect his little enterprise?" Jess asked. "I mean, I've seen people kill for less, but he's not exactly rolling in high-end merchandise or dealing in volume?"

"We still don't have all the pieces to this puzzle, but maybe knowing more about his inventory will help." Alexa took down more serial numbers. After a few minutes, she hoisted the knapsack over her back, and said, "You seen enough?"

"Yeah, I've got a pretty good theory about what's going on here," she whispered. "Let's clear out."

Standing near the exit, they both turned off their flashlights before opening the door. Once again they were in total darkness. Alexa cracked open the door to peer out. When she did, a sliver of light filtered into the unit. Without a word, she nodded, and they both stepped into the night air. They wouldn't be in the clear until they got off the premises. She kept her eyes alert for any sign of movement.

But when Alexa held up her hand and stopped, Jess did too. She had faith in the woman's instincts.

"Saw something. I think we're being watched," the blonde whispered, slinging her knapsack over her shoulder and pulling her weapon. "The gate's sensors should let you out without a keycard. And I'll reset the video cams when I can. Meet you back at the van. Be careful."

Jess gripped her Colt Python, keeping it at her side. When she turned to see where Alexa had gone, the woman was nowhere in sight, and she was alone. Normally, she would have stayed in the shadows, covering her own backside, but there was another way to play this.

Divide and conquer. If someone lurked in the dark, she would either divert attention while her new ally circled behind, or she'd make herself a sitting duck. Trust had never come easy. How much faith did she have in Alexa?

Jess winced. "Time to find out," she whispered.

Luís had seen enough to know the two women had broken into the storage complex using high-tech gear. But while he'd been on the move to get closer, they must have ducked into one of the units. And he couldn't be sure which one.

He'd lost them.

Why they had chosen to break in while on foot had baffled him. If they intended to make a haul, why not load up the van? With a firm grip on his gun, he moved through the shadows and peered down each storage row, looking for the women. All he could do now was hang outside the fence and wait.

But on his second pass along the perimeter, he got caught.

Instinct had cautioned him to stop—too little, too late. He ducked behind a pillar and crouched low. The women had appeared out of nowhere. They emerged from the shadows as he crossed a section of fence, his body silhouetted by a streetlamp.

He wasn't sure what they might have seen, but he couldn't take any chances. He stayed low and moved back the way he had come, hoping to make it to his car. But when he gaped over his shoulder, he spotted only one of the women—the one who drove the van. They had split up.

His gut reflex told him that meant trouble.

"Shit," he muttered. Turning a corner, he jogged down an alley, taking the long way back to his car. His bad luck might have cost him the advantage of being the anonymous watcher. And if he didn't move quickly, trailing the woman in the van wouldn't be an option either.

Alexa had seen movement from the corner of her eye and reacted. After leaving Jessie, she'd scaled the wrought-iron fence and dropped to the sidewalk on the other side. Listening to the sounds of the night, she crouched in the dark and waited. Her eyes peered through the murky black, looking for any sign of movement.

When she sensed it was time, she crossed the street and ducked into an alley. She hunkered near a wall and listened. In the narrow, bricked passageway, sound reverberated off the walls and carried in the night. She closed her eyes to focus on every noise. When she'd slowed her heart and listened with her whole being, she finally heard the crunch of gravel underfoot and the steady footfalls of someone running.

And like a predator, she followed.

Still panting, Luís crouched behind a fence of corrugated metal and peered through slats. He shifted his gaze to split his attention between his vehicle, parked close by, and the woman who sat in the van down the road. After he'd made it back, he fought the urge to unlock his car and jump inside, waiting for the unaccounted-for female to show at the van.

But something had stopped him. He sensed a presence more than he saw or heard one.

Growing up streetwise on the streets of Chicago had honed his skills, and he knew when to lay low. He'd cut a wide swath back to his car, feeling his way through a maze of alleyways, unsure where he was going.

But now something didn't feel right. And it didn't take long for him to understand why.

One of the women emerged from the shadows a half block down. He slowed his breaths, trying not to give himself away. It looked as if she'd been waiting for him to make a mistake, thinking he was home free. There were other cars parked on the street. She had no way of knowing he was hiding nearby or that the dark blue Chevy Impala was his. All he had to do was be patient and wait her out.

But now she moved toward the spot where he hid. She didn't make a sound as she crept closer. And under the bluish haze of moonlight, he caught the glint of her gun and froze. *¡Ay, Dios mío!* Would he have to defend himself . . . and could he shoot a woman to do it? Resisting the impulse to move, he took a deep breath and gripped his weapon as sweat trickled down his spine. What had he gotten himself into?

Earning bonus money meant nothing if he wasn't alive to spend it.

CHAPTER 21

Alexa sensed she was being watched, but nothing gave her any indication where she should look. And time played a part in her decision to move on.

She might already be too late.

The shutdown of the surveillance video at the storage complex had run its course, and the security company responsible might have dispatched a patrol car to check the outage. She kept her eyes alert, watching for any signs of movement on the street as she retrieved the countersurveillance device from her knapsack, the one that had jammed the video signal. She was close enough to bring the video cams back online and worked the controls to get it done. When she looked up again, she gazed down the street to see the murky silhouette of Jessie in the van, waiting.

If someone had been watching them, the few cars parked nearby had the best vantage point. But something caught her eye.

By a dark Chevy Impala, the butt of a cigarette was still lit. It had burned down, leaving a long snake of ash with a spiral of smoke drifting into the still night air.

Someone had lit up and changed their mind in a hurry, tossing the discarded cigarette to the ground. With a faint smile on her face, she made a note of the license tags for the cars parked along the street and headed toward Jessie.

When she got back to her rental car, she ditched her knapsack in the backseat and slipped her gun into a holster she carried at the small of her back. The streets looked quiet, with no security patrols in sight. She headed for the van and opened the passenger door to lean inside and update Jessie.

"I didn't see anyone, but that doesn't mean we didn't have company." She told her about the cigarette butt and the license tags she'd acquired from the cars parked behind them.

"The Surgeon General was right," Jessie said without a smile. "Smoking can be hazardous to your health." She looked tired, and Alexa could see she was hurting. Deep-rooted pain from a beating wasn't easy to mask.

"Keep your eyes on the rearview mirror going home," Alexa advised. "Play it safe. Whoever it is is real cagey."

Jessie nodded, but Alexa reached across the passenger seat and grabbed her arm to make her point more clear. "Get some sleep. I got a feeling we're both gonna need it."

Sitting behind the wheel of the rental car, she watched the van pull from the curb and waited with her eyes on the rearview mirror to see if anyone darted for the cars parked down the street. After giving Jessie a good head start, she pulled away and hit the gas.

By tomorrow, she'd know who owned those vehicles. And she hoped one of the names would stand out as a clear winner for her undivided attention.

Late afternoon

A dark, gloomy day was taking shape, with storm clouds gathering. Even burrowed under the covers of her bed, Jess knew this, but she hadn't arrived at this conclusion by psychic powers. She heard the rumble of distant thunder. And her room was as dark as night, even though she had a general idea what time of day it was.

"Great," she whispered. "Just what I need." Thunder made her edgy.

She flipped on a lamp and looked at her alarm clock. Nearly four o'clock, later than she thought. She'd have only a few hours before she'd stock up for another night of surveillance and hit the road once rush hour died.

After pulling an all-nighter between her stakeout of the nursing home and her criminal romp with Alexa, Jess had slept a few restless hours, still feeling the after-effects of the beating. But since her mind wouldn't turn off, she got dressed and grabbed some coffee while she checked for e-mails from her new partner in crime, Alexa. Good as her word, the woman had sent the electronic file for Beladi's assets, an expansive list that would take time to review.

And she had sent an e-mail with another interesting follow-up to last night.

*Dark Blue sedan, Chevy Impala—registered to a
private investigator named Luís Dante. I think
he's our stalker, but won't know until I talk to
him. Be on the lookout.*

"Yeah, right. You're gonna 'talk' to him?" She
chuckled, reading between the lines of Alexa's e-mail.

But why would a PI be tailing her? The face of
Nadir Beladi flashed through her mind in answer to her
question, sending a prickle down her spine. It had to be
him. She'd have to be more careful. The last thing she
needed was another psychopath finding out where she
lived.

Jess downloaded the financial file on Beladi and had
started the printing process when her cell phone rang.
She checked out the phone display before answering
and recognized the number.

"Hey, Sam. What's up?"

"I wanted to let you know we had to kick Jason
Burke loose. He lawyered up, and we didn't get enough
from him for an arrest. Wish I had better news."

"Yeah, me too."

Jess had been thinking about how she'd tell Sam
what they had found in Burke's storage unit. It would
have been nice if the timing of her tip had been
different, and Alexa could have confirmed the man
was in possession of stolen goods by actual serial
numbers, but with Burke a free man, things had
changed.

"I just got an e-mail from Alexa. Burke had some
noteworthy items on the financials she dug up." Jess

knew she'd have to be careful about how much to tell Sam.

Harper needed the cops to find another viable candidate in Mandy's murder. And it seemed a plausible scenario that the girl could have found out about Burke's side business and tried blackmailing him. Yet telling Sam outright about her break-in at Burke's storage unit would not only put her friend in the middle and compromise her job, it would taint any evidence the cops might acquire as "fruit of the poisonous tree." Anything the police found, as a result of being tipped from the break-in, would be inadmissible in court.

She'd have to find a way to guide Sam's efforts without saying that she and Alexa had already laid eyes on what looked to be stolen goods.

"Burke had a safe-deposit box and paid for an up-scale storage unit using automatic withdrawals from his bank. I figured you could get a warrant to take a peek. Maybe Mandy caught him in a side business he wasn't reporting to the IRS, something the cops might see as motive."

"You got an address on his storage?"

"Yeah, sure." She gave her friend the address and unit number.

Sam was smart and would know how to work it. Jess had a feeling Burke's enterprise would land the guy back in police custody, and he'd have plenty of explaining to do. And it wouldn't hurt Sam's career to look good in front of police brass.

"Anything else?" her friend asked. "Didn't Alexa do other background checks for you?"

Jess wanted time to look over the information she'd just received. And until she did, she opted to stall Sam by blaming Alexa, a convenient dodge.

"She's still working the other names." Jess took a swig of coffee. "I'll let you know. Thanks, Sammie."

She ended the call, thinking about all the despicable men who were capable of ending Mandy's life. But Beladi was still at the top of her hit parade. She had no doubt the man was capable of murder and more. Yet after seeing the storage unit, she wondered if Burke could kill the girl to protect his source of income. And her gut told her that the dude was mean enough to set up Harper to take the fall. He definitely had anger issues.

Jess needed concrete proof for the cops, not just suspicions. Maybe the smoker's financials and his assets would turn up something new. She did a quick scan of the pages Alexa had sent. If she didn't make enough headway, she'd take the pages with her to read later.

But she recognized one street address. Nadir Beladi owned Dirty Monty's, the bar where Seth had been abducted. Now the man's threatening words from the other night, the night Pinzolo had beat her up, rushed to the forefront of her mind.

. . . you came to my turf . . . my place of business . . . setting off grenades at my feet . . .

At the time, she thought he'd taken exception to her treading on his South Side turf, but he had literally meant his place of business, Dirty Monty's. She still had no idea how Beladi owning the bar would play into this, but it was another piece of the puzzle. And Harper being drugged and kidnapped from the man's property had to be something more than a coincidence.

Her thoughts turned to Seth and a twinge of guilt cinched her stomach.

Tonight was Harper's regular time to visit his father. Would he keep his promise? If he stuck to the routine, this might be the best opportunity for her to cross his path. Would she cuff him and turn him over to the police for his own good? Jess clenched her jaw, trying to imagine crossing that line with him. There was only one answer that came to mind.

She'd figure out what to do when she saw him.

Golden Palms Villa
9:45 P.M.

In the rain, the nursing home cleaved to its shadows and looked ominous as lightning assaulted the night sky. Loud cracks of thunder made her tense. Only a few windows shed a pale glow, with most residents in bed by now. And although Jess was grateful Max Jenkins's room was still lit, she knew they'd soon lock the front doors, and there'd be no way into the place.

She looked at her watch, holding her wrist toward the dim light from a streetlamp. Visiting hours were nearly over, and it looked as if Seth wasn't coming.

And with the rain streaking the windows, thoughts of Payton Archer and the night he'd introduced her to his love of the rain, sent her into a morose tailspin. Before she'd met Payton, she hadn't realized how much she craved emotional intimacy. He had accepted her as

she was—with flaws and scars—and seemed to understand intuitively without her having to explain. She
thought about calling him for the comfort of hearing
his voice but decided against it.

"Quit being such a girl," she muttered.

And with Harper missing and in trouble, she felt as
if her life had been highjacked. Her stakeout could
stretch into days and weeks. And she imagined being
relegated to an interminable limbo like Bill Murray in
Groundhog Day repeating the same day over and over.
The interior of the van smelled like stale coffee and the
remnants of fast food, another déjà vu trigger.

"Just take one day at a time, Beckett."

Jess tried to clear her head of all the things she
couldn't control and focus on the here and now. She'd
wait until the on-duty nurse locked the front entrance
and hit the security lights before she headed home and
try again tomorrow. It looked as if Harper would break
his promise to his father, for good reason. Changing
his routine had been prudent, but she had mixed feelings about spending another night without finding him.
No news was definitely not good news—with a brutal
killer in control.

She reached for her binoculars and made another
pass of the facility grounds while she waited for the
night nurse to make her appearance at the front door.

With visiting hours nearly over, Seth arrived by taxi
and instructed the driver to leave him a few blocks
away from the nursing home. Stealth was more important than staying dry. He rushed to a back entrance to

get out of the rain, but the damage had been done. Drops had pelted his jacket and knapsack, drenched his hair, and seeped down his neck onto his T-shirt. With the bad weather, he'd have to rethink his departure. The staff had allowed him to stay overnight before. Maybe the head night nurse would let him do it again.

Through the kitchen, he walked up the back stairs to the second floor, avoiding the scrutiny of the staff. From the many times he'd been at the nursing home, he knew the best way in, completely under the radar of the people who took care of his father. He hadn't intended to avoid them, but he was in no mood for idle chat.

The door to his father's room was shut, but the light from inside seeped onto the floor. After a soft knock, he turned the knob and stepped inside.

"Papa?"

The room was empty. His father was nowhere in sight.

"What the hell?"

"He's here. At the nursing home," Luís said into his cell phone as he sat behind the wheel of his Chevy Impala. "Seth Harper is here, right now. What do you want me to do?"

He found it hard to contain the excitement in his voice, knowing his client would be happy to hear the good news . . . and perhaps be generous as well.

"You've already done it. Good job," the man said. "You've earned your bonus. I'll send it tomorrow as we discussed, but I'll take it from here. Go home, Mr. Dante."

The call ended, leaving Luís confused and more than a little intrigued by it all.

The kid hadn't been easy to track down, but Luís had given his client much more than he'd asked for. He'd anticipated the kid's next move and been waiting when he visited his old man, arriving only a few minutes ago on foot and coming in the back way. The client already had the nursing home address and other pertinent information, thanks to his diligence. And he'd also provided a summary of the old newspaper articles on how Harper's father had saved all those kids from a pedophile, even reading parts of it over the phone.

He'd crossed paths with two mystery women who appeared to be looking for Seth Harper and maybe more. The one in the van was parked down the street now. This time he hadn't had to tail her here. She'd arrived like clockwork.

And now it looked as if the woman was getting out of her vehicle and heading for the nursing facility in the rain.

What is up with her?

Curiosity had piqued his interest again. And even though his client had kicked him loose, Luís had an inclination to stick around and see how things played out—on his own time.

Seth set down his rucksack on the floor as he entered the room. This time of night, he knew his father should have been in his room. Most residents were already in bed, but the nursing staff usually let him stay up for the last hour, an accommodation for his son's visiting routine. He turned to leave, heading for the nurses' station, but the phone on the nightstand rang. Seth hesitated, but eventually he picked it up.

"Hello."

"You wanna know why your old man isn't in his room?" A gruff voice came over the line. "Do I have your attention?"

"Who is this?" He tried to keep his voice calm, but the rest of his body hadn't gotten the message.

"Shut up and listen. I've got your cop father. And if you ever want to see him again, you'll do what I say?"

Seth shut his eyes tight, picturing Max's face and the frail shell of his body.

Damn it! This shouldn't be happening. Not to my dad.

"How did you know I'd be here? No one knew I was coming." He had to know if this was real.

"Oh, baby, I got eyes on you. And I'll know if you're not playin' straight with me. If you tell anyone or come with company, I'll know it, and your old man will be put out of his misery. Am I makin' myself clear?"

Seth fought the sudden rush of emotion. He shook with adrenaline and felt his heart pounding through his chest. And his legs threatened to buckle under him. He had no idea what his father actually saw these days, locked in his head and unable to communicate. It had been painful to picture him adrift in his past without a fragment of his old self to anchor him to the present. But being a former cop, he would know enough to sense danger. And Seth couldn't imagine how frightened his father would be.

"Yeah, perfectly. Tell me what you want me to do. Just don't hurt him," he pleaded, knowing his words meant nothing to the bastard on the other end of the line.

As the man talked, telling him what to do, Seth stared at his own reflection in the window of his father's room until lightning burst across the night sky to wash it away, casting eerie shadows on a rain-streaked window.

He'd brought this to his father's door. Now it was time to end it.

Movement on the second floor had caught her eye—Max's room. She saw the silhouette of a man.

From where she parked, Jess had peered through the windshield in time to see a man's shadow near the window, someone not dressed in a white uniform. But by the time she'd shifted her binoculars for a better look, he wasn't there. She hoped it was Seth, but the rain made it difficult to see. After getting out of the van, she locked it and headed for the front door. Rain pummeled her as she ran. She'd look like a drenched rat when she got inside. And the windbreaker she wore didn't keep out the chill.

"Seth, please let it be you."

Jess pulled open the front door and headed straight for the elevator, avoiding the receptionist on duty.

"Excuse me. Visiting hours are over. You can't just . . ." The uniformed woman did her duty and objected, but Jess had spent a lifetime ignoring authority. A personal campaign.

"I left my car keys upstairs on four. As soon as I find them, I'll be right down. I promise."

Luckily, the elevator arrived so she could pretend not to hear the woman's request to sign in. She punched the buttons for the second and fourth floors, a diversion and a stall tactic. Jess hoped to be gone by the time they came looking. She got off on the second floor and headed for the room of Max Jenkins. When she found the door closed, she eased it open and peered inside.

And came face-to-face with a frantic Seth Harper.

CHAPTER 22

"Jessie, I need my van back. Give me the keys?"

"What's going on, Seth?" She looked into the room. "Where's your father?"

"I gotta go, Jessie. Please . . . I need those keys." He held out his hand, and his fingers were shaking. Something had him really spooked. She'd never seen him like this.

"Let me go with you," she pleaded.

"You can't. I gotta do this alone."

"Do what alone, Seth?"

When she handed him the keys, he brushed by her with a knapsack on his shoulder, heading for the elevator. He was done talking. And her mind raced with the possibilities of what was going on.

Seth had come to visit his father on their usual night, expecting to find him in his room, but his dad was nowhere to be found. And now Seth was rushing out again, only minutes after arriving. Something was very wrong. Add to the mix that Harper was very protective of those he loved and that he'd do anything for his father—despite their differences—and she made a leap in logic. Given all that had happened, it was the only thing that made sense.

"Where's your father, Seth?" she pressed. "Why isn't he here? Does someone have him?"

Harper did a subtle double take as he punished the button to call the elevator, but he didn't answer her questions. And judging by the miserable expression on his face, she'd guessed right, but he held firm and didn't cave with her prying.

"Damn it, Jessie. Please don't make things worse."

"Is that even possible?"

"Thanks for the vote of confidence."

"Tell me what's going on, Seth . . . please."

He clenched his jaw tight and avoided looking her in the eye as the elevator arrived. But he held tough, neither confirming nor denying her suspicions. Reading his face meant nothing if he didn't give her more.

"I've got nothin' to say, Jessie." He shook his head. "Besides . . . where I'm going, you're not gonna want to follow. Trust me. It's best to leave the past buried."

Things looked bleak. And she had no idea how to help, but she wasn't done arguing. She joined Seth for the ride to the first floor with a bad feeling that if she let go of him now, it might be for the last time. Someone depraved enough to use an old man in a wheelchair as bait in order to kill his son wouldn't hesitate to eliminate them both.

A double tap to the head was a cheap fix.

"You have any idea who's behind this?" she asked. When he didn't answer and punched the first-floor button a dozen more times, she didn't hold back. She saw no point in sugarcoating the situation. "You know whoever took your dad is probably gonna kill both of you. The guy's already a murderer, and now he's covering his ass. What's your plan?"

"Stay out of this, Jessie. I'm begging you."

Seth shoved through the elevator doors as they opened on the ground floor. He waved at the nurse on duty and headed outside into the rain. All Jess could do was follow him, her mind reeling with sinister thoughts, each darker than the last. Seth was taking a one-way trip, and she had no idea what was on his mind.

"You gotta let me help you, Seth. This can't be how it goes down. Please . . ." She begged until he turned around, both of them drenched. "At least tell me where you're going. I can meet you . . . and bring help."

Seth stood on the curb in front of the nursing home and stroked her cheek with his fingertips. His eyes were brimming and mixed with the rain trailing down his face. She reached for his hand and held it, pressing it against her cheek—her last-ditch effort to connect with him.

"You've been a good friend, Jessie." A faint smile touched his lips. "I wish . . ."

He never finished his thought. Seth leaned and kissed her cheek, lingering enough for her to feel the warmth of his skin. She shut her eyes and let it happen. But as she opened them again, he had turned and walked away, leaving her standing in the rain as he headed for the van, his knapsack jostling on his shoulder.

"Damn it, Seth," she cursed under her breath and narrowed her eyes. "You're not doing this alone."

He started the van and pulled away, leaving her to watch his red taillights from a distance as he turned a corner. She waited long enough so he wouldn't see her grab her cell phone to make a call. Alexa would be able to track the movement of his van—her last hope.

But Jess was faced with a dilemma.

To get Harper the help he needed, she'd have to ask Alexa to follow the van without wasting precious time picking her up from the nursing home. And that meant she'd be left out of the fight. Nothing pissed her off more than sitting on the sidelines when a friend needed her in the game.

But just as she hit the speed dial for Alexa's number, another car down the street started its engine and flicked on its high beams. She shifted her gaze to the light. The car drove toward her. A dark Chevy Impala. It took a moment for her mind to register what Alexa had told her about the PI on her tail.

"Hey, Jessie." Alexa's voice came on the line. "What's up?"

"Hang on. Something just came up."

Gut instinct gripped Jess by the throat and forced her to move.

She shoved her open cell phone into the pocket of her windbreaker and ran for the Impala. Her feet splashed through puddles on the sidewalk until she cut across grass and vaulted over a low hedge of boxwoods. Darting into the street, she veered into the path of the car. Soaked and panting, she stood in the rain with her hair and clothes clinging to her body. The car's head-lights nearly blinded her.

"No guts. No glory," she muttered, squinting. In a two-fisted grip, she raised her Colt Python and aimed for the driver's head, praying she was right. "Stop . . . or I'll shoot!"

The car screeched to a halt, and she heard a man yelling for her to get out of the road. She held her ground, forcing him to stop.

"Get out of the car. NOW!" she yelled. "I won't ask a second time."

When the man opened the door, he raised his hands and left the car running. "Don't shoot. What's going on? You need a ride?"

"Luís? Is that you?" she asked. The Hispanic man flinched, enough for her to know she was right.

"Yeah, who wants to know?"

"I don't have time to explain. Sorry, man." She nudged the Colt, directing him to back up, and he obliged. "I need your wheels, but trust me, you want no part in this. Hopefully, we can share a brew and talk about it another time."

She directed him to the curb, where he stood in the headlights of the Impala. When he raised a hand to block the glare, she ordered him down on his belly with fingers locked behind his head. And the man did as he was told.

Time to leave. Shivering from the chill of wet clothes, she hit the gas and sped away in his vehicle, taking a peek in the rearview mirror. The PI lunged off the sidewalk and chased after her, flailing his arms and shouting curses in Spanish.

She reached into the pocket of her jacket and pulled out her cell. "You still there?"

"Your powers of persuasion would be more impressive if you didn't let your Colt Python do all the talking."

"Consider me bilingual." She didn't wait for Alexa to counter. "I need you to get in your car now and track the van. Be my eyes, and tell me where it goes."

Alexa didn't hesitate or question her crazy request. Jess heard her move—the rustle of fabric, the ping of a computer, and the woman's shallow breaths as she hustled out the door. And after Alexa gave her a quick reading on where the van was located, Jessie adjusted her course and headed to the general vicinity of Chicago.

"I'm on my way . . . and I've got a clear signal," Alexa told her. "Now talk to me. Tell me what's going on."

"Seth's in trouble. Someone took his father, and Harper's not gonna walk away from this without help." She had a lot of explaining to do and not much time. "I'll explain when I see you. Just follow his van and please . . . don't lose it."

With her cell phone plugged into her ear, Jess listened to Alexa's voice as she called out street names. She gripped the steering wheel of the Impala, speeding along streets she barely recognized, heading blindly in a general direction. Her gut twisted with a knot of fear that she'd be too late to help Harper and his father.

"Damn it!"

With Alexa unfamiliar with the Chicago area, she could only call out intersections as the van crossed. Many of the specific street names didn't hold significance, especially not knowing which block. Jess veered onto freeways trying to make up ground, only to change direction and second-guess her choices.

But all too soon, Alexa's voice came on the line one final time.

"He's stopped. The van has stopped." She gave the street name and the nearest intersection.

Jess hit the gas and sped to the location. She wasn't far away.

Harper's blue van was parked on a dark residential street in a shabby neighborhood—a hodgepodge of smaller dwellings built next to larger boardinghouses and vacated properties boarded up as condemned. Older estates had been converted into projects, once a grander residential neighborhood in the day. Now the structures stood amidst overgrown yards with cheap cyclone fences to catch blowing trash in their mesh. Deep ruts of muddy water and the litter of old tires and hulls of stripped cars on blocks marred front yards that had also seen better days.

Only a few residences had lights on and many of the streetlamps weren't working. The roads were murky with shadows, and gang signs were painted on Dumpsters and on front doors—a show of intimidation—even for those who had no idea what the symbols meant.

But one of the larger houses to the left looked familiar. A recognizable pitch to a roof or its unique window shutters triggered a strange tightening deep in her belly. She glared at the house, searching her memory until she could no longer do it. A wave of nausea forced her to take deep breaths. She grasped the steering wheel tight until the queasy feeling went away.

Stay focused, Jess! For Harper's sake, she had to remain strong and not let her fears take root. This wasn't about her. Seth and his father were depending on her.

"What's going on?"

Jess wondered why anyone would have Seth drive here. She got out of the Chevy and stood in the middle of the street, turning to get her bearings. Down the street, she spotted headlights, and the car slowed as it drew near. She recognized Alexa's rental car. The woman pulled in behind the Impala and parked, keeping headlights burning as she had done. They would need the light on such a dark night. The rain had died to wavering drizzle.

"You okay?" Alexa asked as she got out, drawing her weapon and slamming her car door.

"Yeah." When she shifted her gaze toward the van, her heart lurched. "Let's take a look inside."

She pulled her Colt Python, keeping her eyes on Harper's vehicle, looking for any sign of movement. Alexa spoke to her in a soft voice, telling her she'd take the right side, but she barely heard her. Jess raised her weapon with both hands and headed for the van.

"Seth . . . you there?" she called out, her voice cracking under the weight of her emotion.

No sound came from the van. And the street was deathly quiet. Something about the neighborhood sent shards of dark memories to cut her deep.

Jess felt her eyes sting with tears and a lump wedged in her throat. She imagined Harper slumped behind the driver's seat—dead—his brown eyes staring vacantly into the darkness. Pale skin splattered with his blood.

She blinked back that horrifying picture and tightened the grip on her weapon, creeping closer to the driver's door. After a deep breath, she swallowed hard and reached for the door handle. She yanked it open and aimed her weapon into the dark. Alexa did the same on the other side. Jess's eyes searched the shadows, but nothing.

They were too late.

Seth was gone.

CHAPTER 23

A rush of guilt swept over Jessie as she stared into the shadows of the empty van. She should never have let Harper go. Not without a plan. Her breaths came in shallow pants, and rage stirred hot in her belly. She was just as mad at her own failure as at the bastard who now had Seth.

"This is my fault." She struggled for air, lowering her weapon. "I never should have let him go alone."

Alexa kept her silence for a moment, but eventually said, "Harper made his choice. He did what he had to do . . . for his father's sake." She let that sink in before she added, "And besides, he wasn't really alone, not with a tracking beacon on the van. Whoever did this made a quick . . ." She stopped and turned around, not finishing her thought.

Instead, she searched the area behind her, peering into the shadows for a closer look. Jess watched her move until her eyes gravitated to the eerie shadows of houses on the block, and a familiar sinking feeling roiled in her stomach. The street gave her the creeps.

"What are you looking for?" she finally asked.

Before the woman replied, Jess felt her heart lurch in her chest. She knew the answer before she said anything. Being more objective, Alexa's judgment wasn't clouded with the emotion she felt. If she had distanced herself, she might have done the same thing.

"If they only intended to kill him," her friend replied, "they wouldn't have to take him far."

The idea of Harper being hauled from the van with his body dumped nearby sent a cold chill down her spine. Needles pricked her skin with newfound cruelty. She'd seen far too many ghastly images to last her a lifetime. Picturing Harper's dead body came too easily.

Alexa's attention moved back to the van, and Jess breathed a sigh of relief when she didn't find his lifeless body. But until she found out what had actually happened to Seth, the waiting game would be a miserable gut-wrenching ride of speculation.

Alexa probed the vehicle's interior, and said, "There's a backpack on the floorboard."

"Throw me his bag," she insisted, leaning through the driver's side. "He had it with him at the nursing home. I gotta see what was so important for him to carry."

Harper's bag got tossed onto the driver's seat, and Jess tore into it, searching for any clue where Seth had been taken. The canvas knapsack was damp from the rain, and the main compartment held something heavy, covered in white plastic to protect it. She unrolled the outer covering to see what he had inside, but Alexa's voice distracted her.

"Seth left his cell phone. Why would he do that?" she questioned. "If he'd left an open line, we might have had another way to track him . . . unless he didn't want a crowd."

Engrossed in her own find, Jess barely heard what Alexa said, but from the corner of her eye, she saw that Harper's cell had been left open and illuminated a small spot on the floorboard. Alexa had picked it up and punched buttons until something caught her eye.

"Jessie, you better see this. Maybe this is why he didn't want a crowd." With a grave look on her face, Alexa held Seth's phone toward her. A text message came up on his display, the letters all in caps.

I CAN'T LIVE WITH WHAT I DID. I'M SORRY, FOR MY FATHER MOST OF ALL.

"What the hell is that?" Jess hadn't realized that she'd spoken, her outrage finding voice.

"He sent it to you and others." Alexa hesitated. "You think he's suicidal?"

"No way in hell," she insisted. "You didn't see his face. At the nursing home, he was scared shitless about Max. And he didn't kill Mandy or Jade. You don't know him like I do."

"Relax. I believe you." Alexa narrowed her eyes. "That means someone is covering their ass . . . to make it look as if he'd take his own life and confess in the process. A nice tidy package for the cops."

Jess returned to rummaging through Harper's bag. Plastic crinkled under her touch as a flurry of drizzling rain pelted her neck and damp hair. Everything was conspiring against her, even Mother Nature.

She pulled out the contents of the plastic bag and laid it on the driver's seat. But when she got a good look at it, shock gripped her, and she gasped. Air sucked into her lungs with a harsh sting.

"Oh, God. No."

"What is it?" Alexa raised her voice. "What did you find?"

Jess couldn't make herself speak. Repulsed by what she found, she pulled back her hands as if she'd touched a hot stove. Her skin tingled with heat. And time stopped. Everything around her faded to nothing. A face that had haunted her past came back from the depths of her shame. And the overwhelming feeling of being powerless rushed from her memory, too easily reborn. The sensation had swallowed her, suffocating her in its vacuum.

She had opened Max Jenkins's case file, the one Seth had told her about.

"No . . . this can't be . . . happening." Her own voice sounded as if it came from a long, empty tunnel—the voice of a stranger.

And staring down at the old booking photo of Danny Ray Millstone triggered a surge of images from her past, shadowy memories that were just as threatening as if they'd happened only yesterday. His dead eyes stared back with the same menace.

She felt hands on her and jumped.

"Don't . . . touch me," she pleaded, cowering against a hard surface. Her body shook, and the nausea returned.

"Are you . . ." a woman's distant voice.

But she couldn't shake her deeply rooted fog until strong hands gripped her shoulders and shook her. That's when the voice returned.

"Jessie, are you okay? What's wrong with you?"

She blinked, and the blurred face of a blond woman emerged from the dark. It took a moment for her to recognize Alexa Marlowe.

"Oh, God." She winced. "What happened?"

"You zoned on me, Jessie. What's going on?" Alexa asked, standing next to her. "And what's with this? It looks like a cop's casebook?"

Jess looked down where the woman pointed.

"Yeah, it is. Max Jenkins's case file. Seth's father." Jess shut her eyes tight and took a deep breath as she said, "But we don't have time for a trip down memory lane. We gotta find Harper."

Seth had told her about his father's casebook, but actually seeing it had an impact she never could have imagined. She couldn't afford to let that happen again, yet she knew that would be impossible. It would be no different than telling her body to stop breathing.

Slowly, her brain started to function again as Alexa said, "We should canvass the neighborhood. See if anyone saw anything."

"Not sure we have the time for that either," she muttered. "Besides—in the 'hood—everyone is visually impaired when it comes to being a witness. But maybe Sam can help. I'll give her a call."

She punched the speed dial on her cell, and while it rang, she turned toward Alexa, and asked, "You have the nearest street address or intersection on your laptop? I'll need that."

She followed the woman to her rental car and looked over her shoulder as Alexa worked the keys on her laptop. A map of the area enlarged on the computer monitor as Sam's recorded voice came over the line.

"Damn it. It's rolling into voice mail." Jess left a message, giving the location of the van and what she could share over the phone. She tried Sam's home and work numbers, but had no better luck, so she left similar messages.

"I noticed you left out the suicide text message," Alexa said. When Jess glared at her, she shrugged. "Hey, I just wanted you to know I'm keeping up."

"This isn't about suicide," she explained. "I don't want the cops to think they have a confession and get the wrong idea."

"Sister, we blew past wrong a long time ago. What now?"

Good question. The thought of hitting a dead end left a hole in her heart. Whoever had done this had played it real cagey. Someone had Harper drop the van at a different location and taken him where they would have more privacy . . . and no trail to follow. Frustration wedged a lump in her throat.

But as she stood in the middle of the street, she stared at the houses down the block, and déjà vu hit her hard. Why hadn't she seen it before? She rushed to Alexa's laptop to confirm what she suspected while Seth's words at the nursing home replayed in her head.

Trust me. It's best to leave the past buried.

At the time, she thought the past he'd been talking about had been his own, but maybe he had given her a clue without her realizing it. She knew that she was grasping at straws, but that was all she had. Jess clicked and scrolled through Alexa's laptop until she got her answer, staring down at the street map on the screen—the tracking beacon dead center.

"Unbelievable." Jess took a jagged breath. "I think I know where Seth is."

She stared into the deep shadows on the east side of the street, a narrow gap between two buildings. The moment she did, her heart hammered a staccato beat—an undeniable reaction she couldn't stop. She didn't know if she was ready to do this. But it wasn't about her now—at least it helped her to believe that.

Seth needed her and that's what mattered. And trusting her instincts was the only way to go. She didn't have a choice. With eyes fixed, and without a word, she headed into the darkness and didn't look back. If she explained things to Alexa—and heard the words herself—she might not have the courage to do what must be done.

So she followed a path she'd never been—with dead certainty—that she'd taken her first steps toward a waking nightmare.

"Jessie?" Alexa called. "What's going on? You're scaring me."

Jessie hadn't said a word. She only walked away and got swallowed by the dark. Drizzle sent a shiver crawling over Alexa's skin, but Jessie had more to do with that. The bounty hunter had looked dazed and shaken, channeling demons Alexa knew all too well herself. She locked the vehicles and took off after her, gun in hand.

A nasty feeling nudged her gut, instinct telling her she was going into this blind. More was at play, and she didn't have a clue how to help, but sticking close and keeping her mouth shut felt like the right thing to do.

The darkness and the dying rain made it tough for her to follow, but she kept the bounty hunter in sight, staying a few steps behind. They squeezed through cyclone fences, trespassed over stone walls, and crept down alleys with Jessie making a beeline toward something only she could see. Many houses and converted apartments were lit and occupied, but some were boarded up and overgrown in the rougher section of the neighborhood.

A dog rushed a fence and jolted her heart, a pit bull on a chain leash. They had to run to avoid the owner's curiosity. Alexa took it as a bad sign.

"Damn it, Jessie. How much farther?" she demanded.

If Jessie replied, she didn't hear it. Alexa's heart was still thrashing in her chest. And to make matters worse, the pit bull had set off a reaction in the neighborhood, with other mutts howling in unison—a reminder they didn't belong.

"Just great," she muttered.

The rain had stopped, but the humidity had ramped into high gear and made her sweat. Steamy hot, she felt the steady heat on her cheeks as she straddled another brick wall, staying tight on Jessie's heels. She was pleased to see the bounty hunter stuck to the shadows and avoided being silhouetted by light.

But the farther they went, the more worried she got.

She'd hoped they wouldn't stray far from the cars. Once Sam got Jessie's message, she'd come ready to help. But how would the cop find them now? Alexa had a bad feeling things were about to get worse—and all she'd be able to do was watch. Jessie vanished behind another house, and Alexa quickened her pace to catch up. When she came around the corner, she found Jessie had stopped.

The bounty hunter stood under the bluish haze of a cloud-streaked moon, in the shadow of a deserted three-story mansion. Shattered and boarded-up windows looked more like eyes on an ominous face. And the wide front entry became a gaping mouth. A wall made of stone boulders surrounded the premises. And the grounds—which must have been grand in the day—now were gnarled with brush and weeds. Cracked and uneven cement led to more steps and a massive front door nailed shut with two-by-fours, "X" marking the spot. Vincent Price would have been happy to call this place home, but not Alexa.

She peered at Jessie. Even under the pale light, she saw the look of recognition on her face. The old house was the place she'd been looking for, but why? Had Seth known about this place, or had the killer brought him here?

"I gotta do this," Jessie whispered, a mantra spoken more for her benefit. "For Harper. I gotta do this."

"I'm here, Jess. I'm right here." She wasn't sure Jessie heard her. "You and me . . . we're going in together." She gripped her weapon and waited for the bounty hunter. "But I swear to God, if you shoot me by mistake, I'm gonna be real pissed."

When Jessie didn't respond with her usual smart-ass remark, Alexa knew that something more was going on than Seth and his father, Max. She wished she had Sam's number, knowing Jessie's longtime friend would know more. But the woman needed her help, not her questions. Now was the time for trust.

Without hesitation, Jessie squeezed through a chained wrought-iron gate hinged to the stone wall, and Alexa followed, sticking to the shadows to avoid being seen. If Seth and his father were being held inside, the last thing she wanted was to draw attention.

Once they got to the perimeter, they circled the old house, looking for an easier way in, but only one seemed the path of least resistance with fewer obstacles.

The front door.

Standing under the portico of the main entrance, Jessie took something from her pocket. By the sound, Alexa knew it was a lock pick. She worked the keyhole, hampered by the wooden barrier that had been nailed over it. The door finally creaked opened—the sound grating like fingernails on a chalkboard.

The noise would alert anyone inside that they now had company, but that couldn't be helped. Alexa gripped her weapon and crawled through the boarded entrance, her eyes suddenly blinded by inky black. The stench of mold, stifling humidity, and something more struck her. It was like walking into a wall she hadn't seen coming. She waited for her night vision to kick in, but that didn't help much.

Holding her weapon in a two-fisted grip, she stood inside, listening. The door shut behind her. And for an instant she heard Jessie breathing next to her, but soon that stopped.

"Jessie?" she whispered, barely loud enough for her to hear.

When the bounty hunter didn't respond, Alexa knew she was alone.

CHAPTER 24

Sam had a smile on her face when she walked through the front door to her suburban bungalow, basking in the afterglow of spending time with Ray Garza. Before heading home, she had met him for a drink after work, an impulsive invitation that she couldn't resist extending. And like she had imagined, being with him only made her hungry for more. He had a way of respecting her as a cop while also reminding her she was a desirable woman—an irresistible combination in an intelligent man.

Working the job and being in a man's world had given her tunnel vision. At times it felt like all she knew. She'd thrown herself into her career without a thought for the road not taken. But for a couple of hours, Ray had made her forget all that. And she hadn't let anything get in the way of their time together; it wasn't exactly *Mission Impossible* for her to focus entirely on him.

The man looked incredible by candlelight. Hell, by any light.

His dark eyes smoldered with need that she felt to

her toes. And although she would have preferred to feast on his full lips, she allowed herself to touch him instead. A diversion. Her fingers stroked the back of his hand, feeling the warmth of his skin. An intimate joy. Resisting her urge for more had taken willpower. She wanted their first time together—really together—to be special and not following a drink after work.

Sam dropped her car keys on the console table near her front door and flipped on lights as she walked through her house. When she found the red light blinking on her answering machine in the kitchen, she hit the message button to listen while she took off her gun and hit the fridge for a short glass of milk.

She poured as she listened. A friend had called about getting together for dinner next week. And her mother reminded her of Uncle Larry and Aunt Joyce's wedding anniversary. But the last message—the one from Jessie—stopped her cold.

"My God, Jessie."

She looked at her watch and checked the time stamp for the message. She'd missed the call by only twenty minutes, but in Jessie's world, that could be a lifetime. With a throttling heart, she tried her friend's cell phone, but couldn't get her—she only got a message that Jessie was unavailable. And beyond her cell phone, Sam had no other way to reach her.

"Damn it." She hit her speed dial. And when Ray came on the line, she said, "Jessie's in trouble, Ray. I need your help."

* * *

Jess walked the jagged line between the twilight of bad dreams and the reality of what her life had become. She knew something was dead wrong—that her mind had snapped—but damned if she felt strong enough to break free of its control. The only thing that had kept her going was picturing Harper. He and his father needed help, and it was her turn to step up to the plate, no matter what it would cost.

Once she figured out where the van had been parked in relation to High Street—and vaguely recognized the neighborhood—facing her childhood tragedy had become the only option left for her and Seth. What had happened on High Street had to be the reason Seth's van had been abandoned close by. Any other reason meant he was beyond her help, and she couldn't force herself to consider that.

High Street was all she had left.

She chose to leave her car behind and walk to the house for a low-key arrival. On the side of good news, the location was close enough, and hiking there gave her time to think. But having time to think was also the bad news.

If the killer wanted to stage Harper's suicide, what better way than to force him to come to High Street, hoping to rescue his father. The Millstone residence would begin and end his obsession with his father's cases. In a bent and twisted way, it would make sense to the cops, who already thought he was guilty of being a murderer. His suicide note was as good as a confession. Case closed.

But dread took a firm hold, forcing her to doubt

herself. Could she confront her shameful ordeal even for Harper? When she stepped through the threshold of the old mansion—the torture chamber of the serial pedophile Danny Ray Millstone—she was pulled into the chasm of her worst fears. She felt the man's presence even though she knew he was dead. The windows were boarded up with only slivers of light leaching inside, but Jess saw through the eyes of a tormented child who would never forget what hell looked like.

Little had changed—not for her.

For an instant she shut her eyes. And she still heard the whimpering cries and the menacing footsteps that echoed down hallways and spiraled up stairwells. Those sounds had become a backdrop to her life, especially in the middle of the night. The tragedy she survived had become a part of her. The smell and taste of fear seethed from her pores, a vile reminder.

And by her leaving Alexa behind at the front entrance, anyone might have thought she was confronting her demons head-on and alone. In truth, she had fallen into the same debilitating terror that she'd felt years ago, when she was powerless to save herself. And she couldn't face anyone witnessing her meltdown.

This time she wasn't a child. This time she would walk into it with eyes wide open. This time she had to find the strength to do it for Seth and his father.

Gripping her Colt Python, she edged down a corridor, her back to a wall. She had to remind herself to breathe, but the dank, stagnant air made that tough.

Splayed fingers along a wall guided her in the dark as she looked for any sign of movement . . . or light. And sweat trickled down her back, skittering goose bumps along her skin until . . .

Something brushed against her cheek. It nestled into her hair.

Shit!

She wanted to scream, but jerked a hand up instead. Her sudden move was fraught with a silent panic as she suppressed a cry deep in her throat. It took her a moment to realize she had stepped into a cobweb. Its tendrils clung to her skin and eyelashes. Shaking, she leaned against the wall and filled her lungs. With teeth gritted, she breathed through her nose to steady her heart.

She was losing it . . . *really losing it.* And Harper didn't need her like this.

She made it to the back of the house on the ground floor, to a door she knew well. The basement. Millstone had kept her below. His special place.

Alexa would take the ground floor, but since the large basement needed to be searched, Jess would do that alone. She knew every corner of it, and the search was . . . personal. She reached out her hand until her trembling fingers touched the doorknob. Taking a shaky breath, she turned the knob and peered down narrow wooden steps. A shimmer of light pierced the gloom below, enough to trigger her curiosity. But she recoiled with a mix of hope and dread. Hope that she might find Harper, but dread that she'd already lost him. She'd be too late. Either way, she had to know for sure.

For Harper's sake—and her own—she had to do this.

Sam drove to the intersection Jessie had left on her phone message, white knuckling her steering wheel and driving like a maniac—Code Three—to make up time she didn't have. Jessie had always lived her life on the edge. And Sam fully expected one of these days that she'd get a notification that her friend had been killed, dying by the very sword she wielded in life. Jessie had been dealt cards no one should have to play, but Sam had always respected her underlying strength. Jessie was a survivor.

When she arrived on the scene, she found the blue van and two cars parked behind it, but Jessie was nowhere in sight. She parked her car and peeked into the windows of the other vehicles. The doors were locked, but she found an old case file on the driver's seat in the van. And even looking through the car window on a dimly lit street, she recognized Millstone's arrest photo. It jolted her. And she couldn't imagine how it had made Jessie feel.

"Damn it."

She didn't like how this was shaping up. Ray was on his way. She'd asked for backup, and told him that Seth's father might have been taken hostage. That meant a tactical team would be mobilized. So much for the good part, but she had a bad feeling about how everything else could go.

Max Jenkins was a retired detective, someone every cop had heard of and respected by reputation.

She had no doubt they would get the help they'd need, but with Seth being a suspect in two murders, some might see Harper as the reason Max was in trouble. The situation could turn dangerous in a heartbeat if Seth was considered a threat to his own father.

And then there was the undeniable guilt she felt when it came to Jessie. Guilt had driven her to make mistakes in judgment. She knew it, but that didn't stop her from taking risks for Jessie's sake, trying to prove . . . something. No one took the burden of penance more seriously than a lapsed Catholic.

Most times when she thought of her friend, Sam saw her own failure. She'd ignored her cry for help all those years ago, not understanding what it meant, that tiny finger reaching out from a basement wall. And as a result, others were hurt and Jessie had to endure more at the hands of her sadistic captor. A child herself at the time, Sam had no clue monsters like Danny Ray Millstone existed. But in the end, that didn't matter. She hadn't forgiven herself and probably never would.

Now Jessie needed her again and frustration loomed heavy when she had arrived and her friend was missing. She had started their longtime friendship from a deficit—feeling wholly inadequate—and she'd been trying to make up ground ever since. Now this.

"No way . . . this isn't happening. Not again."

She paced the street, her eyes searching the shadows. She wanted to see Jessie walk into the light with Seth Harper at her side, but that wasn't going to happen. Wishful thinking had no place in her line of work. A cop dealt in reality. She glanced at her watch, wondering if she should call Ray again, but something else stopped her. She turned to gaze at the houses and buildings around her, a sordid mix of run-down properties.

Not too long ago, things had been different. Her grandparents had lived near this intersection. Visiting them had been the reason her path had crossed Jessie's in the first place. The memory of that fateful day stuck in her mind for a reason. It nudged her to think. And the Millstone file had triggered it.

Playing a hunch, she went to her vehicle and scrolled through her onboard computer to pull up a city map for the area. When she found what she was looking for, she stared at the monitor in surprise.

"Oh my God," she gasped. She reached in her pocket and pulled out her cell phone, hitting a speed dial to call Ray again. When he picked up, she said, "I've got a new location for you to meet me."

She gave him the address and told him what she suspected, but left out things too personal to tell him, not now anyway. At some point she might have to answer his questions on the subject of her and Jessie's relationship. And that would mean trusting him with a whole new side of her, but now was not the time.

"Sam, I know you're heading for the house on High Street," he said. "And you've earned the right to see this through, but please wait for backup. Follow protocol. Promise me."

A moment of silence seemed to last an eternity.

"I'm not sure I can make that promise, Ray. Just get there as soon as you can."

Sam ended the call, not waiting for him to reply. She said everything she could and didn't feel the need to lie, not to him. And like Jessie, she headed on foot toward High Street, weapon drawn. With any luck, Ray and his team would get there when she did. They'd arrive loud and proud, Code Three, using sirens and lights. But if she didn't have company, she preferred a more stealthy approach.

Either way, Jessie would get help. Sam would see to that.

Returning to the basement had taken its toll, and Jess knew that any nightmares to come would be fueled by the vivid details of her terror revisited. She crept through the dark with the Colt Python aimed, but could her eyes be trusted? Could her brain assess any real threat?

Sweat trickled from her brow, stinging her eyes. And shadows undulated, playing cruel tricks on her mind. The incessant pounding of her heart kept pulse with her shallow breaths. And her body shook without her ability to control it.

But when a large rat crossed over her foot, she felt its weight and heard its high-pitched shrieks. *That sound. My God, that sound.* It hurled her into the past.

Nightmarish images came back to haunt her in a rush, triggered by that sound. She remembered the scratches of rats as they scurried in the dark basement years ago. As a child, she'd slept with one eye open, afraid the rats would bite her—that she'd wake to find parts of her missing. Fear gripped her like it had back then.

And the rat that darted for cover had triggered a panic attack. Dizziness set her adrift in the dark—her equilibrium challenged—and the nausea returned. She felt as if she were being smothered, unable to catch her breath. And her heart punished her ribs. She almost lost it. Her nerves were fraying, a slow torture.

If she was Harper's last chance, God help him.

She stepped closer to the source of the dim light in the room, a spot behind a wooden post that had been a remnant of an old shelf. As she neared, she knew where the light was coming from, and her eyes brimmed with tears. A glimmer filtered through a hole, one she had dug many years ago. She ducked behind the post and knelt. Trash she'd stuffed into the cavity, to keep the man from finding it, had long since blown away or rotted.

Moonlight and the distant city lights streamed through it now. And a faint breeze touched her cheek as she peered through the crack. She remembered how it felt to see through it for the first time. Back then she'd worn down an old spoon and a few big nails that she'd used as tools to cut through two layers of cracked old brick. The simple comfort of fresh air on her face had made her cry then, as it did now. And images of her first encounter with little Samantha Cooper flooded her mind.

She thought she had been found that day, that someone would come to rescue her, but Sammie must not have understood. And when days went by and help never came, the setback crushed her spirit, finally and completely. She'd never told anyone that, especially not Sam. Hell, she hated admitting it to herself.

She had tried to bury that thought, but being here again was a cruel reminder that Danny Ray Millstone had beaten her down. He'd stolen her innocence and robbed her of ever feeling safe again. He died the day she was rescued, but she got a life sentence. A rush of sadness hit her hard, as if it had happened only yesterday. She clutched a fist to her chest and shut her eyes, fighting back the pain.

"Oh, God," she whispered. "Please." Her version of a prayer.

But Harper needed her now. This wasn't about her demons. She had to find Seth.

She stood on shaky legs. And when she was ready, she ventured into every corner of Millstone's basement. There were lots of places to keep secrets. This had been her world for a time. And she knew it well.

When she got to a familiar air vent, she knelt once more and listened. Jess never thought she would be in this very spot again—the place where she'd first seen Max Jenkins and witnessed the end to her living hell. Struggling to block out a rush of dark memories, she listened at the vent, but her gaze trailed down to the large, dark splatter that stained the floor near her feet.

Stay focused, Jess. She fought to control her breathing.

Shutting her eyes to concentrate, she was surprised how little she'd forgotten. From this point, sounds in the house echoed and traveled through the air vents. Noises from the floors above could be heard by sitting very still and listening. She'd gotten good at deciphering what they meant. It had been her early-warning system when she was held captive. If the man had plans for her, she'd hear it through the air vents first.

But hearing noises from deep within the house also had its price. Every kid crying alone and the torturous screams of others had scarred her. There were nights she still heard them, even now.

She'd never be free of Danny Ray Millstone and his house. Not ever.

As a tear dried on her cheek, she heard a soft footstep above. Her head jerked toward the noise, and she stood. The ground floor was her guess. Although listening through the air vent was tricky, she knew the sound had been too close for it to come from the second or third floor. It could be Alexa, but if she heard the woman's footsteps, then so could someone else—someone who might know the house better than her friend.

She had thoroughly searched the basement and hoped the worst was behind her. Now it was time to find Alexa and put an end to this, but one thing she knew with certainty.

Harper was here. She felt it.

The house on High Street had a vibe to it—the kind that haunted anyone who came here. Alexa sensed the smell of old death and something . . . more. She wasn't one to believe in evil spirits, yet something lingered in this place.

And she hadn't been immune to its force.

She'd nearly finished her search of the first floor, the process slow going in the dark. Her night vision had improved. And she took advantage of every elusive trace of light that had found its way into the gloom.

But the creak of a loose floorboard forced her to stop.

Holding her gun in both hands, she listened for a beat, then crept along a wall, hoping to avoid the same mistake of stepping on a creaky board. Up ahead, she sensed a presence, and the hair on her neck drove goose bumps down her arms. She fixed her eyes on a subtle movement across the floor, a vague shift of light.

Or had she only imagined it?

Jessie. She had to remember that Jessie had gone missing in the house. The shadow up ahead could be her. Alexa gripped her weapon and crept closer, but movement to her right startled her. She turned and aimed her weapon. An open doorway.

That's when she heard it.

"It's me," the bounty hunter whispered from behind cover, then moved into view. Not much more than a shadow, she raised her arms and let herself be seen.

But if Jessie had been to her right, who stood in the shadows ahead?

Alexa wouldn't wait to find out the hard way. Without a word of warning to Jessie, she held up her weapon and headed to the next doorway down the hall. She saw the bounty hunter tense beside her and fall into step.

Down to the left, a shadow moved and eclipsed a very faint light. It drifted as if it were a ghost. And she heard a muffled gasp, at least she thought she had. With her heart hammering her chest and adrenaline coursing through her veins, Alexa pushed her shoulders to a wall and inched closer for a better look.

She held her breath and peered around the corner.

Across the room, she spied a pale glimmer under another door, one with a series of heavy metal brackets, like coat hooks, screwed on the outside of it. And movement obscured the light that spilled onto the floor. Someone was behind the door.

Alexa stepped into the room with Jessie at her back. She moved to the closed door, wedging her body along the far doorjamb. And Jessie took the nearest one. The sparse light from below cast eerie shadows into the room, shedding light on the haunted eyes of the bounty hunter. She'd never seen Jessie frightened like this. The woman was normally rock solid, but something had a firm hold on her.

She nudged her head toward Jessie—her way of asking if she was ready. When the bounty hunter grimaced and gave her attitude with one look, Alexa knew Jessie would back her up.

Being cautious, she listened at the door and heard the soft gasp again. With another nod, she signaled to Jessie and reached for the doorknob. She turned it slowly and realized it was open. One more time she caught the eye of the bounty hunter, then shoved the door open.

Gun drawn, she charged inside, with Jessie close behind. Half the room was steeped in shadows, but a dim light shone from a far corner. It was enough to force her to wince, protecting her night vision.

What the hell . . . ?

It was the last thought she remembered.

Alexa entered the room first, taking the lead into a windowless chamber that was dark except for a single light on the floor. The beam reflected up, positioned against the far wall. With her Colt Python aimed, Jess avoided squinting into the light that would screw with her night vision. Instead her eyes fixed on a dark silhouette of a man sitting across the room. His shoulders were slumped, and the dim light profiled his face.

She didn't see what happened to Alexa until it was too late.

Jess heard a loud thud and caught a glimpse of another man, his movement a blur. Alexa's body blocked her view. And time slowed to a sluggish crawl. She watched as her arm shifted, holding the Colt Python, but Alexa collapsed into her. The blow knocked her off-balance. It took everything she had to hold on to her gun, but Alexa's weapon skittered into the dark.

When Jess hit the floor, Alexa collapsed on top of her. She shoved the woman aside and grappled for her footing. But as she got to her knees, she came face-to-face with a gun muzzle pointed dead center, right between her eyes. That was enough incentive to stop her cold.

Panting, Jess knew she'd been beat. She slowly set her gun down and shoved it toward the man, then raised her hands, hoping he wouldn't shoot.

"Okay . . . okay. You win." She took a quick look down to see if Alexa was still breathing. She never saw what happened. "What did you do to her?"

Alexa had a nasty gash over her eyebrow. Blood pooled under her head, making her blond hair glisten in the faint light. Jess wanted to stop the bleeding, but when she leaned toward the woman, a man's booming voice stopped her.

"You . . . stay put," he ordered, raising his weapon and kicking her gun behind him into the dark. "By the time your friend wakes up, this'll all be over."

He made it seem as if Alexa would walk away from this, but she knew better. Jess shifted her gaze to the spiky-haired man with a nose ring, who had grown careless with his gun, waving it in the air to punctuate his demands. It took her a moment to recognize him, but when she did, surprise made her flinch. And remembering his name had challenged her too.

"Jake Cordell, isn't it?" She forced a smile when he lowered his weapon. "You're a long way from Dirty Monty's. What's this got to do with you?"

She hated admitting her ignorance, but getting him to talk was important. Her mind raced with why Jake was willing to kill to cover his ass. He wasn't a drug-dealing pimp, or a thug with an attitude and a quick knife, or even a guy trying to hide stolen merchandise. The guy was the bartender at Dirty Monty's—a damned barkeep—the bastard who had her chasing after tattoos and no doubt lied about everything he'd told her about Mandy.

In an instant she realized she was back at square one—and completely screwed.

"No way. I got the gun. That means I ask the questions." He narrowed his eyes, anger seething behind them. "This kid should've come alone. Now you're all fucked."

He clenched his jaw, looking real mean. But when he realized that whatever plan he had, it was about to blow up, his face got red, and he yelled, "Why are you here, damn it?"

Spittle ran down his chin. And she heard the panic in his voice. The man looked like it wouldn't take much to shove him over the edge. He walked toward the door, looked outside to make sure they didn't have company, then shut it. Guess he didn't like surprises. Her eyes followed Jake, looking for a way to get a jump on him. But being on her knees gave her a disadvantage.

Recognition flickered in the bartender's eyes. He stared at her, then jabbed his gun into her face, and asked, "Hey . . . didn't you say you worked for an insurance company?" When she shrugged, he spat, "You lied!"

Given all that had happened, the guy was actually pissed at her for lying? Unbelievable.

"Murder trumps lying. Guess you win." When humor

didn't defuse the situation, she tried a distraction. "Where's Seth, by the way?"

She tried to keep the edge from her voice. But when Jake's eyes shifted to the floor behind her, she slowly turned her head to look.

"Oh no," she gasped. "Seth."

CHAPTER 25

Her eyes took in the rest of the room for the first time as Jess rocked back on her haunches, taking the weight off her knees. The gasp they'd heard outside the door must have been Seth's father, Max. At the edge of the shadows, the feeble man sat on a wooden bench, his wheelchair missing. He quietly sobbed, staring down at the body of his son.

That's when she saw Seth. His foot was bent at an odd angle. Belly down, he lay twisted on the floor at his father's feet, with most of his body in darkness. And the familiar tang of blood hit her. She willed him to move, but when he didn't, she searched for any signs of breathing. There were none.

Jess nearly choked. Her body shook. And something deep inside her broke. The onset of another panic attack gripped her, but when she crawled toward Seth, Jake stopped her with a vicious kick. She rolled to lessen the blow, but he'd gotten a piece of her ribs.

"Don't move! Or I'll kill the old man," he yelled, shoving the gun barrel against Max's head. "Nothing you can do for the kid anyway."

She grimaced in pain and fixed her eyes on the man with the gun.

"Is Seth . . ." She couldn't say it.

Looking deranged, Jake paced the floor and ran a nervous hand through his hair, the whites of his eyes showing. His mind elsewhere.

"This is all wrong," he muttered. "It didn't have to go down like this. This was supposed to look like the kid offed himself."

It pained her to think about Seth. And if she had been alone with Jake, with no one else to worry about, she would have taken out her rage on him. But that wasn't the case. Max needed her help, and Seth would have wanted her to take care of his father. That meant she wouldn't wait for a crazy man with a gun to decide their fate. After taking a deep breath, she forced herself to deal with their grim situation and the bastard holding them at gunpoint.

"Tell me about Mandy, Jake."

She'd been careful not to accuse him of killing the girl. And even though reminding the man of his body count was a risk, she had to get him talking to buy time. And maybe with luck, he'd make a mistake.

"Wasn't my fault," he rambled as he fidgeted, scratching his head with the muzzle of his gun. "She brought it on herself. Not me."

"The crank made her crazy?" She gave him an opening to tell his version of the truth, acting as if she were on his side.

Ignoring her—maybe not even hearing her question—Jake pointed his gun at Seth, and ranted, "You know that kid really screwed it up. He had that whore believing she could change her life and get clean. And that bitch believed him," he screamed, his voice cracking. "It was his fault."

Jess saw him losing control and moved a leg to put one foot on the floor, balancing her weight on a knee. In his condition, Jake might not see her shift position, but if she had leverage, she could rush him.

"But why kill her . . . that way?" she asked, keeping her posture passive with head low.

"I asked that, too." He laughed. A strangled guttural sound. "She could've OD'd. That would've done it." He gestured wildly. "And none of us would be here . . . like this."

It took a moment for his words to register.

"Asked who, Jake?" She softened her voice, downplaying her desperate need to know. "Who else was involved in Mandy's murder?"

"No one," he yelled, pointing his gun at her again. "SHUT UP! Just shut up . . . so I can think."

As fast as the guy was unraveling, he didn't strike her as the mastermind behind all this.

"Why was she killed, Jake?" she pressed.

At first, she wasn't sure he'd answer. He shot her a glare and aimed his gun, taking away her breath. But eventually he lowered the weapon.

"Desiree overheard something she shouldn't have," he began. Then in a move that surprised her, Jake added, "It was my fault."

"What do you mean, your fault?"

"She overheard a conversation about a side business I had going." He shook his head. "I thought she'd be cool . . . keep her mouth shut out of . . . gratitude. Hell, I let her operate under Beladi's nose, for cryin' out loud, but that wasn't enough for her."

"She ask you for money?" Her way of asking about Mandy's blackmail scheme.

"Yeah, said she wanted to leave town." Jake raised his voice. "That kid convinced her she could start a new life, like her slate could be wiped clean. Can you believe it?" With his chest heaving, he never slowed his pace. Jake looked like a caged hamster running a wheel, with no place to go. "I would've been okay with payin' her off, but . . ."

He stopped.

"But someone didn't think that was good enough," she took a guess. ". . . and didn't trust your judgment?"

The bartender didn't reply, but if looks could kill, it wouldn't be a stretch to think the lethal laser shooting from his eyes could smoke her.

What the hell had Jake been thinking to lay claim to a piece of the smoker's turf? Nadir Beladi hadn't built his drug and prostitution business by playing nice. The man was smart and a damned viper when it came to controlling what was his. And being surrounded by family, he had others covering his back. That was why the DA had had trouble pinning murders and other crimes on him.

But Jake definitely had an accomplice. Someone more ruthless with an edge of cruelty had tricked him into staging Harper's suicide, which included the heartless murder of an old man with dementia—a move that was lower than low.

"What little enterprise did you have going on the side?" she asked out of curiosity. "Prostitution?"

She remembered what he'd said about allowing Mandy to conduct her blow-and-go freelance work down the street from the bar, a solo act that kept her in crank. Maybe the bartender hadn't lied about everything he'd told her. But when he didn't answer, she guessed something else.

"Fencing stolen merchandise?"

That got a reaction. Jake looked at her with eyes narrowed. Had Mandy been the link between Jake "the snake" Cordell and her old boyfriend, Jason Burke?

"I'm done talking," he said.

But Jess wasn't done asking. "Weren't you afraid Beladi and Pinzolo would find out you were operating under their noses?"

By his sudden reaction, she knew she'd struck a chord. The madman with the wild eyes was back. He aimed his gun at her head, and yelled, "Shut the fuck up!"

Jess knew she had pushed too hard.

It took all her concentration to think through what he'd told her. Keeping her mind off Seth's body had been a challenge. But now she had to focus on getting Max and Alexa out of here—the strain made worse as she glanced toward the old man.

Normally Max had a vacant stare, but now he looked at her. His tear-filled eyes locked onto hers, and his lips moved without a sound, his frustration clear. She had to do something. And without Alexa's help, whatever happened would be up to Jess.

She had no one else.

Sam stood outside the stone wall of the house on High Street, staring at the grounds awash in moonlight. No sign of movement and no lights, but with the windows boarded up, she didn't expect to see much.

Ray hadn't arrived yet, so she was faced with a decision. Should she wait for backup to arrive?

Taking a risk, she gripped her weapon and made her way around the perimeter of the house, looking for any sign that Jessie and Alexa had been there. Soft turf from the earlier rain made it slow going. And her shoes got caked in mud, but she got her answer as she neared the front door.

Muddy footprints.

Even under a cloudy night sky, she saw dark prints on cement. Two different sets. She listened for sounds coming from inside the old mansion. None came. But something else seized her heart in a cruel vise. She ran from the house and stood on the grounds to get a better look from a distance. It took a moment for her to see it.

Through the boards covering the windows, a red glow flickered into the darkness. And soon she felt the heat and smelled the distinct odor of—

"Smoke," she gasped. "Oh, Jessie."

The first floor of the Millstone mansion was on fire. And she had no doubt Jessie and Alexa were inside.

"Damn it!"

Sam holstered her gun and raced to the front entrance. She charged the door and kicked, despite the boards nailed across it. She hit it twice, barely budging it. When that didn't work, she yanked at the boards like a madwoman, hoisting a foot against the doorjamb to give her leverage. After one two-by-four came loose, she tossed it aside and tried again. This time she got a clearer shot and kicked again.

It cracked open. And the heat from a wall of flames nearly blew her back, scorching her skin.

"Jessie!" she yelled, and cowered, raising a hand to cover her face.

When she didn't get an answer, Sam shrugged out of her wet windbreaker and covered her mouth and nose with the damp garment. She took a deep breath and ducked through the door.

She wasn't going to let Jessie down this time.

Jess heard a loud crack echo through the house, and someone yelled, but the words were garbled and she couldn't make them out. She turned to see smoke filtering through the base of the door.

"Fire . . . there's a fire," she cried, and scrambled to her feet.

"No. NO!" Jake aimed his gun at her, but ran for the door. He grabbed the knob and pulled, but the door wouldn't open. "Shit!" With eyes bulging, he backed off and waved his weapon at her again, yelling, "You . . . Open it! Now!"

Jess did as she was told, twisting the knob with both hands. It turned as if it were unlocked, but still didn't open. She yanked on it again, but it wouldn't budge.

"It's not locked, but something is blocking it on the other side. I can feel it." She took a step back and kicked the door. Still nothing. "If it's bolted from the outside, we're in trouble. Since you've got the gun, you gotta decide what to do, Jake."

The bartender had control of their situation, but when she turned, the man's face looked stark white. His chest heaving, Jake looked as if he were hyperventilating. And fear gripped her when she remembered seeing the strange metal brackets screwed to the door. They looked like antique clothes hooks, but now she knew they were more than that. Someone had locked them in, bolted the door from the outside.

"Who's out there, Jake?" she pressed. "Who set you up?"

She could tell by the look on his face that she'd hit the mark.

"No, that can't be . . . I didn't kill her. I swear." Fear replaced Jake's crazed rage. "I never killed anyone."

With the noise in the room, Alexa stirred and moaned, raising a hand to her head. Wincing in pain, she rolled to one side. "What . . . happened?"

Jess dropped to the floor near her and brushed back her hair. "Are you okay? Can you stand?" She helped Alexa to her feet. The woman was groggy and unsteady on her feet, but she quickly recovered.

"Jake was telling me about Mandy, but we got a more pressing problem."

She pointed, and Alexa turned toward the door. When she saw the smoke, she shook her head. "This doesn't look good for the home team."

"Yeah well, Jake's not thrilled with it either. Apparently someone considers him a loose end. He's locked in here, too." She took off her jacket and tossed it to Jake. "Shove this under the door. Maybe we can block the smoke."

They were trapped in a windowless room. The fire would soon raise the temp to an unbearable level. And the air had already grown so hazy with smoke that Max had started to cough. Yet despite a fire burning the roof down over their heads, she thought about what Jake had said.

"Wait a minute. You said you never killed anyone?" She stared at Jake, and he shrugged.

"I lied . . . about the kid," he admitted.

"What?" She turned her back on Jake and stared down at Seth. "If you're jacking with me, I'll . . ."

Jess raced to Harper and dropped to her knees. His head was turned toward the wall, and she couldn't see his face. But she stroked his soft curls, something she wouldn't have done with him conscious. He looked as if he was asleep. Tense and holding her breath, she placed a finger to the side of his neck. His skin was warm to the touch. It took her a moment to find it, but a faint pulse throbbed under her finger. And when she laid a hand to his chest, she felt the gentle rise and fall of very shallow breathing.

"He's alive," she cried, stifling a laugh as her eyes blurred with tears. "Seth's alive."

She turned him onto his back, cradling his head. His eyes fluttered, and he moaned. Pressed against her hand, she felt a large knot on the back of his head, and his hair was sticky with blood. The bartender must have been forced to slug him, not a smart move if he had intended to stage a suicide. All things considered, Jess found herself happy that Jake had a brain the size of a walnut.

But with Seth staying unconscious for so long meant he probably had a concussion or worse. He needed a doctor.

"Jessie?" Seth's dark eyes opened, barely. He struggled to focus. And with the noise from the fire, she almost didn't hear him. But his saying her name sent an adrenaline rush through her body that triggered a smile, despite their circumstances.

"I'm here, Seth." She squeezed his hand. "I'm right here."

"My father . . ."

"He's here, too." She grinned.

Seth shifted his eyes to gaze at his father, but Max surprised them both by reaching out a trembling hand. Harper took it, giving the man a weak smile.

"Very touching, but this ain't gettin' us out of here." Jake jerked an arm toward the door, the one holding the gun.

But this time, Alexa had her fill of the bastard. She stepped between him and Seth, giving Jake a dose of reality.

"Whoever did this wanted you in the house when it went up," the blonde began. "This isn't about making Harper's suicide look convincing. You're the one they want dead, Jake." She glared at him. "And you better decide whose side you're on, 'cause the way I see it—if you put the gun down and help us out of here—we can put in a good word for you with the cops."

"Jesus! You don't know what you're talking about." Jake shook his head, but he finally shoved his gun into the waistband of his jeans.

"Tell me this, tough guy, did you pick this room yourself?" When he didn't answer, Alexa shook her head. "Admit it. You got suckered. No windows. Bolted in. It's a damned death trap."

"No. You see, this was supposed to be the room where that Millstone asshole shot himself in the head," Jake claimed with doubt in his eyes.

"No it's not," Jess interrupted. "And who told you he committed suicide? Max was the detective on the case, and he killed the bastard . . . rescued all the kids here." When all eyes in the room focused on her, she added, "It's true."

"Bullshit! You're a liar," Jake spat. "How do you know so much?"

"'Cause I was one of those kids," she admitted with her voice shaky. "Millstone died in the basement. I saw it happen. He died at my feet."

"Damn." Jake shook his head, finally getting the picture. "We're dead meat."

"Well, I'm not waiting around until I become one big s'more." Alexa ran for the door and tried her luck, kicking a foot into the wood. She yelled and pounded on the door again and again, "Somebody . . . help us. We're in here."

She braved pissing Jake off and went looking for her weapon on the floor. When she found it, Alexa only gave the bartender a threatening glance before she yelled, "Fire in the hole."

Seth made an attempt at shielding his father with Jess's help. And Jake covered his head, cowering in a corner. Alexa nodded over her shoulder, then shot a few rounds into the wood around the doorknob and tried the door again. It moved, but not much.

"Damn it, Jake. Someone really doesn't like you," the blonde said. "Hard to imagine."

Scared as he was, Jake still wasn't talking about his accomplice, but Seth smiled as he watched Alexa.

"I like her. She with you?" he asked, grimacing in pain as he tried to sit up. "Help me up, will you?"

Jess hauled Harper to his feet and wedged a shoulder under him. She helped him sit next to his father and noticed the pain in Seth's eyes. Every move must have hurt, but he tried not to let it show. Looking at Max, he clenched his jaw and wiped away a tear from the old man's face with a gentle stroke of his thumb.

Seeing the love Seth felt for his father should have made her happy, but it didn't. All she could think about was the vile consequence of Danny Ray Millstone. The bastard was dead and still claiming victims.

She forced a smile and put on a brave front for Seth and Max, but the last place she wanted to die was on High Street.

CHAPTER 26

When the smoke got so thick she could barely see, Sam got to her knees and crawled with her wet windbreaker tied over her mouth and nose. Her damp jacket had started to steam with the fierce heat. The only time she lifted the garment was to scream for Jessie, but it didn't take her long to realize she had to conserve energy.

And with the fire getting worse, she was running out of time.

Everywhere she looked, the rooms glowed in blood-red amidst choking black smoke. Flames raged up walls and belched through doorways, consuming everything in sight. She felt the scorching heat on her skin. Even the hair on her arms singed when she got too close to the flames. And she smelled her hair smoldering.

But she forced her mind to focus on her search, despite her growing fear. Another danger posed a problem.

Not knowing what was burning, the closed-in structure made it a real possibility that superheated gases, carbon monoxide or hydrogen cyanide, might build inside the boarded-up house. A rolling structure fire could annihilate an old house in a hurry, but toxic fumes could kill anyone inside long before the fire got to them.

Panic ate at her resolve, but she kept going.

She had gotten through most of the first floor without a sign of Jessie or Alexa. A couple of back rooms were all that remained. With two floors above her, she had to cover ground without wasting time. And until she got upstairs, she had no idea how bad the fire was there.

She pushed herself farther down the hall, making her way to every door, but a loud sound caught her off guard.

"What the hell?" She raised up. "Jessie?"

Sam heard a bang. A series of loud splintering cracks. To her ear it sounded like gunfire, but with the noise reverberating in the house, she couldn't tell which way it came from. As the heat intensified, she crawled faster and deeper into the old mansion, gagging and coughing. She almost turned back but scrambled toward the last open door. Whoever set the blaze must have done it nearby. The flames were more concentrated toward the rear of the first floor.

And a vaguely familiar medicinal odor was still in the air. She had smelled the odor before, yet couldn't quite place it.

But as she neared the door, a man came running from the room. Low as she was, he didn't see her. The man tripped over her, his knee nailing the side of her face. The blow shocked her, and her head snapped back. Shards of pain racked her body as she rolled.

Sam shook her head and blinked, noticing the man had taken a nasty fall. She pulled down the jacket she had covering her nose and mouth. And when her mind cleared enough, she yelled, "Police!"

Ignoring her, he struggled to his feet and turned to run, but the cop in her wouldn't let him go. She reached a hand for his pant leg and toppled him again. This time when he hit the floor, the man grappled her from behind and choked her with his forearm.

She bucked against the death grip he had on her throat and pummeled him with her fists and elbows. But none of her blows did damage. Her muscles were growing weaker the more she struggled. In seconds, she lost feeling in her arms and legs. And her tongue had swollen, blocking any hope for air.

Sheer panic mixed with deathlike indifference as she thrashed against him. She couldn't breathe at all now, and her lungs burned from the strain. Her world faded in and out of black, darkness marred only by spiraling pinpoints of light—her final trace of consciousness.

She was dying. And she knew it.

"Quiet!" Alexa cried, yelling at Jake, who had taken to incoherent rants. "I think I hear voices."

She stepped closer to the doorway, listening. But when the sound faded to nothing, she pounded on the door. And after Jessie retrieved her Colt Python off the floor, she came to help.

"Hey . . . we're in here. Help us! PLEASE!" They

yelled in unison. To make their point, Alexa reached for her gun again and yelled a warning, "Get down."

When the others ducked for cover, she fired a few rounds higher on the wooden door, angled toward the ceiling. She didn't want to hit someone trying to rescue them.

But no one responded. No one was coming.

Alexa wiped her face with a hand. Her head ached as if someone had taken a sledgehammer to it. They had no more time, and she knew it. In desperation, she shoved her gun into the waistband of her pants and got to the floor on her back. She rammed both feet into the bottom half of the door in a mule kick. Once. Twice. The smoky air was making it harder to breathe, and she panted with the effort. And without a word, Jessie got down next to her and kicked with everything she had.

The door was stronger than she would have imagined and her legs stung with every jarring blow. Soon, the heat and thickening smoke would make it impossible to do much damage. The exertion would be too much.

Her thoughts turned to Garrett and the life he had opened her eyes to. She had only just begun to live the way she wanted—on the edge and without holding back for a tomorrow that might never come. It made her kick harder.

She didn't want to die like this.

"Sam's inside." Ray Garza struggled against two firemen who held him back. "You gotta let me go."

He and a CPD tactical team had arrived on the scene about the same time as the fire crew. Both teams wanted to take over and do their jobs, but that couldn't happen. The potential hostage situation with an armed gunman trumped the urgency of the fire—at least for now. That left highly trained firemen frustrated and sitting on the sidelines.

And Ray knew exactly how they felt.

"No one's going inside." A third man stepped in front of him, someone in authority dressed in a fire-department uniform. "You won't be doin' your friend any good if you die tryin' to save him."

Ray glared at the man, letting his words sink in.

"Sam's a woman. A cop," he clarified. "She called it in."

"I'm sorry." The fireman gripped his shoulder. "Real sorry."

Ray quit fighting the two men who braced his arms, and they released him. For Sam's sake, he couldn't afford to lose it. Normally, the fire department had control of a fire, but under a dangerous hostage situation, tactical would have command. Yet knowing cops had the authority hadn't made the waiting easier. He had to let the men do their jobs and accept that he wouldn't be a part of the rescue operation.

He took a deep breath and slumped against the hood of his unmarked police vehicle. Dressed in black BDUs, the tactical team had set up a perimeter to work the scene, but the blaze would dictate everything. A line of firefighters stood to his right. They could only watch as flames ravaged the old Millstone mansion. Each face had a grim expression colored by regret. He understood the anger of being forced to accept defeat before the fight had even begun.

Damn it, Sam! Why didn't you follow protocol and wait for backup?

Dense black smoke tainted the air, and an intense red glow painted the night sky. Police and fire crews continued to arrive Code Three, with bystanders and news crews gathering at a distance. The scene looked and sounded chaotic, but nothing distracted him from imagining the horror Sam faced inside. He knew the minute he arrived and didn't find her that she had gone into the burning building in search of her friend.

Now she might pay the price for going in alone, and he could do nothing to save her. Ray shut his eyes and prayed. He only hoped God would hear him.

A splintering crash brought Sam back, and spiraling heat swept past her. In a stupor, she wasn't sure if she had imagined it. But when her eyes opened, billowing red sparks hung suspended above her head in clouds of swirling black smoke.

The man who'd nearly killed her had let go. And her body had slumped back. A rush of air sucked into her spent lungs, and the effort shocked her already fragile system. Urgent need outweighed the distress of breathing the fiery air. But the act of taking that first breath almost finished the job her assailant had started.

In a coughing jag, she gulped breaths in small measures, her eyes watering. She rolled onto her belly and peered down a murky hallway. The ceiling had collapsed behind her. And the man who had nearly taken her life had made a run for it, but not before he gaped over his shoulder, fixing his gaze on her.

A face blurred in and out of focus, but wasn't clear enough for her to link it with a name, not in her condition.

The man grimaced as she stared back, but he didn't stop. Dodging fallen debris, he disappeared into a wall of flames, leaving Sam alone. She pushed off the floor and sat back until her head cleared enough to stand. Her body had begun to fight her, but she ignored the pain and got to her feet.

Her confrontation had stolen precious time. Sam turned to run deeper into the fire shouting for Jessie between fits of coughing that had her doubled over. She heard another thunderous crash that roared through the old mansion and knew her chances of making it upstairs had run out. The place would soon come crashing down on her.

She'd stayed too long.

CHAPTER 27

"Jessie!" Sam cried. "Where are . . . you?"

One open door remained ahead, and she made a run for it, her last-ditch effort to find her friend. When she looked inside the room, she noticed a strange door. With a makeshift closure, it had a metal pipe lying across steel brackets and was bolted shut. Gaping holes of splintered wood were punched through the closed door. The source of the gunfire. And the blaze had enveloped the walls around the doorjamb.

"Jessie!" she yelled.

Sam raced for the bolted door, careful not to stand in front of it. If someone inside still had a gun, she'd make an easy target. She stood to one side and called out again.

"Jessie . . . you in there?"

"Sam, is that you?"

She heard the muffled voice, and answered, "I'm here. I'm gonna get you out."

Sam wrapped her jacket around her hands and inspected the metal bolt that had them locked inside. It looked hot, but she had no choice. She positioned her hands on one end and shoved. Even through the wrapping on her hands, she felt the trauma of her skin burning, and it sent a jolt through her—searing heat fused with the stark chill of shock. But the metal pipe crashed to the floor at her feet. And the door swept open.

In a blur she felt Jessie rush to her. Barely able to stand, Sam pulled her friend close and drew from her strength.

"Oh Sammie. You did it."

Jess felt Sam collapse in her arms as the others gathered around them. But as her gaze shifted into the larger room and beyond, Jess's mouth opened in shock. Fire had engulfed the house and consumed any hope they had of walking out the way they'd come.

And Sam had risked everything to save her. She clutched her lifelong friend tight, and whispered in her ear, "You saved my life, little sister."

Despite the futility of their predicament, Jess had to return the favor—or die trying. When Alexa joined them, she grabbed Sam by the shoulders to make sure her friend was strong enough.

"Can you walk?" she asked. When Sam nodded, she glanced at Alexa. "It doesn't look like the front door is an option out."

"No way," Sam agreed. "The ceiling caved in. And I'd guess anything upstairs is out, too."

"This shit hole is comin' down," Jake shouted, ". . . and we're gonna die. I can't—"

"Shut up, Jake. You're not helping." Jess turned toward Alexa. "Max and Seth will need a hand. I've got an idea, but you'll have to trust me. We gotta go now."

What she had in mind would be a crapshoot at best, but she didn't have the heart to tell them the truth.

Some people can sit on a sideline content to watch the drama of a game played out, but Ray Garza had never been like that. He had to get involved and make a difference—his way. That was why he'd joined the police force.

He knew that he should have let the tactical team do their thing. And the fire department would have their hands full once they got the go-ahead to move in. But leaving Sam to deal with a full-blown fire and a killer with hostages was too much to ask of a guy—especially a cop.

Ray waited until heads were turned and opened the trunk of his vehicle. A crowbar was the kind of pass-key he needed to gain access fast. He headed down the block, away from the action, then doubled back toward the rear of the burning mansion through an adjoining property.

"Hang on, Coop," he whispered. "Please."

All he could think about was Sam's sweet face—her crooked smile, the way her brow furrowed when she was deep in thought, and the underlying compassion in her eyes that was never far from the surface. And the woman was gutsy, too. Real gutsy.

Even though he had taken issue with her close friendship with Jessica Beckett, he knew that was something he would never change or want to. She cared deeply for those she loved. And her loyalty was steadfast, another quality he admired.

The woman had gotten under his skin in a big way, but damned if he didn't like it.

Ray had hopes for more time with her. He'd never been in love. The possibility of it had always scared him . . . until now. But Sam had opened his eyes to a life outside the job. And he wanted one with her.

"You're not getting out of our bet, Sam."

He forced a smile and picked up his pace. And as he ran through the shadows toward the fireball lighting the night sky, he prayed it wasn't already too late.

"You won't be needing this anymore." Jess pulled the gun Jake carried next to his belly. The bartender looked as if he would object, but backed off. "And since you carried him in here, you're taking Max out. Pick him up."

"No, I don't want him touching my dad," Seth protested. "I'll take him."

Jess was about to put up an argument, but seeing the look in Harper's eyes, she knew better. He tried to mask his pain with a stern expression that she'd never seen before. If there was ever a time that Seth had meant business, this was it.

She pulled him aside, away from the others.

"Take my jacket and cover Max's face. The smoke will be bad where we're going." She squeezed his arm.

"And if you can't do this, don't be the hero. Ask for help, or you'll both die."

"Got it." He nodded. "I trust you, Jessie. Lead the way."

She knew what a concussion felt like firsthand, and Harper was doing a pretty good job covering up. But with the extra load and in his shaky condition, he'd be pushed to his limits. He wouldn't be able to stay low where his chances were better. Carrying Max would put them both at risk for smoke inhalation, but she didn't see an alternative that Harper would tolerate.

"Don't worry. I'll look after him," Alexa reassured her and turned toward Seth, putting a hand on his shoulder. "Let's get your father."

In seconds, they were ready to go, with Jess in front, standing at the door

"Stay as low as you can and stick close," she said. "If you lose sight of the person in front of you . . . yell. We're heading for the kitchen." She waved her hand to show them the direction. "There's a door to the basement below."

"The basement?" Jake questioned, shaking his head. "Goin' deeper into hell is crazy."

"There's a way out down there . . . but we'll have to work at it. If that's not good enough, Jake, there's the door. You feelin' lucky?" She glared at the man who had put them in this situation. When he avoided her eyes and kept his mouth shut, she added, "I didn't think so. Now let's move out."

Jess looked into the eyes of her friends one last time, but when her gaze found Jake, she clenched her jaw and didn't hide her resentment. She didn't trust him, but like it or not, he was part of the group and would need her help out of Millstone's inferno.

Sometimes it sucked to have a conscience.

After they cleared the room, the heat was unbearable. Staying low only made it marginally better. The conditions made her more worried for Seth and his father. She covered her mouth with her forearm and took shallow breaths, dodging fiery obstacles in her path, careful not to lose Harper. He followed her, but the smoke made it nearly impossible to see him. She felt his presence and kept moving. And she prayed the others were close behind. She had underestimated the noise. If one of them got lost now, she wasn't sure she could hear their call for help.

Sam had been right about the upstairs. The staircase had been engulfed in flames, with part of the steps burned through. And the collapsed ceiling at one end of the hall made it impossible to head back the way they'd come in. Eerie sounds roared through the corridors until she heard the loud, splintering rumble of the old mansion coming apart above her. The noise intensified, and her heart beat faster. It sounded as if the second floor was about to come down on top of them.

Jess reached a hand out for Seth. But when she didn't find him, she panicked. She flailed her hands into the murky black and leaned back until she touched something solid—Seth's leg. He stopped, and she gripped his thigh, tugging at his jeans. She pulled him with her and took one step at a time.

She crept toward the back of the house, guided by

her memory. Any familiar traces of the old mansion were burning, soon to be nothing more than charred rubble. But when she got to the basement door, it was open. And pitch-black smoke surged from its depths.

Damn it! Fear twisted her gut when she saw how much smoke came from below. Had she led them to the basement for nothing?

Shaking, she grabbed for Seth again. Harper had trusted her with the safety of his father. Feeling him next to her now—still willing to believe in her—gave Jess comfort. She couldn't let her friends down. Sam had been willing to sacrifice her life to rescue her. And without hesitation, Alexa had accompanied her into a hostage situation, knowing it would be dangerous.

But doubt was a powerful enemy.

Jess second-guessed what she had done and racked her brain, trying to think of another way out. Yet everywhere she turned, their predicament looked more hopeless. The fire had ravaged the ground floor, and the upper stories were ready to fall. And she knew Harper couldn't stand much more.

She ducked down and peered through the door to the basement below. In the distance, fire reflected off the cement floor, but it was a pale comparison to what scorched her back. And the ceiling heaved with dense smoke, a swirling toxic surge that cut the room in half. But her instinct for survival forced her to take that first step down—back into Millstone's torture chamber.

Danny Ray's hellhole would be the key to their survival—or the death of her and those she cared about. The irony wasn't wasted on her.

CHAPTER 28

Jess looked for anything familiar to orient her, but as she crept down the basement stairs, she saw the fire had changed everything. The ventilation system that had been her ears when she was a tormented child now belched smoke that made it hard to see. And sections of the ceiling had collapsed, sending heaps of fiery debris to the cement. Walls had started to catch fire.

But she had to focus and keep going.

Into the cavernous space, she felt her way along the basement wall toward the back. Although the smoke was still bad, the heat from the fire was less intense than it had been on the floor above. And with pockets of flame burning, they made the room bright enough to catch murky glimpses through the deepening haze.

The conditions were marginal, but she had made the right choice—for now.

She kept one hand on Seth and led the way until she found what she was looking for—the familiar wooden post that marked the spot. When she stopped and tugged at Harper's jeans, he collapsed next to her, coughing out of control. But he still held his father in his arms, with her jacket covering the old man's face and head.

"Hang on, Harper. I'm getting you and Max out of here," she promised.

After giving Seth a reassuring squeeze to his shoulder, Jess helped place his father on the floor, propped against a brick wall. Harper slumped next to Max and managed to say "Thanks" before a brutal coughing jag took over. Seeing him so drained scared the hell out of her.

When she felt the others settle next to Seth, she counted heads and breathed a sigh of relief when she realized everyone had made it. But Sam worried her. Unlike her normal feisty self, her friend slid to the floor, exhausted. And her face was streaked with tears, the soot leaving dark tracks on her cheeks. She leaned closer to brush back Sam's hair.

"Catch your breath . . . and pray. God might still listen to you." She kissed her on the forehead and got down to the business of survival.

Jess ran shaky fingers along the basement wall, feeling for every crack and crevice. But when she felt a faint breeze brush her skin, she knew she'd found it—the hole that had given her hope all those years ago—the one she had made as a child.

"This is it," she muttered. When someone touched her shoulder, she turned to see Alexa.

"What is?" The woman dropped to her knees, gasping for air.

She groped for Alexa's hand and helped her find the small gash in the brick wall.

"It isn't much," the blonde whispered, low enough so the others wouldn't hear. "But what's your plan?"

"Help me."

She stood and led Alexa to the wooden post behind them, using her friend as balance when she lifted her leg to kick the base of a two-by-four that had once been part of a storage shelving unit. The base of it had been cemented into the floor. Once Alexa figured out what she was doing, she helped with a few well-placed kicks of her own. Jess heard a crack and grappled the post with her hands, rocking it hard. After it broke free and dropped to the floor, she picked it up and hauled it back to the brick wall with Alexa's help.

"Use it . . . as a battering ram," she explained as her lungs heaved for air. "We'll need . . . help."

Hands came through the shadows and hoisted the two-by-four from her arms.

"I'll take the front." Jake intervened and held the post. "Show me where to hit."

After telling the man what to do, Alexa jumped in behind him and Jess took up the rear. They gripped the makeshift battering ram tight and made their first strike. She had visions of the wall crumbling away, but that didn't happen. They struck the brick again and again.

In the dark, she couldn't tell if they were making progress. She had to leave that up to Jake.

Grit caked her face and arms as sweat poured off her body. And with each driving blow, she felt more drained. The smoke-filled air made it hard to breathe, and every effort depleted her strength. Every time the post hit the wall, a jolt of pain radiated through her arms and shoulders. And wood splinters sliced into her hands with every jarring shove. But she gritted her teeth through the pain and fought back even harder with the next impact.

While they pounded the outer wall, Sam and Seth staggered to their feet, and yelled, "Help us. We're down here . . . in the basement." They screamed, and made noise any way they could. "Please . . . help us."

But after a while Jake stopped and raised his hand. In a strong voice, he cried, "Hold it. I hear somethin'."

Jess winced and blinked her stinging eyes, listening. And in the dark someone gripped her sore, splintered hand. She held her breath and shut her eyes to focus until she heard a rhythmic clinking. The sound was muffled yet clear. And it was far too steady to be an accident.

"What's that?" she asked, her eyes welling with tears of her own.

Ray had run through a stand of trees that separated the back of the Millstone property from the nearest neighbor. The tactical team had set up a perimeter around the premises that had made it difficult to cross without being noticed—but not impossible.

With crowbar in hand, he had picked his spot to give him the best advantage while staying under the radar of the men on duty. Ray saw his opportunity and took it, closing in on the rear wall of the mansion as he stuck to the shadows. The fire had ravaged most of the old home, and the upper floors had started to crater.

But as he crept along the outside wall, he had heard a loud thud. He'd stopped to listen, and distant voices screamed up through the ground—an eerie sound like a message from the grave.

"Sam?"

Using the light off the fire, he found bricks shoved through cracked mortar near ground level but thought his eyes had played tricks on him—a distortion caused by the shadowy fingers of the blaze. Hearing the voices made him take a second look. With his crowbar, he pounded the mortar around the rupture, feeling every vibrating jolt through his muscles. When metal contacted stone, shards of brick flew, and mortar dust hung in the air.

"Sam, are you down there?" he cried, not caring if anyone heard him now.

Jess peered through the haze and saw the small hole she'd started all those years ago cave through when the end of a crowbar wedged into the crack and pried it open. Outside, the silhouette of a man jabbed at the shaft, his body backlit by the night sky. And for the first time in what seemed like an eternity, she felt a cool breeze stroke her cheek.

"Oh my God, we're getting out of here," she whispered.

Tears stung her eyes, but as Jess reached out a hand to help the man outside clear the opening, she got pushed aside and fell to the cement floor. Jake had tossed their battering ram to the ground, shoving her and Alexa aside. He yanked at the remaining bricks to make an opening wide enough for him to crawl through.

"Me first." He hoisted his body up and flung his bulk through the hole, not caring about anyone else. "I did the work."

Jess knew that by the time they all got to safety, the bastard would be long gone. And they'd be back at square one to build a case that would free Harper. Seth would be walking into the hands of the cops who were trying to arrest him—too worried about his father to give a damn about what would happen to him. And without Jake's side of the story, they'd have little proof to shed light on Mandy's and Jade's murders.

"Damn it," she cursed under her breath as she watched Jake fade into the blackness outside.

When the bricks fell away, black smoke rushed out and made it hard for Ray to see. He waved off the haze and leaned to look inside for Sam, but a man muscled through the gaping hole. It happened so fast that he got the sense the guy was making a break for it. Ray tried to block him, but got shoved out of the way.

"Hey . . . Police. Who're you?" he demanded.

The guy didn't answer, but turned to face him. And

in a sudden move, he took a swing. Ray ducked and only caught a glancing blow, but didn't have time to pull his service weapon. Reacting on instinct, he whipped out his crowbar.

"Ah, shit." The man's eyes grew wide and he turned to run.

In one motion, Ray snagged his ankle with the curved end of the crowbar and yanked him off his feet. The bastard hit the ground hard and lay stunned. He wedged the crowbar between his shoulder and neck, pinning him to the ground. And without hesitation, he wrenched an arm back and secured the guy's hands with the Flexicuffs he carried on his belt.

"I wasn't doin' nothin'," he protested, his face in the mud.

"You always take a swing at cops?" Ray shook his head. "Not smart, man."

"I didn't hear you . . . when you said you were a cop. I swear."

"Yeah, right." He grappled with the guy's ankles and bound them, too. "Now you'll stay put."

While he worked, he yelled over his shoulder, "Sam? Can you hear me?"

"Ray? Is that . . . you?" Sam fought a lump in her throat as she called out, "We've got Max Jenkins down here . . . and he needs help. He can't walk."

Sam helped the others hoist Max through the opening. His body was fragile and small, but in her condition, she felt the strain. With Ray's help, they were all lifted from the basement, one by one, with

Sam the last one through the hole. Ray pulled her from the darkness into the night air.

She wanted nothing more than to collapse into his arms, and Ray didn't disappoint her. He pulled her to his chest and lifted her off the ground, cradling her in his arms. The feel of his body next to hers sent a surge of adrenaline rushing through her veins.

"I thought I was never . . ." She couldn't finish.

He pressed his lips to hers and kissed her—hard and sweet. His tongue caressed hers, and as tears trailed down her face, he kissed her cheeks and eyelids. And when he nuzzled her neck with his warmth, he whispered a rush of Spanish into her ear with such tenderness that she swore she understood every word.

"Oh, Ray."

She ran her fingers through his thick dark hair and drank in the scent of his skin, already addicted to his body and the way he made her feel. Over the years they'd worked together, a friendship had been the start of her feelings for him. They had their differences, but she'd seen his respect for her blossom. And on the occasions he'd let it show, she'd seen an arousing hunger in his eyes and knew he wanted her. The feeling was mutual.

But being in his arms now felt so right. And when he kissed her, Sam knew she'd fallen in love with Ray Garza—even before they'd had their first official date.

* * *

While a paramedic examined her, Alexa watched Seth Harper with his confused father. They were sitting on the back of the next ambulance. The old man looked rough, but he had survived the ordeal without suffering from smoke inhalation or burns. The same couldn't be said for the man's son.

The paramedic would be taking Seth to the hospital, accompanied by Chicago's Finest. The police had him under arrest until they sorted things out. And his head trauma, with the likelihood of a concussion, had topped any incidental injuries caused by the fire and forced him to undergo further medical treatment. But at least he wouldn't see the inside of a jail cell for a day or two.

Yet despite the trouble staring him in the face, she knew Seth was more worried about his father. If he could have refused treatment to take care of Max, he would have done it; but CPD had already made the call, and Harper wouldn't have his say.

"If it helps, I can take care of your father, see that he gets home." Alexa smiled at Seth. "Looks like you'll have your hands full."

He looked up in surprise as if he was seeing her for the first time. His dark eyes took her in and held her in place, rooted where she stood. His good looks were stunning up close. Add boyish charm to his innocent sex appeal, and Seth Harper fascinated her, especially when she realized that she'd been holding her breath. No wonder Jessie had become so attached to him.

"That would be great." He fixed his gaze on her, working magical powers he probably didn't know he

THE WRONG SIDE OF DEAD 311

had. "He's at the Golden Palms Villa Nursing Home. I'll get you the address . . . and thanks. They're probably real worried about him by now. I'll call to let them know you're bringing him."

"And you better give me your keys to the van," she added. "Jessie will need her wheels. Preferably a vehicle not reported as stolen." When he looked confused, she added, "It's . . . complicated."

"Yeah . . . well, I'm not exactly in the mood for complicated." He reached into his pocket and pulled out a set of keys. "You've been a good friend to Jessie. She could use one."

He slumped against the door of the ambulance, looking exhausted. When he winced in pain, she took it as a sign for her to leave him alone. A real pity.

"Well . . . I'll make sure she gets these." She jingled the keys in her hand. "You take care of yourself." She reached out a hand and touched his face. The gesture surprised him, but when he looked at her, he smiled.

"Yeah, sure." He nodded. "And thanks . . . Alexa."

With Sam at his side, Ray escorted Jake in cuffs to a waiting officer, who took the man into custody. Breathing in the night air had revived her, but not half as much as seeing Ray up close and feeling his hand at the small of her back. Considering what had nearly happened, she felt lucky to be alive. And although having someone take care of her now wasn't entirely necessary, it did feel damned good to let go—just this once.

"From his ID, he's Jake Culver. Get him checked by

the paramedic before we take him for a ride," he told the officer, then pointed a finger at her. "And you're next. No argument."

"Yes, sir." She saluted.

"Detective Garza?" An officer from the tactical team waved Ray over to another squad car. And Sam came along, not wanting to let him out of her sight.

"Thought you should know," the cop said. "We found a guy on the premises. He claims not to know anything about what happened in there, but he was behaving suspiciously so we're bringing him in for questioning. He's got no ID and was not in a sharing mood."

Sam leaned down to get a better look into the vehicle and a cop flipped on an interior light. She squinted into the backseat, but smiled and shook her head at the man who avoided her eyes.

"That's Sal Pinzolo." She stood and told Ray and the other officer. "He's muscle for Nadir Beladi, a major drug dealer who runs hookers, too. Jessie thought the guy might have something to do with Mandy Vincent's murder and gave me his driver's license to run."

"What?" Ray asked. "How . . . never mind."

He narrowed his eyes and smirked—probably realizing that she'd been keeping secrets on Harper's case—her attempt to edge him out on their bet.

"Yeah, and he might have been the guy who tried to kill me inside, but I can't swear to that. I was pretty messed up, not seein' real clear." She winced. "But if the fire crew finds charred remains inside, then I'd have serious doubts about who I saw. We'll have to wait and see."

"That son of a bitch," Ray cursed, and glared at Pinzolo. "Are you sure you can't ID the bastard?"

"Sorry. Wish I could." She sighed. "But if I know Jessie, she probably has some theories on what happened. I'll bring her in tomorrow . . . see if she learned anything from Jake while they were locked up. Alexa, too."

"Good idea. We'll get a chance to sweat these guys during interrogation." He stroked her hair but turned toward the other cop. "Keep this joker separated from the guy I arrested, especially at the station house. I don't want him playing intimidation head games."

But when Jake got into the back of the next police cruiser, the interior light came on, and the bartender got a good look at the man in the next vehicle. Pinzolo glared back. Sam knew by the look on Jake's face that Pinzolo had delivered his message without using a word.

"Too late." She nudged her head and Ray caught Pinzolo staring at Jake. "I'd say the damage is done."

"We'll see about that," he assured her. "If this asshole is involved, we'll get them talking."

She had faith in Ray. He was a solid interrogator. But Beladi and Pinzolo had evaded the DA for a reason. Once they lawyered up, it would be business as usual. And Jake didn't have the backbone to be more than an expendable pawn in their game. If it turned out any other way, she'd be surprised.

She had her mind on the job when Ray took her hand to lead her to a paramedic. He was taking charge of her well-being, and she was happy to let him. But having Ray holding her hand made it difficult to suppress a smile, even though she gave it her best shot.

And failed miserably.

Jess found it hard to turn away—the fire mesmerized her. It had become addictive, with an unrelenting pull, similar to the torturous hold Danny Ray Millstone had had on her . . . until now.

A part of her wanted to watch the bastard's place burn to ashes with no remnants left except for the scars she would always carry, both inside and out. Fire crews had moved in to control the blaze, but the old mansion had fallen. It would no longer stand as an affront to the life she'd made.

"Alexa made sure Max got home okay." Sam interrupted her melancholy moment. "And she gave me the van keys that she got from Harper." She handed her the keys. "I'd say she's been a nice addition to your circle of friends."

Jess took a deep breath, unable to look away from the dying blaze.

"Yeah. I agree," she said. "And I might have to rethink how I feel about Ray Garza. The guy's growing on me . . . like a tumor, Harper would say."

Jess tried to smile, but her heart wasn't in it. Her thoughts still plagued her.

"Can you come by the station house tomorrow?" Sam asked. "We'll need your statement . . . see if you can help us piece this together. Sal Pinzolo was arrested on the property."

"What?"

"He claims not to know anything about what happened, but anyone connected to a guy like Beladi has his own agenda."

"Yeah, especially that mean bastard." She crossed her arms, and added, "Jake had a lot to say in there. If he's smart, he'll keep talking. And Harper could use the help."

Jess thought of the implications of Pinzolo getting caught red-handed on Millstone's property. He could have come to kill Jake on the orders of Beladi and set up the dumb jerk for the murders to throw suspicion off his employer. And someone had started the fire and locked them in that room with the door bolted shut from the outside.

Adding Pinzolo to the equation—killer turned arsonist—gave her theory a certain plausible ring. But that left her wondering about motive. Had Jake told her the truth about having a side business that Mandy found out about? Did Beladi and Pinzolo uncover the enterprise that Jake ran under their noses and come for their pound of flesh? And who had been the brains behind framing Harper?

She had a feeling the case would hinge on what the bartender had to say. Surely, Jake would see that telling the cops what really happened was his best insurance to stay alive, even if he had to implicate himself. If he served up Beladi on a platter to the DA, he might get an offer of witness protection and start a new life somewhere else. She didn't like the idea that Jake could get off scot-free, but that option was the lesser of two evils.

Men like Beladi and Pinzolo had to be stopped.

"You want to stay with me tonight?" Sam offered. "I don't want you to be alone . . . not after what happened."

"No . . . I'll be okay." She glanced at Sam. "Besides, you might get lucky. I saw how Ray looked at you. And from where I stood, the feeling looked mutual."

They watched the fire in silence. Jess knew Sam had her own demons, that had started the day her life crossed Millstone's path. And she couldn't think of anyone else that she'd rather share this moment with than Sam—a woman who'd risked her life to save a friend.

"You know, Sammie. Nothing says 'I love you' more than running into hell for a friend. Hallmark doesn't make a card that says 'I'd die for you,' but maybe they should."

"I didn't run into a burning building thinking I was gonna die, Jessie. I only wanted you to live."

Despite all they'd been through tonight, Jess had to smile. "The only good thing that ever happened here . . . was that I met you."

She put her arm around her friend and watched as Danny Ray Millstone's mansion burned to the ground. Jess felt the heat radiating on her skin, heat that would purge away only a fraction of her ordeal. In her heart she knew her nightmare would never end—the psychological wounds had cut too deep and would remain—but seeing Millstone's legacy go up in smoke had given her closure to a part of her life she wanted to forget.

Like the phoenix from Greek mythology, she felt

reborn to a new life she had earned, rising out of the ashes of her degradation—a resurrection that would be forever grounded in pain.

People say that whatever doesn't kill a person makes them stronger. But for her that wasn't much consolation when the lesson came at a price she never wanted to pay.

CHAPTER 29

Next morning

After she and Alexa made their formal statements to the police, Jess convinced Sam to let them observe part of Jake's interrogation from behind a two-way mirror. Ray joined them. In a dark room, they watched as Jake went through the motions. His arrogance was gone, replaced by his fear of an unknown future. He looked pale under the lights and slumped in his chair like a whipped dog.

But Jess hadn't felt sorry for the bastard. She had come to the police station for answers, especially where Seth's *own* future was concerned. What she discovered was something she didn't expect. Jake had confessed to everything, letting Seth off the hook for murder. After the hospital released him, Harper would be free to go. And she couldn't have been happier.

Yet her relief over his good news was tainted by the fact that Pinzolo had become Mr. Teflon.

"It's too early for this." Alexa took another gulp of coffee.

"Yeah, tell me about it." Ray heaved a sigh, clearly not happy with the situation. "Pinzolo lawyered up. But we didn't have enough to file charges on him anyway. We cut him loose this morning. And Jake is too stupid to see that using the same lawyer isn't in his best interest."

"You've got to be kidding." Jess grimaced.

"Wish we were," Sam added. "And whatever intimidation game Pinzolo played on Jake is protected under attorney-client privilege."

"This is insane," she ranted. "What happened to Jake's story . . . the one he told me? He could be a witness for the DA against Pinzolo and his boss."

"That's why I think Jake was played," Ray clarified. "He kept his mouth shut until his lawyer showed. The next thing we know, he's saying that he killed Desiree because he found out she was still seeing her ex-boyfriend." He turned toward her. "And when he got wind off the street that you wanted to question Jade, he decided to kill her. He's in there making his formal statement now."

"So why frame Harper?"

"He claims Harper was set up out of pure meanness. A fit of jealousy over the time he spent with Desiree. The kid smacked of money, and he wanted to put him in his place."

"No, no way." She crossed her arms, shifting her gaze between Ray and Sam. "This wasn't a crime of passion about jealousy. Hell, Jake's no Casanova. And like I said, he told me Mandy found out about a business he was running on the side . . . right under the devil's nose. Now I can't see him taking on Beladi and Pinzolo alone, but then again, stupidity is more Jake's speed."

"I second that." Alexa raised a finger.

"Hey, I believe you two," Ray said. "But he hasn't corroborated Jessie's version of the story. And a written confession aces any rendition of 'he said she said.' Not that it matters, but did anyone else hear Jake confess?" He pointed to Alexa. "Did you?"

"Sorry. Can't help you. I was down for the count," the blonde said. "But even if I was willing to lie— which I do quite well by the way—it wouldn't add up to much with dick-for-brains in there willing to confess."

Jess clenched her jaw to temper the rage churning in her belly.

"She's right." She glared at Jake in the next room. "Max won't make a credible witness, and no one else but me heard Jake. Plus, I'm guessing any good defense attorney would say my relationship with Harper is plenty of motivation for me to accuse someone else."

"If we can't get Jake to turn state's evidence against Beladi and Pinzolo, then Sal will walk away from this a free man." Sam sighed. "Nothing definitive places him inside that house. And without a real confession from Jake, we can't pin those murders on Pinzolo as an accomplice either."

"This smells like a cover-up, but I'm missing pieces to the puzzle." Jess shook her head. "Someone had to lock us inside that room. The door was bolted from the outside. That's attempted murder. And my gut tells me Pinzolo set that fire. What about an arson charge?"

Now she was grasping at straws, scheming for any way to lock Pinzolo up.

"The arson investigator is our next stop." Sam nodded. "He's giving us his preliminary findings. Very unofficial. But maybe he'll give us something meaty to chew on. I'll let you know. Call me later."

"Yeah . . . thanks." She nodded.

"Oh and before I forget," Sam added. "A private investigator, Luís Dante, came in to file a report . . . said you stole his car. When he heard what happened, he dropped the charges. But he told me to say that you owe him a beer. Does that make sense?"

"Yeah . . . sort of," she muttered. "Thanks, Sam."

Rapt in thought, Jess left the observation room with Alexa, heading for the parking lot. Sal Pinzolo walking away clean made her skin crawl. She'd faced him before and witnessed his cruelty, especially when he had the advantage. She'd have to watch her back. Next time, he wouldn't settle for a beating.

"Well . . . one good thing might come of this," Jess observed with a sideways glance.

"Oh, yeah. What's that?"

"Jake will be out of the gene pool." She shrugged. "Darwin's theory is intact."

Alexa raised an eyebrow. "I feel better already."

Sam walked into the meeting room with Ray, noticing that another man stood in the far corner, waiting for them to arrive. Dressed in uniform, arson investigator Captain Joe Collins, was a tall, lean man with alert blue eyes and short-cropped dark hair, cut military style. By reputation, he was a quiet man and an unconventional thinker with a penchant for details. Good qualities for an investigator.

"Good morning, Captain. Glad you could make it." She smiled. "I'm Detective Sam Cooper, and this is Detective Ray Garza."

Sam liked him the instant he shook her hand with a firm grip, not the limp grasp some men thought women preferred.

"Call me, Joe." A corner of his lip curled into a half smile.

"First names work for us, too," she said, offering the man a seat at the conference-room table. They sat as she began. "I know this is much too early in your investigation to make this official, but anything you can tell us might help move our case forward."

"Well, bottom line, nothing I found thus far points to arson," the captain said. "To put out the blaze, fire did their basic surround and drown, lots of water dumped. And as you might imagine, any trace evidence got hit with it, too. I used arson dogs to detect the use of accelerants, and they came up empty. But let me ask you a question . . . since you were inside."

"Yeah . . . shoot." She nodded.

"Was there any room in the house that seemed like the source of the blaze . . . an area that was more engulfed in flames than the rest of the house?" the man asked.

"Yeah, toward the back on the first floor, near the room that had been bolted shut." She crossed her arms and fixed her gaze on the arson investigator.

"In a vacant house with no electricity, fires don't start by accident, especially if the fire was concentrated the way you describe. That raises a red flag for me as an investigator." He narrowed his eyes. "Do you remember smelling anything unusual at that location?"

She thought about it a long moment, delving into the horror of last night. When she didn't answer right away, Ray leaned closer.

"Sam? What are you thinking? Just spit it out. Say the first thing that comes to mind."

"I smelled something"—she wrinkled her nose—"medicinal. But I couldn't place it."

"Could it have been rubbing alcohol?" Collins asked. "Or some other household product?"

"Yeah, it could have been. Why?"

"The dogs in our K-9 unit are trained to detect certain types of petroleum-based accelerants, but not the entire range of flammable household products." He shook his head, his face grim. "Isopropyl alcohol is water soluble and can be washed away. No trace evidence left behind. If your firebug used rubbing alcohol or some other similar product to set that blaze, then I'm afraid we'll never prove it."

"Don't you have other ways to test . . . for the presence of rubbing alcohol, at least?" she asked.

"Dogs can smell the smallest unit of measure better than our electronic detectors can quantify," Collins explained. "In short, if the dogs fail, then we don't have much. Plus our K–9 unit is only a tool in our investigation. We confirm anything the dogs find with trace analysis from the crime lab. But in this case, that didn't happen. We're still talking to possible witnesses, but I'm afraid arson is a long shot."

The captain got to his feet. "That's all I've got, but I'll call if that changes."

"It is what it is, Joe." Ray stood and shook the man's hand. "Thanks for coming."

"Anytime," Collins said as he gripped Sam's hand.

After the arson investigator left, Sam stood and stared out the window, disappointment setting in. Ray shut the conference-room door to give them privacy.

"What now?" he asked, his voice low. "We got nothing on Sal Pinzolo. I can still work Jake under the radar of his lawyer if you want. But with Pinzolo on the loose, I know you must be concerned for Jessie."

"Yeah, I am. Real concerned."

Harper was free to go, and Jess was very satisfied with that even though Mandy's murder case was far from over. Despite the uncertainty in the police investigation, she was pleased that her trip home would include a stop at the hospital with good news for Seth. She couldn't wait to deliver it personally. But as they stepped outside heading for their cars, Alexa surprised her.

"So tell me. Is Seth seeing anyone?"

"What?" She shot her a sideways glance, wrapping her head around the abrupt question. "He's a little young, isn't he?"

"Young for what? And are we talking about the same man?" Her friend laughed. "Besides, young is the whole point. You have to admit there's something about a younger lover that appeals to . . . an experienced woman. There's no pretense. There's only need. And don't you think he's gorgeous with a capital G?"

"I hadn't noticed," she lied.

"Then you haven't staked a claim, right? Because if you're interested in him, I'll back off. He's all yours."

"No . . . no claim." A pang of jealousy hit hard, confusing her. "But you don't live here. Why would you . . . ?"

"I'm not talking about setting up house. I just want to . . . have a little taste." The woman smiled, her eyes glazing over as if she were somewhere else. And Jess had a pretty good notion where.

"TMI, my friend." She raised a hand. "Whatever you two decide to do is none of my business."

But as she came to the blue van—still disturbed by their conversation and her reaction to it—she noticed that her vehicle had a flat tire.

"What the hell . . . ?" She walked around the van and corrected her count to two flat tires. And with only one spare, that meant she had a bigger problem. *Damn it!*

"Oh, wow. Not good," Alexa commiserated, dropping to a knee for a better look. "I've got my rental around the corner. I can give you a lift wherever you need to go to get this fixed."

"Why me?" She shook her head and knelt beside her friend.

But a voice coming from behind brought Jess to her feet.

"Maybe because you don't know how to mind your own business. You're thickheaded. And unlucky things can happen to stupid people."

She turned to see Sal Pinzolo leaning against a brick wall near an alley. A broad-shouldered mammoth, the guy blocked the sun when he stepped closer. He had cleaned up since the fire, but no one could wash away the smell of mean. And with him here, she knew one thing.

Her flat tires were no accident.

Her mind reeled with what to say, and anger got the better of her. Being a woman who'd eaten tough for breakfast ever since she was a kid, Jess didn't hesitate to go for his jugular.

"What's so special about you, Sal? I mean, really." She eyed him up and down. "Without Beladi, who the hell are you? You're just hired muscle. That's it."

Pinzolo glared at her, his eye twitching. This time she took his facial tic as a sign she had hit her target dead center and kept going.

"And news flash, stud, you're not as young as you used to be. I sure hope you have a retirement plan." She stopped and narrowed her eyes, hitting on a different tack. "Or did Jake ruin that for you?"

When he didn't ask what she meant and kept his silence, she kept talking.

"I bet you two had your own 401(k) plan operating under Beladi's radar. And you covered it up . . . kept the big boss in the dark. Now *that's* stupid."

She let her mouth run and had thrown out anything she knew would rile the guy. But when she alluded to him and Jake working together—without his boss's knowledge—Sal's facial tic got worse. And her speculation made sense, even if she had made it up on the fly. She had stumbled on the truth but had no proof to back it up, only Sal's unexpected reaction.

"You got a big mouth. And you don't know what you're talkin' about. That asshole killed two hookers. That would have shamed my boss. He's got pride. And I was only protecting his interests."

"Oh . . . the drug dealer? In his organization, I thought murder would be grounds for promotion." She smiled and placed her hand over her heart. "But sorry, Sal. I didn't realize you were so sensitive. I'd hate to besmirch your employer's sterling reputation."

"You're a regular smart-ass, but the cops got nothin', and neither do you. Jake killed those whores. End of story. If you know what's good for you, you'll let it go."

"That sounds like a threat, Sal."

"Whatever works for you, bitch," he spat.

When Alexa closed ranks, Pinzolo nudged his chin in challenge and waved her on.

"You got somethin' to say?" he asked.

Alexa smiled with a slow easy curve to her lips.

"Yeah, indulge me," she replied in a low, throaty voice. "You see, I made you a promise when we met . . . when I warned *you* to let it go. Apparently, listening isn't a strong suit of yours, but I'm a girl who keeps her promises."

"Sounds like trash talk, but you're on my list, blondie." He grinned. "You better have eyes in the back of your head."

"Oh I do, Sal." She smiled and cocked her head.

"And please . . . make me number one. I tend to be an overachiever."

By the look of Sal's pulsing facial tic, her cavalier attitude really pissed him off—no doubt exactly what Alexa had in mind. Bullies always expected to dish it out, but never knew how to take it. Pinzolo was no different. And being confronted by women had probably never happened to him before.

"Be careful what you ask for." Pinzolo pointed at Alexa, then glared at Jess before he walked away, an iron-fisted hulking load of badass.

She knew big talking was a weapon in her arsenal—a pure defense mechanism. Her bluster made it look as if she weren't afraid of the bastard, but Jess knew the man posed a real threat. And it wouldn't end here.

"Flaunting is a highly unattractive quality, don't you think?" Alexa stared at the man as he turned a corner. "And guys like Sal never know when to leave well enough alone."

"Yeah, unless they learn the hard way." Jess chewed the inside corner of her lip.

"Honey, I doubt the hard way would make an impression on Sal, but he'll get what's coming to him. I can assure you."

"Yeah, that's a sure bet. And I'd pay serious coin to be there when it happened."

Midnight

Nadir Beladi opened his eyes and stared into the dark shadows of his bedroom, not recognizing where he was at first. It took him a moment to get his bearings. With alcohol on his breath and the smell of sex on his sheets, he remembered the hooker he had brought to his room earlier, but she had been taken away after he was done with her. His men had seen to that.

But something had awakened him. He was sure of it.

And as he held his breath to listen, he felt a presence in the room. He remained still—his body taut—and peered through the dark for any signs of movement. Nothing. When he raised his head off the pillow, he heard a chilling sound. Someone had racked the slide of a gun and shoved the muzzle next to his ear, pressing it hard to the back of his skull.

When the trespasser didn't shoot, he dared to take a breath.

"Who are you?" he asked. "And how did you get in here?" Not waiting for a reply, he ventured the real question on his mind. "Do you have any idea who I am?"

"I know exactly who you are, Nadir." A woman's voice.

She barely spoke above a whisper. And he did not detect an accent. He looked for any reflection of her face in a mirror. There was none. And he tried to place the voice, but nothing came.

"If this is your idea of foreplay, I must say it is working. My cock is hard for you. Please . . . let me see your face." He tried flattery, anything to keep her talking.

She nudged the gun and thumped his head.

"Ah." He winced, but kept still. "What do you want?"

The bitch had dared to injure him. Surely he would have a bruise by morning, if he survived.

"Let's get one thing straight," the woman whispered. "I've got nothing but contempt for men like you. And I can only pray that you learn from your parents' mistake and use birth control."

"Surely you did not come here merely to insult me."

"Why is *that* hard to believe?" She hesitated, then added, "But you're right. And insulting a man like you is too easy. I'm here about justice. And believe me, you'll want to hear what I've got to say."

The woman spoke and he listened. At first he was reluctant to believe what she had to say about Sal Pinzolo, his number one man. Even she admitted her conjectures were only speculative, but what she told him eventually made sense in light of his own observations. In the end she had planted a fertile seed of doubt and made him a believer.

In America, a man was presumed innocent until proven guilty, a noble belief that had served him well in his many brushes with the local police. But in his world he could not afford such idealistic sentimentality. Such a view would be a weakness, to be sure. And men like Sal Pinzolo could be easily dealt with and replaced. The way he saw it, he had nothing to lose by ridding his house of a suspected traitor.

Nothing.

CHAPTER 30

Two days later

"Glad you could meet me on such short notice." Sam shoved into a corner booth in the back of the Funky Buddha Lounge, hitting the bar for an early drink before it got crowded. It was a trendy metro watering hole with mural-covered walls and antique lighting that was more her friend's style. Sam waited until the waitress brought their drink orders before she gave Jess the news.

"Earlier today someone at the Adler Planetarium called to report a body floating in Lake Michigan off Lakeshore Drive. The medical examiner ID'd the body as Sal Pinzolo. He was capped twice in the back of the head, but not before someone carved him up. And the fish of Lake Michigan had their fill of Sal . . . like the rest of us. Can't say I'm sorry he's gone, for your sake."

Jess narrowed her eyes and stared at Sam before she took a long swig of her single malt scotch. In her world, mustering sympathy for anyone like Pinzolo wasn't going to happen. The guy lived by the knife and died by it. Beladi must have found out what Sal had done. Or maybe his suspicions were enough reason to torture him for a real confession. But she had no doubt, the murder of Sal Pinzolo would end up a cold case with no leads.

"I gave Jake Cordell the news, too. I think he had thoughts about recanting his story, but he's probably even more afraid of Beladi with Sal not being his safety net, if he ever was." Sam looked up from her drink. "You don't seem too surprised."

Jess shook her head. "In my gut I know that Sal was the one who tortured those women, Sam. Their knife wounds had his signature all over them. He got what he deserved." She downed the rest of her drink and gestured for the waitress to bring another. "And if Jake served Harper the Mickey, I doubt he was there when Sal killed Mandy. Jake was an ass, but I couldn't see him standing by and watching that girl die, not like that."

Sam nodded, a grim look on her face. "I bet Jake was the anonymous caller, but he's never admitted it."

"My gut tells me he was the driver who tailed me out to the murder scene the night I first met him at Dirty Monty's, too." She narrowed her eyes. "He got someone to cover for him, then waited until I drove away. That had to be him. I left Pinzolo and Beladi kissing the pavement."

"Kissing the pavement?"

She'd never told Sam about the stun grenade, and now was not the time for true confessions.

"Just a figure of speech." She waggled her finger at Sam to change the subject. "But you know, there was a time I would have pegged Jason Burke as a killer."

Sam stared at her for a long moment but eventually went with the flow. No questions asked. "Yeah, me too. But get this. That jerk was fencing stolen merchandise on *eBay*."

"No, say it ain't so." Jess had to laugh. "Him sitting behind a computer would be a stretch, but having the balls to sell online is real chutzpah."

"Kind of creative, actually. With the anonymity of the Internet and the lack of online controls to monitor that kind of thing, Jason Burke was living on the cutting edge of technology . . . until we arrested him."

"Couldn't happen to a nicer guy," Jess grinned. "Speaking of a *real* nice guy, how's Ray?"

"Ray is damned fine, sista." Sam crooked her lip into a lazy smile and lowered her eyes, lost in a memory. And Jess couldn't be happier for her childhood friend.

"Yeah, I'd second that," she agreed. "And whatever came of that bet you two had? Now that Harper's a free man, you have to spill the details."

"Ray acknowledged that I won, but I think he knew I tag teamed him by using your help and Alexa's. But the way I worked it, we'll both win."

"Anyone ever tell you that you're a real tease, Sam Cooper?"

Her friend knew how to milk a story, so Jess settled into her seat with an elbow on the table and her chin resting on her palm.

"You love him, don't you?"

Sam looked as if she'd object or deny, but in the end she only smiled. "I was going to have him paint my house, but after he kissed me, I came up with another idea. Now we're taking a long-overdue vacation together. I pick the place, and he pays."

"Sounds nice," Jess admitted. "And what if he had won?"

"He told me he wanted me to cook for him, some family recipes from his mother. No pressure there."

Unlike her, Sam was an excellent cook. She would have aced any test Ray could have conjured up.

"Ah, that's kind of sweet." Jess cocked her head. "In a 'me Tarzan, you Jane' sort of way. Add candles, ditch the chimp, and I see real romance potential."

Sam chuckled. "No matter how it would've turned out, if I got more time with him, I would've been a winner either way."

"I'm happy for you, Sammie. No one deserves love more than you." She raised her glass. "I feel that we've both made it a dark tunnel and come out on the other side, together. So let's drink to new beginnings."

"To new beginnings." Her friend held up her glass and took a sip.

Jess drank to Sam's prospects. Her friend had always lived a charmed life compared to hers. Despite the fact that Sal Pinzolo would no longer be a threat—and she could stop sleeping with her Colt Python under her pillow—too much remained unsettled in Jess's life to make her feel good about her future. And although she had come full circle, with the destruction of Millstone's mansion closing that chapter in her life, she felt restless and anxious for something new to happen.

Without having any idea what it should be.

A week later

The morning held the promise of an early fall as a crisp breeze jostled the trees of the Chapel Hill Cemetery. Not a cloud marred the pale blue sky. If not for the nip in the air, the day had the feel of spring and new beginnings.

A strange contrast to why she'd come.

Dressed in a dark pantsuit and holding a dozen white roses, Jess spotted Harper standing alone by a grave, staring down at the modest headstone. Since his usual Jerry Springer tee and jeans weren't fitting for the solemn occasion, Seth wore a navy suit and gray-striped tie, looking more like the man Alexa had talked about.

Why hadn't she seen it before?

When she got closer, he looked up, not hiding his sadness—not from her.

"Hey, Jessie." He took a deep breath. "When I said I'd be here this morning, I really didn't expect you to come. But I'm glad you did."

She'd come for him. And despite not knowing Mandy, she'd come to recognize the occasion and acknowledge her passing from this life. In the end, she felt a connection to her. Mandy had been a girl unable to deal with what life had dished out. And thanks to

Seth, he'd helped her see beyond the labels of hooker and drug addict to find the human being Mandy Vincent had been before she met Danny Ray Millstone. Except for the mercy of a higher power—or a fortunate roll of the dice—Jess might have turned out the same.

She placed her roses at the base of the headstone, next to the elegant pastel lilies he had brought. Jess smelled the earthy aroma of the freshly turned soil at her feet. And she watched a hawk make lazy circles in the sky, content to stand next to Harper in silence until she found a way to comfort him.

"You picked a real nice spot, Harper." She stared across the horizon and took a breath. "It's peaceful."

Seth had paid for Mandy's funeral expenses. She'd been buried two days ago, with Jess and a handful of others in attendance, but today would have been her birthday. Mandy would have been twenty-three years old.

"You know, Jake told me that you made a difference with her." She watched the breeze blow his hair, but he didn't look up. "She had gone to him for money, to start a new life somewhere else. I think that's why she called you . . . that day."

He turned to look at her, a questioning expression on his face. She could tell he didn't believe what she said.

"Despite Jake being an asshole"—she furrowed her brow—"I don't think he lied about that."

When a tear rolled down Seth's cheek, she knew he was struggling to find the words to share what he was feeling. And she was content to let the quiet moment linger between them.

"I was the one who got her killed," he said. "I put her in the line of fire."

"No, you only tried to help her." She touched his arm. "Mandy made the wrong choices in her life, long before you came along. I think meeting you gave her hope . . . that things could change for her."

He shut his eyes tight, then slowly looked down at her grave.

"No really, just think about it. You have . . ." She tugged at his sleeve until he looked into her eyes. When he did, her breath caught in her throat. ". . . such a big heart. This wasn't only about your father and your search for the kids in his casebook. Once you found who you were looking for . . ."

His eyes made it hard for her to continue—especially when her gaze lingered on his lips. She swallowed and took a deep breath.

". . . you wanted to make a difference. And you have. Believe me, you have." She nodded and let go of his arm. "I mean, you did. With Mandy."

For an instant, his eyes softened and his guilt-ridden grief faded long enough for her to imagine he might kiss her again. She held her breath, waiting for that moment. That second chance. But when he didn't, she saved face by shifting the conversation.

"So . . . have you reconciled your past with Max? I mean, are you still planning on using that old case file to track down the kids he saved? I know it's none of my business now, but—"

He stared at her, blinking. The shift in topic had

thrown him. He cleared his throat and ran a hand through his hair.

"I don't know, Jessie." He shook his head. "When I found you, I realized you were a strong, capable woman, making it on your own. You didn't need me. Mandy was different. If I did make a difference with her, maybe I should still pursue this . . . quest of mine. And you're right. It's not about my father anymore."

"Oh, I think Max has a great deal to do with this." She grinned, feeling the heat of her blushing cheeks. "You inherited his good-guy genes . . . and his courage. You've had a connection to your father all along, smart guy."

Seth nudged his lips into a crooked half smile, an expression Jess wanted to remember. And after he touched Mandy's headstone one more time, he headed for his car. Jess walked with him, but halfway there she got a call on her cell. She reached into her pocket and recognized the number. Area code 907. Payton Archer.

"I gotta take this. It won't take long," she assured him. "Don't leave me— "

He interrupted her by saying, "Never."

"At least, not without saying good-bye," she added.

Seth watched her walk away, but not before he saw her smile, and say, "Hey, Payton. Yeah, it's good to hear your voice too."

And his heart sank.

He should have been happy for her. Jessie had found someone she cared about, yet seeing her happy with another man only made him miserable. It had been the reason he had walked out of her life months ago, something he'd never told her. He could see being a friend to her eventually, but his heart wasn't ready to let go.

Most men would see Payton Archer—a former NFL quarterback—as a major rival. But Payton was a good man and not the problem. It was Jessie. She thought of him as a kid and had no feelings for him beyond friendship. And hearing the phrase "let's be friends" would zap the love muscle out of commission. He couldn't face hearing those words from her.

By the time he got to his Mustang, he blocked out the world by plugging music into his ears as he waited for Jessie. When Secondhand Serenade launched into "Fall For You," he slumped against his passenger door and shut his eyes, letting the lyrics do a number on his heart. He was so rapt in his misery that he never saw Alexa walk up. She pulled the earbuds out to get his attention.

"Hey there, Harper." She slid next to him and nudged his shoulder with hers. "I came by to steal you away. Nothing fancy. Just you and me."

"I thought you left town after the funeral." He let his eyes search for Jessie. When he found her, he wished he hadn't. He heard her laugh from where he stood.

"No, I thought you might need a friend." Her hand brushed his hip as she leaned against his car.

"A friend, huh?" he asked, finding it hard to hide his disappointment at hearing the word "friend" from another woman.

"For starters," she said in a low husky voice.

His eyes grew wide when Alexa raised an eyebrow and lowered her gaze to his lips and beyond. But she shocked him even more when she loosened his tie. She straddled his legs and leaned close, tugging at his tie and unbuttoning his shirt, not taking her eyes off his. He swallowed, hard. And when her perfume drifted to him on the wind, goose bumps raced across his skin. And his reaction had nothing to do with the chill of a stiff breeze.

"Don't you want to hear what I have in mind?" She winked.

Jess ended her conversation with Payton, promising she'd call later when she had more time. After the fire, she'd called him, and they had talked. And he'd called to check on her several times since then, yet with the time difference between Alaska and Illinois, they had played phone tag all day. A part of her wished he lived closer to Chicago. The close emotional bond they had formed, while searching for his niece, had been hard to live without these past few months. But Jess knew in her heart that a visit from Payton would only complicate things.

She'd been in denial and had to deal with her feelings for Seth, whatever they might be.

Was she trying to sabotage her long-distance relationship with Payton, protecting her heart before he broke it off? Or were her feelings for Harper real? Two good men. And she had no idea if the choice was even hers to make. Maybe both of them would open their eyes and see her more clearly—a familiar pattern she'd noticed for the men in her life.

When she headed toward Seth, she looked up to see Alexa unbuttoning his shirt. The intimacy of her stance disturbed her. And Harper couldn't take his eyes off the tall blonde.

"Damn it, Beckett," she muttered.

Jess veered toward the van, hoping they wouldn't see her. She had no right to be jealous. She'd cleared the path for Alexa. And Seth deserved a good woman in his life. But if she truly believed that, why did she have this damned lump in her throat?

"Hey, Jessie. Where are you going?"

She stopped when she heard Alexa's voice, but she stayed where she was, and yelled back, "Something came up. I gotta go."

Alexa narrowed her eyes and left Harper behind, walking toward her. The woman's eyes never left her, and she found it hard to hide what was in her heart.

"You're welcome to join us. We're just grabbing a bite to eat . . . and take things from there."

"No, really. I've gotta go." She tried to smile, but couldn't. "Take it easy on that Midwest boy. Break him in real slow, you hear?"

Alexa touched her arm as she turned to leave. "Are you okay with me . . . and Seth? Seriously. I'll back off if you're not."

Jess stared at Harper standing on the curb near his vehicle. He'd tossed his suit jacket in the car and stood in shirtsleeves minus the tie, looking anxious. Alexa had given her one more chance to make her choice. But for Harper's sake, she couldn't do it.

She'd never be anyone's prize.

"No, I'm okay with it. He could use a good woman in his life. It should be you." She hugged Alexa, and this time she smiled at Seth and waved good-bye. "Thanks for all your help, Alexa. We couldn't have done it without you. Have a safe trip back."

"Well, I was hoping I wouldn't go back to New York City alone," the blonde said.

"Oh?" Jess's heart lurched in her chest.

Was Alexa going to take Harper with her? Harper had shallow roots in Chicago. None that couldn't be uprooted for something better. The thought of that kind of finality with him gripped her stomach.

"Yeah, Garrett would like to meet you. I think he wants to make you an offer you can't refuse. Wielding your own justice can be addictive . . . and empowering. Think about what we could do." Her friend smiled. "You game?"

Jess had almost forgotten about Garrett Wheeler's interest in her. And after the background check she had done on the man, what little she'd found only made her more intrigued. Linked to the most powerful and influential men on the planet, Wheeler had access to money, resources, and connections she could only fantasize about.

And he wanted *her*. Jessica Beckett.

Was she ready for the big leagues? Could she be the kind of woman he was looking for? It only took her a moment to make up her mind. Jess took a deep breath with her heart throttling her rib cage. A big change was coming. She felt it.

"Hell, yeah, I'm game."

Downtown Chicago
Midmorning
Days later

Seth Harper had come to the realization that for him, women should come with warning labels—something fitting yet blatant like the tag he'd seen on a kid's Superman costume that stated *Wearing of this garment does not enable you to fly.* Or another warning had hit home with a message from a Swedish chain saw, *Do not attempt to stop the blade with your hand.* Most people might find such advice obvious, but in his case when it came to women, *nothing* should be taken for granted. Considering his boneheaded moves with Jessie Beckett, could taking flight in spandex or stopping a chain saw with his bare hands be that far behind?

Those options certainly would have been less painful.

In his limited experience, he found that being in love exposed a guy to losing a vital body part—the heart in most cases—unless your name happened to be John Wayne Bobbitt. But the hazards in love weren't readily apparent or tagged with a warning. And he saw no easy way out of his current predicament.

Especially since things weren't up to him anymore.

It had been days since he had seen Jessie at the cemetery, and she was ignoring his phone calls again. After leaving a couple of messages, he figured the ball was in her court, and she knew how to reach him. But playing hard to get was not his gig. And no guy in his right mind *ever* sounded convincing in that role, not with a strong, intelligent woman like Jessie.

She had put distance between them. And he had no say in the matter.

So this morning he'd agreed to join Jonathan Humphries for breakfast, something they did from time to time, but his heart wasn't in it. His heart was with Jessie. He knew he'd be lame company for Jonathan, but he'd made a promise to the man. They walked together to a nearby hotel café and he pretended to enjoy it despite how he felt.

"Great day, isn't it?" the older man prompted.

"Yeah, sure is. I'm glad you suggested this." He forced a smile with hands in his slacks and barely glanced up. Ignoring the beautiful weather and his good friend, Seth had only one thing on his mind.

How could Jessie cut him out of her life so easily?

After the question formed in his mind, he realized how stupid it sounded. He had done the same to her not long ago when he walked out of her life after she left for Alaska in search of a missing girl. And he had been as miserable then as he was now.

"Allow me." Jonathan pulled open a glass door and stood to one side, extending a hand into the Ritz-Carlton Hotel on East Pearson Street. Seth had been so distracted he'd forgotten his manners.

"No, here, Jonathan. Let me." He reached for the door and let the man go first.

The café served a fine breakfast and overlooked the lobby. They were seated and ordered, but halfway through their meal Jonathan eased back in his chair and stopped talking. He stared at Seth as if he were a science experiment that had gone bust.

"What?" He'd kept up his side of the conversation, hadn't he?

"You're putting up a good front, but you can't fool me, young man. If I had to guess, I'd say a woman was at the root of it."

Seth winced at him, hating to be so transparent. But he'd known Jonathan Humphries too long to continue faking a good mood.

"Why are women so . . . complicated?"

Jonathan raised an eyebrow. "Do you really expect another man to answer that?"

Seth crooked his lip into a smile and shook his head. "Guess not."

"Dare I ask the young woman's name?" the man questioned.

But as Seth thought about what to say, someone caught his eye in the lobby below. He saw Alexa Marlowe, Jessie's friend. And seeing her gave him a good excuse to avoid answering Jonathan's question. The man knew Jessie and might voice his disapproval, something Seth was in no mood to hear.

And even though he appreciated that his friend had his best interest at heart, when it came to how Seth felt about Jessie, he wasn't ready to deal with the stark reality that she had no interest in him. *None.* He wanted to believe that love was a gift between two people and that it had all the durability of Super Glue—without being toxic to small animals.

Yet with Jessie, things were never that simple.

"Excuse me, Jonathan. I see someone I know. Do you mind? I won't be long."

Alexa glanced over the hotel lobby, looking for Jessie. They had made plans to eat breakfast together somewhere close and talk about the job her boss Garrett Wheeler would propose. If the bounty hunter still felt like making the trip to New York City with her, she would arrange for another passenger on Garrett's jet, a departure already set for three days from now.

But a male voice calling her name forced her to turn around. Seth Harper was a very pleasant sight to see as he walked toward her, dressed in navy slacks and a pale blue dress shirt. The only thing better would have been to see him naked under her bedsheets—an image that warmed her skin and other places.

"Good morning, Alexa. Great to see you. Are you staying at this hotel?" he asked.

A cute smile graced his lips, and his dark eyes held her in place as they usually did. His physical beauty always took her breath, especially when he stood near her like this. Beyond decency, she inched closer as if they were already lovers and playfully tugged at a button on his shirt. By the look on his face, her intimacy surprised him, but she loved teasing to keep him off-balance.

"Yes, but I'm only here for a few more days unfortunately. I'd love to see more of your city . . . and you."

After being Garrett Wheeler's lover, she'd learned how to please a man but had been obsessed by the idea of taking on a younger lover. And Seth Harper would be perfect. *Sensitive. Expressive. Giving.* And she had no doubt he'd be eager once she exposed him to her needs.

"What are you doing here, Seth?"

He told her something about having breakfast with a friend at the café and went on to polite conversation about Chicago, but she couldn't keep her eyes off his full, sensual lips. She imagined them on her nipples, along with the warm sensation of his tongue. Her skin rippled with goose bumps, and her body flushed with heat. The faint pulse of her heart throbbed in her ear with a steady urgency as images of him flooded her mind.

Those lips probably tasted like—

Without thinking, she let her body react.

"Hold that thought." She placed a finger to his lips, relishing the feel of them coupled with the blush of his skin. "There's something I have to do. And I hope you'll allow me."

From having a confident and aggressive man like Garrett as a lover, she'd learned to take what she wanted. Life was too short to waste time with playing coy.

She tugged at his shirt to draw him closer—and kissed those irresistible lips. Surprised by her sudden move, he tensed his body. When she felt him pull away, her hands found the small of his back and his muscled shoulders. That was when Seth gave in—and let it happen.

At least, that's how she chose to remember the moment.

Jess shoved through the hotel's revolving glass door and into the lobby in time to witness Alexa locking lips with Harper. A two-by-four in the face would have hurt less. Her heart stopped midbeat. Jess had seen enough. She slipped behind a column to hide and leaned on it for strength with eyes shut tight. When she opened them again, she saw her own reflection in a window. A scarred face stared back. *Her face.* An unbending reminder of what everyone else saw when they looked at her.

And the image of Seth kissing Alexa had been seared into her memory. Salt in a very old wound.

Being faced with what she'd given up hit her hard. Seth Harper. Even if she felt confident enough to compete with someone like Alexa, it was too late. What appeared to be the "morning after," the beautiful blonde had seduced Harper here at her hotel. And Seth wasn't the kind of guy who crossed that line easily. If he had made love to Alexa, he'd apparently moved on with his life. And she had to respect that.

Jess knew she had no special hold over him. Hell, they'd only kissed once, and she'd been the one to pull away. She'd become a part of his past. And all of it happened after she'd given her worthless blessing to Alexa, as if she had the right to give the green light on

Harper's life . . . and heart. She had only herself to blame for how things had turned out.

If she hadn't arrived when she did, she might have missed the whole encounter between Seth and Alexa. Would that have been better . . . the old ignorance-is-bliss routine? Not one to live in denial, Jess felt her gut twist with the agony of what she'd seen. She obviously had feelings for Seth, but in the harsh light of truth, he needed someone whole, someone undamaged, who could give him the stable kind of love he deserved.

Yet if he was moving on with his life, and she had claimed to be okay with that, then why did she ache all over?

She slipped through a side door of the hotel and headed back to her vehicle, but stopped when she got far enough away to use her cell phone. She placed a call, and when Alexa answered, it took a moment to find her voice.

"Hey . . . Alexa. It's me." A tear slid down her cheek. She brushed it aside and tried to sound casual. "Look, I gotta cancel our breakfast. Something's come up. Rain check?"

"Yeah, but . . ." Alexa began.

"And I've been thinking," Jess interrupted. "Can we bump up our flight to New York to tomorrow morning, first thing? I'm anxious to meet Garrett and hear what he's got to say. I'm ready to . . . move on with things."

"Yeah, sure. I'll rearrange his private charter. And I'll call you when I have details. Are you okay?"

"Yeah, thanks. See you tomorrow." She ended the

call, ignoring the noticeable concern in Alexa's voice.

She had already made up her mind. If Garrett Wheeler proposed a reasonable job offer, she would accept it. Sticking around Chicago had lost its appeal.

"I gotta get out of this town." Jess headed for the parking garage. "Time for a change in scenery."

She needed a major distraction to get a guy like Seth Harper out of her mind. And if things worked out, Garrett and his secret organization of wealthy and influential vigilantes might hold the key to a much-needed change in her life—in more ways than one.

Compared to Alexa, Jess had a lot to learn when it came to the higher stakes of an international scene filled with savvy criminals who had impressive resources. And higher stakes meant she had to develop her "A" game to a level she didn't have yet. She'd have to work hard to prove herself worthy of Alexa's faith in her, no matter how many months it would take her to prepare.

In truth, Jess knew she wasn't up to the job now. Yet with the combination punch of Garrett's backing and her stubborn streak, she'd be ready to confront a clever and more dangerous adversary.

Jess took a deep breath and wiped another tear from her cheek—swearing she'd be more than ready.

And now

A sneak peek at the next book from

Jordan Dane

Available Fall 2010
from Avon Books

Not even the mesmerizing beauty of the sea at night calmed Luc Toussaint.

The moon dappled undulating waves with shimmer as his slow-moving trawler navigated the Atlantic toward the Canal de la Tortue. Haiti and Port de Paix lay dead ahead. The crew of the *Aquilina* made ready for docking and had left Luc at the helm, alone with his thoughts. As captain of the commercial vessel, he normally took pleasure in the solitary feeling at this hour and drew comfort from being one with the sea. That feeling of serene isolation reminded him of the old days when he was a younger man—but not tonight.

He had other things on his mind.

To settle his nerves, he had smoked far too many cigarettes and kept an alert eye on the horizon as he peered through the dim glow of the wheelhouse and the reflection of the boat's running lights on the water. Earning extra money for his family, he carried additional cargo in a special compartment known only to him and the men he worked for on the side. He played a small part in a smuggling operation with a splinter faction of a drug cartel, and his crew had no idea. His men knew nothing about any contraband on board.

For that matter, he didn't know much more.

For the sake of his wife and children, he only cared about the money and merely played his part as blind courier between South America and Miami, Florida. What had been stowed below was none of his concern. And even though the Dominicans had cut into his action and ramped up their role by becoming wholesaler to many cities on the East Coast of the United States, Luc wanted no part in that.

On most nights, the limits he'd set made him feel absolved of the crime. A more palatable rationale.

When he first saw the city lights of Port de Paix—a distant glow that had robbed the skyline of stars—he had called in his position and estimated time of arrival using the special cellular phone he'd been given. As an agreed-upon security measure, he avoided using the high-frequency radio transmission, the equipment he had in the wheelhouse. Luc blew smoke from his nose and glanced at his watch one more time. When he looked up, he spotted a searchlight on the water dead ahead. The Haitian national police were about to intercept him.

After speaking to his South American contact, he had expected the marked patrol boat, but making it through an inspection at sea always made him nervous these days.

Luc only hoped his part would be over soon.

He breathed a sigh of relief when he spotted the familiar face of a Haitian inspector as the man boarded his vessel, an official he'd seen before and knew by reputation. The hulking man in uniform lumbered across the deck—Gerard Heriveaux—a big man with a pronounced slouch. He and his men knew how to look the other way. And knowing that allowed Luc to relax until the man pulled him aside.

"We must break protocol," the inspector said in French. "I'm here to intervene on behalf of our mutual friends. Contact your man and confirm this. I will wait."

One of the inspector's men handed him a canvas duffel bag. Luc had no idea why Heriveaux would need it.

"I do not understand," he said. "What is happening?"

The Haitian officer looked over his shoulder and kept his voice low. "We've received word that the counter-narcotics unit will raid your vessel when you dock. If you want to be held harmless, you will contact your man to confirm and let me do my part. Now is that clear enough?"

Luc stared at the older man, unable to control the escalating beat of his heart. Nothing like this had ever happened before. The threat of a raid would put him in the middle, between dangerous drug smugglers and an unforgiving Haitian government. Even the hint of an illegal operation would mark him by local officials. He had not been so foolish as to deny this possibility, but being faced with it turned his stomach sour.

God help him.

"Yes, very clear," he nodded. "I will make the call."

Luc headed for the privacy of the wheelhouse to use his cellular phone. When the man on the other end of the line made it easy for him to explain—offering his take on the raid—it made him more confident he would be doing the right thing and reinforced that he'd not be held accountable. His contact told him what to do.

When he returned to the Haitian inspector on the leeward deck, Luc made sure his crew was distracted by the official inspection and delegated the paperwork to one of his men before he waved the officer forward, "Come. Follow me."

In privacy, he led Heriveaux to his personal cabin below. Behind a large wooden panel on the back of his bunk, he yanked at one side and opened a secret compartment. Bolted down and welded, a large combination safe was secured inside.

A safe he didn't know how to open.

"If you have the trust of my contact, you will know how to access what's inside. I do not," Luc told the man. "And I have no wish to be involved. I'll be outside my cabin until you have secured . . . whatever is in that safe."

As he opened his duffel bag, Heriveaux acted surprised by his reaction, but smiled. "You are a smart man, Captain. Go. Do what you must. I will be with you shortly."

Luc shut the door behind him and stood outside his cabin, waiting for the inspector. With the trawler adrift on the sea, the *Aquilina* pitched in the rolling waves, forcing him to widen his stance for balance. His stomach roiled with the motion, the start of nausea more attributable to the sudden change in plan. He wiped both hands over his face and waited.

Luc Toussaint prayed he'd done the right thing.

* * *

Once the *Aquilina* was moored to the pier at Port de Paix, Luc's crew got to work unloading the documented cargo. But a familiar face on the dock below caught the eye of the captain. He quickly disembarked down the gangway and walked toward Inspector Gerard Heriveaux. The man barely glanced at him, as if nothing was the matter.

"Why are you here?" He shrugged as he stood before the Haitian official. "Has something else happened?"

"What are you talking about?" the inspector questioned. "I'm here to inspect your vessel and collect your port fee."

Heriveaux scribbled on a document clipped to a board and prepared another inspection form—a form Luc already had signed and had in his possession, stuffed into his pocket. He retrieved the executed document, unfolded it, and pulled the man aside.

Lowering his voice, Luc said, "But I already paid you. And don't you think it's unwise to duplicate the paperwork? Someone might notice."

With a confused look on his face, Inspector Heriveaux knitted his brow, cocked his head and opened his mouth to speak. But the ringing of the private cell phone clipped to Luc's belt distracted him.

When he recognized the number, he raised a finger and said, "Please . . . I must take this. Excuse me."

Heriveaux grumbled and turned back to his paperwork with a show of indignation as the harsh voice of his South American contact stole Luc's attention.

"Why have I not heard from you? You were supposed to call by now. What's your position?"

Luc's eyes grew wide and his jaw dropped. But as he stared at the annoyed inspector standing in front of him on the pier, it did not take long for him to realize—

He'd been pirated and put out of business by a slick operator.

"I c-can . . ." He choked on words he'd never believe himself. ". . . explain."

The Haitian patrol boat set course for Tortuga Island, the historically infamous Pirate Island across from Port de Paix. En route, every decal, flag, and uniform that designated the identity of the boat and its personnel would be removed, bagged, and thrown overboard with weights. No evidence of their piracy would remain.

In his cabin below deck, Jackson Kinkaid stripped out of his uniform to his skivvies and stared at the age-ravaged face and thinning gray hair of Inspector Gerard Heriveaux in the mirror one last time. Being a chameleon, he admired his work. His best disguise to date.

What had taken him hours to create would be gone in minutes.

Kinkaid removed his brown-tinted contact lenses and dug his fingernails into the skin at his cheek, tearing at the latex until his own face emerged, dotted with adhesive. He bent over a small sink to scrub off the last remnants of the disguise and wet down his dark hair. When he looked into the mirror again, familiar green eyes stared back. And he straightened his spine and shoulders to regain his youth . . . and attitude.

"You won't have to worry about old age, Kinkaid," he smirked at his reflection. "You won't live that long."

Before he dressed, he sat on his bunk with eyes closed and listened to a digital recording on an iPod. He needed to hear it like he was compelled to breathe, and he'd made this special time a ritual—a self-inflicted reminder of how much he had changed. The recording also never let him forget that his life hadn't always been empty.

While he took his personal downtime, his team headed for Tortuga Island, where his men would separate, and a helicopter awaited him. Not too long ago, the island had served as the filming locale of a sequel to *Pirates of the Caribbean*. Kinkaid appreciated the irony, especially considering what he had just pulled off.

Forty-five minutes later

"Boss, we're here." The voice of his number one man, Joe LaClaire, called to him from on deck.

Kinkaid knew from the plan that they would be docking in a discreet cove on the island, away from curious eyes. For security reasons, they randomly selected the location, but this spot had a unique attribute. A helipad was nearby, and a Bell 210 helicopter awaited his arrival.

By the time he emerged topside, Kinkaid garnered his men's attention when he came out wearing a navy Armani suit with a light gray shirt and burgundy-striped tie. The stark contrast of dress attire on board generated a flurry of whistles and verbal abuse he found hard to ignore.

"Cut the crap, you bastards," he yelled. A rumble of

good-natured laughter from his men made Kinkaid smile. He gripped the shoulder of the short dark-haired man standing in front of him and lowered his voice. "Get the cash where it needs to go, Joe. You're in charge now."

He trusted Joe with his life, so relying on him to secure what they had plundered wasn't an issue. The drug money taken off the trawler had been easy pickings, especially with an inside track to the drug cartel. Eavesdropping on the international maritime satellite communication network helped determine what cargo to hit and the level of risk involved—all part of their usual meticulous homework. And the anxious trawler captain had given him plenty of time to break into the safe when the man left him alone in his cabin.

But commandeering the trawler's private cell phone—pretending to be the captain's smuggler contact—had been a stroke of genius Joe had orchestrated. It had saved the trawler crew from having to face Kinkaid's plan B if anyone had resisted.

"I'll see you at the rendezvous point tomorrow morning. Eight sharp," he said.

These days he had few friends. He'd severed ties and kept moving to avoid dealing with the baggage. Friends expected too much. And they knew when he was lying and called him on his shit. LaClaire understood the way things were. He rarely pushed and didn't take it personal when he drew the line. And that was okay, most days.

"Just watch your ass." Joe narrowed his eyes. "I don't want to dip into my hard-earned funds to bail you out." He leaned in and whispered. "There was close to a half million in that safe."

"Good haul." Kinkaid forced a smile. "I gotta go."

"I hate not leaving together after an operation. You sure you won't need me to stick around?" Joe asked.

"No, I have obligations." Kinkaid adjusted his cuff links, thinking about the second half of his evening. He was already late.

After his helicopter touched down, he had arranged for a taxi to get him to his next stop. A taxi service in Port de Paix was a high-risk sport. The vehicles were nothing more than unmarked junk heaps without meters. But given his timetable, he didn't want to risk not finding one.

The charity event he'd be attending was an affair put on by a determined Catholic nun.

"People are waiting for me, Joe." He raised an eyebrow. "Hell, I'm the damned guest of honor."

Port de Paix, Haiti

When Kinkaid arrived late to the party, the fundraiser for the St. Thomas Aquinas Academy was in full swing, an occasion that marked the tenth anniversary of the missionary school. With its aqua stucco walls and red-tiled rooftop, Dumont Hall was a civic building on the fringe of town and near the academy.

Not much more than an impoverished village with dirt streets, Port de Paix had few buildings suitable for such an event, but the organizers had done well, and it looked as if some of the expected supporters had traveled to attend. Women in fancy dresses accompanied men in suits with children playing dress-up. Partygoers could be seen through the windows and on the front steps of the building. And the music of a small quartet wafted into the night air as Kinkaid's taxi pulled to the curb.

He cringed at the thought of walking into an event he knew he didn't belong. And if he believed in divine intervention, the course that had led him to this fiasco had a real hinky vibe to it, like an unavoidable retribution for his sins.

Four years ago, he'd crossed paths with a very persistent Catholic nun, Sister Mary Katherine, when her need for cash outweighed her common sense. Their meeting had been a surprise for both of them. It had not been their first. After his arrival in Haiti—under the guise of an American businessman traveling the islands—the woman had tracked him down, looking for donations. How she'd found him, she never said. And she'd followed his lead in not talking about the past. She had left that up to him, which meant the topic never came up.

The nun had no idea what he'd become. And he never told her otherwise, but being with her was a constant reminder for him. *Deserved penance.*

Standing on the curb with the taxi driving away, he stalled making his entrance. He took a breath of fresh air to dispel the smell of the taxi from his nostrils. Despite his usual swagger—a product of the flamboyant public image he had cultivated out of necessity over the years—he hated being the center of attention. But tonight he'd have to put up with it. If Sister Kate hadn't specifically asked him to attend and made such a big deal about it, he would have turned her down flat.

"Only for you, Kate."

Killing time, he avoided the main hall and headed for a spot in the garden to the left of the entrance. Dirt and gravel crunched under his shoes when he entered a courtyard. The pungent aroma of flowers mixed with the scent of the ocean off a warm breeze, but something more lingered in the air. His eyes trailed to a far corner of the garden, where he searched the shadows for what he knew he'd find. He had taken a gamble that he wouldn't be alone, and he was right.

In the dark, under the dim glow of moonlight, he saw Sister Mary Katherine. Her dark silhouette stood out against the stonework behind her. A faint yet ghostly twist hung low around her head like an aura, and he grinned at the faint impression of a halo. Sister Kate was too grounded in the reality of life to ever be mistaken for an ethereal saint, despite the fact that he couldn't think of anyone more deserving.

The nun was sneaking a cigarette—her one true vice—and billowing smoke like a flume. She smoked when she was nervous. And even from a distance, he recognized another of her anxious habits. She fidgeted and tapped her toe, unable to keep her feet still. When she saw him, she didn't bother to hide what she was doing.

"Come here." She waved her free hand. "Let me get a good look at you."

"Okay, you got me at this shindig. Now what?" With

arms crossed, Kinkaid slouched against the stone wall next to the Catholic nun, who was dressed in a traditional black tunic and veil with starched white collar.

Sister Mary Katherine flicked her cigarette away to glance at him, top to bottom.

"You clean up real nice, Jackson. You change the color of your skin to suit the occasion."

"You have no idea, Kate." He crooked his lip into a smile until he noticed that Dumont Hall had uniformed guards with weapons at key locations, not exactly low-profile. "This event is supposed to be about the kids. What's with all the firepower?"

"Now that's where you're wrong," the nun argued, waggling a finger. "What we do at the school is for the kids, yes. But this event? It's about you, Jackson Kinkaid. I'm proud of you. And people are curious about the wealthy American, my dear." She cocked her head. "Curious enough to make a donation if they like what they see. So play nice, will you? Do it for the children."

Over the years, he'd gotten a bit of a reputation in certain circles. Partly due to his involvement with Sister Kate's pet project, the media had initially placed the spotlight on him, but when other more influential people took notice, he had to invent a persona that people and the police would buy. One thing led to another, and things got out of control fast. He'd been mistaken that the local media would get tired of covering his story—and now he was stuck with the aftermath. No good deed went unpunished.

He'd never told Kate that she'd brought trouble to his

door the day she'd found him in Haiti and brought the past colliding into the present for him. She thought she had done him a good turn—drawing attention to what she believed to be his philanthropic nature—and the academy's kids had benefited from it. The choices he'd made in his life were not their problem.

Sister Kate walked with him toward the main building, but not before she wiped stone dust from the back of his jacket like a nervous mother hen. With her arm in his, the nun explained how the local papers had circulated the news of the charitable event for the St. Thomas Aquinas Academy and that the local police thought it would be wise to add security. She told him that she had little to say about it.

"In truth, the police are here for you, Jackson."

"That's not funny, Kate. Armed men in uniform aren't my idea of a good time," he protested.

"But an armed man who is well dressed in designer threads is perfectly acceptable?" She reached over and tugged at the lapel of his suit. "I noticed you were packing heat."

Under his jacket, he wore a .45-caliber Glock 30 in a holster.

"Packing heat?" He laughed. "You've been watching too many Bogart flicks."

"And you're ignoring my question." She crossed her arms and stood in front of him. "You're a man with secrets, Jackson Kinkaid. You always have been. Don't bother to deny it."

"Wouldn't if I could," he agreed.

"You've always struck me as someone I can trust,

but I have a feeling I'd never really know you in a lifetime. Why is that?"

"Why you trust me?" He smirked. "Good question."

"That's not what I meant, and you know it." She poked his arm.

"I could say the same about you." He shrugged. "I trust you, but I haven't scratched the surface of really knowing you. You're not exactly an open book."

"I'm a nun. What's to know?" She brushed off her habit. "Besides, being trustworthy comes with the uniform."

"Not in my world, Kate." Kinkaid grinned. "You're a complicated and uncompromising woman who respects secrets. And I like that." He looked away and broke the hold she had on him. "Besides, you don't want to know who I really am. Men like me are the reason you pray."

"You're not the only reason I pray, Jackson. Not by a long shot."

He caught the glint of her eyes in the moonlight and knew she was staring at him, trying to understand what he'd said. And maybe she'd revealed a little about herself in the process. Kinkaid was satisfied with status quo when it came to Sister Kate. The nun had a past that she kept secret, too—a feeling he got from a kindred spirit—someone who had taken a very different path than the one he'd chosen.

When she didn't say anything more, he knew that she understood not to ask questions. If she ever did, he would tell her the truth, and that might change everything between them. She had accepted him into her life, and that was good enough for him. And for a reason he didn't want to think about, it mattered what she thought of him. But that didn't mean he wanted to risk crossing the line—to tell her the truth about his life.

"Come on. Let's get this over with . . . for both our sakes." She took his arm again and headed for Dumont Hall, muttering under her breath, "Who invited the likes of you and me anyway?"

"Someone with exceedingly low standards." He smiled. "But remember. This is all for the children."

"That it is, my dear." She patted his arm and grinned at him. "That it is."

New York City
Lower East Side
9:30 P.M.

Alexa knocked on the apartment door and peeked through the peephole. From the outside looking in, nothing was very clear through the lens, but she spied a light on inside. That was good enough for her to decide that someone was home, although that didn't ensure her knock would get answered. Straightening her blond hair, she took a step back into the hall so she'd be visible through the peephole—and waited.

Jessie Beckett opened the door without a hint of whether she was pleased to see her. And she didn't feel the need to break the ice by talking either. Dressed in faded jeans and a black Chicago Bulls tee, the former bounty hunter could play poker with the best, yet she'd never make a good politician since she spoke her mind, short and sweet—one of the reasons the woman had grown on her.

"You don't call . . . you don't write." Alexa leaned a shoulder against the doorjamb with her arms crossed. "Can I come in?"

Jessie stared at her a moment, then backed away to let her in. Alexa entered the small apartment before Jessie had a chance to change her mind.

"I've been busy, that's all," she said. "You didn't tell me what hard work it would be. Garrett's people have me jumping, but it's all good . . . I think."

"From what I hear, you're a star," Alexa replied, unbuttoning her light tweed jacket and putting her hands into the pockets of her khaki pants.

She glanced around the tiny living room, sparse with cheap rental furniture and worn cardboard boxes stacked in a corner. The mundane room was colored in varying degrees of brown and looked like something anyone would scrape off their shoe. And it smelled a little musty, with the faint scent of pine and ammonia.

Although it was clear that Jessie had made an attempt to clean, she barely looked like she lived there. No personal effects could be seen, only the essentials for her to eat and sleep in the apartment that Garrett Wheeler—the liaison to the Sentinels—had leased for her after she'd picked it. The woman definitely gravitated toward the simpler life, having no tolerance for the more-upscale lifestyle he would have provided.

But that only made Garrett peeved that he hadn't gotten her total buy-in. Lavish gifts and posh living quarters were more his style. Yet she had refused his usual ploys to make her feel obligated to him—and to add insult to injury—the woman could pick up and go in a heartbeat. Garrett didn't like that. So knowing Jessie had worked late, Alexa had been sent to check on her even at this hour, a task she would have done on her own without his prompting.

She had something personal on her mind, and she had to get it off her chest.

Alexa turned to face her and get a closer look at her new partner. Jessie looked tired, and the spark of her usual defiance had been dulled. Alexa knew about going stir-crazy until that first assignment came along. Living in luxury had made the wait tolerable for her, but Jessie didn't have such a distraction. Plus, the Sentinels instruction program for its operatives was consuming, a twenty-four/seven schedule that had kept them apart until this week, when she'd be officially assigned her new partner.

Jessie was ready, and they both knew it.

"Rumor has it that you're the one to beat. You had top honors," Jessie reminded her. "I'm just trying to make a good first impression."

"Spoken like a true overachiever who's been smacked by the humility stick." She chose a chair across from the small sofa and sat.

"Can I get you a beer?" Jessie asked.

Beer was not Alexa's drink of choice, but for Jessie's sake, she said, "Sure, as long as you don't force me to go bowling after."

"Deal."

Alexa had gotten various reports from Jessie's trainers as her instruction progressed. Top marks on all levels except when it came to a consistent concern. Her instructors had agreed that Jessie was both physically and mentally tough and would make a gifted operative, but she was a definite loner. In the world of the Sentinels, this was not a bad thing, but not everyone was convinced she'd make a good partner until Alexa spoke up for her.

That helped Garrett make up his mind. He needed to test her with the real deal. Soon they'd be assigned a case, another reason for Alexa to make contact with Jessie.

"Garrett told me we'd get one of the next assignments. You up for it?"

"Hell, yeah." Jessie handed her a beer without a glass. "I'd take my urine test over just to feel I'm making progress."

"I'll mention that to the HR department."

Jessie plopped onto a sofa across from Alexa and took a long pull from her bottle before she spoke again, "I mean, it's not that I'm ungrateful for all Garrett's done for me. The training has been interesting. And I've never been in such good shape physically. The first few weeks were a killer. But lately I've been pulling longer hours to stay . . . focused. Just hanging out like this is driving me crazier than usual. Without a bail-jumping scumbag in sight, I'm going through arrest withdrawals."

"Yeah, I figured."

Alexa knew that Jessie hadn't been back to Chicago

since her training started nearly six months ago except to pack a few personal belongings. Garrett was maintaining her Chicago apartment in case she changed her mind. Plus he'd given her the option of flying back on a few occasions—at his expense—but she'd never taken him up on the offer. She hadn't even gone back to see her cop friend, Sam Cooper. Although Alexa didn't know her well, that behavior smacked of avoidance and seemed out of character, even for someone as detached as Jessie.

That left Alexa with questions. And before they worked together, she had to clear the air by testing a theory she had for the reason Jessie had severed her link to Chicago.

"What are you doing tomorrow morning?"

"Not much. Why?"

"I thought you might want to ride with me to the airport. I invited your friend Seth Harper to town for the weekend."

The look on Jessie's face told her everything she wanted to know. Alexa knew her plans with Seth and her playful weekend of seduction had gotten complicated.

Port de Paix, Haiti
10:00 P.M.

"And are you single, Mr. Kinkaid?" In a coy gesture, the older woman stroked the stem of her wineglass, not taking her eyes off him. Before Kinkaid replied, she added, "My daughter is studying finance back in the

States. I'm sure she'd love to meet you . . . to discuss your . . . assets."

He forced a polite smile and downed a full martini, wishing he had a second one on deck. He took a deep breath and gazed across the room to catch Sister Kate smirking. She stood with a small group of contributors, holding the hand of a little Haitian boy. Although she smiled and carried on conversation, her feet were fidgeting enough to almost keep time with the music. And whenever she could, Kate glanced his way, watching over him. Kinkaid could tell that the nun took devilish delight in his uneasiness. Misery did indeed love company. He narrowed his eyes and shook his head at her, but Kate had supplied him with all the excuse he'd need.

"Best wishes to your daughter in her studies. But if you'll excuse me, Sister Mary Katherine is calling."

He made what he hoped was a diplomatic exit and went looking for a drink. But as he walked away, he caught the matchmaking woman checking his assets head to toe. She smiled and waved, without any sign of embarrassment. And from a distance, Kinkaid raised his empty glass in reply.

Sorry, lady. For your daughter's sake, you shouldn't troll in these waters. You've got no idea what lurks deep.

Kinkaid took a detour to the nearest cash bar as he listened to the music and took in the room. The musicians weren't bad, especially after a few drinks. And the food looked great. Sister Kate and her organizers had put on a fine spread. When he crossed the room, dodging partygoers and avoiding eye contact, he shifted his gaze to the exits. At first nothing seemed out of the ordinary. And he would have let the nagging sensation go, except for one thing.

It wasn't what he saw, but what he didn't see that bothered him. He stopped and turned. Not one local policeman was at his post. The uniforms were gone.

"What the hell . . ." He turned toward Sister Kate with a look of concern on his face. She noticed his expression right away and shrugged to convey she didn't understand.

Neither of them saw what happened next until it was too late.

A blast of automatic gunfire erupted and echoed through the room. A deafening sound. He reached for his Glock as plaster rained down on his head, and he ran for cover. Complete and utter chaos followed. People ran screaming and jammed the exits. Gunmen dressed in black grabbed the guests. Men, women, and children were ordered to the floor, facedown. The assailants wore masks. Only their eyes and mouths were visible, making them appear more sinister.

Kinkaid caught a glimpse of Sister Kate across the room. She herded children and headed them for a door, helping them to escape. Her black habit was hard to miss. And for the first time, he'd seen terror in her eyes when she stared back—although he knew her fear wasn't for her own safety.

But the gunmen shut down the mass exodus, and Kinkaid was too far away to help Kate.

"Jackson . . . Kinkaid."

He heard his name called out. The armed men were looking for him. *Damn it!* But why? Had he brought this down on Sister Kate? Or were these men just looking to abduct a wealthy American businessman?

"Kinkaid," a man yelled, and searched the cowering people on the floor. No one looked him in the eye as he raged and spat at his hostages.

Kinkaid stayed hunched behind a column, considering his limited options. By his estimation, he'd be the only guest with a weapon. If he guessed wrong on what to do next, people could die, and he'd be taken out of the equation, unable to help. Yet he had to do something.

Slowly he wedged his gun at the small of his back and hid it under his jacket. If one of the men got close enough to search him for a weapon, they'd find an empty holster. And that small diversion might give him time to pull his handgun and get some answers. Risking his neck might be worth the gamble if he found out what the men wanted and could stop the gunplay. He stood and raised his hands, ready to come out and identify himself.

But before he could, more shots rang out. This time the bastards aimed into the frantic crowds who packed the exits—a cruel, sadistic show of power meant to terrorize already helpless victims.

"No, no." His lips moved, but his voice sounded muffled in his head. His hearing was trashed from the gunfire. And all he could do was watch. Everything happened too fast.

Two bodies fell. A man in a suit got shot in the back.

The round hit his body with a meaty thud and sent him sprawling to the floor. And a gray-haired woman in a blue dress snapped her head back and tumbled. A crimson mist hung in the air as her body fell. When she hit the floor, the back of her head slammed hard, and a pool of her blood seeped onto the carpet. Her vacant dead eyes stared accusingly at a young girl who stood over her. The kid couldn't have been much more than eight years old.

"Oh, shit," Kinkaid muttered.

For a split second, everything in the room stopped as he watched the girl. He tuned everything out. Complete tunnel vision. He couldn't take his eyes off her, but the instant was gone in a flash.

A shrill scream rose above the panicked cries of men and women as they fled. The sound of the pitiable wail triggered a dark memory—one he'd never forget. He shut his eyes and tried to shake the past, but nothing would break him free until the blond girl screamed again.

His eyes fixed on her and grounded him in the moment. Even from a distance he saw the little girl tremble. And her face had turned a vivid red as tears streaked her cheeks. She stared at the woman's body in shock, unable to move. One of the attackers turned toward the crying child and yelled something in a language Kinkaid didn't understand. The masked man raised his weapon and aimed at the little girl.

The bastard was going to shoot.

HOT ROMANCE AND
COLD SUSPENSE FROM
JORDAN DANE

NO ONE HEARD HER SCREAM
978-0-06-125278-5

They never found her sister's body, but Detective Rebecca Montgomery knows her murderer is still out there. In the five months since Danielle went missing, there have been two more brutal abductions.

NO ONE LEFT TO TELL
978-0-06-125375-1

The body of a brutally slain man is found on the holy grounds of a chapel. Detective Raven Mackenzie and her partner uncover the dead man's connections to a powerful female crime boss, and her mysterious head of security who is the prime suspect.

NO ONE LIVES FOREVER
978-0-06-125376-8

Jasmine Lee needs Christian Delacorte's help freeing her kidnapped lover, a powerful mogul linked to Chicago's underworld. Christian doesn't trust her, but Jasmine entices him to leave behind the woman he loves, Detective Raven Mackenzie, to help her.

EVIL WITHOUT A FACE
978-0-06-147412-5

Jessica Beckett is a bounty hunter used to bringing lowlifes to justice, but now she has agreed to help former NFL quarterback Payton Archer find his missing niece.

Visit www.AuthorTracker.com for exclusive
information on your favorite HarperCollins authors.

DAN 0809

Available wherever books are sold or please call 1-800-331-3761 to order.

NEED SOMETHING NEW TO READ?

Download it Now!

Visit www.harpercollinsebooks.com
to choose from thousands of titles
you can easily download to your
computer or PDA.

Save 20% off the printed book price.
Ordering is easy and secure.

HarperCollins e-books

Download to your laptop, PDA, or phone for
convenient, immediate, or on-the-go reading. Visit
www.harpercollinsebooks.com or other online
e-book retailers.

Visit www.AuthorTracker.com for exclusive
information on your favorite HarperCollins authors.

Available wherever books are sold or please call 1-800-331-3761 to order.

HRE 0307